BORN
OF THE
SUN

Adventures in Our Solar System

edited by
MIKE ASHLEY

This collection first published in 2020 by
The British Library
96 Euston Road
London NW1 2DB

Selection, introduction and notes © 2020 Mike Ashley

Cataloguing in Publication Data
A catalogue record for this publication is available from the British Library

ISBN 978 0 7123 5356 4
e-ISBN 978 0 7123 6766 0

The frontispiece illustration and illustrations on pages 10, 38, 88, 108, 214, 238,
258, 284 and 320 are reproduced from *Sur les Autre Mondes* by Lucien Rudaux,
Librairie Larousse, Paris, 1937. The captions have been translated and adapted.
The illustration and caption on page 168 are reproduced from *The New Book of
Knowledge* edited by Sir John Hammerton, Waverley Book Co., Ltd., Glasgow, 1953.

Front cover illustration: Nova melting a hypothetical planet, 1950 by
Chesley Bonestell. Reproduced courtesy of Bonestell LLC.

Front cover design by Jason Anscomb
Text design and typesetting by Tetragon, London
Printed and bound by TJ International, Padstow, Cornwall

BORN
OF THE
SUN

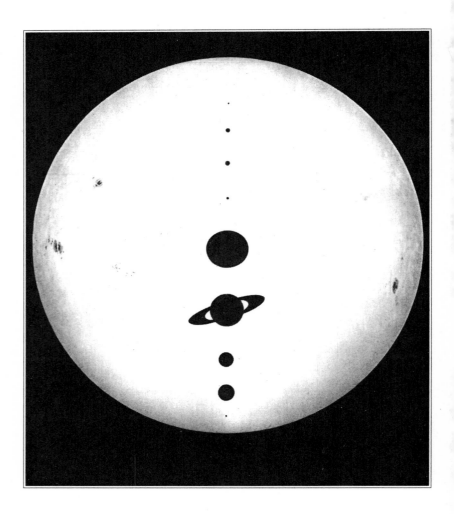

CONTENTS

INTRODUCTION

Solar Tour

We are going on a tour of the solar system—the old solar system, beloved of writers of science fiction, before the space probes discovered what was really out there.

For decades little was known about most of the planets—Pluto was not even discovered until 1930—so science fiction writers had a fairly free hand in creating adventures on these worlds. Sometimes, too free a hand. Although we have known for many years that Jupiter and Saturn were gas giants and unlikely to have a solid rock surface, that did not stop space adventurers landing there and having adventures amongst aliens as if they'd landed on a set at Universal Studios.

For this volume I wanted to select stories that took at least some notice of the scientific understanding of the day and set their adventures on a world that was feasible, as suspected in the first half of this century. In order for the stories to be reasonably scientific most included here are from the 1940s and 1950s, with two from the 1960s, but I have included two from the dawn of the science-fiction magazines. One of these, "The Hell Planet", explores a planet that does not exist but which had been suggested as possible in 1859 by the French astronomer Urbain Le Verrier. He called it Vulcan, and it was supposed to orbit near the Sun, within the orbit of Mercury. Its existence was more or less dismissed in 1915, but the name persists as the home of Mr. Spock and his fellow Vulcans in *Star Trek*, though his world is not of our solar system.

Pluto was demoted to a dwarf planet in 2006, which seems unfair, especially as the *New Horizons* probe in 2015 showed such an active, complicated world. But in the heyday of the science-fiction pulps it was a proper planet and is restored to its rightful place here.

I have not included the Earth or the Moon in this tour of the solar system, though my anthology *Moonrise*, also published in this series, provides eleven visions of our nearest neighbour. But I could not exclude Mars, despite having already provided various visions of that world in *Lost Mars*, and I have included a story here that was too long for that anthology and has never been reprinted, so it's a true lost Martian tale. Also, although Saturn does not have a story of its own, its major moon Titan, does.

The history of each planet and how we have imagined it is itself a fascinating study and, as a preface to each story I have provided a potted history of each world in both fact and fiction.

So strap yourself in and prepare for a kaleidoscope of worlds.

MIKE ASHLEY

A SPECTATOR PLACED ON MERCURY WOULD SEE THE SUN AS AN ENORMOUS
DISC COMPARED TO ITS DIMENSIONS AS VIEWED FROM EARTH

MERCURY

Sunrise on Mercury   Robert Silverberg

Mercury is the closest planet to the sun and the smallest (if we exclude Pluto). It has a diameter of 4,880km (3,032 miles) so is not much bigger than our Moon (3,475km; 2,159 miles). Its orbit is eccentric, so although we may say its average distance from the Sun is around 58 million kilometres (36 million miles), it actually ranges from 46 million kilometres (28.6 million miles) to 69.82 million kilometres (43.4 million miles).

Those figures show how close Mercury ventures to the Sun. During its day the surface temperature at the equator can reach 427°C, higher than the melting points of both lead and tin. At night the temperature can drop to -170°C, so it is a world of extremes.

In 1893 Giovanni Schiaparelli claimed that Mercury was tidally locked with the Sun, meaning the planet always has one face toward the Sun and one in shadow. This gave rise to the idea that Mercury had a perpetually hot side and a dark, extremely cold side, with a narrow zone between that was in twilight, and where the temperature might just be hospitable. This was disproved in 1965 when it was discovered Mercury rotated very slowly with one Mercurian year lasting 58.6 Earth years. The science-fiction writer Larry Niven was poorly treated by this discovery because, just as it was announced, his debut story, "The Coldest Place" was published where it is only revealed at the end that explorers on the coldest planet in the solar system are on Mercury.

Being so close to the Sun, Mercury is at the mercy of the Sun's gravitational pull, but it stays free by being the fastest planet in the solar system, zipping along at over 47km (29 miles) per second. That's how it earned its name. The ancient Babylonians called it Nabu after the messenger to the gods. The Greeks did not realize that the planet seen low on the horizon in the morning and the evening were the same world, so they named the morning world Apollo and the evening world Hermes. When Pythagoras returned from his travels through Babylon in the mid-sixth century B.C., he passed on the knowledge that the two worlds were the same, and the name Hermes remained, after the Greek messenger to the gods. The Roman equivalent was Mercury.

Mercury's eccentric orbit suggests something must have happened to the planet in the distant past. Recent probes have discovered that the planet has more volatile elements, like sulphur and potassium, than you'd expect, as the Sun's heat should have long burned them away. The theory has been proposed that Mercury was formed much farther from the Sun, perhaps close to the orbit of Mars, and was knocked from that orbit billions of years ago and propelled towards the Sun. Remarkably, this idea had already been used by the wonderfully named Homer Eon Flint back in 1919 in his novella "The Lord of Death". An expedition visits a lifeless Mercury but finds evidence that a civilization had once existed when the world was further from the Sun—close to the orbit of Earth.

Much of what we know about Mercury has been discovered in the last fifty years or so and the possibilities to explore the planet in fiction were open to much conjecture. Most early space stories were either on the Moon or Mars or, at a stretch, Venus. Yet a French author set an adventure on Mercury as far back as 1750. That was when *Relation du monde de mercure* by Chevalier de Béthune was published, but Brian Stableford, in his ground-breaking study of early French science fiction, *The Plurality of Imaginary Worlds* (2016), has suggested it may have been written as early as 1715. The book is not so much a novel as a discourse on life and creation, but the author speculates on possible inhabitants. The Mercurians are short, winged humanoids who enjoy basking in the Sun. There are also intelligent fish and birds. The Chevalier hints at parallels between the planet's Solar Emperor and France's Louis XIV, known as the Sun King.

Béthune's book was a one-off, way ahead of its time. Although the occasional philosophical reference to Mercury appeared, if we leave aside the anonymous political satire, *Man Abroad* (1886), which projects America's foreign policy to a future where all of the solar system is colonized and Mercury is prone to attack because of its vast gold deposits, the first true attempt to apply some scientific rationale to Mercury was in an occasional series "Letters from the Planets" by the Anglican clergyman W.S. Lach-Szyrma. He was fascinated with the prospect that there was life throughout the cosmos and had already explored it in *A Voice from Another World* (1874) and *Aleriel* (1883). Aleriel is a Venusian who explores the solar system in his ether-car but it was not until later that he reached Mercury in "A Journey to the Regions of the Sun". Lach-Szyrma was seeking to educate his public about the planets and this series appeared in *Cassell's Family Magazine* periodically from 1887 to 1893. Aleriel's stay on Mercury is short but he discovers that its scientists are far ahead of others and that although the planet is small the inhabitants take advantage of its lesser gravity and float around in "cars" and tiny "islets".

After Schiaparelli's pronouncement, Mercury became a less attractive world and writers gave it scant attention. In *A Trip to Venus* (1897), John Munro's voyagers pass by Mercury and find it uninhabited except for various extreme creatures, such as dragons. William Wallace Cook presents an extremely hot Mercury in "Adrift in the Unknown" (serial, 1904–5) but inhabited by two-foot high creatures who live in caves.

Once we enter the world of the pulp magazine Mercury became fair game for anything. In *The Fire People* (serial 1922), Ray Cummings—at one time the most popular writer of sf for the pulps, but one who never wasted a good idea on one story when he could string it out over a dozen or so—has the Mercutians (his parlance) invade the Earth. He has Mercury divided into various zones, the Dark Country, the Twilight Zone and the Light Country, in the centre of which is the Fire Country. Cummings returned to Mercury in several serials, all formulaic planetary adventures, including *Tama of the Light Country* (serial 1930) and *Tama, Princess of Mercury* (serial, 1931).

Other pulpsters presented us with Mercurian beetle men, molemen, frog-like beings, mushroom creatures, and, rather more interestingly, energy beings, as suggested by the long forgotten Clifton B. Kruse in "W62 to Mercury" (1935) and Frank Belknap Long in "Cones" (1936). But if we ignore the variously described fauna of Mercury, there were more serious themes emerging. In both "The Last Planet" (1934) by R.F. Starzl and the serial "Dawn to Dusk" (serial, 1934–5) by Eando Binder, Mercury is seen as the last refuge of humanity millennia hence as the Sun grows cold. In many stories, starting with Clifford Simak's "Mutiny on Mercury" (1932), Mercury is a valuable source of minerals. Leigh Brackett wrote a series of stories set around Mercurian mines starting with "The Demons of

Darkside" (1941). We later learn that her hero Eric John Stark, who first appeared in "Queen of the Martian Catacombs" (1949), had been born on Mercury where his parents were involved in mining. Mining is still key to Mercury's importance in Arthur C. Clarke's *A Rendezvous with Rama* (1973).

Mercury is also a source for harnessing solar energy which Clifford Simak had explored in "Masquerade" (1941) and Isaac Asimov in his book for young adults, *Lucky Starr and the Big Sun of Mercury* (1956). Asimov used Mercury as a setting for several stories, most significantly an early robot story, "Runaround" (1942), where a robot finds itself in a dilemma between obeying a vague order or protecting itself from the hostile environment. This was the first story to relate Asimov's Three Laws of Robotics in detail.

For most of the post-war years, until the revelation that Mercury did turn on its axis, the majority of Mercurian adventures were either set in the twilight zone or had expeditions venturing into the hot side. In "Ride the Twilight Rail" (1953) by E.R. James, a monorail is constructed across the twilight zone which allows a transmitting station to be maintained. In "Sunrise on Mercury" (1957) by Robert Silverberg, reprinted here, an expedition finds itself at the mercy of the rising Sun. "Brightside Crossing" (1956) by Alan E. Nourse has the extreme endurance of crossing the planet's hot side.

Perhaps the last great story to be set on a tidally locked Mercury was "Hot Planet" (1963) by Hal Clement where a team of scientists, trying to discover why Mercury is developing an atmosphere, are forced on to the planet's surface amidst suddenly erupting volcanos. It was a suitable farewell to the old world.

The fact that Mercury does rotate, albeit very slowly—it's possible to walk over Mercury's surface and keep the Sun in the same position in the sky all the time—has not stopped writers exploring the world.

In *The Memory of Whiteness* (1985), Kim Stanley Robinson has a solar energy station on rails that keeps the Sun forever in twilight. David Brin has a base on Mercury in *Sundiver* (1980) from where to observe the bizarre sun-ghosts which exist in the Sun's chromosphere. Whilst in *Manifold: Space* (2000) Stephen Baxter takes us back to the vision of the pulp writers to show Mercury as the last home of humanity where it has sought refuge from aliens who have destroyed Earth.

Far from being a distant and hostile world, Mercury has proved popular amongst writers and may yet have its importance for mankind.

Robert Silverberg (b. 1935) is one of the giants of science fiction with a career that stretches back to 1952, with his first story in a paying magazine—albeit a small-press title—"The Sacred River" in *The Avalonian*. His first professional sale was to the Scottish magazine *Nebula SF* where "Gorgon Planet" appeared early in 1954. During the 1950s he sold prolifically to all of the science-fiction magazines of the day (and there were many of them then) and to plenty more magazines besides. His output shifted to writing non-fiction books at the turn of the decade but he returned to science fiction with a vengeance in the early 1960s and his stories soon began to win the Hugo and Nebula Awards. Silverberg has been so prolific that I hesitate to say just how many books he has had published as obscure ones under little-known pseudonyms still surface from time to time—his website lists almost 300 novels alone, let alone story collections, anthologies and many non-fiction books. But Silverberg was not simply a writing machine. His stories, especially from the mid-1960s on, explored new ideas and concepts often in original and unusual ways. Amongst his major novels are *Nightwings* (1969), *Son of Man* (1971), *Dying Inside* (1972), *The Book of Skulls* (1972), *The Stochastic Man* (1975) and *Lord Valentine's Castle* (1980).

The following story was inspired by a painting by artist Ed Emshwiller which showed two men running away from a melting glass dome on the surface of Mercury. Both cover and story ran in the May 1957 issue of *Science Fiction Stories*.

NINE MILLION MILES TO THE SUNWARD OF MERCURY, with the *Leverrier* swinging into the series of spirals that would bring it down on the Solar System's smallest world, Second Astrogator Lon Curtis decided to end his life.

Curtis had been lounging in a webfoam cradle waiting for the landing to be effected; his job in the operation was over, at least until the *Leverrier's* landing-jacks touched Mercury's blistered surface. The ship's efficient sodium-coolant system negated the efforts of the swollen sun visible through the rear screen. For Curtis and his seven shipmates, no problems presented themselves; they had only to wait while the autopilot brought the ship down for Man's second landing on Mercury.

Flight Commander Harry Ross was sitting near Curtis when he noticed the sudden momentary stiffening of the astrogator's jaws. Curtis abruptly reached for the control nozzle. From the spinnerets that had spun the webfoam, came a quick green burst of dissolving fluorochrene; the cradle vanished. Curtis stood up.

"Going somewhere?" Ross asked.

Curtis' voice was harsh. "Just—just taking a walk."

Ross returned his attention to his microbook for a moment as Curtis walked away. There was the ratchety sound of a bulkhead dog being manipulated, and Ross felt a momentary chill as the cooler air of the super-refrigerated reactor-compartment drifted in.

He punched a stud, turning the page. Then—
What the hell is he doing in the reactor compartment?

The autopilot would be controlling the fuel flow, handling it down to the milligram, in a way no human system could. The reactor was primed for the landing, the fuel was stoked, the compartment was dogged shut. No one—least of all a Second Astrogator—had any business going back there.

Ross had the foam cradle dissolved in an instant, and was on his feet in another. He dashed down the companionway and through the open bulkhead door into the coolness of the reactor compartment.

Curtis was standing by the converter door, toying with the release-tripper. As Ross approached, he saw the astrogator get the door open and put one foot to the chute that led downship to the nuclear pile.

"Curtis, you idiot! Get away from there! You'll kill us all!"

The astrogator turned, looked blankly at Ross for an instant, and drew up his other foot. Ross leaped.

He caught Curtis' booted foot in his hands and, despite a barrage of kicks from the astrogator's free boot managed to drag Curtis off the chute. The astrogator tugged and pulled, attempting to break free. Ross saw the man's pale cheeks quivering; Curtis had cracked, but thoroughly.

Grunting, Ross yanked Curtis away from the yawning reactor chute and slammed the door shut. He dragged him out into the main section again, and slapped him hard.

"Why'd you want to do that? Don't you know what your mass would do to the ship if it got into the converter? You know the fuel intake's been calibrated already; a hundred eighty extra pounds and we'd arc right into the sun. What's wrong with you, Curtis?"

The astrogator fixed unshaking, unexpressive eyes on Ross. "I want to die," he said simply. "Why couldn't you let me die?"

He wanted to die. Ross shrugged, feeling a cold tremor run down his back. There was no guarding against this disease.

Just as aqualungers beneath the sea's surface suffered from *l'ivresse des grandes profondeurs*—rapture of the deeps—and knew no cure for the strange, depth-induced drunkenness that prompted them to remove their breathing-tubes fifty fathoms below, so did spacemen run the risk of this nameless malady, this inexplicable urge to self-destruction.

It struck anywhere. A repairman wielding a torch on a recalcitrant strut of an orbiting wheel might abruptly rip open his facemask and drink Vacuum; a radioman rigging an antenna on the skin of his ship might suddenly cut his line, fire his directional-pistol, and send himself drifting away sunward. Or a Second Astrogator might decide to climb into the converter.

Psych Officer Spangler appeared, an expression of concern fixed on his smooth pink face. "Trouble?"

Ross nodded. "Curtis. Tried to jump into the fuelchute. He's got it, Doc."

Scowling, Spangler rubbed his cheek, then said: "They always pick the best times, dammit. It's swell having a psycho on a Mercury run."

"That's the way it is," Ross said wearily. "Better put him in stasis till we get home. I'd hate to have him running loose looking for different ways of doing himself in."

"Why can't you let me die?" Curtis asked. His face was bleak. "Why'd you have to stop me?"

"Because, you lunatic, you'd have killed all the rest of us by your fool dive into the converter. Go walk out the airlock if you want to die—but don't take us with you."

Spangler glared warningly at him. "Harry—"

"Okay," Ross said. "Take him away."

The psychman led Curtis within. The astrogator would be given a tranquillizing injection and locked in an insoluble webfoam jacket for the rest of the journey. There was a chance he could be restored to sanity, once they returned to Earth, but Ross knew that the astrogator would make a beeline for the nearest method of suicide the moment he was let loose in space.

Brooding, Ross turned away. A man spends his boyhood dreaming about space, he thought, spends four years at the Academy and two more making dummy runs. Then he finally gets up where it counts, and he cracks up. Curtis was an astrogation machine, not a normal human being; and he had just disqualified himself permanently from the only job he knew how to do.

Ross shivered, feeling chill despite the bloated bulk of the sun filling the rear screen. It could happen to anyone… even him. He thought of Curtis lying in a foam cradle somewhere in the back of the ship, blankly thinking over and over again *I want to die*, while Doc Spangler muttered soothing things at him. A human being was really a frail form of life, Ross reflected.

Death seemed to hang over the ship; the gloomy aura of Curtis' suicide-wish polluted the atmosphere.

Ross shook his head and punched down savagely on the signal to prepare for deceleration. The unspinning globe that was Mercury bobbed up ahead. He spotted it through the front screen.

They were approaching the tiny planet middle-on. He could see the neat division now: the brightness of Sunside, the unapproachable inferno where zinc ran in rivers, and the icy blackness of Darkside, dull with its unlit plains of frozen CO_2.

Down the heart of the planet ran the Twilight Belt, that narrow area of not-cold and not-heat where Sunside and Darkside met to provide a thin band of barely-tolerable territory, a ring nine thousand miles in circumference and ten or twenty miles wide.

The *Leverrier* plunged downward. "Downward" was actually a misnomer—space has no ups or downs—but it was the simplest way for Ross to visualize the approach. He allowed his jangled nerves to calm. The ship was in the hands of the autopilot; the orbit was precomputed and the analogue banks in the drive were happily following the taped programme, bringing the ship to rest smack in the middle of—

My God!

Ross went cold from head to toe. The precomputed tape had been fed to the analogue banks—had been prepared by—had been the work of—

Curtis.

A suicidal madman had worked out the *Leverrier's* landing programme.

Ross' hands began to shake. How easy it would have been, he thought, for death-bent Curtis to work out an orbit that would plant the *Leverrier* in a smoking river of molten lead—or in the mortuary chill of Darkside.

His false security vanished. There was no trusting the automatic pilot; they'd have to risk a manual landing.

Ross jabbed down on the communicator button. "I want Brainerd," he said hoarsely.

The First Astrogator appeared a few seconds later, peering in cautiously. "What goes, Captain?"

"We've just carted your assistant Curtis off to the pokey. He tried to jump into the converter."

"He—?"

Ross nodded. "Attempted suicide; I nabbed him in time. But in view of the circumstances I think we'd better discard the tape you had him prepare and bring the ship down manually, yes?"

The First Astrogator moistened his lips. "Maybe that's a good idea," he said.

"Damn right it is," Ross said, glowering.

As the ship touched down, Ross thought, *Mercury is two hells in one.*

It was the cold, ice-bound kingdom of Dante's deepest pit—and it was also the brimstone empire of another conception. The two met, fire and frost, each hemisphere its own kind of hell.

He lifted his head and flicked a quick glance at the instrument panel above his deceleration cradle. The dials all checked: weight displacement was proper, stability 100%, external temperature a manageable 108F., indicating they had made their landing a little to the sunward of the Twilight Belt's exact middle. It had been a sound landing.

He snapped on the communicator. "Brainerd?"

"All OK, Captain."

"How was the landing? You used manual, didn't you?"

"I had to," the astrogator said. "I ran a quick check on Curtis' tape and it was all cockeyed. We'd have grazed Mercury's orbit by a whisker and kept going—straight for the sun. Nice?"

"Sweet," Ross said. "But don't be too hard on the kid; it's not his fault he went psycho. Good landing, anyway. We seem to be pretty close to the centre of the Twilight Belt, give or take a mile or two."

He broke the contact and unwebbed himself. "We're here," he announced over the shipwide circuit. "All hands to fore double pronto."

★

The men got there quickly enough—Brainerd first, then Doc Spangler followed by Accumulator Tech Krinsky and the three crewmen. Ross waited until the entire group had assembled.

They were looking around curiously for Curtis, all but Brainerd and Spangler. Crisply, Ross said, "Astrogator Curtis won't be with us. He's aft in the psycho bin; luckily, we can shift without him on this tour."

He waited till the implications of that statement had sunk in. The men adjusted to it well, he thought, judging from the swiftness with which the horror faded from their faces.

"All right," he said. "Schedule calls for us to spend a maximum of thirty-two hours on Mercury before departure. Brainerd, how does that check with our location?"

The astrogator frowned and made some mental calculations. "Current position is a trifle to the sunward edge of the Twilight Belt; but as I figure it, the sun won't be high enough to put the Fahrenheit much above 120 for at least a week. Our suits can handle that sort of temperature with ease."

"Good. Llewellyn, you and Falbridge break out the radar inflaters and get the tower set up as far to the east as you can go without roasting. Take the crawler, but be sure to keep an eye on the thermometer. We've only got one heat-suit, and that's for Krinsky."

Llewellyn, a thin, sunken-eyed spaceman, shifted uneasily. "How far to the east do you suggest, sir?"

"The Twilight Belt covers about a quarter of Mercury's surface," Ross said. "You've got a strip 47 degrees wide to move around in—but I don't suggest you go much more than twenty-five miles or so. It starts getting hot after that, and keeps going up."

"Yes, sir."

Ross turned to Krinsky. The Accumulator Tech was the key man of the expedition; it was his job to check the readings on the pair of

Solar Accumulators that had been left here by the first expedition. He was to measure the amount of stress created by solar energies here, so close to the source of radiation, study force-lines operating in the strange magnetic field of the little world, and re-prime the Accumulators for further testing at a later date.

Krinsky was a tall, powerfully-built man, the sort of man who could stand up to the crushing weight of a heat-suit almost cheerfully. The heat-suit was necessary for prolonged work in the Sunside zone, where the Accumulators were—and even a giant like Krinsky could stand the strain only for a few hours at a time.

"When Llewellyn and Falbridge have the radar tower set up, Krinsky, get into your heat-suit and be ready to move. As soon as we've got the Accumulator Station located, Dominic will drive you as far east as possible and drop you off. The rest is up to you. We'll be telemetering your readings, but we'd like to have you back alive."

"Yes, sir."

"That's about it," Ross said. "Let's get rolling."

Ross' own job was purely administrative—and, as the men of his crew moved busily about their allotted tasks, he realized unhappily that he himself was condemned to temporary idleness. His function was that of overseer; like the conductor of a symphony orchestra, he played no instrument himself, and was on hand mostly to keep the group moving in harmony toward the finish.

Now, he had only to wait.

Llewellyn and Falbridge departed, riding the segmented, thermo-resistant crawler carried in the belly of the *Leverrier*. Their job was simple: they were to erect the inflatable plastic radar tower far to sunward. The tower that had been left by the first expedition had long since librated into a Sunside zone and been liquefied; the plastic base and parabola, covered with a light reflective surface of aluminium, could hardly withstand the searing heat of Sunside.

Out there, it got up to 700 degrees when the sun was at its closest; the eccentricities of Mercury's orbit accounted for considerable Sunside temperature variations; but the thermometer never showed lower than 300 degrees on Sunside, even during aphelion. On Darkside, there was little variation; temperature hung down near absolute zero, and frozen drifts of heavy gases covered the surface of the land.

From where he stood, Ross could see neither sunside nor Darkside. The Twilight Belt was nearly a thousand miles broad, and as the planet dipped in its orbit the sun would first slide above the horizon, then dip back. For a twenty-mile strip through the heart of the belt, the heat of Sunside and the cold of Darkside cancelled out into a fairly stable temperate climate; for five hundred miles on either side, the Twilight Belt gradually tracked toward the areas of cold and raging heat.

It was a strange and forbidding planet. Humans could endure it only for short times; the sort of life that *would* be able to exist permanently on Mercury was beyond his conception. Standing outside the *Leverrier* in his spacesuit, Ross nudged the chin control that lowered a pane of optical glass He peered first toward Darkside, where he thought he saw a thin line of encroaching black—only illusion, he knew—and then toward Sunside.

In the distance, Llewellyn and Falbridge were erecting the spidery parabola that was the radar tower. He could see the clumsy shape outlined against the sky now—and behind it? A faint line of brightness rimming the bordering peaks? Illusion also, he knew. Brainerd had calculated that the sun's radiation would not be visible here for a week. And in a week's time they'd be back on Earth.

He turned to Krinsky. "The tower's nearly up. They'll be back with the crawler any minute. You'd better get ready to make your trip."

Krinsky nodded. "I'll suit up, sir."

As the technician swung up the handholds and into the ship, Ross' thoughts turned to Curtis. The young astrogator had prattled of seeing Mercury, all the way out—and now that they were actually here, Curtis lay in a web of foam deep within the ship, moodily demanding the right to die.

Krinsky returned, now wearing the insulating bulk of the heat-suit over his standard rebreathing outfit. He look like a small tank rather than a man. "Is the crawler approaching, sir?"

"I'll take a look."

Ross adjusted the lensplate in his mask and narrowed his eyes. It seemed to him that the temperature had risen somewhat. Another illusion, he thought, as he squinted into the distance.

His eyes picked out the radar tower far off toward Sunside. His mouth sagged open.

"Something the matter, sir?"

"I'll say!" Ross squeezed his eyes tight shut and looked again. And—yes—the newly-erected radar tower was drooping soggily, and beginning to melt. He saw two tiny figures racing madly over the flat, pumice-covered ground to the silvery oblong that was the crawler. And—impossibly—the first glow of an unmistakeable brightness was beginning to shimmer on the mountains behind the tower.

The sun was rising—a week ahead of schedule!

Ross gasped and ran back into the ship, followed by the lumbering Krinsky. In the airlock, mechanical hands descended to help him out of his spacesuit; he signalled to Krinsky to remain in the heat-suit, and dashed through into the main cabin.

"Brainerd! Brainerd! Where in hell are you?"

The senior astrogator appeared, looking puzzled. "Yes, Captain?"

"Look out the screen," Ross said in a strangled voice. "Look at the radar tower!"

"It's—*melting*," Brainerd said, astonished. "But that's—that's—"

"I know. It's impossible." Ross glanced at the instrument panel. External temperature had risen to 112—a jump of four degrees. And as he watched it clicked up to 114.

It would take a heat of at least 500 degrees to melt the radar tower that way. Ross squinted at the screen, and saw the crawler come swinging dizzily toward them: Llewellyn and Falbridge were still alive, then—though they probably had had a good cooking out there. The temperature outside the ship was up to 116. It would probably be near 200 by the time the two men returned.

Angrily, Ross faced the astrogator. "I thought you were bringing us down in the safety strip," he snapped. "Check your figures again and find out where the hell we *really* are. Then work out a blasting orbit. That's the *sun* coming up over those hills."

"I know," Brainerd said.

The temperature reached 120. The ship's cooling system would be able to keep things under control and comfortable until about 250; beyond that, there was danger of an overload. The crawler continued to draw near; it was probably hellish in the little landcar, he thought.

His mind weighed alternatives. If the external temperature went much over 250, he would run the risk of wrecking the ship's cooling system by waiting for the two in the crawler to arrive. He decided he'd give them until it hit 275 to get back and then clear out. It was foolish to try to save two lives at a cost of five. External temperature had hit 130. Its rate of increase was jumping rapidly.

The ship's crew knew what was going on now. Without direct orders from Ross, they were readying the *Leverrier* for an emergency blastoff.

The crawler inched forward. The two men weren't much more than ten miles away now; and at an average speed of forty miles an hour they'd be back within fifteen minutes. Outside it was 133. Long fingers of shimmering sunlight stretched toward them from the horizon.

Brainerd looked up from his calculations. "I can't work it. The damned figures don't come out."

"Huh?"

"I'm computing our location—and I can't do the arithmetic. My head's all foggy."

What the hell, Ross thought. This was when a captain earned his pay. "Get out of the way," he snapped. "Let me do it."

He sat down at the desk and started figuring. He saw Brainerd's hasty notations scratched out everywhere. It was as if the astrogator had totally forgotten how to do his job.

Let's see now, If we're—

His pencil flew over the pad—but as he worked he saw that it was all wrong. His mind felt bleary, strange; he couldn't seem to handle the computations. Looking up, he said, "Tell Krinsky to get down there and be ready to help those men out of the crawler when it gets here. They're probably half-crooked."

Temperature 146. He looked back at the pad. Damn; it shouldn't be that hard to do simple trig, he thought.

Doc Spangler appeared. "I cut Curtis free," he announced. "He isn't safe during takeoff in that cradle."

From within came a steady mutter. "Just let me die... just let me die..."

"Tell him he's likely to have his wish," Ross murmured. "If I can't work out a blastoff orbit we'll all roast here."

"How come *you're* doing it? What's the matter with Brainerd?"

"Choked up. Couldn't do the figures. And come to think of it, I feel pretty funny myself."

Fingers of fog seemed to wrap around his mind. He glanced at the dial. Temperature 152 outside. That gave the boys in the crawler 123 degrees to get back here... or was it 321? He was confused, utterly bewildered.

Doc Spangler looked strange too. The psych officer was frowning curiously. "I feel very lethargic suddenly," Spangler declared. "I know I really should get back to Curtis, but—"

The madman was keeping up a steady babble inside. The part of Ross' mind that could still think clearly realized that if left unattended Curtis was capable of almost anything.

Temperature 158. The crawler seemed nearer. On the horizon, the radar tower was becoming a crazy shambles.

There was a shriek. "It's Curtis!" Ross yelled, his mind returning to awareness hurriedly, and peeled out from behind the desk. He ran aft, followed by Spangler, but it was too late.

Curtis lay on the floor in a bloody puddle. He had found a pair of shears somewhere.

Spangler bent. "He's dead."

"Of course. He's dead," Ross echoed. His brain felt totally clear now; at the moment of Curtis' death, the fog had lifted. Leaving Spangler to attend to the body, he returned to the desk and glanced at the computations.

With icy clarity he determined their location. They had come down better than three hundred miles to sunward of where they thought they had been. The instruments hadn't lied—but someone's eyes had. The orbit Brainerd that had so solemnly assured him was a "safe" one was actually almost as deadly as the one Curtis had computed.

He looked outside. The crawler was almost there; temperature was 167. There was plenty of time. They would make it with a few minutes to spare, thanks to the warning they had received from the melting radar tower.

But why had it happened? There was no answer to that.

Gigantic in his heat-suit, Krinsky brought Llewellyn and Falbridge aboard. They peeled out of their spacesuits and wobbled unsteadily, then collapsed. They looked like a pair of just-boiled lobsters.

"Heat prostration," Ross said. "Krinsky, get them into takeoff cradles. Dominic, you in your suit yet?"

The spaceman appeared at the airlock entrance and nodded.

"Good. Get down there and drive the crawler into the hold. We can't afford to leave it here. Double-quick, and then we'll blast off. Brainerd, that new orbit ready?"

"Yes, sir."

The thermometer grazed 200. The cooling system was beginning to suffer—but its agonies were to be short-lived. Within minutes, the *Leverrier* had lifted from Mercury's surface—minutes ahead of the relentless advance of the sun—and swung into a temporary planet-circling orbit.

As they hung there, virtually catching their breaths, just one question rose in Ross' mind: *why*? Why did Brainerd's orbit bring them down in a danger zone instead of the safety strip? Why had both Brainerd and Ross been unable to compute a blasting-pattern, the simplest of elementary astrogation techniques? And why had Spangler's wits utterly failed him—just long enough to let the unhappy Curtis kill himself?

Ross could see the same question reflected on everyone's face: *why?*

He felt an itchy feeling at the base of his skull. And suddenly, an image forced its way across his mind in answer.

It was a great pool of molten zinc, lying shimmering between two jagged crests somewhere on Sunside. It had been there thousands of years; it would be there thousands, perhaps millions of years from now.

Its surface quivered. The sun's brightness upon the pool was intolerable even to the mind's eye.

Radiation beat down on the zinc pool—the sun's radiation, hard and unending, and then a new radiation, an electromagnetic emanation and with it a meaningful commutation:

I want to die.

The pool of zinc stirred fretfully with sudden impulses of helpfulness.

The vision passed as quickly as it came. Stunned, Ross looked up hesitantly. The expression on the six faces surrounding him told him what he wanted to know.

"You felt it too," he said.

Spangler nodded, then Krinsky and the rest of them.

"Yes," Krinsky said. "What the devil was it?"

Brainerd turned to Spangler. "Are we all nuts, Doc?"

The psych officer shrugged "Mass hallucination... collective hypnosis..."

"No, Doc." Ross leaned forward. "You know it as well as I do. That thing was real; it's down there, out on Sunside."

"What do you mean?"

"I mean that wasn't any hallucination we had. That's *life*— or as close to it as Mercury can come." Ross' hands shook; he forced them to subside. "We've stumbled over something very big," he said.

Spangler stirred uneasily. "Harry—"

"No, I'm not out of my head! Don't you see—that thing down there, whatever it is, is sensitive to our thoughts! It picked up Curtis' godawful caterwauling the way a radar set grabs electromagnetic waves. His were the strongest thoughts coming through; so it acted on them and did its damnedest to help Curtis' wish come true."

"You mean by fogging our minds, and deluding us into thinking we were in safe territory, when actually we were right near sunrise territory?"

"But why would it go to all that trouble?" Krinsky objected. "If it wanted to help poor Curtis kill himself, why didn't it just fix it so we came down right *in* Sunside? We'd cook a lot quicker that way."

Ross shook his head. "It knew that the rest of us *didn't* want to die. The thing down there must be a multi-valued thinker. It took the conflicting emanations of Curtis and the rest of us, and fixed things so that he'd die, and we wouldn't." He shivered. "Once Curtis was out of the way, it acted to help the surviving crewmembers get off to safety. If you'll remember, we all thought and moved a lot quicker the instant Curtis was dead"

"Damned if that's not so," Spangler said. "But—"

"What I want to know is, do we go back down?" Krinsky asked. "If that thing is what you say it is, I'm not so sure I want to go within reach of it again. Who knows what it might make us do *this* time?"

"It wants to help us," Ross said stubbornly. "It's not hostile. You're not afraid, are you? I was counting on you to go out and scout for it in the heat-suit."

"Not me!" Krinsky said hastily.

Ross scowled. "But this is the first intelligent life-form we've hit in the Solar System yet. We can't simply run away and hide!" To Brainerd he said, "Set up an orbit that'll take us back down again—and this time put us down where we won't melt."

"I can't do it, sir," Brainerd said flatly. "I believe the safety of the crew will be best served by returning to Earth at once."

Facing the group of them, Ross glanced quickly from one to the next. There was fear evident on the faces of all of them. He knew what each of them was thinking: *I don't want to go back to Mercury.*

Six of them; one of him. And the helpful thing below.

They had outnumbered Curtis seven to one—but unmixed by the death-wish. Ross knew he could never generate enough strength of thought to counteract the fear-ridden thoughts of the other six.

This is mutiny, he thought, but somehow he did not care to speak the thought aloud. Here was a case where a superior officer might legitimately be removed from command for the common good, and he knew it.

The creature below was ready to offer its services. But, multivalued as it might be, there was still only one spaceship, and one of the two parties—either he or the rest of them—would have to be denied its wishes.

Yet, he thought, the pool had contrived to satisfy both the man who wished to die and whose who wished to stay alive. Now, six wanted to return—but could the voice of the seventh be ignored? *You're not being fair to me*, Ross thought, directing his angry outburst toward the planet below. *I want to see you. I want to study you. Don't let them drag me back to Earth.*

When the *Leverrier* returned to Earth, a week later, the six survivors of the Second Mercury Expedition could all describe in detail

how a fierce death-wish had overtaken Second Astrogator Curtis
and caused his suicide. But not one of them could recall what had
happened to Flight Commander Ross, or why the heat-suit had been
left behind on Mercury.

THE NIGHT SKY FROM MERCURY, WHICH WOULD BE COMPARABLE
TO THAT WHICH WOULD BE SEEN FROM VULCAN. THE EARTH
AND VENUS SHINE PARTICULARLY BRIGHTLY.

VULCAN

The Hell Planet   Leslie F. Stone

This is not the Vulcan of Mr. Spock from *Star Trek* though, like that Vulcan, this one does not exist. But it seemed to, for a while.

During the 1850s the French astronomer Urbain Le Verrier who, as we shall see, calculated the position of Neptune with pin-point accuracy, was trying to obtain more data on the orbit of Mercury. By 1859 Le Verrier had become convinced that there had to be something else acting upon Mercury to explain the perturbations in the planet's orbit, and he suggested there must be an inner planet, closer to the Sun, which he called Vulcan. Following Le Verrier's calculations, the amateur astronomer, Dr. Edmond Lescarbault announced he had seen Vulcan and, over time, other astronomers made the claim. However, their data suggested a planet too small to have a sufficient effect upon Mercury's orbit, and Le Verrier began to wonder whether there was an asteroid belt close to the Sun. He died in 1877 without having resolved the problem.

Despite claims by others that they had also seen an inner planet, there were more claims by those who had seen nothing, but it was difficult to dismiss entirely. Any such planet would be seen only briefly at sunset and sunrise, and so close to the Sun that its glare could hide the planet. With the advent of astro-photography it became easier to observe the heavens in minute detail. Vulcan proved too elusive and by 1909 it had been all but dismissed. When Albert Einstein published his General Theory of Relativity in 1915, it was realized that the immensity of the Sun's gravitational pull had an even stronger secondary effect upon any nearby object and this was enough to explain Le Verrier's anomaly.

There was no Vulcan.

But for fifty years or more there just might have been, and its possibility continued to linger in the imaginations of many. The astronomer and meteorologist Donald Horner included Vulcan in his fanciful tour of the heavens *By Aeroplane to the Sun* (1910), but said nothing about it. The pulp writers took it to their heart, though. It is a valuable source of a rare element in Leslie F. Stone's "The Hell Planet" (1931), reprinted here. It's a penal colony in Harl Vincent's "Vulcan's Workshop" (1932) and it's an artificial world in Ross Rocklynne's "At the Centre of Gravity" (1936) where two men are trapped inside the planet. John Russell Fearn was at his most imaginative in "Mathematica" (1936) and its sequel where Vulcan was not only an artificial world, but the place from which the solar system was created. Vulcan is at its most vivid in Leigh Brackett's "Child of the Sun" (1942), with its surface like "splinters of black glass" and its underworld beings of living fire. In the Captain Future novel "Outlaw World" (1946) by Edmond Hamilton, Vulcan is also a hollow world, inhabited within.

The possibility of Vulcan lingered at least until the publication of *Mission to Mercury* (1965), a young-adult novel by Hugh Walters, in which our heroes observe Vulcan in its orbit. But the concept has not gone altogether. In "Vulcan's Forge" (1983), Poul Anderson has scientists on Mercury discover a near molten asteroid in orbit around the Sun.

The solar system will certainly have more surprises.

⸻

Leslie F. Stone (1905–1991) was one of the pioneer women contributors to the early science-fiction pulps. She had trained as a journalist and married fellow newspaperman William Silberberg in 1927 but she retained her maiden name for all her published work. Her first appearance, besides some fairy tales in her local newspaper, was with "Men with Wings" (1929) about human glandular manipulation that brought forth winged humans. Her first sale had been "Out of the Void" (1929) which appeared later, and besides its super-scientific paraphernalia was one of the rare stories from those early days to include a transvestite, who becomes the first female space captain. In fact, Stone should be applauded for challenging the barriers. Her Saturnian hero in "The Fall of Mercury" (1935) is a black man. The society in "The Conquest of Gola" (1931) is a matriarchy that defeats the male invaders from Earth. Stone sold some twenty stories to the sf pulps until the change in the market in the 1940s drove her away. Her work was reprinted, though, keeping her name alive, and in 1967 she revised "Out of the Void" for book publication, but further efforts came to naught. By then she had become more interested in gardening and ceramics and worked for the National Institute of Health. Their gain was almost certainly science fiction's loss.

I

"**T**HERE HE IS. LORD! WHAT A HOT LITTLE PLACE. Can't say I look forward to landing there particularly. Rather well named, what? Vulcan, master of the forge, maker of the armour of the mighty gods from the white heat of the flame!"

"It's the find of the century, Gorely, no question of that, if only it yields a third the amount of *cosmicite*[*] Wendell says it will. If so we'll be multi-millionaires after this trip."

"Well, at least, we won't be in the same straits that the Sellers crowd were. We know what we're up against with Wendell on hand. What a fight he must have put up to come through alone."

"Hush… here he comes…"

The pair, Tom Gorley and Jack Morgan, were standing in the forward turret of the space ship *Adventure*. Both were seasoned explorers as were all Captain Timothy Beale's crew. They had been in many odd places together, to Diane on the very edge of the solar system, but this was their first time so close to Sol, beyond Mercury. They wore the dark glasses and insulated refrigerated suits necessary scarcely more than twenty-five millions of miles from the sun.

---

[*]   Cosmicite seems to have been that rare metal possessing the ability to absorb and reflect practically all rays, no matter what their wavelength. Its use on earth as a heat-insulator would have been revolutionary if sufficient quantities were to be had.

The refrigerant units of the *Adventure*, despite the heat insulating coating of *cosmicite*, were hard taxed to keep a liveable temperature within the shell of the space flyer, but the men were not heeding the heat. They were looking forward to their descent upon the orphan of the solar system, Vulcan, innermost planet, discovered by the crew of the *Corsair* four months before.

Astronomically speaking, Vulcan had for many years in the past been conceded as a possibility by scientists. The perihelion of the orbit of Mercury moves somewhat faster than it should if the planet were acted upon only by known forces, and this fact had led astronomers to believe in an intra-Mercurian planet. The peculiarity of Mercury's motion pointed toward an attraction of a planet whose orbit lay between that world and the sun. A planet in this position could be observed only with difficulty, for its elongation from the sun would always be small. Several times in the past it was supposed to have been observed, yet others disputed the truth of such a discovery. Naturally it would be next to impossible to see this tiny planet against the glare of the sun's disc.

It had taken Captain Boris Sellers to find it; but he had not survived his discovery. Every man of his crew had died a horrible death, except Bill Wendell who alone managed to pilot the *Corsair* back to Earth with its gruesome burden of dead men, and his tale of discovery. That awful journey had left its mark on him as one could see at a glance, as he came into the *Adventure's* turret.

Although only thirty-four he looked a man of sixty. His hair had turned snowy white, his eyes were dimmed, still filled with some nameless horror which lurked in their depths. Heavy lines creased the flesh about his mouth; and his walk was that of a man whose body is tortured by the pains of senility.

Only the lure of the vast deposits of *cosmicite*, that priceless metal without which no ship could dare travel the void, had brought him back to Vulcan. He had the guarantee that half the wealth the *Adventure* would unearth would go to him and to the families of those men who had lost their lives on the ill-fated journey of discovery.

The men of the *Adventure* were diffident about addressing Wendell. He seemed to move in a world of his own, annoyed if others sought intrusion there. But today was different—he had come seeking the company of those in the turret.

He stood gazing out the thick port giving view to the world they were approaching. The window, like all the shell, was daubed with a covering of *cosmicite* put on with a spray so that it was so thin as to be transparent. But for that coating, the crew of the *Adventure* could not have withstood the terrible emanations of the cosmic and heat rays that pervaded space.

The discovery of *cosmicite* is a story in itself. One remembers the first intrepid space explorers who lost their lives in attempting to conquer space with no knowledge of the danger they faced when they plunged out of the Earth's atmospheric blanket. Oddly enough the man who discovered the only material impervious to the dangerous rays was one by the name of John Cosmo!

"A few hours and we'll be there," Wendell was saying in his quavering voice more to himself than those in the chamber with him. "Vulcan, the monster itself in beauty, festering in poison... Sellers, Tomlin, Berber, Keep, Lassier, Morton, Chin... all dead... and only I am alive to tell the story!"

"But you found the mines, didn't you?" Gorely asked timidly, suddenly realizing how little they knew of what lay before them. Wendell had, of course, explained everything to Captain Beale, but for the most part the men were ignorant of what they were to face. Men of space never asked questions; their trust lay in their leaders.

Wendell looked up in surprise at the other's voice. He studied the man before him as if seeing him for the first time in his life, though purposely he had come here seeking companionship.

"The mines... the... oh, you mean the *cosmicite* mines. No! We did not find the mines. The natives had it. Ingots of it, statues, shields, arrows and spears tipped with it... they worship it like a god! *Cosmicite. Dasie* they called it. Believed it protected them from their enemies. A backward people, but they mined the metal.

"And they thought we were gods. A kindly people. They wined and dined us... only not me. I had a bad stomach, a recurrence of sickness of years back. I was confined to the *Corsair*, on a soft diet... too sick to eat or walk. I was put out by it, I imagined my companions receiving gifts I could not share. I was jealous! I avoided them.

"The fourth day I felt better. I went out to meet them as they came into the ship laden with gifts—strange fruits, meats, wines and *cosmicite*. I picked up a bunch of fruit that resembled grapes. I ate one. Then... then Berber, my buddy... he pitched to the floor screaming and retching. He was sick, something was tearing at his vitals, he said... he was burning up... fever. A few minutes and he could not speak. We carried him to his berth, dosed him up... then Lassier was taken sick. We put him to bed, but he wasn't the last. Another and another were taken ill... then the captain.

"There were only Chin and I left to treat our fellows. We went from one to another giving medicine that seemed to do no good. Berber could not raise his chest to breathe now. It... it was as if his bones could no longer support the flesh... they were rotting away! The others were the same. Now Chin could no longer walk. Oh it was... damnable. My friends dying... I unable to ease them. Berber died, then Lassier... they all died before my eyes. Captain Sellers alone knew what it was… he told me… the fruit, the water… all poison. It was radium… the soil, the water, the growing things… even the natives were impregnated with it… and it was too rich in solution for men of Earth. It was killing them.

"I remembered the single grape I had eaten… I thought I felt stomach pangs already, but I had to stand by and listen to Captain Sellers telling me what to do. 'They think us gods,' he said, speaking of the natives. 'They must not know of this… that we die. You, Wendell, take the *Corsair* back home with all of us in it! You must not bury us here… There is a fortune on Vulcan… it is stupendous. *Cosmicite* is scarce throughout the solar worlds, but this planet is filthy with it… and radium… you must get home… tell others what we have seen… bring an expedition to mine it. Treat the natives well… they may be induced to tell where their mines lay… then all the solar system will be ours… thousands of space flyers can be built in place of the paltry fifty or sixty now in existence… but let no man *eat or drink of this world!*'

"He said more, then began to babble, and like the others it grew difficult for him to breathe. I turned away, forced my stomach to give up that bit of fruit I had eaten. I was frantic with the moans of my fellow-men in my ears. Men dying like flies…" He lapsed into silence while he remembered.

After a pause the young-old man began to speak again. "I tried my best to ease their pain, some died more quickly than others… according to the proportion in which they had eaten the food of the natives. But they had had four days of it. Sellers was last to go, though quite out of his head by then. It was not easy to drive the *Corsair* without help, to plot my course and watch out for meteorites. It meant days of continual vigilance at the controls. And there were the bodies of my fellows below.

"I could not move them... they were already rotting... putrefaction had set in almost immediately with their passing. I could only cover them with sheets... soon the ship smelled like a charnel house.

"And I began to feel real pains in my stomach. The single grape had poured poison into my system before I got rid of it. Lucky that I had eaten no more... else I would not be here to tell the tale. I suffered... my stomach was a fiery pit, my head spun like a top, my knees were weak, and with it all I had to stay at my controls. I fought it off somehow... as a result I am a sick man for the rest of my days. I... well here I am back for more... and if you value your lives, men, if you do not want to die an evil death, do not be tempted by the sweet luscious fruit and sparkling waters of Vulcan... it's..."

He would have said more but Jimson, Beale's lieutenant, had appeared in the doorway. "Mr. Wendell," he called, "the captain wants to see you in the control-room."

Wendell went with him. Beale was studying the world that rapidly edged closer. They had come halfway around the sun to meet it, and now Vulcan lay in quadrature to them, its first quarter, showing them half its illuminated side. At most it was but 1200 miles in diameter, a small world whose mass was surprisingly great in proportion to its size. Wendell had already explained to Beale that Vulcan's surface gravity was in excess of that felt by men of Earth when upon the moon. That was because it was made up of the heaviest of metals. Now the captain wanted to know if Wendell knew where they were to land.

In half an hour the little world looked like a bowl with its upturned edges. They were circling it, passing from the light into the darkness twice. They saw it had no really large areas of water. There were innumerable lakes and rivers, but nothing that could be rightfully called a sea. There were mountains in one hemisphere, but for the most it was flat or slightly rolling country. One thing was particularly noticeable about the night side, the fact that the vegetation gave off a ghostly light, glowed of itself like phosphorus. The lakes were molten silver, the jungles a riot of wild colour.

As they dropped closer Beale saw that landing was to be a problem. Never had he seen a more fecund world. Nowhere could they see the ground, so heavily was it grown with tall spiky trees, fleshy vines and spreading shrubs. Even the banks of the waterways were overgrown, heavy with life. At Beale's query, Wendell shook his head. Just so had the *Corsair* found Vulcan. They could blast an opening in the trees for themselves, but if they wished to find natives it would be best to cruise about until they sighted a clearing, a man-made clearing.

By laboriously pulling out the trees, the men of Vulcan made a council-hall for themselves. In one of these clearings the *Corsair* had found a ready berth, nor had the natives appeared to resent their using it. The *Corsair* had found the village near the north pole. Wendell had left too hurriedly to be sure of finding it again, but he imagined they could find another like it.

Every man able to get near a port-hole was made a lookout. Twice they circled Vulcan again and were rewarded. A circular opening in the jungle lay below, just large enough for the *Adventure* to fit with little room to spare. Wendell did not believe it the same clearing in which the *Corsair* had landed, but it was likely enough with a promise of a village nearby.

With wondering eyes the men stared at the queer life about them, for it was even stranger than it had appeared from above. The trees were for the most part a hundred feet high, straight, slender with trunks that resembled those of a palm tree: smooth, glistening, barkless; but the branches that jutted from their crowns were unlike anything they had ever seen. They were long, stiff, needle-pointed spikes with a feathery lacy froth of needles. The branches were no more than three to four feet in length, solitary and uncrowded. The only shade cast by the whole tree was the straight unvarying image of its pole-like length.

Vines clung somehow to the unyielding trees, vines that dropped festoons of needles from their length linking the jungle trees together. Around the trees was growing a veritable mat of stiff-stalked young trees; bushes, stocky plants, all with underdeveloped spiky leaves and branches. Only on the ground was there a growth with a fleshier leaf—broad and flat, prone to the soil. The bushes mostly resembled palmettos and cacti.

Nature, at first lavish, had turned about-face and with niggardly hand finished her work, stinting the land of her natural abundance. Then she had remembered and was more prolific, for on each tree, weighing down the vines, bending the backs of the shrubs, palmettos and cacti were the fruit clusters. Red, yellow, blue, orange, green they were; long banana-shaped fruit, globulars of all sizes, berries, melons—round, oval, cylindrical, every shape and form; luscious peaches, over-sized pears, mouth-watering berries, scarlet cherries, purple grapes, juicy plums, golden oranges... all were here in wild profusion, in wild fecundity.

"It's the sun," explained Wendell. "Were the leaves of the trees broad they would absorb too much vitality beside that already partaken of from the radioactive soil, hence they would shrivel and die under the glare of the white-hot sun. Nature can be more prodigal with the fruit because there are enough to make use of it... See..." He pointed out flocks of tiny birds, no larger than humming birds darting among the fruit, the swarms of insects feeding in armies, the dainty head of some animal feeding on fruit fallen to the ground.

Another creature that looked like a cross between a bear and a monkey was climbing a tall tree toward an especially appetizing cluster of fruit hanging by a slender cord from a vine. The fruit proved just out of reach of the animal, but with infinite patience the bear angled for the prize with long forelegs. At last, unable to gain the fruit by that means, it let go its hold upon the tree-trunk to make a lunge for the fruit cluster, and landed upon it with all four feet. The vine held and the animal went about the prosaic business of harvesting its dinner without a care as to what would happen when it ate away its support.

A shadow fell against the trees and ground. Glancing up the men saw an unusually large, brightly-plumaged bird plunging downward. Through the thick walls of the ship they could not hear its cry, but they could see its paralysing effect upon the flock of humming birds which for the nonce seemed suspended on quivering wings unable to move forward or backward. The killer had time to swoop down, gobble a third of their number before their brains began to function properly again, and they could escape. The big fellow made no attempt to follow. He simply turned to the fruit nearest at hand and commenced to gorge himself.

Beale and Jimson, standing with Wendell, grew aware of even more life in the jungle. Birds of every size and description flew through the trees, creatures lurked among the vines, snakes and tiny furred things raced up and down tree trunks and vines, flinging themselves through the air. There was life on the ground, peering from between the heavy, thick leaves of the vines that crawled upon the earth's bosom. Suddenly Wendell was pointing out a strange apparition to his companions.

It stood staring back at them from between two tree trunks, a creature five feet tall, upright on two legs. It had a small pointed face that was fox-like, yet faintly resembled a human face! The head was round, bulging upward from heavy beetling brows. The ears that came to a point at the top were set on the side of the head slightly below the level of the large black eyes. The nose was long, pointed—the cheeks and jowls sloped forward adding to its animal-like appearance. The mouth was wide, the chin rather heavy-set, incongruous looking to the rest of the face, giving it its humanness that was otherwise lacking except in the rather intelligent set of the large beady black eyes.

II

Men of Vulcan

The face and body were bare of hair, the skin a slate brown. The body was proportionately slender to its height, in repose it leaned forward so that the thin arms dangled below the knee. Hands like the face were free of fur, delicately-boned, almost claws.

"It's the man of Vulcan," averred Wendell. "Or at least we called it a man, for such were the creatures we encountered before. This clearing is their meeting hall. They live back among the trees. If these little fellows are like the others they will have *cosmicite* in plenty!" He was excited.

"What shall we do?" queried Beale.

"Nothing. Wait. More will come. They are peaceable, or so the others were. Let them see we mean no harm. Let the men stay at the windows—come and go—act natural."

For two days no attempt was made to communicate with the strange little "men" of Vulcan. All the crew were now familiar with their bizarre appearance, their fox-like faces, their twitching ears that always seemed in movement, their stiff gawky walk, their strangely shiny bodies. For the most part they seemed unarmed, only a few carried a strange type of ridiculously small bows and arrows. What interested the Tellurians the most was the fact that the arrows and a few spears that appeared now and then were tipped with white metal cosmicite! The metal seemed in common use among the Vulcanites, yet at the same time was held in veneration. They wore strings of it about their necks from which dangled either round nuggets of the same material, or tiny, crudely-carved figurines, amulets. They wore queer elbow and knee-shields of cosmicite, curved plates that fitted over the joints and were held in place with thongs. Some had bits of cosmicite wire twisted about both head and body, and a few carried broad round shields of it on the left arm.

The very inactivity of the Adventure's crew seemed to have gained the confidence of the natives. They had drawn nearer and nearer to the space ship, studying its exterior first from afar, then dared to lay reverent hands upon its shell. They appeared to have discovered that it was coated with cosmicite, and this homely truth had wiped away the last vestige of their fear. They could understand that!

One little fellow, more daring than the rest, enticed two of his fellows to form a living ladder for him to climb upon their shoulders. That brought him up to the level of one port-hole in the ship's side. There were two of the men within, and for several moments the three stared at each other—the two curious, the fox-man awed by his own daring. From them his eyes flitted to the room beyond. For the moment the savage forgot everything else as he stared at the strange furnishings. Then suddenly he swayed and toppled from their sight. His ladder had given way!

He picked himself up, and they saw him racing across the clearing and into the jungle, all atitter to tell his friends what wonders he had seen.

On the third day Wendell, Beale and Jimson sallied forth from the flyer. They wore the lead-mesh under-suits Wendell had insisted be brought along, shoes with thin lead soles, helmets of lead-mesh that had visors over the face that could be raised at will. Their gloves were heavy with lead. Lead alone would protect them from the radium emanations that had killed the men of the *Corsair*. Besides this they wore dark glasses to protect the eyes against the excessive sunlight of Vulcan. Only the small gravitation on Vulcan's surface, but one-sixth that on earth, permitted the men of earth to burden themselves with hundreds of pounds of lead. The men knew, were they to obtain sufficient *cosmicite*, that a thin covering of it would protect them from all dangerous rays, and these ungainly space suits would no longer be necessary.

Through the trees they could see fox-men scurrying away in sudden fright. Wendell led his party to the edge of the clearing, then deliberately stood there gesturing broadly to his companions as if explaining things to them. The natives did not run far, soon the three were aware of many eyes upon them. A half hour was wasted away as the Tellurians permitted the Vulcanites to grow accustomed to their strange appearance. Now Wendell drew forth his light service air-pressure gun and with a great show of pantomime pointed out to his companions a giant bird that hovered over the clearing. He aimed his gun. There was no explosion, but the bird fell almost at the men's feet.

It was Jimson's cue. He acted as if Wendell's feat were too simple for words, and pointing out a cluster of high-hanging fruit he drew his needle-beam pistol. Scathing fire leaped from the gun, played on the fruit and charred it so that it hung there a mass of cinders. Whereupon Beale with wider gestures drew forth the more deadly weapon, the cathode atom-destroyer. A thousand feet away stood an unusually tall tree, rising almost two hundred feet into the air. Upon it Beale turned his ray. The white light was blinding and the tree was no more!

Without a word the three turned and hurried back to the flyer. A great burst of sound rose from the jungle, the awed voices of the fox-men. Surely, come what may, they would carry in their hearts a deep reverence for the men of the *Adventure*.

The following day the three again went into the clearing. The men crowded about every window port to watch their reception by the natives. They could see a number of the little fellows lurking among the trees. The appearance of the three in the open seemed to be a signal long awaited, the undergrowth was suddenly thick with the shiny-skinned men. There was some hesitation among these, but after a few minutes of this indecision the three realized they were merely awaiting the arrival of several personages who could be seen hurrying down the path that led from their village.

These were seven creatures from whose path the others crowded away. They were taller than the average fox-man, broader of shoulder, heavier of limb, with faces that were shrewd, intelligent. Like their fellows they were unclothed and they, too, were ornamented with bits of *cosmicite*—but their shields were larger and heavier.

What made them stand out from the others was the colour of their skin. It has been noted that the natural colour of the Vulcanites was a brownish-grey, whereas in the case of the seven chiefs (for such they proved to be) no two were alike. The foremost was white, a pure virgin white made possible by some bleaching agent. The second was red, a bright naked red. He was followed by a third whose skin was green, a fourth blue, and so on through the colours of the spectrum, bright garish colours like those that filled the jungle.

★

The white-coated native was evidently the leader. He came striding forward filled with the importance of this occasion, cynosure of all eyes. As he drew near the Tellurians saw that in addition to his *cosmicite* trinkets he wore a head-dress of feathers that stuck up from his pate several feet, permanent fixtures glued tightly in place. Also he wore wristlets of the precious white metal besides his knee and elbow shields, and when he turned about they saw a long hairless tail of some animal securely fastened to his person.

Later when the Tellurians learned enough of the rudimentary language of Vulcan, a common tongue used by all tribes, they discovered this imposing creature was Rafel, elected chieftain of his tribe that numbered no less than three thousand males. (Females and young were not counted in the census.) There were six hereditary chiefs (*tuco**) who once every six years[†] were selected from among their families, one chosen to be their official representative. Once elected he could not be deposed during his reign, the very chiefs who put him at their head were as much his subjects as the lowliest *muli*.[‡] His power was of life and death.

Rafel not only directed the civil welfare of his people, but was also their spiritual leader. And since there were no less than a thousand gods and devils in their Pantheon, his job was not one to be sneered at. Yet, with it all, he turned out to be a kindly if not kingly fellow. His dignity sat not too heavily upon his shoulders and he proved open

*   It is difficult to give Earthly equivalent to Vulcanite terms. There were scarcely more than a hundred words in the vocabulary, and many proved obscure to the Tellurians. The term *tuco* was applied by the fox-men to anyone or thing of high rank. Gods, men and devils were all *tuco*!

†   The year of Vulcan is only fifty-four Earth days long, but since Vulcan rotates on its axis once every 19 hours its sidereal year is sixty-eight and a fraction Vulcan days long.

‡   *muli*... captive, applies to both man and animal. The main motive of war between tribes is for the securing of slaves. Rafel's tribe numbered more than four thousand *muli*, male and female.

to reason. Like all savages he feared most to lose face, to be made a fool of! He believed without question that the *Adventure* had come from the sun. Had he not seen the "sky-boat" come out of the sun itself? He considered his tribe unduly honoured by the visit.

He came leading the procession of emblazoned *tucos* forward, halting at the edge of the clearing. Wendell, Beale and Jimson had taken but a half dozen steps from the airlock, permitting the first move to their "hosts." And for all his apparent efficiency, Rafel was for the moment at a loss as to what he should do on this unprecedented occasion. A chieftain of three thousand adult males, however, must have recourse to doing the right thing at the right moment. After his single minute of indecision he was suddenly a typical "greeter."

Standing just within the clearing with the circlet of trees at his back, the chieftain threw wide his arms as if to embrace the universe, and began to recite what was undoubtedly a prepared welcome speech. It was long, twenty minutes of it. Jimson nudged his chief. "The chairman of the Rotary Club back home ought to be in on this. All that's missing is the key to the city."

"Hush, I think it's coming now," whispered Beale.

For Rafel had raised one arm high above his head in signal to those behind him. Now the six elaborately-coloured *tucos* came forward bearing a burden between them. It lay suspended upon a square of woven grasses, a tiny statuette. No more than six inches tall it was of exceedingly crude workmanship, a figure of *cosmicite*. It took Beale and Jimson several moments to discover that it depicted a rather ugly little fox-man, shiny-skin, squatting on his heels and holding a round globe (also of *cosmicite*) between its knees which it contemplated.

"It's a god, possibly the god of the sun," explained Wendell, who had seen a like figurine on his first landing upon Vulcan. They could see that the six carriers held the figure in deep veneration. They halted before Wendell, waiting for him to do something about it. Jimson nudged him. "Take it!"

Wendell did not listen to him, but merely raised a hand as if in blessing, and by the expression on Rafel's face they saw he had done the right thing. The seven were grinning broadly. Then, at Rafel's signal, the six *tucos* retreated back into the trees carrying their god with them.

"That's one up for our side," grinned Jimson.

Rafel waited until his companions were out of sight, then gave a second signal to his people. This time it was not the gaily-coloured chiefs who answered his summons, but a dozen slate-brown *mulis*, each carrying a grass-matting basket on his head. At Rafel's signal they lowered them to the ground. They contained a variety of fruit, a sort of meal-cake, the raw flesh of strange animals, water and nuggets of *cosmicite*.

Wendell made no motion to accept the fruit, but he did stride over to the single basket of *cosmicite* and select from the top a single nugget. He motioned for the captain and Jimson to do likewise. When that was done he waved an arm over the baskets. But this time Rafel did not understand. A frown appeared between his beady eyes.

In a rasping voice he called out three words. There seemed to be some delay, but after five minutes or so a dozen more slaves came running forward with twelve more baskets on their heads. These contained the same variety of food, the twelfth, *cosmicite*. Rafel watched Wendell anxiously, but he only shook his head, and sought again to wave the baskets away. Again Rafel called out three words, and though the delay was longer than before, twelve more baskets appeared!

Wendell realized if something was not done to halt the procession the *Adventure* would be surrounded by baskets. It took him ten full minutes to make Rafel understand that his men and he had no use for the food and water, but that the *cosmicite* was acceptable.

The chieftain understood at last. He called a word to his bearers to carry off their burdens again, leaving the three baskets of metal. Jimson turned to the ship, motioned for men to come through the lock and carry away the baskets. Rafel waited quietly with arms crossed while this was done. With signs he made the men understand they were now to follow him.

He led the way down a well-worn path through the trees. The natives stood back from the path watching them pass. They had glimpses of both women and children with dumb animal faces and round pot-bellied figures.

A hundred yards from the clearing the village began, if such could be termed a village. There were no houses, just burrows in the ground entered by round holes covered by a trapdoor of matted grass, vines and jungle debris. When dropped in place no one could guess at the teeming life that dwelt below. The jungle life went on above ground undisturbed, food ready for the hand of man.

After passing a dozen openings Rafel led his guests through a trap only more imposing than its fellows because of its larger size. There was a crude ladder of pegs set in the straight wall ten feet down. Down the ladder they found a large room roughly fifteen feet square. It was not dark, for the walls sparkled with bits of shining pebbles that gave off a dim eerie light; while in the centre of the chamber was a large piece of jagged ore, the size of a man's head, emitting light.

Jimson pointed out that this light-bearing ore was one of the several radioactive salts. He had been to the radium mines of Luna and had seen like ores. With that inexhaustible supply of the precious element so close to home it would be centuries before men of Tellus would turn to Vulcan for their needs. Beale was glad they were wearing their leaden suits. No wonder Sellers and his crew had died so horribly. A few hours' exposure to those rays and death was inevitable!

Evidently the bombardment of the radioactive rays did not affect the fox-men. Instead, were they taken from their natural environment they would most likely perish for the lack of the emanations that were part of their beings. Poison to one, life to another! Possibly, too, the food of the Tellurians would be as poison to them as the fruits of Vulcan were to the Tellurians!

Glancing about the room the three wondered about furniture, but for some mats of moss in one corner the chamber was quite bare. Rafel solved the problem by pointing to the floor. The six *tucos* who had followed them into the chamber squatted behind Rafel who took his place facing the white men. The chieftain made several queer cabalistic passes through the air and a number of women came down the passage with metal bowls of food which were placed before each man. There was some half-cooked meat, fruits and a thick gruel. Wendell motioned to show that neither he nor his companions would partake, but that did not deter Rafel and his fellows. They nodded their understanding and "fell to" noisily. For the next half hour the three had the pleasure of watching their hosts gorge themselves.

After the first few minutes of watching the fox-men enjoy their fare, Beale decided it not amiss to discuss their situation. As the three talked Rafel eyed them covertly, but his glance was only friendly interest.

Judging by the three half-filled baskets of *cosmicite* presented to them, Wendell conjectured that the metal was not too plentiful in the village. There was no sign of any in the room in which they sat, except upon the persons of the chiefs. Possibly the three baskets were all the superfluous metal in the village. By force of arms they might denude their hosts of what remained on their persons, but that was not what they wanted. They must know the source, the location of the mines themselves. There was but one way to find out. They must learn the language of the fox-men. Beale decided upon taking the easiest and quickest course.

III

The Gods Speak

Attracting Rafel's attention, he pointed to himself and said "Beale." After a moment's hesitation Rafel pointed one thin finger at himself saying "Beel." The captain shook his head, and it took him a number of minutes to make the chieftain grasp the fact there was only one Beale. After Rafel got that into his head it was easier, and with some coaching they learned his name. It was slow progress, but Rafel at last learned that Jimson was "Jimso" as he called him, and Wendell was "Wemdal." Then elaborately he named all his six fellows.

With that lesson fairly well learned, Beale pointed to Wendell, Jimson and himself collectively, and again after a great deal of waving of arms and patience he learned that the fox-men were called "Tolis."

Henceforth it was simpler. Beale had but to point to an object to obtain its name. Jimson had found a pencil and pad and jotted down each new word with its equivalent much to the fox-men's wonder. The room in which they sat was a "kel," the floor, and this included the ground as well, was "get," good "gimgim," *cosmicite*, "*dasie*" and so on.

When his teachers began to yawn unselfconsciously, Beale realized how late it must be. Rafel appeared disappointed they would not stay the night. Wendell, Jimson and he were feeling their own hunger now and were anxious to get out of their heavy suits. Rafel ushered them forth into the growing dusk with great aplomb.

Even before all the light of the sun was gone, the jungle was changing in aspect—the ground, the trees, the very fruit and even the bodies of the men of Vulcan were beginning to glow of their own light. It was as weirdly beautiful as it was strange. Beale and Jimson recalled they had seen the same thing on the night-side of the planet with their arrival. Wendell pointed out that everything here was luminous because of the high percentage of radium that was absorbed by every organic thing.

By the time they reached the *Adventure*, the full wonder of the eerie night was upon them. Every tree trunk, every tendril of the vines, every separate spiney leaf, every berry was plainly outlined as though in silver. Night insects just beginning to stir, carried their own lanterns; the birds were streaks of brilliance against the black moonless sky. Altogether Vulcan was an unusual world.

It was more than a week before their real mission could be spoken of to Rafel. During that time Wendell, Beale and Jimson spent most of their time in the company of the chieftain, learning his tongue and the customs of these savage little people. Twice Rafel had been taken into the *Adventure*. He seemed quite willing to devote all his time to the strangers; awed by their presence, he took childish delight in their company. He did not question. If they wished to enlighten him about themselves of their own will that was sufficient. The *Adventure* was something outside his realm, incogitable.

The men of the crew were not so patient. They could see no good reason for this dalliance. They recommended stripping the natives of their ornaments and forcing them under pain of death to tell where more was to be had. They were free to wander about the "settle-ment" as they pleased, but in most cases one visit to the burrows of the Tolis was enough. Only a few of their number bothered to learn the tongue of the shiny fox-men. Then they had their first "accident."

It was nearing sunset of the short Vulcanite day, when Jimson standing at one of the ports saw Warren and Yarbow running through the trees as if in mortal terror of their lives. Wendell was at his side.

"Good Lord!" cried Jimson at sight of the racing men. "Have they gone crazy?" His eyes went beyond the men, trying to discover if they were being chased by natives, but in the deceptive ghost light of the verdure it was difficult to see.

"They run from themselves..." said Wendell quietly. "Get them into the ship before any natives see them as they are..."

"What do you mean? What has happened?"

"Go, open the lock, I tell you!"

Jimson cast one more look out the window. The men had reached the clearing, but Warren had stumbled over a vine and sprawled on the ground. Instead of picking himself up he was rolling about wildly, clutching at himself, trying to reach a dozen places at once, but Yarbow stumbled forward unaware of his companion's antics, his face a horrible mask of twisted pain.

Jimson needed no further urging to get down to the lock. He passed a man in a corridor and ordered him to follow. Yarbow fell through the doorway as it was pulled open from within, but Jimson did not pause; he ran out to where Warren still squirmed in the throes of some mysterious attack. The poor fellow was almost gone when he reached him; and Jimson had to carry him, a dead weight, into the ship.

Beale had been summoned and was trying to ease Yarbow's pain, but the pair were beyond help. They moaned and screamed alternately, seemed unable to breathe; their eyes grew glazed rapidly. In half an hour Yarbow was dead, Warren followed quickly.

Wendell had a ready explanation. "Two days ago I saw them eat some fruit... I warned them, but they laughed at me. I've been watching them, but they must have slipped out this afternoon behind my back. Lucky they had sense to get back here without the natives seeing them die. You'll have to bury them in the dark..." He turned and went away without another word.

Someone muttered behind his back, another began to curse this unnatural world. Beale demanded silence. Tomorrow, he promised, he would confer with Rafel about the mines.

In a world abounding with the heavier metals, the Tolis were a race possessed of little science. They used stone knives and hatchets, stone-headed spears and arrows. They knew fire, but nothing of smelting ores. *Cosmicite* was found in nuggets, and these they fashioned by laborious hammering. They had nothing that might be considered luxuries. Because of the nature of the planet they had no need for clothing. Everything beyond their limited comprehension was magic, every tree and bush had its god. The sun that lighted their day was the Great Leader. The spirit of the *cosmicite*, or *dasie* as it was known to them, was their second-best god, considered superior in many ways.

An arrow or spearhead tipped with a pellet of *dasie* went true to its mark regardless of the aim. The archer who failed to kill his enemy was impure of heart, therefore undeserving of the fidelity of the god! The same was true of food eaten from plates of *dasie*. If the food poisoned the diner, his unclean touch had vitiated the power of the god's strength.

True to his word, Captain Beale addressed Rafel the next morning. He managed to convey to the chieftain in the mongrel dialect the Earthmen were using to make themselves understood, the fact that there was a shortage of *dasie* in the land of the sun. He explained that he and his men might easily have taken as much *dasie* as they desired without the men of Tolis being the wiser, but the ways of the Gods were not thus. The *dasie* belonged to the Tolis by right of virtue, and therefore the Gods instead of taking what they wished by force were asking as a favour, an adequate supply of the precious "stone." The three baskets Rafel had so open-heartedly given were but a drop to their real need.

As he spoke Beale was watching Rafel narrowly. He saw the frown that came into the chieftain's face and knew he was treading delicate ground. The coming of the Gods to the fox-men was a great event in their lives, an unprecedented break in the monotony of the jungle, and thus far had cost merely three baskets of *dasie*. This demand for more *dasie* was different, and Rafel wisely knew it was a demand. Rafel had been witness to the target practice of the Gods on the third day of their coming, and he was intelligent enough to know that what had been done to birds and trees could be accomplished on man.

Beale said a little more, but knew he had already won his point. Magnanimously he gave Rafel until the following morning for his answer, knowing well enough what the answer would be!

And sure enough the first hint of the rising sun brought Rafel into the clearing. He began the ceremony with flowery protestation of undying goodwill, exhorting the captain to carry to the Great Leader word of his worthiness. Then he was waving to his fellows who came bearing between them on its cloth the little statue they had seen the first day.

When the figurine was borne away Rafel gave his second signal. Only ten days before the coming of the "sun-boat" Rafel had been to the mines. And here came twenty men bearing on their heads well-filled baskets of white metal. The eyes of the crew of the *Adventure* glittered at the sight. Nuggets ranged from the size of peas to double the size of a man's fist. This meant vast fortune for them all, even after Wendell had taken his lion's share!

Forgotten were the mines, the possibility of even greater wealth, but not so Wendell. He could not forget.

Afraid the sight of the metal had robbed Beale of his reason, Wendell took the fore. He scarcely glanced at the baskets. Then he cried. "No, no, take it away!"

Rafel's surprise was no greater than that of Beale and Jimson. The men staring out the windows of the *Adventure* did not grasp what Wendell was doing. Beale and Jimson wanted to protest, but Wendell flung them both an eloquent glance from his heavy brows. Rafel was protesting, unable to comprehend. Not enough? He paused but a moment, waved again to his men and they went off—to return with twenty more baskets. Rafel looked to Wendell for approbation. The eyes of the others were starting from their heads, unbelieving.

And all Wendell did was to shake his head. "Take it away, all of it," he told Rafel.

Rafel struggled between two emotions, one of joy that the *dasie* was not to be accepted after all, the other... fear for the same reason. Beale and Jimson murmured protest behind Wendell, but he did not appear to hear them.

Instead he stood by stoically waiting until every basket had been carted away. In the *Adventure* men cursed, cried against Wendell, but unknown to them... he had securely locked the heavy porte of the ship from the outside!

Now he gave his full attention to Rafel, to explain through the poor medium of the savage tongue what the trouble was... That the Great Leader would consider it a great sin if his messengers deprived the fox-men of their precious stone.

In answer Rafel grinned. Surely, he thought, the Great Leader would know that there was more *dasie* to be had, that it was but a five-sun walk to the mines. He and his men could replenish their stores quickly enough. The Tolis gave with willing heart. Let the men bring back their burdens!

Still Wendell shook his head. He sought again to make Rafel understand. The *dasie* of the Tolis was of no use to the Gods. It was, as all other "stone," useless. The Gods could not dare accept that which had come to them from other hands. Just as the *dasie* of the Tolis was contaminated if touched by alien hands, so was the *dasie* defiled that had been handled by any but the Gods themselves!

And this time Rafel comprehended it. He was abject in his misery. In his generosity he had not considered this contingency. He was only glad the Gods had not struck him down in their anger. He must go now to discover when the spirit of the *dasie* would concede it propitious for a new expedition to start for the mines, when he and his fellows might lead the way.

Wendell had to be agreeable to that, and Rafel went away with a promise to be back on the morrow. Now he had to placate the men of the *Adventure* for his refusal of the forty baskets of *dasie*, pointing out that if he had his way there would be forty times forty baskets to be had, more than the *Adventure* could hold if they but listened to him.

The next day Rafel came to advise them they must wait two days before they could start for the mines; for so his spiritual aides had decreed.

The men grumbled, but otherwise were quiet. They strolled about the village watching the preparations taking place for the march, particularly those of Rafel who had something in a pot that boiled without fire. And the chieftain was eating *cosmicite*. An open dish in the centre of his burrow held a pebbly dust of it, and whenever he thought of it he would take out a small crumb and placidly chew and swallow it.

At last Rafel was ready to announce the start. To the men of the *Adventure* it did not look like much of an expedition. There were ten natives in the party—Rafel, the six *tucos* and three youngsters, sons of two of the *tucos*. In small sacks of woven grass each man carried a supply of sun-dried meat, and except for two of the boys carrying heavy stone knives to cut their path through the jungle, they were otherwise unarmed. Rafel carried several implements of his trade, one *tuco* carried a bowl of what turned out to be holy water. Their drinking water and supplementary diet of fruit would be found on the way.

Beale had expected to go with his men in the *Adventure* to take the natives with them to point out the way, but Rafel piously vetoed such a suggestion. First, he declared, the trek to the mines must be made in a spirit of humility, the "sun-boat" made too much racket, and the spirits demanded silence; second there was no clearing large enough to contain the *Adventure* within many walks of the fields! No, they must go afoot as his forebears had gone afoot for a hundred generations.

This put a different complexion on things. It meant five days of marching in heavy leaden suits under the burning sun, the matter of carrying enough food tablets and water to last the entire trip, beside their mining implements. Beale tried to argue. The *Adventure* could make its own clearing a day's march from the mine, but in this Rafel proved adamantine.

There was a short conference in the *Adventure*. There would be no need for all to go. At most six men could do the work. They would locate the mine, take its position by sun and stars as well as landmarks, and bring away only samples, a small supply that each man could carry comfortably. Later when the natives thought they had returned to the sun, they would drop upon the mine, blast a clearing for the ship and load it with all it could carry.

It was decided Beale would stay with his ship. Jimson would take charge of the expedition. Five were chosen to accompany him: Arth, Morgan, Talbot, Ware and Petrie, the youngest and heartiest of the crew.

The trip would consume ten days of travel, and with a day stop-over at the mine it would mean eleven days in all. Against accident they would carry food in the shape of tablets and water in airtight canteens, each man his own share, a twelve-day supply. In addition to other things, Jimson carried a tiny wireless to keep in touch with Beale once they reached the mine.

It was noon before they could start and Rafel was impatient at the delay. The men's packs were hastily packed, but at the first stop that night they would straighten them out. Each man carried his revolver against unforeseen dangers. It was with much misgivings that Beale saw them go weighted down like deep-sea divers. Did he have a premonition of disaster? He managed to shake off his forebodings to wave cheerily as they disappeared into the trees.

Their direction lay opposite to the village, but for half an hour the men could still glimpse the towering outline of the *Adventure* through the trees. Then they dropped into a low valley, and it was gone from sight. They were now entirely dependent upon Rafel and his garishly-tinted crew.

After a few hours under the brilliant sun, Jimson wished they might make the march in the cool of the night, but the fox-men feared the night with its ghostly shapes. The eerie appearance of the luminous vegetation coupled with the fact that the *yal*, a catlike creature, roved the night, forbade them stirring from camp with the setting of the sun. Instead they must travel beneath the hot sun; and there was little shade to be had amid that forest of narrow trees with their sharp, spiny blades of leaves.

The natives, naturally, were not discommoded by the heat. Whatever it was in their blood or chemical structure that permitted them to eat freely of the radium-impregnated food, also made the terrific heat of this world as nothing to them. The three youths cutting the path through the thick jungle seemed scarcely wearied after a day of wielding the machetes with which Beale had provided them to replace their own heavy stone knives.

I V

The Lure of the Planet

Under Jimson's vigilant eye his men husbanded their water carefully, drinking only four times during the day and then sparingly. At each meal (the natives ate four times during the nine-hour day) they ate two of their food lozenges. Health sustaining though they were, however, they were none too appetizing and had to be taken with water to wash them down. All in all it was gruelling work to push through the fetid jungle; but these men were accustomed to work of this sort. They had chosen this life in preference to sitting behind a stuffy desk in their own stuffy world, and this was not their first experience in an alien jungle. The new thing was the terrific furnace heat.

Heads down, eyes turned to the ground, sweating under heavy suits, averting eyes from the luscious fruit that hung invitingly everywhere in clusters from the trees and vines, the men pushed on. They turned their backs, perforce, upon the water when camp was made beside some creek, river or small lake. They talked among themselves of other things when the strange drilling of the *webe* bird, a creature like a woodpecker, became too nerve-wracking, and they counted themselves lucky that the swarms of insects rising at every step from the rich mould underfoot could not find them through their heavy garments. Balm in Gilead! They slept deeply, and of-times on the march broke out into gay song. So have men of the past given chase to elusive fortune, and so will they in the future.

Rafel, following on the heels of Jimson, listened reverently to the chatter of the Tellurians. His heart swelled at the sound of their song. Since the spirits had been agreeable concerning the coming of the Gods to the abode of the *dasie*, he knew no qualms. He appreciated the fact that he was deeply honoured in that the Gods had sought him out to be their guide and friend. The Tolis never lifted their voices in song, but by the time the party reached the mines the fox-men could repeat the words and hum the tune of Jimson's favourite song, "When you and I were young, Maggie!"

It was on the noon of the fourth day that it was discovered that Ware had only brought one canteen of water with him! In the excitement he had left the others prepared for him. It was a blow to all six, for it meant the rest would have to share their precious store with him. They managed to laugh it off and make ribald jokes for the benefit of the culprit. But Jimson worried. An accident like that could cripple the whole expedition. Lucky they carried an extra day's supply.

Then they came to the mine. The "mine" was situated in a cave of an underground river. The cave's entrance was cleverly hidden, but before it could be opened Rafel and his fellows had to perform rites to propitiate the god. This solemn ceremony included a soundless dance, the sprinkling of holy water around the surrounding terri-tory, and a long silent prayer in which all nine shiny men squatted

in a row, heads touching their knees for three hours. Using this time
to their own advantage Jimson and his men crept over the ground,
carefully taking their position by the sun, studying landmarks and
the lay of the land. They explained their absence as to having to do
with their own rituals.

At last, to the satisfaction of everyone, the cave was opened. They
went within, stopping every few feet while Rafel said prayers and sup-
plicated the spirit residing herein. The cave was almost as brilliant as
day, due to radium salts imbedded in the walls and ceiling, and by its
light they saw they were on a shelving beach of a subterranean river.
Its banks for several hundred yards in both directions was strewn with
nuggets of *cosmicite*, nuggets of every size, many as large as a man's
head. They could see the metal shining on the shallow bottom of
the river, lying in full sight, waiting for the picking!

Jimson and his men were filled with boundless joy. Because of
the double curve of the river at this point they could see but a small
portion, and could only guess what lay the full length of the river,
and at its source. It was unbelieveable. They wanted to fill their sacks
immediately, to rush back to Beale with their news. But Rafel was
not through with his rites. It was dark outside when he finished, and
that meant they must eat, sleep and await the new day before they
might gather the metal. It was really four days before Rafel was ready
to return to the village!

A different prayer had to be said over each nugget as it was
plucked from its bed. Then Rafel insisted that each man take away
in his knapsack as much as he could carry! He stood by while each
bag was filled, making careful estimate of the weight of each man in
proportion to how much he could rightfully bear on his back. With
each man laden down there was more prayer, and the ceremony
of putting the lid back upon the cave's mouth. This took a full day

for Rafel had to be satisfied that the cave entrance was safe from detection. And another full day of prayer before they could dare take their departure!

Jimson was beside himself with chagrin long before that. And he was deeply worried. His men were already on short rations. Prepared at the most for twelve days, they had been out nine days already and the return trip still to be made! He could not believe Rafel had purposely not mentioned this enforced stay-over. On being asked how long the journey would take he had truthfully told them five days each way. The natives did not care how long the entire trip consumed. Was there not food and water in plenty all along the way?

And there was the matter of water. Ware's shortage made their predicament worse. Water inadequate for five had to be divided among six. And to make matters worse Jimson could not communicate with Beale. The wireless was useless, there was too much interference. All he could raise was static; the radioactivity of the planet made wireless impossible. The men waved aside his fears. "We can do on four lozenges a day instead of eight, and we'll go easy with the water. Don't worry, Bill, we can't lose out now…" They had known times as bad as this before.

At night Jimson lost good hours of sleep tinkering with the radio. If only he could reach the *Adventure*… it could meet them halfway. But he was without success. Then they were ready for the return. Some of the men surreptitiously dumped a portion of the *cosmicite* from their knapsacks, but the others were more greedy. Beale had promised they could keep all they brought with them without counting it among what was to be taken aboard later.

During the first day of the march they showed no sign of fatigue. They sang and joked as they strode along behind the machete wielders. They were not returning the way they had come. Rafel explained that to do so would mark their path too plainly for lurking enemies; other tribesmen were always on the lookout for new *dasie* mines. Hence they struck off on a slightly changed course, and on the second day arrived at an impassable river!

It meant building a bridge to cross it. The fox-men had become highly excited at the sight of the vicious river. They claimed the gods of the river was angry and had to be pacified before they could cross!

Half a day was spent in prayers before trees were felled to make the bridge. That in turn had to be tossed into the river once they were across. Here the Tellurians suffered their third misfortune. As they crossed the rude bridge Talbot fell! Losing his balance he was gone before the others could come to his aid. He toppled into the torrent and was swept from sight immediately, drawn down into the whirlpools, broken on the ragged rocks a quarter of a mile below.

Jimson placated Rafel with the explanation that Talbot had suddenly decided to return to his heavenly abode in the sun via the river. The Great Leader had recalled him. Eager to believe, Rafel accepted the story. He was awed beyond measure to have been witness to the passing of a god!

It was a pity Talbot had carried his water with him, however. Jimson had told him he was carrying too much *cosmicite* for his own good, but he had been one of the greedy. That was perhaps the reason for his fall. Morgan averred Talbot had picked up nuggets discarded by others.

Altogether they spent a day and a half beside the river.

The next day they found their canteens dry! With all their precautions the terrific heat of the unshaded sun had evaporated all that remained. The sun winked out at last, lay low on the horizon. A cool breeze stirred the tops of the jungle trees, relief of a sort. The men knew what they faced. Four days under a pitiless sun, four days without water and without food, since they could neither swallow or digest the food tablets without the aid of water... Hunger was not the worst... it was the thirst! And the natives had camped them beside a shallow gurgling brook...

Somehow the five fell asleep, but morning was worse. Above all they must not let Rafel and his crew know the truth. They must keep upon their feet steadily, not dare to stumble. There was no singing in the line that day, and very little talk.

With the third stop of the day, during which the fox-men ate their fruit and slaked their thirst Jimson noticed a spot of blood on Ware's lip. He wondered about that, so that he began to watch the other until to his horror he saw Ware put a wrist to his mouth, and heard the sibilant sound as the man sucked upon his flesh!

Pulling Ware to his side he saw the truth. There was fresh blood on his lips. The man was sucking his own blood. He whimpered when Jimson accused him. "I cut my wrist on a vine a way back, and it... well... it sort of quenches some of my thirst..." he explained.

"You fool," moaned Wendell, "you fool!" And he watched Ware for the rest of the day. It was horrible enough to think of a man doing such a thing, but Jimson feared also that the open cut would be his end, the poison from the plant that had made the cut... would it prove deadly?

In the next few hours he forgot Ware's predicament in his own. Water, water. God, would this never end? Like an automaton he found himself pushing one foot forward... then the other. The heat, the odours of stinking jungle. Swarms of insects rising in clouds in a man's face at each step. The rank odour exuded by the large fleshy leaves of the ground creepers. *Webes* drilling on all sides. Brightly-plumaged birds darting from their coming; paining the eyes with the slash of their colour.

Food! Fruit on every side, hanging in clusters within reach; fat, juicy, peach-like gobulars, scarlet cherries, purple plums. Luscious and poisonous. Tempting a man to stop, pluck and eat; to quench the thirst in their juice and let consequences be damned!

But one remembers Wendell's white hair, Warren and Yarbow. A monstrous planet this. Wrapped in beauty, festering in poison. And the water. God!

Now John Arth stumbles ahead. He's reeling, unable to stand the gaff. Ah, well, what's the odds... what if Rafel knows they aren't Gods? They'll die soon enough, they'll die on their feet of starvation... thirst... with food and water in full sight and reach of the hand. Must try to get Beale on the wireless tonight. Last chance... then... then to give up, welter in the poisonous water, sate one's self with lush fruit. Metal. Riches. All for the sake of a white metal dragging at their shoulders, eating into the flesh, burning a deep scar on their consciousness.

It's night again, blessed silvery night filled with luminous shapes, the ghosts of all those who have died for thirst in this life. Sneering at them, jeering... Pointing long fingers at the water beside which the natives have camped for the night, beckoning for them to come; partake of the liquid flood; bask in it; to live again if only for one moment of exquisite joy.

Was ever there a world with more water? Since leaving the *cosmicite* fields the party had followed the course of a river, the same that had swallowed Talbot. Sometimes they lost it, sometimes they crossed it on a worm-eaten log; darting from stone to stone. But this was a lake beside which Rafel had camped, possibly an inlet of the same river, but it seemed to stretch for miles—cool, limpid, inviting...

"I can't stand it anymore, I can't, I can't." That was Morgan. "Water, water," he moaned, "water, please." Jimson remembered the immortal verse, "Water, water, everywhere and not a drop to drink!" So had the Ancient Mariner felt... only not so bad... he could not have been so thirsty... surely...

"Quiet, Jack, you'll arouse the natives. That Rafel's smart. He sits close to us at night to listen to us talk, repeats words to himself. Please, boy, keep quiet." How fuzzy my tongue is. My words are thick in my ears.

"I can't. I tell you, I can't stand it any more. I'm dying of thirst in sight of all that water..."

"We all are. We're hit hard."

"How d'we know it's all poison? Maybe it was only in that place where the *Corsair* landed... maybe just one little pool..."

"No... no, it's the whole planet, the radium... too high in solution... and there were Warren and Yarbow, Jack." He sighed. "Please, please, have patience. Rafel hurries home. We'll be back to the *Adventure* in three days..."

"Three days... three days!" The last was a shriek. "We'll be dead by then... all. I'm dying now. Ah, I know!" his eyes were suddenly crafty... "I'll show 'em! I'll take my clothes off... I'll stand in the lake... it won't hurt... I'm burning up, burning up..."

"No, no, Jack, you daren't. It will kill you. Why even to remove your clothes exposes you to the emanations!"

"I won't drink... and only for a minute... just to stand in it?" He was begging like a child.

"It'll seep through your pores, it will burn your skin... it will kill you... the damned unnatural stuff!"

Jimson tried to hold the other back, to prevent him from flinging off his clothes, but Morgan was strong with desire, and Jimson
was weak... weak.

He watched with heart in his mouth. Morgan was so young,
just twenty-four. Perhaps after all it wouldn't hurt him. If only he'd
be content with one dip, hurry back into his clothes. Ah, he was
returning.

Morgan was revived. "It's marvellous," he averred. "I feel as if
I'd eaten a full meal, my mouth is no longer parched. Come, all of
you. See... I'm strong again!" He turned a neat cartwheel for their
edification. Jimson knew. It was the radium. Of course he felt good
for the time being... but what afterwards?

"No, it's suicide!" Jimson sought to hold the others back, harangue
them, but they paid him no heed. Sitting on the bank he watched
them disport themselves in the water, his own mouth so dry his
tongue was like a piece of flannel. Every few minutes they tried
to entice him to join them. He was tempted. "Why not?" he asked
himself. There would be relief, instant relief. What did he care, for
death was on the way regardless. Better death in the cool serenity
of the lake than on that sun-beaten hell that was the way back to
the ship.

They were far out in the lake, several hundred yards distant
when with a wild call they turned in unison to swim back to shore.
Unconsciously Jimson's weary eyes numbered them... one, two,
three... one, two three... and there should have been four! He jumped
to his feet, scanned the lake on all sides, but with the exception of
those three bobbing figures racing toward him the lake was empty!

Arth wasn't out of the water before he began to yell. "Ware...
went down..." Then they were on shore dripping water at his feet.
"He went down like a stone... suddenly," they told him. "We dived

for him, but he was dead already!" They were shivering even though the night was warm.

What was the use of saying "I told you so!" Death was riding their shoulders already. Nor did he tell them about the cut on Ware's wrist that was possibly the real reason for his early death... that and the polluted water. Tomorrow... if they lived... they might be tempted to ape Ware.

Then Jimson saw Rafel, a luminous figure standing beside a tree watching them. Did he guess? Did he know? Had he understood their words, their want? Did he see that one of their number was missing again? Could he know how they suffered? Well, what of it... they were men, starving, thirsty men.

V

Water!

Without a word Arth, Morgan and Petrie donned their clothing again. They dropped Ware's garments and his load of nuggets in the water. They lay on the ground close together as if seeking safety in their numbers. Jimson turned to the radio again. It was useless. He grew drowsy, his head nodded. He dreamed he too swam crystal-clear water where there was no shore, where he kept on swimming, swimming...

With the arrival of morning he found the three still alive, unharmed it appeared. They were ready for the march, their eyes bright, their bodies filled with new vigour; their fear of the previous night was gone. On the march they gave surreptitious help to Jimson over the roughest part of the trail as the natives cut through the heavy growth that seemed to spring anew with their passing.

The day was a repetition of the past one, the nerve-trying sounds of the jungle, the myriad insects, the awful heat of the sun beating down upon heavy helmets, the bands of their knapsacks biting into their shoulders. Later Jimson was to wonder how he had ever managed to cling to the *cosmicite* as he did. Only force of will kept him on his feet—the will to live, to enjoy the fortune upon his back.

Then came the mid-morning halt. He noticed that Arth was groggy. He had dropped to the ground with a heavy thud; lay where he had fallen, eyes closed, mouth strangely grim. Morgan and Petrie was almost as bad. Arth groaned, but the others set their teeth against the animal expression of the body.

When the signal came to start, Arth could not get up. He moaned, but was unable to speak. He lay there staring up into Jimson's face, his eyes big and glassy like the eyes of a dog Jimson had seen die once. He would recall Arth's face many days to come. Morgan and Petrie just stared at them, gritting their teeth so hard their jaws made clicking sounds. Jimson tried to bring Arth to his feet. He was a sack of meal, boneless in his grasp. He had to let him fall back to the ground.

"He drank some of it," Petrie said through stiff jaws, meaning the water of the lake.

Rafel and his men stood by watching, curious. They saw the glazed condition of Arth's eyes; they knew death. They glowered at the white men. Then Rafel spoke. "He die... like men!"

Jimson hesitated, then shook his head. "He die like man because he sin," he said in the jargon they used to make themselves understood by the fox-men. "God eat only food and drink water of God!" He tapped his knapsack significantly. "If God eat, drink, food meant for man he die... for then... there not be plenty for man!" He could hardly force the words from his swollen lips, but he thought his answer was masterful. Let the beggars get around that!

"The one who die in water... he sin, too?" asked Rafel. Then thoughtfully. "There plenty for God and man!" and waved an eloquent hand to take in the fruit-bearing trees, the glimmer of the river a hundred yards to the right. Jimson's eyes following his hand bulged at the sight; he forgot for the moment what he was about as he too considered the plenitude of water in this wild land. He caught himself, hurried to cover his pause.

He shrugged his shoulders. "Great Leader say different. He say it taboo..."

Rafel, whose land suffered with too many taboos, could appreciate that, but by listening to the men during their long days of companionship he had learned a smattering of their tongue. Now he said: "You eat all food..." here he tapped Jimson's knapsack... "your water—gone. You die for water... and Gods no die! So it is told!"

Jimson wanted to cry out, to tell him the truth, to find sympathy in the beady eyes before him, but he dared not. Rafel was a mighty man among his kind, he would not endure being made a fool of! He would lose face with his people were it known the white men had but made a pawn of him.

"We Gods!" Jimson was belligerent now. "You know we Gods... or you die!" He tapped his pistol. It was the last chance, for Rafel had seen what the pistol could do. He would at least believe in that.

The fox-man nodded. "We believe," and he ordered his men to bury the now dead Arth, for Arth had died as they argued. The natives whispered among themselves at the decay already setting in upon the body. It rotted before their eyes. They had never seen the like. This if nothing else convinced them that these men were indeed different than they. The march continued.

Now it was Jimson who seemed strong in comparison to the others... Morgan and Petrie who were weak. They stumbled at every unevenness of the road. At last Rafel came to Jimson's side. "They die... too!" he muttered. Jimson nodded, not daring to speak.

"You men... no Gods!" The chieftain spoke with real conviction now. "Gods no die. You men like us. You come from another place.* I listen, I know. Other place!" he said accusingly.

Jimson lost his head. "Sure... we're men. It's this damned poisonous world... it's..." he realized what he had been saying... but he was speaking English... perhaps Rafel could not understand after all.

"Men like us... you... you..." but the fox-man could not find words to express his black thoughts. He knew but one thing. He and his people had been betrayed. He called to his fellows, halting their march, and broke into a flood of liquid tones that Jimson could not follow. Their faces were sombre.

Suddenly Morgan pitched to the ground, felled like a tree. Petrie was easing himself after him, unable to sustain his own weight longer. He had dropped his pack somewhere behind. Rafel gave them no heed. He was screaming at Jimson. "You make lie. You spoil magic... the *dasie* cries for revenge..." He was working himself into a black rage. Jimson found it in himself to sneer.

"Well?" he wanted to know. "What does it matter?"

"Men from other place. You make sky-boat swim ocean between places. You want *dasie*... you act like Gods to fool us. But you no return. You no tell others. My people... they make you die!" A bow and arrow appeared in his hands as if by miracle from its holder at his back. His companions were armed likewise, an evil circle of *cosmicite*-tipped arrowheads pointed at Jimson's heart.

---

* It is to be questioned if Rafel truly understood that they had come from another world. The Tolis' word for world is place, as is any other part of their planet which is foreign to them.

He dared not draw forth his revolver and he was afraid. He who had faced death for three days was afraid of it in this form. "Wait," he shrieked. "Rafel wait! Talbot... him God; Wendell and Beale who wait in big boat of the sun... them Gods. We... others... we not Gods... we Men-Gods... men who serve Gods. You understand? Someone must serve Gods... like *muli* serve men. You understand?"

Rafel hesitated. Jimson could see in his eyes that the poor fellow wanted to believe if only he dared. He needed to save his face. He was wavering now. "You lie one time, maybe you lie again... the *dasie* wants revenge!"

"No, no, the *dasie* is unharmed. It's they who die..." he pointed to Morgan and Petrie. "The taboo... they broke it. I not die because I not sin. Wendell, Beale true Gods... they not die. I swear it, I swear it!" There was panic in Jimson's voice. His throat creaked with every word.

After a minute long pause Rafel nodded, lowered his bow. "We wait... Beale, Wendell must show them true Gods!"

Weak with relief Jimson wanted to cry, but he was a dried-out husk. He turned sadly to his companions. Morgan was breathing with difficulty. Petrie had placed himself flat on his back. Jimson leaned over Morgan. He picked up one arm to feel his pulse. It bent weirdly in the middle of the forearm. Petrie saw it. "It's in the bones... its eats... away... the lime..." he explained. Morgan's eyes had glazed; they stared at the brilliant swollen sun directly without seeing Petrie was going too. A few minutes and he could not raise his chest to breathe or moan.

Rafel's men refused to help Jimson bury his dead, and he was too weak to scratch out even the shallowest grave. He wanted to say a prayer, but his cracked lips refused utterance. He had to leave the pair where they had fallen, boneless things, decaying already. Soon they'd be devilish masses of putrefaction shunned by the meanest scavenger of the jungle.

The natives paid him no heed as he stumbled on after them. The machetes flashed in the sun. Rafel no longer waited for him to pass on ahead.

On, on, push on! Swing the damn machetes. On, on, one step, now two, a third and another. What if these weighted feet refused to obey? The *cosmicite* on his back... it was dragging him down... Lord... he didn't have the strength to pull his arms out of the straps. If there were only some water, a drop, a thimbleful. What is that? A slow-moving river. Water! *Water!* WATER!

How thick the grass has grown, vines pull at arms and legs... why... the machete wielders have gone... gone, here... oh God... was he? Ah, yes... the water... water... there ahead!

Funny noise! Crack... crack! *Webes* didn't make a sound like that. Yet familiar... strangely familiar. Jimson! Jimson! Why all the jungle was calling his name. Jimson! What a joke. Why there they are. Talbot, Ware, Arth, Morgan, Petrie... coming to meet him. Good fellows... they wouldn't leave a pal behind. Not them. And they'd go swimming together... all of them this time...

Funny... lying here... hurry... hurry can't you see the water ahead... not ten feet away. Why only animals crawl... what's wrong? What's the weight on one's back... something lying heavily on one's back, holding one down... oh yes... one's old man of the mountain... the *cosmicite*... the fortune with which to buy a space ship of one's own. The sun... it's gone... the world is black... this then... is death... death. Silly to have feared it. It's cool... clean.

Water, water! Oceans of it running over his mouth. Feeble fingers reach to catch escaping drops... the flood withdrawn. More, more, I say! More!

"Easy, easy, Bill!" Funny Beale's voice here. "Take it easy like a good fellow. There, a little more now. You're all right, old man!" Beale... good ole Beale... don't know he's too late... don't know that I'm dead!

"I'm dead... a dead man... only a man... not a God!" Jimson could hear that strange voice at his ear. It took several moments to recognize those hollow tones for his own.

"You're not dead, though you were darned near it. The others, Bill, what happened?"

"They weren't Gods... they sinned... they bathed in the lake... their bones... dissolved like... water."

"My God! Wendell warned you!"

"I told 'em you were God... not us..."

"Yes, I know. The fellow Rafel took a pot-shot at me. Lucky I wore my lead mess shirt. The soft tip of the *cosmicite* blunted... and the arrow fell to the ground. They are certain now that I am a God. But what a price to pay. Five men gone in one blow... and all of the *Corsair's* crew but Wendell... you almost..."

"I've got the stuff, Captain. Look... sixty pounds of it, and pure... pure..."

"Yes, Bill, you're a wealthy man now. You can buy an estate and marry a wife and play at life, but you won't, you poor fool, you won't. You'll go on and on... looking for new fortunes, peeping into all the strange corners of the universe... and if you're lucky you'll see many new things and make many fortunes, but one of these days in some strange jungle like this it'll get you... and you'll die like the rest of us... with... with boots on... Wealth, fortune, Lady Luck! It'll get you.

"And the others, men who will come after us to Vulcan. These poor untutored savages will fight to preserve their rights. Thousands will die before they learn their lesson; the rest will become slaves to dig out the ore. Our own men... poor devils... they'll sweat and toil in this noisome jungle, under the blistering sun, living on food lozenges... on water so filtered that it is dead. Craving baths in the cool inviting lakes, tempted by the growing fruits on the vines. Some will succumb... and their bones... will rot!

"Riches! Man's damnable desire to conquer, to nose in where he don't belong. In the future men will point to you and me. They will say... 'those pioneers... they were men!' Bah! Sheep! That's what we are... pigs for the slaughter... pigs for slaughter!" A wild laugh broke upon the jungle.

SEEN FROM VENUS, THE SUN'S DISC APPEARS AROUND TWO TIMES
AS LARGE AS IT DOES VIEWED FROM THE EARTH'S SURFACE.

VENUS

Foundling on Venus   John and Dorothy De Courcy

Although Venus is our nearest neighbour and comparable to Earth in size, it long remained a complete mystery, because the planet is covered in thick, impenetrable clouds. Until Russian and American probes reached the planet in the early/mid 1960s it was impossible to say whether the surface of Venus was Earth-like, a water-world, or a desert. Such speculation allowed for endless but often quite formulaic adventures.

Some of those speculations were encouraged by our attitude to Venus over the centuries. Because it is enshrouded in cloud, Venus reflects much of the sunlight. It has the highest albedo of any planet—it reflects around 75% of all sunlight it receives. By comparison, Earth reflects about a third. This brightness makes it easily visible in the night sky, even though it does not rise that high above the horizon. Like Mercury, Venus is visible early in the morning and again in the evening and, as with Mercury, the ancient Greeks thought it was two planets. They named the Evening Star Hesperos ("evening") and the Morning Star Phosphoros ("light-bringer"). The

Babylonians knew better, having calculated it was the same world and, as it was so bright and beautiful they named it Ishtar after their goddess of beauty and love. Once Pythagoras set the matter straight in the Greek world, they renamed the planet Aphrodite, after their goddess of love, and the Roman equivalent was Venus.

By association with the goddess of love, the inhabitants of Venus were assumed to be superior to humans both spiritually and artistically. In his 1686 work translated as *A Discourse on the Plurality of Worlds*, the French philosopher Bernard de Fontenelle speculated that the Venusians would be "full of wit and animation, always in love, always making verses, listening to music, having galas, dances and tournaments."

There was another theory that affected how we saw Venus. In 1798 the French astronomer Pierre de Laplace suggested that the planets had been formed from a huge ball of gas that periodically ejected material which condensed into a planet. This suggested that the earliest planets formed were those first ejected and were therefore further out, which is why many came to believe that Mars must be an older planet than Earth, and Venus a younger world. As our understanding of our own prehistory emerged, it became fashionable to consider that Venus was like our prehistoric past, perhaps the Mesozoic or Jurassic, and therefore full of dinosaurs and primitive humans.

These two views of an Edenic or primitive Venus do not sit well together and gave rise to two schools of fiction. The first author known to use Venus as the primary setting for a novel was the erstwhile French lawyer Achille Eyraud. In *Voyage à Vénus* (1865), he chose the superior form, though his novel—believed to be the first to use rocket propulsion as a means of travel—is really a utopian satire complaining about the state of French politics and society. Eyraud was, though, in favour of equality for women.

The rather more spiritual, Edenic state was favoured by W.S. Lach-Szyrma in *Voice from Another World* (1877) where he shows Venus as scientifically and socially advanced and its beings angelic. Marie Corelli also depicts happy spiritual people, highly advanced in the arts, in *A Romance of Two Worlds* (1886). Likewise, George Griffith, whose protagonist takes his new wife on their honeymoon around the solar system in *A Honeymoon in Space* (1901), finds Venus a paradise with humanoid flying beings who communicate by music. John Munro had also seen Venus as an idyllic utopia in *A Trip to Venus* (1897). The ultimate novel of an Edenic Venus is C.S. Lewis's *Perelandra* (1943) which depicts a perfect world which must be saved from corruption.

Fred T. Jane had a rather different view. In *To Venus in Five Seconds* (1897) he sees two races of Venusians. The native race looks like an elephantine fly but is intellectually advanced, especially in science. A second race is descended from the ancient Egyptians who had invented a matter transmitter and could not only move about the Earth instantaneously (that's why there are pyramids in Central America as well as Egypt) but also travel to Venus!

The idea of rival races on Venus rather took hold, especially with Schiaparelli's conviction that Venus might be like Mercury and tidally locked to the Sun. In *A Columbus in Space* (serial, 1909), Garrett P. Serviss describes a Venusian darkside, populated by primitive ape-like people, and a lightside with a humanoid, more enlightened race. Alas, neither of them are prepared for those rare moments when the clouds part and they see the Sun. It drives them mad!

During the pulp era, few writers showed much ingenuity and settled for formulaic adventures on, generally, a tropical Venus, often with dinosaurs. Amongst the more original was Homer Eon Flint, whom we have already seen was way ahead of his contemporaries. In "The Queen of Life" (1919), Venus is highly reflective because the entire sphere is covered by a glass shell to protect everyone from harmful radiation. Leslie F. Stone was another who showed initiative, though stretched credulity in the process. In "Women with Wings" (1930), both human and Venusian races are becoming degenerate. The Venusians had evolved from a form of flying fish, but were sufficiently human that the two races could interbreed, strengthening the bloodline.

Ralph Milne Farley had a long series about the adventures of Miles Cabot, who perfects a matter transmitter (like Jane's ancient Egyptians) and sends himself to Venus, hence the title *The Radio Man* (serial, 1924). He describes a jungle world, but with boiling oceans. Farley's series was inspired by the works of Edgar Rice Burroughs, especially his series set on Mars. Otis Adelbert Kline was another Burroughs imitator who chose Venus for his battleground in *The Planet of Peril* (serial, 1929) and sequels. Burroughs eventually reached Venus (or Amtor) with *Pirates of Venus* (serial, 1932), featuring explorer Carson Napier. The most distinctive feature of Burroughs's Venus is the giant trees over 1800 metres (6000 feet) high. None of these planetary romances considers Venus seriously and simply create an exotic world for fantastic adventures.

The idea that Venus was a water-world became the predominant image for most writers at this time. Laurence Manning employs such a setting in "The Voyage of the *Asteroid*" (1932), with Venus inhabited by dinosaurs and humanoid reptiles. Leigh Brackett describes a watery Venus in "Terror Out of Space" (1944). C.S. Lewis's Perelandra is also a water-world with one Fixed Land point. Isaac Asimov has the same setting in several stories, including his young-adult book *Lucky Starr and the Oceans of Venus* (1954). The classic work of the Venusian oceans is the two-story sequence "Clash by Night" (1943) and "Fury" (serial, 1947) by Henry Kuttner and C.L. Moore. Earth has been devastated and humanity has taken refuge on Venus in domed undersea citadels, called "keeps", ruled by an "immortal" elite. For some writers, such as Ray Bradbury in "All Summer in a Day" (1954), Venus not only had oceans, but it rained incessantly.

The 1950s saw some authors taking note of recent research which suggested Venus was far from a watery world. Leading the way was Poul Anderson. In "The Big Rain" (1954) he describes a harsh, sweltering Venus that, when it does rain, rains formaldehyde. The story considers how Venus might be terraformed, using the formaldehyde locked in Venus's clouds. Airmaker machines, spread all over Venus, accelerate a reaction with the formaldehyde, ammonia and methane to produce hydrocarbons and oxygen, whilst bombs reinvigorate volcanos so that in time it starts to rain—and rains for over a hundred years, by which time Venus starts to be Earth-like.

By the early 1960s it was clear from the Russian space probes that Venus was a hostile planet. Its mean surface temperature is 464°C, hotter than Mercury, the heat trapped by the clouds generating what we call the "greenhouse" effect. Larry Niven recognized the inevitable and produced "Becalmed in Hell" (1965), whilst Roger Zelazny wrote a tribute to the old watery Venus in "The Doors of His Face, the Lamps of His Mouth" (1965). Writers had to face facts, and the idea of exploring Venus, where the surface pressure is over ninety times that of Earth, and the atmosphere almost entirely carbon dioxide, was daunting to say the least.

That did not stop authors trying. In *The Merchants of Venus* (1972) Frederik Pohl introduced the mysterious Heechee, an alien race that had once colonized Venus and, though long gone, their constructions, including tunnels and underground chambers, can be adapted to human use. Pamela Sargent takes us through a terraformed Venus in *Venus of Dreams* (1986) and its sequels, whilst Ben Bova tackles the challenge head on in *Venus* (2001) where two expeditions face the harsh conditions and struggle to trace a scientist whose mission had unaccountably failed.

Venus is an object lesson in fate. It has been adopted by those warning of climate change to show what might happen to Earth if the greenhouse effect accelerates due to too much carbon dioxide in the atmosphere. Earth has benefitted from what is charmingly called the "Goldilocks Zone", neither too hot nor too cold, which we endanger at our peril.

There have been several husband-and-wife writing teams in science fiction. The best known are Henry Kuttner and Catherine Moore, but there were also Edmond Hamilton and Leigh Brackett and A.E. van Vogt and Edna Mayne Hull—though both very occasionally—and, more recently, Isaac Asimov and Janet Jeppson, Alexei and Cory Panshin, and David and Leigh Eddings, to name but a few. In most cases the partner also wrote separately, and the only married writing team I can think of who always wrote together and not separately were John and Dorothy De Courcy. They were married for over sixty years until Dorothy's death in 2010 at the age of 87. John died just two years later in 2012 having reached 90. They started writing soon after the Second World War and between them wrote twenty-one stories over the next eight years and then, inexplicably, stopped. Most of their work was for the sister pulps *Amazing Stories* and *Fantastic Adventures* during the editorship of Raymond A. Palmer, when the magazines were filled with stories about the Shaver Mystery and other strange phenomena. The De Courcys became interested in the lost world of Agharti and wrote three stories, featuring the intrepid explorer Ira Travers, and this mystical empire, "Morton's Fork" (1946), "The Man from Agharti" (1948) and "The Golden Mask of Agharti" (1950). Most of their stories feature some form of mysticism or the bizarre, including an earlier story they wrote set on Venus, "Alchemy" (1950), where the history of the planet is revealed through a vision. The following was their last published story and needs reading more than once for its full impact.

U NLIKE GAUL, THE NORTH CONTINENT OF VENUS IS divided into *four* parts. No Caesar has set foot here either, nor shall one—for the dank, stinging, caustic air swallows up the lives of men and only Venus may say, *I conquered*.

This is colonized Venus, where one may walk without the threat of sudden death—except from other men—the most bitterly fought for, the dearest, bloodiest, most worthless land in the solar system.

Separated by men into East and West at the centre of the Twilight Zone, the division across the continent is the irregular, jagged line of Mud River, springing from the Great Serpent Range.

The African Republic holds one quarter which they exploit as best they can, encumbered by filter masks and protective clothing.

The Asians still actually try to colonize their quarter, while the Venusian primitives neither help nor hinder the bitter game of power-politics, secret murder, and misery—most of all, misery.

The men from Mars understand this better, for their quarter is a penal colony. Sleepy-eyed, phlegmatic Martians, self-condemned for minute violations of their incredible and complex mores—without guards save themselves—will return to the subterranean cities, complex philosophies, and cool, dry air of Mars when they have declared their own sentences to be at an end.

Meanwhile, they labour to extract the wealth of Venus without the bitterness and hate, without the savagery and fear of their neighbours. Hence, they are regarded by all with the greatest suspicion.

The Federated States, after their fashion, plunder the land and send screaming ships to North America laden with booty and with men grown suddenly rich—and with men who will never care for riches or anything else again. These are the fortunate dead. The rest are received into the sloppy breast of Venus where even a tombstone or marker is swallowed in a few, short weeks. And they die quickly on Venus, and often.

From the arbitrary point where the four territories met, New Reno flung its sprawling, dirty carcass over the muddy soil and roared and hooted endlessly, laughed with the rough boisterousness of miners and spacemen, rang with the brittle, brassy laughter of women following a trade older than New Reno. It clanged and shouted and bellowed so loudly that quiet sobbing was never heard.

But a strange sound hung in the air, the crying of a child. A tiny child, a boy, he sat begrimed by mud at the edge of the street where an occasional ground car flung fresh contamination on his small form until he became almost indistinguishable from the muddy street. His whimpering changed to prolonged wailing sobs. He didn't turn to look at any of the giant passers-by nor did they even notice him.

But finally one passer-by stopped. She was young and probably from the Federated States. She was not painted nor was she well-dressed. She had nothing to distinguish her, except that she stopped.

"Oh, my!" she breathed, bending over the tiny form. "You poor thing. Where's your mama?"

The little figure rubbed its face, looked at her blankly and heaved a long, shuddering sigh.

"I can't leave you sitting here in the mud!" She pulled out a handkerchief and tried to wipe away some of the mud and then helped him up. His clothes were rags, his feet bare. She took him by the hand and as they walked along she talked to him. But he seemed not to hear.

Soon they reached the dirty, plastic front of the Elite Cafe. Once through the double portals, she pulled the respirator from her face. The air inside was dirty and smelly but it was breathable. People were eating noisily, boisterously, with all the lusty, unclean young life that was Venus. They clamoured, banged and threw things for no reason other than to throw them.

She guided the little one past the tables filled with people and into the kitchen. The door closed with a bang, shutting out much of the noise from the big room. Gingerly she sat him down on a stool, and with detergent and water she began removing the mud. His eyes were horribly red-rimmed.

"It's a wonder you didn't die out there," she murmured. "Poor little thing!"

"Hey! Are you going to work or aren't you, Jane?" a voice boomed.

A large ruddy man in white had entered the kitchen and he stood frowning at the girl. Women weren't rare on Venus, and she was only a waitress...

"What in the blue blazes is that!" He pointed to the child.

"He was outside," the girl explained, "sitting in the street. He didn't have a respirator."

The ruddy man scowled at the boy speculatively. "His lungs all right?"

"He isn't coughing much," she replied.

"But what are you going to do with him?" the man asked Jane.

"I don't know," she said. "Something. Tell the Patrol about him, I guess."

The beefy man hesitated. "It's been a long time since I've seen a kid this young on Venus. They always ship 'em home. Could have been dumped. Maybe his parents left him on purpose."

The girl flinched.

He grunted disgustedly, his face mirroring his thoughts. *Stringy hair... plain face... and soft as Venus slime clear through!* He shrugged. "Anyway, he's got to eat." He looked at the small figure. "Want to eat, kid? Would you like a glass of milk?" He opened a refrigerator, took out a plastic bottle and poured milk in a glass.

Chubby hands reached out for the glass.

"There, that's better," the cook said. "Pete will see that you get fed all right." He turned to the girl. "Could he belong to someone around here?"

Jane shook her head. "I don't know. I've never seen him before."

"Well, he can stay in the kitchen while you work the shift. I'll watch him."

She nodded, took an apron down from a hook and tied it around her waist. Then she patted the sober-faced youngster on his tousled head and left.

The beefy man studied the boy. "I think I'll put you over there," he said. He lifted him, stool and all, and carried him across the kitchen. "You can watch through that panel. See? That's Jane in there. She'll come back and forth, pass right by here. Is that all right?"

The little one nodded.

"Oh?" Pete raised his eyebrows. "So, you *do* know what I'm saying." He watched the child for a few minutes, then turned his attention to the range. The rush hour was on and he soon forgot the little boy on the stool...

Whenever possible during the lunch-hour rush, Jane stopped to smile and talk to the child. Once she asked, "Don't you know where your mama and daddy are?"

He just stared at her, unblinking, his big eyes soft and sad-looking.

The girl studied him for a moment, then she picked up a cookie and gave it to him. "Can you tell me your name?" she asked hopefully.

His lips parted. Cookie crumbs fell off his chin and from the corners of his mouth, but he spoke no words.

She sighed, turned, and went out to the clattering throng with laden plates of food.

For a while Jane was so busy, she almost forgot the young one. But finally people began to linger more over their food, the clinking of dishes grew quieter and Pete took time for a cup of coffee. His sweating face was haggard. He stared sullenly at the little boy and shook his head.

"Shouldn't be such things as kids," he muttered. "Nothing but a pain in the neck!"

Jane came through the door. "It gets worse all the time," she groaned. She turned to the little boy. "Did you have something to eat?"

"I didn't know what to fix for him," Pete said. "How about some beef stew? Do you think he'd go for that?"

Jane hesitated. "I—I don't know. Try it."

Pete ladled up a bowl of steaming stew. Jane took it and put it on the table. She took a bit on a spoon, blew on it, then held it out. The child opened his mouth. She smiled and slowly fed him the stew.

"How old do you think he is?" Pete asked.

The girl hesitated, opened her mouth, but said nothing.

"About two and a half, I'd guess," Pete answered himself. "Maybe three." Jane nodded and he turned back to cleaning the stove.

"Don't you want some more stew?" Jane asked as she offered the small one another spoonful.

The little mouth didn't open.

"Guess you've had enough," she said, smiling.

Pete glanced up. "Why don't you leave now, Jane. You're going to have to see the Patrol about that kid. I can take care of things here."

She stood thinking for a moment. "Can I use an extra respirator?"

"You can't take him out without one!" Pete replied. He opened a locker and pulled out a transparent facepiece. "I think this'll tighten down enough to fit his face."

She took it and walked over to the youngster. His large eyes had followed all her movements and he drew back slightly as she held out the respirator. "It won't hurt," she coaxed. "You have to wear it. The air outside stings."

The little face remained steady but the eyes were fearful as Jane slid the transparent mask over his head and tightened the elastic. It pulsed slightly with his breathing.

"Better wrap him in this," Pete suggested, pulling a duroplast jacket out of the locker. "Air's tough on skin."

The girl nodded, pulling on her own respirator. She stepped quickly into her duroplast suit and tied it. "Thanks a lot, Pete," she said, her voice slightly muffled. "See you tomorrow."

Pete grunted as he watched her wrap the tiny form in the jacket, lift it gently in her arms, then push through the door.

The girl walked swiftly up the street. It was quieter now, but in a short time the noise and stench and garishness of New Reno would begin rising to another cacophonous climax.

The strange pair reached a wretched metal structure with an askew sign reading, "El Grande Hotel." Jane hurried through the double portals, the swish of air flapping her outer garments as the air conditioning unit fought savagely to keep out the rival atmosphere of the planet.

There was no one at the desk and no one in the lobby. It was a forlorn place, musty and damp. Venus humidity seemed to eat through everything, even metal, leaving it limp, faded, and stinking.

She hesitated, looked at the visiphone, then impulsively pulled a chair over out of the line of sight of the viewing plate and gently set the little boy on it. She pulled the respirator from her face, pressed the button under the blank visiphone disk. The plate lit up and hummed faintly.

"Patrol Office," Jane said.

There was a click and a middle-aged, square-faced man with blue-coated shoulders appeared. "Patrol Office," he repeated.

"This is Jane Grant. I work at the Elite Cafe. Has anyone lost a little boy?"

The patrolman's eyebrows raised slightly. "Little boy? Did you find one?"

"Well—I—I saw one earlier this evening," she faltered. "He was sitting at the edge of the street and I took him into the cafe and fed him."

"Well, there aren't many children in town," he replied. "Let's see." He glanced at a record sheet. "No, none's reported missing. He with you now?"

"Ah—no."

He shook his head again, still looking downward. He said slowly, "His parents must have found him. If he was wandering we'd have picked him up. There is a family that live around there who have a ten-year-old kid who wanders off once in a while. Blond, stutters a little. Was it him?"

"Well, I—" she began. She paused, said firmly, "No."

"Well, we don't have any reports on lost children. Haven't had for some time. If the boy was lost his parents must have found him. Thank you for calling." He broke the connection.

Jane stood staring at the blank plate. No one had reported a little boy missing. In all the maddening confusion that was New Reno, no one had missed a little boy.

She looked at the small bundle, walked over and slipped off his respirator. "I should have told the truth," she murmured to him softly. "But you're so tiny and helpless. Poor little thing!"

He looked up at her, then around the lobby, his brown eyes resting on first one object, then another. His little chin began to quiver.

The girl picked him up and stroked his hair. "Don't cry," she soothed. "Everything's going to be all right."

She walked down a hall, fumbling inside her coveralls for a key. At the end of the hall she stopped, unlocked a door, and carried him inside. As an afterthought she locked the door, still holding the small bundle in her arms. Then she placed him on a bed, removed the jacket and threw it on a chair.

"I don't know why I should go to all this trouble," she said, removing her protective coveralls. "I'll probably get picked up by the Patrol. But *somebody's* got to look after you."

She sat down beside him. "Aren't you even a bit sleepy?"

He smiled a little.

"Maybe now you can tell me your name," she said. "Don't you know your name?"

His expression didn't change.

She pointed to herself. "Jane." Then she hesitated, looked downward for a moment. "Jana, I was called before I came here."

The little face looked up at her. The small mouth opened. "Jana." It was half whisper, half whistle.

"That's right," she replied, stroking his hair. "My, but your throat must be sore. I hope you won't be sick from breathing too much of that awful air."

She regarded him quizzically. "You know, I've never seen many little boys. I don't quite know how to treat one. But I know you should get some sleep."

She smiled and reached over to take off the rags. He pulled away suddenly.

"Don't be afraid," she said reassuringly. "I wouldn't hurt you."

He clutched the little ragged shirt tightly.

"Don't be afraid," she repeated soothingly. "I'll tell you what. You lie down and I'll put this blanket over you," she said, rising. "Will that be all right?"

She laid him down and covered the small form with a blanket. He lay there watching her with his large eyes.

"You don't look very sleepy," she said. "Perhaps I had better turn the light down." She did so, slowly, so as not to alarm him. But he was silent, watchful, never taking his eyes from her.

She smiled and sat down next to him. "Now I'll tell you a story and then you must go to sleep," she said softly.

He smiled—just a little smile—and she was pleased.

"Fine," she cried. "Well—once upon a time there was a beautiful planet, not at all like this one. There were lovely flowers and cool-running streams and it only rained once in a while. You'd like it there for it's a very nice place. But there were people there who liked to travel—to see strange places and new things, and one day they left in a great big ship."

She paused again, frowning in thought. "Well, they travelled a long, long way and saw many things. Then one day something went wrong."

Her voice was low and soft. It had the quality of a dream, the texture of a zephyr, but the little boy was still wide awake.

"Something went very, very wrong and they tried to land so they could fix it. But when they tried to land they found they couldn't—and they fell and just barely managed to save themselves. The big, beautiful ship was all broken. Well, since they couldn't fix the ship at all now, they set out on foot to find out where they were and to see if they could get help. Then they found that they were in a land of great big giants, and the people were very fierce."

The little boy's dark eyes were watching her intently but she went on, hardly noticing.

"So they went back to the broken ship and tried to decide what to do. They couldn't get in touch with their home because the radio part of the ship was all broken up. And the giants were horrible and wanted everything for themselves and were cruel and mean and probably would have hurt the poor shipwrecked people if they had known they were there.

"So—do you know what they did? They got some things from the ship and they went and built a giant. And they put little motors inside and things to make it run and talk so that the giants wouldn't be able to tell that it wasn't another giant just like themselves."

She paused, straightening slightly.

"And then they made a space inside the giant where somebody could sit and run this big giant and talk and move around—and the giants wouldn't ever know that she was there. They made it a *she*. In fact, she was the only person who could do it because she could learn to talk all sorts of languages—that's what she could do best. So she went out in the giant suit and mingled with the giants and worked just like they did.

"But every once in a while she'd go back to the others, bringing them things they needed. And she would bring back news. That was their only hope—news of a ship which might be looking for them, which might take them home—"

She broke off. "I wonder what the end of the story will be?" she murmured.

For some time she had not been using English. She had been speaking in a soft, fluid language unlike anything ever heard on Venus. But now she had stopped speaking entirely.

After a slight pause—another voice spoke—in the same melodious, alien tongue! It said, "I think I know the end of the story. I think someone has come for you poor people and is going to take you home."

She gasped—for she realized it had not been her voice. Her artificial eyes watched, stunned, as the little boy began peeling off a skin-tight, flexible baby-faced mask, revealing underneath the face of a little man.

THE REDUCED SIZE OF THE SUN VIEWED FROM THE CANALLED SURFACE
OF MARS, COMPARED WITH THE SUN SEEN FROM EARTH.

M A R S

The Lonely Path   John Ashcroft

With Venus seen as impossible for humans to colonize, Mars becomes the only planet in the solar system where humans might be able to live, despite its harsh environment. It's a comparatively small planet, its equatorial diameter being roughly 6,790km (4,220 miles) compared to Earth's 12,742km (7,920 miles), and its surface gravity is about a third of Earth's. Because it has no magnetic field Mars has lost much of its atmosphere, blown away by the solar wind. What remains is rarefied, and is 96% carbon dioxide. Its surface temperature, on a good day, might reach 35°C, but at night it can plummet to -143°C. Humans can only live there in fabricated units which would have to be brought all the way from Earth, and spacesuits would always have to be worn when out on the surface. Mars is not a natural place for humans.

It was not always so. In fiction, for decades, Mars was regarded as a likely home for human habitation, maybe inevitably if Earth was made inhospitable by nuclear war or other catastrophes. Ray Bradbury's *The Martian Chronicles* (1950), one of the classic texts on the human colonization of Mars, depicts a very hospitable planet where mankind settles and the native Martians die out.

It was long thought that Mars must have intelligent life, especially after newspapers reported in 1882 that the Italian astronomer Giovanni Schiaparelli had discovered canals on Mars. What he'd actually said was that he had seen *canali*, or channels, but that was interpreted as canals, and since canals are artificial, there had to be intelligent life. This was promoted relentlessly by the American astronomer Percival Lowell in a series of books starting with *Mars* in 1895. Linked with the belief that Mars was older than the Earth, allowing intelligent life a head start, it was likely that Martians were far in advance of humans. So, when H.G. Wells had Earth invaded by Martians in *The War of the Worlds* (serial, 1897), with their superior war machines and heat ray, it was entirely believable and, for the next seventy years or so, we clung to the belief that perhaps there really were "little green men" on Mars.

Thoughts about Mars were prejudiced by its name. It has a distinctive red colour, noticeable even to the naked eye, arising from the high iron content in its soil. Red suggests blood, which suggests conflict. The Babylonians called it Nergal, after their war-god, and in turn the Greeks called it Ares and the Romans, Mars. Wells's novel combined the ideas of an advanced Martian race and a warlike one, and that image lasted for a long time.

A "red" planet was also an obvious setting for a socialist state in *Krasnaia Zvezda* ("Red Star", 1908) by Alexander Bogdanov, which emphasized the benefits of socialism. The book was popular in Russia, especially at the time of the 1917 revolution, but it was not translated into English until 1984. Kim Stanley Robinson claimed it served as an influence for his *Red Mars* (1992), the first of his trilogy about terraforming the planet.

Until Wells's novel, the Martians were generally seen as benign and spiritual. The earliest fictional journey to Mars was *Der Geschwinde Reise* ("The Speedy Journey", 1744) by the German astronomer Eberhard Christian Kindermann. Most surprising is that this journey is to a Martian moon. The two moons of Mars, Phobos and Deimos, were not discovered until 1877 but Kindermann was convinced he had seen one. His explorers are led to the moon by an angelic guide. The inhabitants are humanoid and the travellers present themselves as gods. Much of the discussion with the natives is about religion. They reveal that this moon was the first object created by God.

Religion would feature in quite a few Martian stories over the next century or two. The little-known Charles Cole was especially daring in *Visitors from Mars* (1901) where he suggests that Jesus had been raised on Mars and sent to Earth to help. The Martians rescued him at his crucifixion and brought him back to Mars. *Out of the Silent Planet* (1938) by C.S. Lewis, the first book in his Cosmic Trilogy, is a religious allegory. The lead character, Ransom, represents the "ransom sacrifice" that God made of Jesus on behalf of mankind. Ransom is taken to Mars so that mankind, which has proved evil and warlike, can be redeemed. A decade later in "The Man" (1949), Ray Bradbury describes how an expedition to Mars is ignored because Jesus had just appeared to the Martians.

At the same time that H.G. Wells was transfixing the nation with his invading Martians, the German educator Kurd Lasswitz presented a different approach in *Auf Zwei Planeten* ("Of Two Planets"). Humanoid Martians have established bases at the North and South Poles. They are benign and want to help humanity in exchange for air and energy to supplement their planet's diminishing supplies. Alas, the English fail to appreciate the offer. The Martians overwhelm

Earth but despite their efforts to improve the planet, further hos-
tilities erupt. Lasswitz's novel was translated into many European
languages, but the first English translation was an abridged version
published in the USA in 1971.

After H.G. Wells and Jules Verne, the biggest early influence
on science fiction was Edgar Rice Burroughs who wrote chiefly
for the pulp magazines. His first Martian novel, *A Princess of Mars*
(1917) had been serialized as "Under the Moons of Mars" in 1912.
John Carter, a Civil War veteran, is overcome by fumes and finds
his astral self on Mars. Mars is mostly desert, irrigated by canals,
and with a thin atmosphere, but Carter finds he has great strength
and agility because of the lesser gravity. There are two Martian
races, one green-skinned race with two sets of arms, who are
warriors, and a scientifically advanced red-skinned race. Carter
rescues a beautiful princess, Dejah Thoris, but they are separated
and most of the first novel is Carter's efforts to rescue her from
the various warring factions. It's an exciting adventure story and
it set a trend for the planetary romance. There have been many
imitators, including Otis Adelbert Kline, Robert E. Howard, Lin
Carter, Philip Jose Farmer, Michael Moorcock and Marion Zimmer
Bradley, though the Queen of the Planetary Romance was Leigh
Brackett. She brought to the field a sense of alienation and wonder
that made her stories, which began with "Martian Quest" (1940),
strange but welcoming.

Homer Eon Flint's Mars, in "The Planeteer" (1918), is ruled by
a totalitarian regime, but the planet is dying. The Martians believe
they will benefit by moving Mars closer to Saturn, which has turned
into a new Sun, but their plans fail and Mars is destroyed. Moving
planets around the solar system was one of the cosmic stunts of
pulp writers. In "Across Space" (1926), Edmond Hamilton reveals

that Martians have built a ray that will draw Mars towards Earth and allow the surviving Martians to fly across.

Although the planetary romance and cosmic super-science have never gone away, during the 1930s and beyond some writers strove to bring more realism to their adventures. Edmond Hamilton led the way here. Both his "The Conquest of Two Worlds" (1932) and P. Schuyler Miller's "The Forgotten Man of Space" (1933) showed how Mars and its ecology needed to be protected against the excesses of colonialism. In Laurence Manning's serial "The Wreck of the *Asteroid*" (1933), pioneer explorers crash on Mars and struggle to survive in the alien environment. A popular story of the day was "A Martian Odyssey" (1934) by Stanley G. Weinbaum, which depicted a wonderful array of Martian life each suitably adapted to its environment.

As our knowledge of Mars grew, including the realization in 1947 that its atmosphere is almost entirely carbon dioxide, writers took a grim approach to Martian exploration. Both J.T. McIntosh in *One in Three Hundred* (1953) and E.C. Tubb in *Alien Dust* (1955) depict the harsh reality of trying to establish a base on Mars, whilst in *Outpost Mars* (1952), Judith Merril and Cyril Kornbluth (writing as Cyril Judd) contrast the dilemma between trying to establish a suitable colony and to make it pay by plundering the planet's resources. Arthur C. Clarke managed to blend both romance and realism in *The Sands of Mars* (1951) where he proposed a balanced way to develop a Martian colony, which also helps the native life.

Even if Mars has no life today it might have had once, and there have been several stories, such as H. Beam Piper's "Omnilingual" (1957) and John Ashcroft's "The Lonely Path" (1961), which is reprinted here, where explorers try to decipher ancient ruins. As he had with Venus, Roger Zelazny wrote a farewell to the old-style Mars in "A

Rose for Ecclesiastes" (1963) by showing how a fading Martian race can be revived.

The idea of discovering evidence of a lost Martian civilization continues to intrigue and has been explored by Ben Bova in *Mars* (1992) and its sequels, Allen Steele in *Labyrinth of Night* (1992) and Ian Douglas in *Semper Mars* (1998). The prospect of any life on Mars, no matter how remote, can still generate a fascinating story as Ian Watson demonstrated in *The Martian Inca* (1978) and Gregory Benford in *The Martian Race* (1999).

Kim Stanley Robinson's series that began with *Red Mars* (1992) is perhaps the most detailed exploration of recent years in how to terraform Mars, though there have been many other examples over the years, from as early as Clarke's *The Sands of Mars*, to such recent works as A.A. Attanasio's *Solis* (1994) and Alexander Jablokov's *River of Dust* (1996).

Mars will continue to exert a strong sense of wonder because, as our least inhospitable neighbour, it holds our only hope for possible refuge should disaster strike. Equally our fascination in humans pitted against great odds brings comparisons to some of our great explorers such as Ernest Shackleton in the Antarctic or Sir John Franklin in the North-West Passage. The extremes of surviving on Mars are shown in great detail in *Mars Crossing* (2000) by Geoffrey A. Landis and with the protagonist's defiant struggle for survival in Andy Weir's *The Martian* (2011).

There is little doubt that we will never give up hope about Mars. [*]

---

[*] For a more detailed study of Mars in early science fiction see my introduction to *Lost Mars* (2018), also published by the British Library.

John Ashcroft (1936–1997) was a journalist who worked for much of his life as a night supervisor in the Telephone Newsroom at the Liverpool *Daily Post*. He was a dedicated science fiction and astronomy fan and sold just ten stories to the British sf magazines in the 1950s and early 1960s, starting with "Dawn of Peace Eternal" in 1954. To my knowledge nothing by him has ever been reprinted, so it is a pleasure to reprint here a novelette about a discovery on Mars. Ashcroft wrote a sequel to this story, "No Longer Alone" (1961) and the two stories were reworked into a novel which, alas, never sold and is now lost.

I

S ANDERSON STOOD UP AND ABSENTLY KICKED AT the ground, and thick red clouds boiled up.

"For Heaven's sake—do you mind?" protested Platt, scrambling aside. "I know it can't get in our eyes, but damn it all, it's nice when you can see."

"Sorry," said Sanderson, chuckling. "I didn't expect it to do that. It's queer stuff—too thin for sand, and not fine enough for self-respecting dust. It must be nearly as light as the air—if you can call it air—to hang like that."

A sudden breeze brushed away the dust, carrying it in sparse puffs among the limonite hills.

"Let him play sandcastles if he likes," said Kennedy acidly. "It can't get in our helmets—unless they spring a leak, of course," he added brightly.

Sanderson grinned and looked round at the scenery.

Ahead lay the undulant desert, patched with brown and orange and streaks of ruddy oxides, glowing against the dark sky. Here and there rose snags of black rock. The brighter stars already glittered in the east. Over on the left, clattering sounded thinly as someone put the finishing touches to a building in the camp. Behind, the sun neared the horizon.

"Three degrees off plumb," mused Wallanstein, staring at the Tower. "It seems impossible in something so high."

"It… well, it's ugly," said Cortot.

"Yes? Just because it makes the Eiffel Tower look like a kid's whim?" asked Platt.

"No," protested Cortot. "There is more design in one rivet of the Eiffel Tower than in all of this thing. Nobody with a soul could leave a monument like that."

"It may not be a monument, don't forget," said Sanderson, sitting down again.

"Cortot's scared it will divert the tourists from Paris," said Kennedy.

Minhov, sitting on the dune's crest, ran gloved fingers tracing patterns in the sand, and uttered a guffaw that rang in everyone's helmets. "It would be funny to discover that the Tower *was* built as a tourist attraction."

"Tourist repulsion, perhaps," conceded Cortot.

"Well," said Sanderson defensively, "it attracted *us*, and we came forty million miles as the crow flies for a closer look."

"And I'll bet that would surprise the builders," said Platt.

"I don't know so much," said Kennedy. "It might have been built purely to attract attention, and you must admit it worked."

"Yes," said Cortot. "But there's a difference between attraction and pure curiosity."

"Soon be twilight," said Platt. "I missed it last night—I happened to be glancing the other way at the time."

"Olaf says the Tower was originally embedded in a mountain," said Wallanstein. "I don't mind somebody wanting his creation to endure, but when he plans it to outlast a mountain—well, that's too ambitious."

"Depends on how much importance they attached to it," said Sanderson.

"Then they must have considered it vital," said Wallanstein drily. "That's all I can say."

"We'll find it's just a monument after all," predicted Platt.

"I prefer the signpost idea," said Minhov. "Our preliminary scans would have detected any buildings as big as normal houses, even if they were buried. It seems unlikely that the builders of the Tower would vanish leaving no other trace—unless they weren't native to the planet. I think the Tower was left as an indicator of some kind. For all we know, it may be as prosaic to its builders as a traffic sign is to a motorist."

"I feel insignificant enough without your saying things like that," said Sanderson. "Your theory makes us look like the babies of the galaxy."

"Aren't we?" asked Kennedy sourly.

Sanderson felt the old familiar acid burn within him. True, there had been progress in the thirty years since the launching of the first unmanned satellites, but, as always, technical improvements outdistanced social ones. Even now, a brief flicker of hostility between nations had the power to chill. Mankind had not quite walked out from the shadow of the mushroom clouds.

And Sanderson knew, as they all knew, that the next decade might be the deciding one: humanity had a precarious grip with fingers and toes on the cliff that led to the stars, and the only hope lay in climbing higher to where the ledges were wider and breath could be regained. A fall now would be crippling, if not fatal.

He looked almost angrily at the Tower, and wondered if its discovery might prove more harmful than beneficial to human morale: there was a difference between being soberly awed and utterly humiliated.

The breeze whispered again, ruffling the sand and blowing distorted clouds of it across the desert. The Tower stood thin and dull, lent a vague sheen by the ebbing sunlight. The niches were just visible as dark specks.

"I haven't seen either Phobos or Deimos yet," complained Platt.

"Give them a chance," said Kennedy. "We only landed last night. Anyway, they'll be no more impressive than the met-satellites back home."

"The Tower must have had a purpose," said Wallanstein. "If only that of reminding whoever came this way that someone very powerful had been around."

"Not on a merely local scale, either," added Minhov. "It was meant to be seen from a hell of a distance."

"I agree with you," said Kennedy, suddenly serious. "I think that someone from outside the solar system left it as a sign. You know, we're like the small fish that plucks up courage to stick his head out of the water—and the first thing he sees is a lighthouse."

Behind them, the sun finally dipped below the hills. Pools of shadow lapped in the hollows and flowed together in a tide that drowned the crests of the dunes, and the sky darkened abruptly. Night and cold marched silently overhead, a spectral army with a banner of frozen stars. Its base no longer visible save as a silhouette against the stars, the Tower seemingly hung suspended in the air: the great shaft caught the light of the departed sun, glinting dully while the hills below were clad in darkness.

Kennedy uttered a half admiring obscenity.

Night wind rippled around, plucking at protective clothing and toying with the dust.

Platt shivered slightly. He heaved himself to his feet.

"Come on," he said. "If we hang around much longer we'll all get the willies for keeps. And MacDunn will have us for being MacLate."

They began shuffling down the dune. The fine sand was as tiring and treacherous as snow. Sanderson glanced upwards and his feet slid from beneath him and he finished the descent on buttocks and heels.

"Watch it," cautioned Kennedy. "Those bits of stone will carve chunks off your backside."

"They just about did," said Sanderson ruefully, brushing himself down in the dark.

They trudged towards where the incomplete camp was an oasis of noise and metal and light in the bleak evening. Every so often someone glanced back to watch the steady progress of the dull glow up the side of the Tower: now the column stood like a sentinel among the stars, rising three thousand feet in the frigid night.

"I owe you all an apology," said MacDunn cheerfully. He leaned against the alloy wall and hurriedly shifted his weight back on to his feet as the wall swayed. Grins appeared on a few faces.

"I know you all wanted to be away for a squint at the Tower this morning: but I thought it would be convenient if we had somewhere to live as well as something to look at. I hope Butterfield didn't drive you too hard. Anyway, while you were erecting this glorified shanty-town, three of us sent Bluebottle out to scan the Tower. Let's have the results, please, Helmut."

Wallanstein switched on the projector and someone dimmed the lights. A few people coughed; others eased into more comfortable positions.

That morning, while sections of alloy wall were being pulled from the landing ship to the camp site, someone had shouted and pointed: everyone had downed tools to watch MacDunn releasing the Bluebottle, like an armoured knight launching a falcon. The mechanism had circled, glittering in the cold sky, then dwindled into a spark that sped towards the Tower.

"We guided it round at various heights," explained Mac Dunn. "This is the view at ground level."

Cortot leaned forward to peer at the screen. "What about the niches?" he asked.

"We checked all of them," said MacDunn. "They're identical—and bleak, as if eighteen foot cubes had been cut out at seventy-foot intervals all the way up the Tower. You can see that only the top five feet of this first niche is visible. That worries me, because the rest of it is obviously below ground, and the ground happens to be bare and very firm rock."

"That suggests that the Tower came first," protested Cortot.

"It probably did, in a way," said Foster. "When you can build such a thing, it may be child's play to melt a bit of igneous rock to sink it into."

"Wait," said MacDunn, arresting the birth of a hubbub. "You see the scratches on the rock? They must have been extremely deep to remain faintly visible at all—they were caused by hard boulders being moved in the grip of ice, gouging the softer rock beneath. So the Tower has survived at least one glacier passage. And that," he added caustically, "was when our ancestors were still in the branches and chucking nuts at one another. Nor is that all—how long did it take Mars to lose a three thousand feet high mountain range? Olaf is convinced that when the Tower was built only a few feet of it projected above rock level."

"Oh, hell, no," cried someone. "That's going too far. The glacier, maybe—but not that…"

*

"It's beyond argument," said Sorenson, defending himself. "The geological evidence is clear, and, also, the Tower does show very faint traces of weathering. Hardly noticeable, without detailed inspection. And there are indications that only the highest niche once lay above ground level."

Sanderson's pulse was racing, but he felt his wilder dreams dying. Against all probability, he had hoped that some trace of the builders might remain, and that humanity might actually meet them. So much for his hopes—the builders had been forgotten when the seas first washed the shores of Earth's known continents.

"So close," growled Lymann disgustedly. "So close, and so far. It seems a long time, but on a solar scale we only just missed them. The odds against civilizations co-existing locally within such margins—well, the miracle is that we missed them so narrowly. Ships that pass in the night of time, you might call it. It's tragic, but it's still a thing to marvel at. I wish we could have met them."

To Sanderson, the words held a bittersweet truth. During the years since observation from the early satellites had detected the Tower and the survey by the unmanned *Bonestell III* had confirmed its existence, he had dreaded finding a mere tombstone. He had never regarded matters quite in this light, however: the narrowness of the margin hurt, yes, but some of the wonder remained.

"All this leaves the bigger headaches," remarked Thomas. "That is, Why, What, and Who—or perhaps What again."

"I'd say it's just a monument," said Ziolkowski. "And a highly effective one. But why are there no other traces?"

"No," said Minhov. "I still think it was left by a visiting race—a marker, or signal, or some such thing."

"I think it was a native creation," said MacDunn. "That's enough to accept without bringing interstellar flight into the argument.

But there's more to it than meets the eye—literally. I'd like to know how far down it extends—no, listen, let me explain. The material isn't anything we can identify yet. We do know it must be infernally tough—not only has it survived the weathering that removed a mountain from around it, but also it must be rooted damned firmly and deeply or it would have fallen long ago, ripping its foundations out of the ground as it toppled. It leans outside its centre of gravity, which, for a thing so high, is well nigh incredible. In fact, were it not strong it would snap under its own weight, however deep its roots. I'm frightened, honestly frightened, to imagine how far down it continues. The builders wanted it to outlast everything around it, and I'm wondering just how long it is expected to stay there."

"Those niches..." said Cortot softly. "As you said that, the odd idea came to me that the niches might be like marks on a sundial—could this be a measuring implement that uses the weathering of rock instead of the movement of shadow?"

"That scares the hell out of me," drawled Winter.

"I think it scares all of us," admitted MacDunn.

"I take it you will be having a personal look at the Tower tomorrow?" asked Platt hopefully.

"Yes. Even though there should be no risk whatsoever, we'll go cautiously at first. I can't get Kennedy's idea of booby-traps out of my mind. Helmut and I will be going in the morning for a preliminary recce, and we shall want four others who—Oh Lord, don't trample me to death. I can see we shall have to draw lots."

Someone ripped sheets off a memo pad, tore them into strips and passed them round: names were inscribed, and the strips were folded, dumped into a helmet and shaken up.

MacDunn pulled out the first one. "Kennedy."

"Poetic justice if there *is* a booby-trap," said Platt.

Minhov shrugged complacently as he was chosen. Then Sanderson heard his name announced and wanted to dance. Summers, the last one, a scrawny biochemist, frowned gloomily and joined Kennedy in predicting disaster.

MacDunn ran through the film in more detail and then called a break for a meal. As usual, Platt was first through the airlock. He burst back in excitedly, all but sabotaging the entire exit. "Hey, look at this," he said. "We never noticed it last night."

"Phobos?" asked Sanderson eagerly.

"No," said Platt scornfully. "I'm talking about the Evening Star."

For a moment the phrase failed to register, and someone said, "So what?" And then a laughing rush began and they all tried to leave the hut together. They ran out to stand and grin like children at the cold drop of silver, shining steadily above the night desert.

Here, of course, the Evening Star was the Earth.

II

Ironic cheers rang for a moment over the noise of machinery. MacDunn grinned from the vehicle and waved rather rudely at the men who had stopped work to watch the departure. Then the Potamus swerved out of the camp and trundled into the desert. Sanderson glanced down at the dust billowing from the fat tyres, and then gave all his attention to the land around hin. Wallanstein drove carefully, using the smoother dunes wherever possible, and avoiding an occasional rock that had defied the polish of time and sand. Summers swore enthusiastically each time the vehicle dipped and rattled over a rough patch.

Minhov studied the colours of the desert, the drab brown and the patches of red or yellow oxides and the streaks that fired the landscape. "Gauguin might have done a lot with this scenery," he remarked. "I wish I had brought my paints with me—it's worth sketching."

"This is a scientific expedition, not a travelling art scholarship," grunted MacDunn. "We want results, not a pile of pretty pictures."

"Kilted barbarian," growled Minhov.

The Potamus slithered sickeningly down into a dry gully and lurched groaning up the opposite slope. The immensity of the Tower was becoming evident as the distance shrank. Summers regarded it cynically.

"I wish we had landed in one of those mossy areas," he said. "We'll learn as much from the local lichen as we will from this ungodly whatnot."

"You're as eager to reach it as I am," said MacDunn. "Forget your puir wee bonny lichens, can't ye?"

"Hear that?" said Kennedy eagerly. "He's reverting to the language of his ancestors."

"Aw, shaddup," said MacDunn.

Wallanstein halted the Potamus at the edge of the shallow mound of rock from which the Tower rose. They clambered down to the sand. Summers loped up the mound, followed by the others.

"Look at this," said MacDunn. "The material simply meets the rock with scarcely a visible joint."

Sanderson stood staring up along the face of the Tower.

"You get dizzy doing that," remarked Kennedy.

"You also get a stiff neck," said Sanderson, "I feel like an ant at the foot of a telegraph pole."

"Let's have a look in the niche," suggested Minhov.

They followed the curve of the Tower till they reached the shadowed cave.

"If anything is to be found, it will be in there—or in one of the others," said MacDunn. "Its pretty dim in there, though, and we could easily miss something. Hold on—I'll get a torch"

"Here," said Kennedy. "I brought mine."

"Thanks, Alan." MacDunn prowled into the recess until he reached the wall eighteen feet inside. The others followed, studying the patch of light thrown by the torch. Voices, already made inhuman by the microphones, sounded still hollower, and the adoption of a crouching posture produced a closed-in feeling. Sanderson recalled the stream that had frozen in a long-ago winter; with his friends he had walked twenty yards on the ice beneath a stone culvert, flashing a treasured torch and marvelling at the grip of the ice on the walls. This was very similar.

MacDunn murmured in satisfaction. "See… the Bluebottle would never have detected this. There's a slight change of colour—if you can call it that—a lighter shade of jet black…"

They crouched around, breathing harshly.

The patch was evidently artificial. Only a strip several inches wide showed above the rock, but the straightness of its upper edge revealed it as no freak stain. It extended to within two feet of the right side of the niche: probably it similarly approached the other side, but the rock was not level and sloped up to conceal several feet of it.

Kennedy produced a set of lenses and scrutinized the surface beneath concentrated light from the torch.

"I believe there may be a joint… but incredibly fine. This is superb craftsmanship."

"Could it be a door?" asked Sanderson. "Like the sealing stone or whatever you call it on a pyramid?"

"If it *is* a door," grunted Minhov, "we can't open it; and even if we could, we couldn't get through it."

"I think we should all go home and watch cricket," said Summers.

"I wonder if…" MacDunn walked out of the niche, straightened thankfully and stared upwards. "I wonder if the other niches are the same? I think we're on to something."

"I'll rouse the Bluebottle," said Wallanstein hastily. "I should be doing so, anyway, and if Mac is going to perform acrobatics with his fancy ladder I might take some entertaining film."

MacDunn and Minhov went with him to the Potamus.

Wallanstein settled himself at the controls. Lazily the Bluebottle droned skyward to hover sixty feet above, cameras scanning and recording. Wallanstein monitored the film, using the screen on the portable equipment.

MacDunn and Minhov unclipped the ladder mounting and carried it up to the Tower.

"We'll never be poor again," remarked Summers happily. "What with film rights, recordings, memoirs, and our share of the ladder company's profits, plus our wages, we'll be set up for life."

"If this ladder contraption goes wrong," said Kennedy, "we'll break our necks, the company won't market the thing, the inventor will commit suicide, and our relatives will be swindled out of compensation by the company's lawyers. It's a hard and wicked world, my friend."

MacDunn struggled with the supports, swearing grimly.

"I remember my first Meccano set," mused Summers.

"It's as simple as a deck chair and as hard to sort out," said Sanderson, watching helpfully.

"Hold this on the wall," begged MacDunn. "One of you twist that bar—right." He switched on the motor. Rubberoid seals clamped like thirsty lips on the smooth wall. The mounting clung limpet-like to the Tower.

"I don't believe it," said Sanderson. "Even with the lower gravity, it can't stay up in this air pressure."

Minhov and Kennedy connected the twelve-foot sections of frail-looking ladder until an eighty-four foot length lay on the desert. MacDunn dragged the near end into position and clipped it to the base; Summers pulled a lever and delicately the ladder pivoted into a vertical stance.

MacDunn gripped the rungs, tried to shake them or wrench the ladder from the wall, climbed a few feet, repeated his efforts, then shrugged and continued climbing. They watched until his bulky shape reached the second niche and he slid sideways and entered it.

Wallanstein, watching the Bluebottle's view, actually saw what happened before MacDunn himself did. The others knew nothing until a head poked from the niche and an arm beckoned excitedly.

"Now we're getting somewhere," said Sanderson as Summers began climbing.

"One at a time," said Kennedy. "Let's not push our luck too far with the ladder—I still mistrust the damned thing."

As Summers entered the niche, Sanderson began climbing, fumbling in his eagerness. Near the niche he looked down, catching a glimpse of endless lurid land and the distant flash of sunlight on metal from the camp. Below, Minhov stood with one foot on the ladder, and Kennedy was gesturing impatiently and impolitely. Sanderson hurriedly finished the ascent, conscious of the Bluebottle buzzing somewhere behind him. Several feet of ladder rose alongside the opening of the niche; cautiously he slid across, grateful for the way Summers jerked on his arm to help him inside.

The interior of the great shadowed niche was bare, except for the end wall where he saw MacDunn's discovery.

"Discovery is a bad word," said MacDunn. "It implies that I found it, whereas I have a nasty feeling that *it* found *me*."

"What happened?"

"Well, when I first looked, there was only the very slightly lighter patch, as on the other niche wall. I did some prodding and hammering, then turned to wave you all up, and the panel opened behind me with a loud hiss." He chuckled richly. "I don't mind admitting that it scared the liver and lights out of me."

"I've figured it out," said Summers confidently. "I'm no mathematician, but I can see the obvious."

"Thank you very much," said Sanderson. "I remain ignorant."

"It's clear enough," said Summers.

"It also looks harmless," said MacDunn. "But it could be a trap for grave-robbers—for all we know, this place may be a mass mausoleum."

Minhov entered, followed by Kennedy. They studied the discovery.

The panel in the wall had become a recess several inches deep and roughly sixteen feet square. Evenly spaced across the bottom few feet of the panel were nine strips of some brown metallic substance, each twelve feet long and two inches wide. Each strip was studied with four rows of tiny holes.

In a small cavity at the base of the recess lay two small metal pins. Sanderson peered down at them.

"What are these?" he asked. And, even as he spoke, he began to realize.

Bluebottle buzzed to and fro like a dog hinting that a walk was necessary.

"What's up with the thing?" demanded MacDunn. He walked to the edge of the niche and looked down. An arm was waving energetically from the Potamus. In realization, MacDunn switched on the radio speaker in his helmet and let everyone have the benefit of Wallanstein's curses.

"Sorry about that," he said. "I forgot about it. But can't you pick us up by the normal mikes in the Bluebottle?"

"Of course," said Wallanstein. "Don't worry—your comments are being recorded here for posterity—but I like to talk as well as listen."

Sanderson was examining the brown strips, trying to detect a key to the puzzle.

Apparently at random, a pin had been inserted into one hole in each of the seven lower strips. No pin had been inserted into any hole on the top two strips, but two spare ones lay ready for use.

The men crowded round. Bluebottle hovered over their heads, buzzing and squinting. Minhov scowled balefully at it and wished aloud for a fly-swatter.

"Fathomed it out yet, Sandy?" asked Summers.

"No. There are too many possibilities. We don't know which way to read it—up, down, across, or what. I mean, it might depend on addition, subtraction, geometrical progression or cube roots or any damned sequence."

"Heaven preserve us," muttered Kennedy.

"It's actually simple," said Summers.

"I can spot it," remarked Minhov.

"Of course, it might be a red herring," said Summers. "But it seems innocent. I've gloated long enough—here, look."

He pointed at the bottom brown strip. "The puzzle must start from the bottom and work upwards, if the last two parts to complete are the top ones."

"Not necessarily," objected Sanderson. "They might have wanted us to deduct the beginning—it's just as probable."

"Stand back a bit," said Summers. "You'll see the pattern on the first three strips."

"Ah…" said Sanderson. "Now I'm with you."

"Yes," said Summers triumphantly. "On the bottom strip, the pin is in the fifth hole from the right, on the bottom row. On the second strip, it's in the fifteenth hole from the right. On the third strip, the forty-fifth: a simple matter of multiplying by three each time. Of course, once you exceed the length of one row of holes you lose the visual sequence. But we can work it out easily."

Minhov pointed confidently at a hole in the eighth strip and then at one in the ninth strip. "Those are where the spare pins go," he said.

"Hark at Genius," said Kennedy. "I got stuck at the fifth strip."

"If you're right," said Sanderson, "and we don't deny it, and we do stick those pins in—what'll happen?"

Kennedy predicted that a door would open releasing the biggest and hungriest beast ever imagined. "There's an Arabian Nights flavour here," he added, "and I'm not sure that I like it."

"My mathematics are correct," said Minhov positively. "I accept no responsibility for the results of their practical application."

They looked at each other, grinning in their helmets with excitement.

"Can't we chance it?" asked Sanderson. "Surely it's only a combined intelligence test and locking device?"

"One never knows," said MacDunn. "It might be a booby-trap left by some long gone spiteful laddie, ready to blow up half the planet with whoever set it off."

Minhov wished everyone a happy Christmas.

"Seriously," said Summers, "I think we'll find a museum, records, mausoleum or something of historical value—it was left like this to preserve its contents from primitive natives or animals until a race with some amount of intelligence arrived."

"Why bother with a test?" asked Sanderson. "An advanced race could break in anyway."

"Yes?" replied Summers sceptically. "Could *we* do it? I have my doubts. It was built to last indefinitely, but it has a simple device to reveal its contents. It seems a very smart plan to me."

"Perhaps they had a war," said MacDunn in a determinedly grim mood, "and were losing, and left this as a trap for their enemy, and—"

"Oh, for God's sake," complained Sanderson.

He stared at the puzzle and then looked back at the red land whose bones had been picked by time. He wanted to complete the pattern, but, as Kennedy had said, it was almost too inviting, and nasty doubts nagged him.

"The hiss as it opened was probably air escaping from some-where," said MacDunn. "Which suggests that it had never been opened since the atmosphere was far denser."

"Well?" said a metallic voice. Wallanstein, speaking through MacDunn's helmet, made everyone start slightly. "You already know how old the Tower is. Forget the gossip and have a sensible discussion."

"It's all right for you," said MacDunn irritably. "You can sit down there warming a seat while we stand up here and wonder what the blazes will happen if we stick those pins in."

"Listen," replied Wallanstein calmly. "I'm as excited as any of you, and I have my own theories, but I think I may be seeing things with better mental as well as physical perspective. We have no right to make a decision—especially as Henry said that his solution might only be a red herring. We need time to go over this with the computer and ensure there is no alternative solution. Shift aside and let the Bluebottle take detailed pictures. Then we go back and thrash it out with everyone else. We can't act without consulting the others, not in a case like this. We found it, and may not want to lose any further credit, but we'd be ill-advised and selfish to go ahead by ourselves. If the majority in camp think it might be dangerous we shall have to leave it for a while. In any case, we should let the Earth know—and if Earth cries 'Verboten' we'll forget about it till a later decision is made. For Heaven's sake, let's be sensible about this."

MacDunn shrugged. "That's the best way," he admitted. "Thanks, Helmut. We're on the way down. Go ahead with Bluebottle."

None of them knew whether to feel secretly relieved or cheated. They began descending the ladder while the Bluebottle buzzed and snuffled at the puzzle. MacDunn went last. As he swung on to the ladder he uttered a startled exclamation. The Bluebottle was hovering baffled before a blank wall.

"The damned thing's gone," he said anxiously. "Wait…"

He stepped back into the niche and the puzzle reappeared as the panel slid upwards.

"It must somehow register my presence," he announced to Wallanstein. "See what happens when I get back on the ladder. Yes, closed again… Ah well, I hope you've got all the pictures you wanted, Helmut?"

He reached the ground and stood with the others.

"What the devil are you doing?" he asked.

Kennedy straightened from the Tower's face with an apologetic expression and put the pencil back in his pocket and zipped it. "I was trying to write 'Carruthers was here before Kilroy' on the wall," he said sadly, "but it won't show against this black stuff."

Minhov snorted at this irreverent attitude to something older than Mankind's hairy ancestors, and Sanderson smiled.

Cold wind blew about them, furrowing the dust.

"I predict a rowdy meeting," said MacDunn with glum satisfaction. They carried the motor from the ladder to the Potamus, and Wallanstein recalled the Bluebottle; fat tyres churned the sand, and they drove back over the wilderness towards the camp.

The meeting was, if anything, restrained. It was generally agreed that the Puzzle should be completed. News of progress was relayed up to the parent ship anchored against Phobos, sent across to the moon and down to Earth; the eventual reply amounted to "Congratulations—proceed with caution."

"Which hands the can neatly back to us," remarked Summers.

Every man in the camp worked out the Puzzle to his own satisfaction, no one being willing to accept anyone else's mathematics. Even when the computer confirmed the general findings, one cynical surveyor considered this good reason to re-check his mathematics. The computer failed to detect any other possible solution to the Puzzle (like the Tower, the Puzzle had by now earned the distinction of a capital letter.)

A further journey to the niche was made, and the holes indicated by the calculations were ringed with paint. MacDunn decided that the Bluebottle should be controlled from camp, and not by a member of the exploration team, "just in case any unforeseen result should cause local damage."

"Of course," said Kennedy, "a lot depends on what is meant by the word 'local.' To the builders, 'local' might have meant merely planetary."

I I I

Sanderson stepped thankfully from the ladder into the niche, enjoying the feeling of solidity beneath his feet. "That's better," he said. "I still have doubts about that patent invention."

He looked back. Bluebottle hovered, relaying the scene to the camp. Stars burned above the motionless desert. There was no hint of the cold that hugged the land; rather, the ochre hills glowed with a suggestion of heat. The wilderness rippled away, red and brown and orange, to form a dimpled and oddly apparent horizon. Far out where the sand met the dark sky glittered the metal of the camp, alien in the richly hued waste. The shadow of the Tower was a long path across the dunes.

"Come on," urged Minhov. "Sandy's right—let's organize ourselves. We can only die once."

"Cheerful wretch," said MacDunn. He crouched before the Puzzle and picked up one of the two spare pins, holding it clumsily in his gloved hand.

"Steady," urged Sanderson. "We don't know what'll happen if it goes into the wrong place."

Minhov made the obvious comment that no one knew what would happen if the pin filled the correct place either, and added that this might lead to something far worse.

"Well," said Sanderson, "if what springs out is half as ugly as the thing Kennedy sketched last night, I'll go steaming over the horizon at a mighty rate of knots. Let's know the worst."

Typically, MacDunn ignored the paintmarks and counted out the Puzzle again, much to the chagrin of some watchers in the camp who regarded this as sheer sarcasm. He confirmed the results, and slid the pin into the hole on the eighth strip. His breathing was loud in his helmet as he picked up the second pin. Sanderson, stooping over him, felt perspiration on his back. Then MacDunn had inserted the pin into the hole on the ninth strip. Around them pressed the black and featureless walls of the niche. There came a silence in which Sanderson could feel the beating of his heart, and his breath slipped slowly from him.

Nothing happened. The key had been turned in the lock left by the builders, and no door opened.

The three of them straightened slowly and looked at each other. Tension eased into anticlimax.

MacDunn uttered a bitter laugh, and shrugged.

Behind them, the Bluebottle broadcast the magnificent failure back to the camp.

Then a glimmer of hope, mingled with apprehension, lit Sanderson's mind. "The other niches," he said. "What if we have to complete a Puzzle in every one of them?"

"No…" protested MacDunn. "Please, no—it would take weeks…"

"You know," said Minhov, "there is one alternative." He smiled behind his mask, certain that he had guessed the truth. He pulled out the pins and exchanged their positions, and, with quiet deliberation, the sixteen-foot square of the Puzzle slid aside and the way into the Tower lay black and wide before them.

*

Sanderson recalled someone saying that the Tower was a mausoleum holding the dead of the builders. And someone had said that it was a museum preserving their memory and culture from the ruin of age. And others who pronounced it a monument to the flowering of life before the world grew waste. Or a signpost left by long gone travellers, pointing the way to stars for whoever followed later in the morning of Time. And the pessimists who predicted that it might be guarded against vandals, and those who feared a trap left amid a war that was forgotten before humanity made weapons of flint.

And then he felt a horrid tremor within his mind—a glimpse of two identical images not quite superimposed, rousing an echo along corridors of nerve and a sudden acceleration of his blood. He stood frightened and must have shuddered visibly for a moment.

"Got the creeps?" asked MacDunn.

"Yes," he admitted sheepishly. "Forget it… I got one of those deja-vu sensations—you know the kind of thing. My mind's suffering from the tension. It all goes back to the time I opened a forbidden door and stole jam at one in the morning."

"Whatever's inside the Tower," said MacDunn drily, "you can be sure it isn't jam. Daddy won't come and box your wee lugs this time—although something far more horrible than Daddy might get you."

"Do we walk in?" asked Minhov. "This reminds me of the spider inviting the fly to supper. Let's send the Bluebottle first—"

"Very appropriate if there *is* a spider," said MacDunn.

"We can manufacture another Bluebottle in a week," said Minhov. "It took thirty seven years to develop me to my present state—I feel suddenly irreplacable."

Jarvis, back in base camp operated the controls. The Bluebottle buzzed purposefully forward into the niche, steadied itself, steered at the entrance and glided cautiously into the gloom till it was gone from sight.

Into MacDunn's helmet, Jarvis gave a harsh and crackling commentary.

"There's a blank wall about... say... twenty yards ahead. Yes... and a side turning. I'll guide her down it. Looks like another blank corridor—oh, no—reception's fading and the controls are sluggish. The walls must block me somehow—damned queer. I'm pulling her out before we lose her altogether..."

In the darkness, Bluebottle prowled and peered with lensed eyes that needed no light. The men stared, till a feeble metallic glint came, and the machine buzzed out under control again.

"All but lost her then," complained Jarvis. "I think one of you will have to go in. At least, Bluebottle didn't set off any booby-traps."

"Yes," said MacDunn cynically. "And it couldn't make the puzzle appear, either. Any traps here may only react to something alive."

"I'll take the chance," volunteered Minhov.

"We all will," said Sanderson.

"Oh no, we won't," retorted MacDunn. "What if the Puzzle closed with us inside? And didn't open again?"

"The best idea," said Jarvis, "is for one of you to go in while the other two keep watch—meanwhile, two more can come out from camp here and relieve you so that all three of you can go in."

There was general agreement on this. Eventually, Jarvis announced that Laurie and Reinhardt were leaving the camp.

"While they're on the way," said Minhov, "I'll have a look inside. Don't worry about losing contact—it's inevitable, even if we all had radio. And don't worry about my taking chances—I place a high value on my neck."

He switched on his torch and walked into the Tower. All around him light suddenly glowed from the walls and ceiling. He halted and looked about. The entrance and the side turning were now fully illuminated.

"That was thoughtful of them," he remarked. The casual comment brought shivers to Sanderson's flesh. Minhov grinned and waved and then deliberately walked on and stepped into the side corridor.

Minutes passed in silence. Sanderson and MacDunn stalked to and fro within the niche, glancing at their watches.

In the distance sunlight flashed on the Ocerous as it scuttled like a beetle across the desert: then the driver followed the shadow of the Tower through the gaudy desolation. The vehicle halted beside the Potamus. Two figures emerged and ran clumsily to the base of the Tower. A few moments later, Laurie clambered into the niche, followed by Reinhardt. They stared in fascination at the lit entrance.

"Any news yet?" demanded Laurie eagerly. "Is Alex in there?"

"Yes," said MacDunn. "And now you're as wise as we are."

Seventeen minutes passed before Minhov walked from the side corridor and greeted them. He was grinning in unashamed excitement and triumph.

"Where in the name of God have you been?" demanded MacDunn, half relieved, half angry.

Minhov's eyes sparkled and he guffawed with sheer delight.

"To the top of the Tower," he said.

Into the hush he added exultantly, "And to the bottom, too, just for the free ride."

"How?" asked Sanderson. "You mean there's a lift?"

"Yes—I'll show you."

"Just a minute," said MacDunn. "Not everybody. Three of us will go, as arranged. If we get back with no trouble, I think we can consider it completely safe."

"Yes," said Reinhardt gloomily. "Maybe the big black beasties won't close the door until enough of us are inside to make a good meal."

Their footfalls echoed thinly from the walls and high ceiling as Minhov led the way down the corridors. Then they walked into a room whose dimensions were slightly smaller than the cross section of the corridors.

"This is the lift," explained Minhov. "Look." He indicated a vertical row of holes on one wall, and a pin resting in a recess.

"They were fond of puzzles," said Sanderson caustically.

"Simplest way of ensuring that only intelligence can find its way around in here," said Minhov. "Anyway, this isn't a puzzle—it's too obvious. You see the hole nearly half way up—the one with the blue light in it? I spotted that it was the forty-second hole from the top of the row."

Sanderson thought about this for a moment, and then said, "So what?"

Minhov gave him a hurt look. "This niche entrance is the forty-second one from the top of the Tower. So this was obviously the selection panel of a lift."

"It may be obvious to a genius like you," said MacDunn. "I would never have seen it in a month of Sundays."

"Listen," said Sanderson. "If you're right—"

"I am," interrupted Minhov indignantly. "No ifs—I checked it."

"Yes, but it means that the ruddy Tower extends down nearly as far as it sticks up. That's fantastic."

"Don't you remember," said Minhov patiently, "someone saying that the Tower might be built to last far longer than it has? And Mac saying it must be deeply embedded to remain standing at all? Why shouldn't it be drilled another twenty-seven hundred feet into the rock? Anyway, I've been down there, and I know it does."

"All right. I surrender. How does this lift work?"

"You can't even see that?" asked Minhov despairingly.

He took up the pin and inserted it into a hole at random. The floor pressed itself up at them and their bodies tensed in the smooth acceleration. The blue glow left the hole and appeared progressively in the holes above, ascending the column until it reached the pin. Motion ceased. The end wall, which had sealed itself silently, opened. Beyond lay a white-lit corridor as bare as the others.

"Shall we go all the way up?" asked Minhov. "Or down?"

"You didn't leave the lift, then?" asked Sanderson.

"No—I thought I had gone as far as I should, alone."

"If there's anything to be found, it will be at the bottom, surely," said MacDunn.

"The top is just as logical," said Minhov.

"I'll take the casting vote," said Sanderson. "I suggest the top. The thought of going all the way down gives me cold shudders."

Minhov said something sarcastic about scientific method and democracy, and tugged out the pin and pushed it into the top hole. The lift closed and rose smoothly, faster and faster, and they watched the blue light climbing the row.

"I would never have risked going all the way up and down this alone," confessed Sanderson.

"I had a few bad moments," admitted Minhov. "Such as when I panicked at the bottom and miscounted the holes coming back up—it gave me a nasty feeling."

"The lift must have come automatically to the floor on which the niche was opened," surmised MacDunn. "Probably the niches all have identical Puzzles: the builders wanted to make it easy for us to find an entrance, so they put entrances all the way up."

"One for every few million years," said Minhov.

"Mars years, that is," said Sanderson happily.

The lift eased to a halt and opened.

They walked out into the empty corridor. It turned twice at right angles, and then led into a dead end. They tapped the wall and sought some sign of a joint.

Then MacDunn glanced back and his heart thumped unevenly.

"Don't look now," he said with ominous calm, "but they've locked us in."

The walls met another dead end behind them. They were trapped in a twenty yard length of corridor. They banged the walls and swore and strode up and down; then, before panic could tighten its hold on them, the original end wall slid aside and an utterly unexpected feeling hit them—that of their protective clothing slackening as air rushed in around them.

MacDunn checked the pressure with his wrist-gauge.

"Nearly Earth normal," he announced.

The temperature was 18 degrees Centigrade; allowing for a slight oxygen deficiency, the air could be breathed without discomfort.

A thrill crept in Sanderson's flesh. Suddenly he sensed the presence of someone or something in the walls around him, the touch of two minds in darkness, and a birth of fear.

MacDunn and Minhov looked questioningly at one another, and then gave strained smiles and walked forward. Almost reluctantly, Sanderson followed.

The passage led into a wider one in which an alcove had been hollowed out. Sanderson felt something stir in his mind, a moth fluttering just beyond the glow of the fire of his reason, and a hideous fascination drew him forward. He walked to the recess while perspiration shone on his face, and abruptly his vision blurred and he fell sickly down a night of nothingness where a great black hand flung him.

MacDunn turned to make some comment to Minhov, and saw Minhov's eyes widening incredulously, and he swung round to find the alcove empty. There was no trace of Sanderson; he had vanished, utterly and soundlessly.

And as they stood in shock, a panel opened behind them and they heard the approach of unsteady footsteps.

I V

There was warmth and darkness. Memory walked the tunnels of his mind, opening a door here and there, and it seemed that a limitless list of words and concepts unreeled from his brain like tape winding into emptiness. And there was a voice in the darkness, gentle, insistent, repeating his name, and somewhere grew recognition of himself. Feeling returned, and a yielding surface was cushioning him. His first effort at speech was a coughing mumble, then his throat relaxed and he drew a hoarse breath and flexed his arms and legs in the night.

"Relax, Sanderson," came MacDunn's voice from far above. "It's all right."

"Let's have some light," he complained. "I must have fainted. I... ah, that's it."

The dark dissipated like rising mist, and his eyes narrowed at the gradual return of light.

"I was in that corridor... the alcove..."

Appearing more clearly overhead was an unfamiliar ceiling. He stared up, trying to identify it, and then he looked sideways and saw strange walls. He pushed himself up on one elbow into a half-sitting position, suffering momentary dizziness, then his eyes cleared and he looked bewilderedly at the block of substance—a form of rubber, surely—which supported him. He found with a surge of embarrassment and indignation that he was naked. More anxiously, he looked about him.

"Where is this? Mac, where the devil are you?"

"Don't be alarmed," said the voice. "You must prepare yourself for a certain amount of shock."

The voice was MacDunn's, but a slight trace of care in the pronunciation gnawed at Sanderson's nerves, and the truth began to engulf him, frighteningly.

"We must apologize," said the voice, "for acting as we did. Urgency alone justified our treatment of you."

Sanderson felt cold, and he shook slightly, but his own voice, though unnaturally taut, held more self-control than he anticipated. "Who are you?" he asked quietly. "I remember entering the Tower... your Tower? Where am I now? Where are my friends?"

"You're still inside the Tower," replied the voice reassuringly. The uncanny resemblance to MacDunn's voice emphasized the strangeness of the situation. The voice was beautifully resonant, or perhaps amplified, suggesting power and confidence and sheer size.

"You've been asleep—one might call it that—a form of induced trance—for almost two days."

Shaken, he said, "And you are the—well, the builders?"

"Yes."

There was a pause. He gripped the edge of the block of rubbery substance with tight hands, and swallowed. His rapid pulse was the sole physical indication that this was not an extension of—had he dreamed? Images were still fading behind a veil in his mind. After a few seconds he smiled and then uttered an unsteady laugh.

"That was the one thing we didn't seriously expect," he admitted. "We thought the planet had been dead for... oh, a very long time. We thought the Tower was a monument, a museum, or even a burial place. What is it, then—a living place?"

"One could call it that," was the rather evasive reply.

"The language... the voice... what's happened to my friends?"

"The language was learned from your mind while you slept, and the voice was chosen because it was that of someone you trusted," answered the voice candidly. "I am afraid that you were examined in detail while unconscious. I apologize, not merely for the physical possession which was taken of you, but also for the intrusion made into your mind. Both acts were contrary to our ethics and distressed us considerably. We tried to filter out all matters not connected with your language, although other associations did of course enter our recordings. We hope that you will forgive us when you see the urgency of the situation."

After a brief silence, Sanderson said, "But what about my friends?"

"They are unharmed, though they will be disturbed at your disappearance. You will be returned to them at the earliest opportunity."

He sat in the empty room with resentment and fear lurking in his mind for a while, but both feelings faded. The trick of using MacDunn's voice annoyed him at first, then he saw that he appeared to be in no immediate danger, and his curiosity began to conquer his dread.

"I feel uneasy like this," he said. "Where are my clothes?"

And he smiled at the thought of this request being among the first words between Mankind and another race. As an ambassador, he felt utterly inadequate.

"That," said the voice in a puzzled tone, "was a matter which defeated our understanding. We considered these coverings to be a protection against an alien environment, but from your mind we gained impressions of some social or racial connection, and we did not press further. I hope that no discomfort has been caused. I'll bring your clothes in to you."

Unready for a physical meeting, he stiffened as a panel opened and something walked into the room. After the first shock, he realized that the thing was mechanical—strolling on three jointed legs with a peculiar rhythmic motion. The legs met at a body roughly the size of his own helmet, from which hung other flexible limbs, two of which held out his clothes almost deferentially.

Gingerly he took the clothes from the delicate grip. On closer inspection, as he dressed, he saw that the machine was made partly of metal and partly of polished red wood, the result having a touch of craftsmanship suggestive of a piece of graceful furniture. Erect, it stood level with his chest. There were lens-like panels in the curved wood, and some metallic attachments that resembled antennae.

"I hope that the clothes are in good condition," said the machine. The deep Scottish voice filled the room. "We tried to correct certain defects in them."

Certainly the clothes had been washed and pressed, and he felt far happier as he zipped them around him.

"What exactly are you?" he asked the machine.

"Call me Guide. This is an indirect method of accompanying you, but we consider it the best. Our true nature might have a disturbing effect on you, and also there is a slight risk of mutual bacteriological contamination—no decision has yet been reached on either problem."

"You mean that you're controlling this machine—using it as a—well, an interpreter, or a go-between?"

"Yes."

He eyed the device as it swayed to and fro, comfortably, like a farmer standing with his back to a hearth.

"We gained the impression from your mind and your comments that the outer world is dead," said Guide, in a curiously wistful manner. "Is this true?"

"You mean that you don't *know*?" he demanded incredulously.

Guide paused for a few moments. "What is outside? Describe it for me."

With a sense of unreality, Sanderson said, "Well, there's little vegetation—just scraps of moss and lichen and some fernlike plants, mainly bordering the bigger canyons. We haven't explored widely, but from spatial observation we feel confident about that. The air's too thin to breathe—mainly nitrogen—most of the oxygen combined chemically with the desert long ago, limonite and other oxides, and so on. And the desert covers most of the planet. I suppose you sealed yourselves off in here? Is this your natural atmosphere? I remember an airlock on the way in—you're native to this planet, surely?"

A definite sadness coloured the voice as Guide answered.

"That was as we feared. Oh, we knew it would happen, but to accept the death of one's world is not pleasant."

"But why didn't you know?"

Guide turned to the door and asked him to follow. He walked with the machine along corridors until a dead end blocked their way. "This leads to the open air," said Guide.

"Wait—my helmet—my breathing equipment—"

"They won't be needed," said Guide.

The end of the corridor opened and a refreshing wind blew in, and Guide beckoned with a rubbery limb and walked forward, and Sanderson stepped from the Tower, his mind numbing under the shock.

There was grass beneath his feet, and trees feathered their foliage in the distance. Beyond, stood mountains, oddly steep, with massed cloud drifting over them. And the air was rich with the scent of large red flowers that drank the sunlight all around.

He turned, stunned, and saw that the Tower was a building thirty feet high, black and alien in the park. Almost this might have been Earth, but the gravity was still low, and he saw that the grass was not quite grass, and the flowers were unknown, and there was a subtle difference in the wind and sky and the slenderness of the mountains.

He clenched his fists as the sight clawed at his reason.

"This is the world we love and inhabit," said Guide. "Hence my sorrow at your description of what it will become."

His knees felt weak as the possibility struck him.

"There has, of course, been a transference across the dimension which you call Time."

Sanderson stood on the lawn in the grip of aching fear.

"What year is this?" he asked shakily.

"That would mean nothing to you," said Guide chidingly. "We can tell you the exact extent of your transference, but the figure would be too large to hold any personal reality for you. It can only be measured in millions of our years."

And nearly twice as many of *mine*, he thought bleakly.

Fighting to control his voice, he asked, "But—why have you done this?"

"It seemed inevitable," said Guide, "that in the far future another intelligent race would visit the world we had left. We were very lonely, and we wanted desperately to meet whoever came after us."

Sanderson stood amid flaring flowers while the clouds moved high above. And the utter sincerity in the voice of Guide drove away the fear that had filled him.

Later, he sat on the grass with the sun warming his back just sufficiently to render him comfortably lazy. This might have been a late summer day in Norway, and he guessed that the night would be very cool. Somewhere an analyst, either living or mechanical, had confirmed that the local fruit would nourish him, and he chewed hungrily at a thing resembling an apple but with a jucier flavour.

"So the Tower," he said between mouthfuls, "was built to project future visitors back to this time. Have any others ever come?"

"No," said Guide softly. "The power accumulated was enough for one projection only. In bringing you here, the Tower has fulfilled its purpose. Some of my race said that we were being pessimistic in building the Tower to endure so long: now, I think that the pessimism was justified. We expected visitors from outside the solar system—the planned age of the Tower was a safety measure in case none came before life evolved into intelligence on your world. Ironically, you are very early, and the expected visitors are either very late or non-existent."

"Then," said Sanderson, "in all the gap between this moment and the year from which I came, not one other race has found your planet?"

"So it seems," said Guide. "We must both accept the bitter fact that our races are alone in a considerable section of this galaxy."

It was a sobering thought. Sanderson visualized the shoals of stars receding unthinkably into darkness—surely, within those depths, other beings must be fumbling their lonely way; and surely, in such a span of time, other beings must have roamed into the solar system, however isolated it might be from the richer clusters of suns? He felt the tingling chill of utter loneliness.

"This," he said thoughtfully, "makes it seem all the more miraculous that intelligent life has appeared twice in this system."

"Yes," said Guide. "We were extremely surprised and—forgive me for saying so—disappointed when we learned from your mind that you had come from our neighbour planet, and not from outside the solar system."

Sanderson chuckled wrily. "We think we're pretty clever to hop from one planet to the next," he said. "It will be a long time before we seriously consider venturing towards another star."

"That was our situation," said Guide, "until circumstances demanded a solution to the problem."

Sanderson stared at the wooden and metal globe above him, and as the implications of the remark struck him the fruit hung unbitten before his open mouth. "You mean that you *have* interstellar travel?"

"Yes," answered Guide, sounding more weary or resigned than proud. "It was developed in emergency conditions, as was the Tower. Both projects had been theoretically possible for over a century, but until a few years ago we saw no necessity for a practical application. Our race is leaving the solar system and we wanted to meet whoever visited our birthplace, hence the sudden decision to use the projects. We did expect intelligent life to evolve on your world, but you are astonishingly early. Actually, we expected something insectile. The only promising creatures there at this time are the ants."

"They got locked in a fixed pattern and never developed further," said Sanderson.

"A pity," remarked Guide.

"I don't think so," retorted Sanderson.

"I didn't consider it from your viewpoint," said Guide, with a suggestion of very human amusement.

"There are some who say that if we all murder each other—and we've come close to doing so twice in my short lifetime—then the ants will be our inheritors, if we haven't killed them as well as ourselves. But that's beside the point. You said that your race plans to leave this system?"

"The fleet is in orbit now," said Guide. "I, controlling this machine, am the only member of my race on the planet."

"You're all leaving *now*?"

"Yes."

He looked about him at the flowers and trees and the serene peaks.

"But why?" he demanded.

"We know that our world will die," said Guide, "and we wish to find another elsewhere." It paused, and added, "The decision was not a pleasant one to make. We would have preferred to remain and meet your race in a more natural manner. Also, of course, we love this world, and it hurts all of us to leave it."

"But there's so much time yet," protested Sanderson. "The end is millions of years away."

"No," answered Guide, and the word was full of unmistakeable pain.

V

The night was cool, and the peaks stood darkly against the stars. Soon a pale glow seeped into the sky, silhouetting the mountains.

A cold white curve slid from beyond the rim of the world, and the curve grew into a segment with the peaks gnawing at it like black teeth, and with immense slowness the shining hulk crept higher, dwarfing the man who raised his eyes to watch the fateful majesty of its ascent, and reflecting its light from the metal of the machine that stood beside him. Now the intruder cleared the peaks, to bathe the scene in ghostly radiance. It sprawled in the eastern sky, drowning the stars in its glow, staring down with pits of eyes and the pockmarks of lesser craters. The weight of it seemingly pressed down on Sanderson. His skin prickled.

"There will be no collision," said Guide quietly. "But it will be very, very close."

Sanderson sought words and found none.

"The effect of the passing will be disastrous. Your presence testifies that our world will survive intact, but it will no longer be the world that we know. Its very orbit will be changed."

"In my time," said Sanderson, "this world has an eccentric orbit."

"At present, its orbit is as close to a circle as an ellipse can ever be."

Mockery flared in the sky. The flowers and trees and the individual blades of grass were limned in the phantom light.

"Its diameter is slightly less than that of this world," said Guide. "The closest approach will be at this time tomorrow. My race will be moving away before then, and you will be returning to your own time."

"How long have you known about this... thing?"

"We realized several years ago that evacuation was necessary. We used those years to plan and build the fleet and to put into practise the theory behind the Tower." The suggestion of a bitter smile tinted the voice. "At least, on the cosmic scale, one receives fair warning of the approach of disaster."

Sanderson looked up at the shining threat that had banished the stars, and suddenly he felt ill.

A lifeless, unthinking wreck of rock and metal creeping eternally amid the stars, its journey having no purpose or beginning or ending or path, merely a line that meandered through infinity, curving in the drag of an occasional sun, and now swinging across the solar system to bring ruin to a world—the absence of meaning was agony to Sanderson.

"Life is a rare thing forever poised on the brink of death," said Guide drily. "It is essential that life should help other life against the common dangers. We were prepared to wait while intelligence evolved on your world and then to safeguard it without interfering with its birthright. But that is no longer possible. In fact, this brief meeting will probably be the last between our races."

"But surely, Guide, with your technical knowledge, you could return afterwards and restore your world?"

"We considered doing so," admitted Guide. "But there are other considerations. Dispersal is a method of protection: should any further accident occur in this system, such as the growth of the sun into a supernova, what may be the only intelligent life in this galaxy would be destroyed. Life is too rare and too precious for this risk to be taken."

"That," said Sanderson bleakly, "is not a happy thought."

"It's a realistic one," retorted Guide. "And you already know that we will not return—if we were to decide to do that, the present situation would never have arisen."

"I see." This had not occurred to Sanderson, obvious though it seemed on second thought.

"We would like to take records of your race with us, so that your experience and memory will not be lost in the event of further disaster."

"You're still being pessimistic," he commented with a wry smile.

"Realistic," corrected Guide again. "We consider that every scrap of information and knowledge may be vital to the universal civilization which we hope will develop."

"What exactly do you want me to do? There's so little time."

"We wish to record directly from your mind. A complete recording, not merely the learning of language. No mental or physical harm can result, but it does entail utter loss of privacy from birth to the beginning of the recording."

Sanderson pondered for a while, and then said, "Yes—of course. It's a fair exchange—in fact, I'm still getting the best of the bargain. Your knowledge of my race will be very hazy and biased."

He remembered the wealth of historical recordings in the Tower, covering the entire history of life on the planet. There had been no time to study them—merely time enough for Guide to teach him how to operate the recordings. On his return, he could provide humanity with an immense store of information.

"You can have my every thought," he said. "I only hope you don't get too bad an impression of my race—I tend to be cynical about our progress. But if we do destroy ourselves, it will be some consolation to know that something of us will survive somewhere."

"Somewhere, yes," said Guide. "But where?"

"You have no specific destination?"

"Well," said Guide, in a very human fashion, "there appears to be a lack of planets within a radius of thirty light years. We are first aiming for a star at roughly that distance where there's a slender chance of finding suitable planets, but we're fully prepared to let this be merely the commencement of our real journey."

The calmness of the statement was impressive. The man regarded the machine and marvelled at the sheer courage of its builders. To sail out into the stars demanded determination, but to do so blindly, driven by hope alone—that was the act of either the inspired or the insane. With more bluntness than he had intended, he said so.

In tones that suggested a broad smile, Guide said, "Call us fanatics, then. We believe that life was not created with a purpose, but we think that life has the right to adopt a purpose. If we perish in our attempt to survive, it will have been a worthwhile effort if one member of your race learns something from us, and preserves our respect for the urge to live and to help other life to live."

Sanderson thought angrily of the rumours of war that yet rumbled in corners of the Earth, and then he thought of the knowledge locked in the Tower and of the key which had been handed to him, and a savage determination filled him: the knowledge could be turned into wisdom that might ensure humanity's survival, and it was his own responsibility to let the knowledge be used for that end only.

"I shall do whatever I can," he promised.

A shoal of minnows in a backwater at the brink of a great black river, the emigration fleet hung amid the stars. He began to count the vessels, but there were too many, and he sat mutely before the screen with awe on his face.

Would we, he thought, have risen like this to such a challenge? Faced with the ruination of the Earth, would we have united our industries to create a titanic convoy, capable of carrying us with our plants and animals and stored history? And, given the fleet, would we have found the courage to launch ourselves into the chartless deeps, in the hope—the very slender hope—of finding somewhere a shelter?

And he knew that humanity would have found the courage.

But would we have devoted our last Earthly days to the leaving of our beliefs with whatever beings might stumble on our birthplace in the ages to come?

It was possible. But humanity was young and still obsessed with the squabbles of the young, and the day of the adult lay far in Sanderson's future. He gazed at the silent fleet that awaited the exodus, and through him ran a wild and glad exhilaration at the thought of any life reacting in this manner to the threat of annihilation.

"This is a tremendous achievement," he said soberly. "It may well be unique in all the galaxy."

"Perhaps," said Guide, and added with disturbing dryness, "and also, among variable stars, it may be as frequent as the migration of birds at the approach of winter."

"The psychological effect on my race should be immense. Beneficial, too. This may make our view of life more mature—we have a long way to go before we grow up."

"But you have evolved incredibly fast," said Guide. "Your race is a freak of evolution, and a considerable part of the future of the galaxy may yet depend on you."

"If we don't wipe ourselves out," he retorted bitterly.

"This self-destructive activity is puzzling. Whilst learning your language we gained some blurred glimpses of conditions on your world, few of which made sense to us."

"The full recording may leave you just as baffled," said Sanderson cynically. A thought which had been in his mind for some time arose. "Can I see my world? I feel curious."

"Certainly," said Guide, manipulating controls at the side of the screen. The fleet faded. A silvery globe appeared, and beyond it the distant familiar moon. Then the view changed with startling rapidity.

"Here are your earliest rivals," said Guide.

Rock and earth filled the screen. Artificial mounds of some substance akin to clay stood here and there. The view came into such close detail that the grain of the rock was visible. Amid the mounds streamed down rivers of ants, some unburdened, others carrying particles of soil as if from an excavation.

"This is surely a film," protested Sanderson.

"No, it's direct reception—allowing for the minutes during which the light is travelling across space. Your world is not in proximity to ours at the moment."

The technical skill implied was overwhelming. Sanderson smiled rather weakly, and then could not suppress a rather superior chuckle as he watched the toiling insects.

"Is there no chance of life evolving on any of the other planets?" he asked.

"No," said Guide. "It is unlikely that even rudimentary forms will appear elsewhere, even by the time that your race reaches the other planets."

Sanderson suddenly grinned, recalling one of MacDunn's favourite sayings. It would have been appropriate had Guide said, "There's only me and thee here, laddie—and as soon as I've laced me boots there'll only be thee..."

The stray mass moved ever nearer the helpless world ahead. Already its attraction insidiously plucked at the water, and for the first time there were vastly rising tides. Hanging swollen and bleached from a night that had become an eerie noon, the destroyer reflected its face in the heaving oceans. On the sunward side, wind was whistling plaintively over the Tower. Sanderson lay motionless while apparatus drank at the well of his mind. Guide stood over him, and the creature that used the eyes of the machine felt deep kindship and compassion and the burn of frustration: its race and humanity might have walked the lonely path of tomorrow together, but the whim of time and evolution had decreed otherwise. One brief meeting was permitted, and then a farewell that might be eternal. For if the exodus succeeded, and the race flourished elsewhere, surely Sanderson's world would have been visited by returning pilgrims. No, it seemed that a lonelier destiny would follow the parting.

The apparatus drank quietly. The recording took several hours, and the classification and analysis of the material would take as many years. But the result would provide extensive knowledge of a race that would not be born for a million centuries.

"Transport is on its way now," announced Guide. "Soon I shall be leaving. You're sure you don't regret the choice you made regarding your method of return?"

"No, I don't regret it. I'm grateful to you for making it possible— the chance was too priceless to miss."

"I'm glad," said Guide simply. "It was the least we could do to help you."

He looked down at the machine, and absently clasped his hands behind his back. Wind moaned, tugging at his hair and clothing, and the air was cool. In his nostrils burned the acrid fumes of a volcano that had erupted on the horizon. The grass no longer felt secure beneath his feet.

"Will I see you before you go?" he asked. "You said that you are merely using the machine to communicate with me. Where are you, actually? And what are you? You've been evasive from the start, haven't you?"

"Yes," admitted Guide candidly. "At first there was the question of mutually harmful bacteria, but that was found to be negligible— otherwise you could never have left the Tower without protective clothing."

"Then why are you hiding?"

"There is something similar to us in shape within your mind," said Guide slowly. "It was associated with deeply rooted fear—possibly ancestral. No doubt the full recordings will explain this—we did not probe too far while learning your language. But, until your complete confidence had been gained, we considered it best not to let you see us."

"Will I be allowed to see you at all?" he asked. A sense of desperation filled him.

"Yes, I think the time has come for a personal meeting," said Guide. "If you find the sight of me too distressing, say so, and I shall leave immediately. Our acquaintance has been pleasant, and I don't want to spoil it at this stage."

Overhead, storm clouds gathered, thick with ash from the riven peak. The wind played about with newfound power which would soon be unleashed in an orgy of demolition. From the distance came a faint sound of thunder. Sanderson's heart beat faster as it had on his awakening within the Tower, and he rubbed his palms on his hips, nervously.

"Go on," he invited. "I want to see you, whatever you may be."

For a few seconds there was silence. The machine stood as if switched off. Slowly Sanderson turned and looked at the wide door of the Tower. A slight metallic sound came from beside him, and he turned, startled. The three slim legs of the machine buckled and folded, and its spherical body rested gently on the grass. A panel opened in its side, and something brown and sinuous emerged. Sanderson uttered no cry, but he stepped back instinctively, impelled by a horror that swept aside his reason. Revulsion chilled his stomach, and in him leapt the memory of a sickening moment in his childhood. His lips writhed as he tried to speak. Ever since that long-ago night in the cellar, when his childish hand had brushed something that bit and sprang, he had been nauseated at the very thought of a rat.

"Would you prefer me out of sight?" came the anxious Scottish voice from the machine.

Those eyes, bright and wickedly wise—the perfect tiny hands—the sleekness of the thing as it sat on its haunches and swayed slightly, looking up at him; but the fur was glossier than a rat's, and the limbs were jointed differently, and the head was rounder, and the tail—the ropy grey tail that had once coiled obscenely amid his fingers—the tail was missing.

And there came a sudden flood of relief like sunlight pouring through an opened door to clear the shadows and reveal the dimly frightening shapes for the harmless things they were, and his fear drained away, and with sheer reaction as his limbs relaxed he began to laugh.

He stooped and picked Guide up in gentle steady hands and held him before his face and smiled. The dainty lips and tiny sharp teeth of the creature formed a grimace that held no threat, and he realized that Guide shared more human emotions than he would have dared to guess. Then the creature ran along his arm, clawing delicately at the fabric of his clothing to keep a grip, and sat on his shoulder and rubbed its side against his cheek like a contented cat. Sanderson thrilled to an almost physical sense of brotherhood, while his brain cleansed itself to poison that had clogged it for thirty years. He felt suddenly healthier. Then far away a spurt of fire lit the underside of the clouds, and later came a shudder in the ground. With Guide squatting comfortably on his shoulder, in a meeting that required no words, he all but cried like a child.

Overhead glittered something silver.

The ship was arriving.

Guide scampered over the grass, leapt into the entrance lock of the vessel, and turned with one hand raised in farewell. Sanderson waved back, not trusting his voice. Then Guide moved aside, and the lock sealed itself, and the small craft rose without a sound and he watched until it was lost amid the boiling clouds.

The machine lay empty and dead on the grass, where already dust was settling to whiten the green. Sanderson felt a choking grief and desolation as he stared about him. The gale roared strongly, and the volcano coughed flame at the scudding ash that blotted out the sun. In the tradition of executioners, the wandering fragment would strike with a masked face. The daylit side of the world was rolling ponderously to meet the destroyer, and the seas were washing amid the hills and the rock was trembling. He was alone now, unutterably alone, and the cataclysm was very near.

Forlorn, he raised unseeing eyes to where the emigration fleet was carrying a civilization a thousand times as old as Man's. His mind formed a final farewell, and then with an abrupt fear of the tumultuous world he turned and walked slowly into the Tower and sealed the entrance behind him.

That evening blackness veiled the sky and the blackness was lit by fire that spurted from the rocks, and the spectral splendour of lightning stalked among the hills. Rivers boiled up slopes as the world and the intruder grappled for control of wind and water. Seas surged over the cities, and the tide swirled on, and the mountain caps became islands ripped bare by the gales that shrieked. And the rocks were opened, and slow rivers of flame crept from the heart of the world, to explode in scalding steam when the oceans poured upon them. Seabeds rose and continents moved and the hills sank foaming. The Tower shivered and tilted, and Sanderson stood fearfully while it slowly righted itself. Once, a stupendous detonation ripped aside the ash and soot, and he glimpsed the sightless face of the destroyer, pitted and agonized, and saw a jagged crack that was seventy miles wide go zigzagging across it like a black line sketched on the forehead of a skull; and then the clouds rolled inward, fired redly in the glare of a sundered mountain. Smoke filled the screen.

The world twitched and groaned in pain for thirty hours while the hulk moved by in the darkness, and then, stealthily, the grinding chaos abated. The ash-shrouded sky flickered fitfully over the fire of adjusting rock, and somewhere burned the steadier glow of lava, and once or twice sounded the petulant mutter of mountains subsiding in search of a new balance. And the tension and terror took its toll on Sanderson, and with his sweat stale in the room for none to smell but himself, he slipped into the collapse of utter exhaustion.

He woke with a headache, and with a foul taste in his mouth, but a shower and some fruit refreshed him. Guide's race, in the limited time at their disposal, had done their best to provide all modern conveniences, and he stood little chance of going hungry. He wondered briefly what the camp botanists would say when he showed them the fruit.

Then he felt an apprehensive eagerness to see the outer world. The direct view from the wall that could be made transparent was blocked: on using the screen, he found that the Tower had been submerged under a river of rock. He was thankful that the builders had unerringly chosen the firmest part of the planet—apart from the splitting of one small peak, whence flowed the lava, the local mountains were little damaged.

Elsewhere, however, lay utter devastation. Seas had emptied, leaving cracked plains sprinkled with ash, and there were lakes where hills had stood. And distant mountains raged torrents as the great rain fell and the shifted oceans sought their former shores, and the boulders were rolled down in frothing rivers and the soil was scoured away. Here and there sprawled fragments of architecture, and there yet lived scraps of forest, seared and sooted in areas, and with smouldering pits where cosmic bombardment had occurred. The air was slightly thinner and the sky was dark with dust that would hang for years to redden the sun. A long crescent in the haze, the destroyer was travelling on, lividly scarred and wrapped in a wisp of dust and vapour.

Sanderson felt older. With the desolation all around him, he sat in thought for a few hours, and then he set the equipment and lay down and let the stream of time be dammed into a still pool within the room.

He woke a century later in a healing world. The seas were settled and the hills had lost their rawness. Plants fought greenly against the desert. The intruder had dwindled from sight, lost amid glittering millions of stars. Somewhere out there hung the fleet, tiny in the stare of infinity.

"No getting away from it," he thought, "the blighters have got guts—more than Mankind may ever have—when there *is* a Mankind, that is." He chuckled at the thought. Then he roved with the screen from blistered Mercury to the shrunken cold of the world beyond Pluto, a world which had no name because there lived no man to name it.

"But there is a man," he realized. "There's *me*."

And he laughed, and named it Sanderson's Planet, and slept again for a thousand years.

On his ninth awakening a hundred centuries had gone, and he glimpsed small animals whose ancestors had survived the forgotten catastrophe. He studied the Earth, watching the beasts that slithered and mated and fought and died in swamps where fire and the wheel would be used by a race unborn. He was alone in the solar system, yet his path was far less lonely than the one the fleet had chosen. Out amid frozen splendour in distances that deadened the imagination, the children of Guide's descendants were forging a home? or perhaps the fleet had perished a thousand years ago, drowned by a wave in the dark and indifferent sea.

He himself could never know, but he hoped that his own descendants would one day learn.

With a sense of isolation that would haunt him till his death, he set the controls and slept for another hundred thousand years.

And Sanderson returned, taking ever longer steps down the path of time, and on each awakening the Tower stood taller as the rock was worn away. Once he woke at night to find rain falling on the dark land, a thin pitiful rain, perhaps the last the desert would know. The thinning wind rubbed patiently at the mountains. And as he walked with million year strides the forests lost their ancient fight, and the last seas gave way and shrank in surrender to the dust. Then he woke to find the fifth planet destroyed by some cataclysm far greater than the one that had left Mars crippled and dying: there remained merely a gradual spilling out of rocks and dust, two fragments destined to be the moons of Mars, others to form a sparse band about the sun.

He considered delving into the ceaseless recordings of the Tower to locate the event, but a queer dullness prevented him: isolation was killing his curiosity.

One more time he woke. The system was deep in a cosmic dust cloud. Ice sheathed the desert under a pale red sun that did not dazzle him. Nowhere was there motion: in awful silence the Tower stood black and slender from the glacier that hugged its base. Thin wind mourned the stillness. On Earth ended the reign of the mammoth as ice crept into the forests. Sanderson felt horror ripple through his flesh as he watched alone in the dark winter.

The equipment would continue to record: mechanisms knew no misery and did not fear the madness of despair. He had seen enough and suffered enough, and with empty eyes and trembling hands he lay down and sought the refuge of the long sleep.

And the sleep brought dreams, where a door opened and a machine hummed forward into gloom, and there came the certainty that this had happened before, a long time ago; and he was in a room that rose tirelessly, and suddenly he walked with other men down a corridor into an alcove, and he tried to scream as the equipment switched itself off and woke him, and he lay ill and shaking for a moment, and then stood up and opened the door and lurched out into the passage.

MacDunn and Minhov stared, stupefied, as he approached. In his face was the wisdom and concentration of a man more than half drunk.

"Sandy," said MacDunn. "Where have you been? For God's sake, man, what's happened to you? Where's your helmet?"

They tried to grip his arms to steady him, but he struggled free and led them into the room.

"Look," he said in a voice which they scarcely recognized, and he pressed a button.

The wall shimmered into transparency. Sanderson shook his head and grinned tiredly as reaction swam in him, and he looked ruefully at the fruit which had slept with him and which he had forgotten to eat. Through the wall, he gestured at where the base camp was a metal discord in the dirge of the desert and the wind.

"What's going on?" demanded Minhov. "What's happened?"

Sanderson swayed. "We'll succeed," he said in a choked voice. "When we sort out the knowledge in here. When we understand, this will put us on the road once and for all." He giggled as his nerves affected him. "They called us a big freak—but we haven't really started yet. We'll even go and find them..." He coughed hoarsely, and then he laughed and said he was hungry, and with an apologetic grin he leaned on the wall and abruptly slid down to the floor.

MacDunn knelt over him and examined him.

"He's just fainted—sheer exhaustion, it looks like. But how the hell—I mean he only vanished for a minute..."

Minhov found Sanderson's helmet and breathing equipment and connected it and fitted it on to him. "See the shadows under his eyes," he said. "He looks years older."

MacDunn peered uneasily up and down the passage. He felt cold.

Minhov slid his arms under Sanderson and lifted him gently.

"Let's get him off to camp and let him rest," he said. "I think the explanations can come later. He looks as if he's been through hell."

They walked through the obediently opening airlock and into the lift. On the way down, MacDunn said, "The others will be getting worried about us, too. We've been away too long."

And the lift halted and they walked out to the niche, and the lights in the Tower died behind them.

THE ASTEROID EROS:

"LIKE A MOUNTAIN TUMBLING THROUGH THE SKY."

ASTEROID BELT

Garden in the Void   Poul Anderson

The word "asteroid", coined in 1802 by astronomer William Herschel, meaning star-like, applies to any small object or planetoid that orbits the Sun. It is usually distinguished from comets and dwarf planets, especially those orbiting beyond Neptune, and typically applies to those that orbit between Mars and Jupiter. Some have extremely eccentric orbits and periodically swoop close to the Sun, passing through the orbit of Earth. These are known as near-Earth asteroids or Earth-grazers, and some come worryingly close. An early work of science fiction to consider an Earth-grazer (as distinct from a comet) was "The Moon Maker" (serial, 1916–17) by Arthur Train and Robert W. Wood in which an asteroid whose orbit is affected by a comet, heads for Earth. Scientists send a manned probe, equipped with a special ray to deflect the asteroid.

The largest of the asteroids is Ceres with a diameter of 939km (584 miles). A better idea of its size is its surface area which is 2,770,000 square kilometres (1,070,000 square miles) or roughly the size of Argentina. It is spherical and even has a tenuous atmosphere so is a

genuine dwarf planet. The other large asteroids, Vesta, Pallas and
Hygeia are each roughly twice the size of Sweden. It has been estimated that there could be up to two million asteroids with a diameter
greater than one kilometre.

Ceres was discovered on New Year's Day 1801 by Giuseppi Piazzi
who found it by chance. Piazzi fell ill and was not able to pursue
his study of Ceres, but Heinrich Olbers, a physician and amateur
astronomer, took up the chase. He had already been looking for a
planet between the orbits of Mars and Jupiter based on Bode's Law.
In 1772 Johann Bode had shown how each planet fits into a rough
mathematical sequence away from the Sun, but there was a gap
between Mars and Jupiter. Once Olbers heard of Piazzi's discovery
he searched further and discovered Pallas in 1802 and Vesta in 1807,
whilst fellow astronomer Karl Harding discovered Juno in 1804. It
was not until 1845 that the fifth asteroid was discovered, Astraea, and
thereafter discoveries followed rapidly.

It was Olbers who suggested that the asteroids might be the
remains of a major planet that had been destroyed. He even gave
this planet a name, Phaeton, and there were various theories about
its fate—pulled apart by Jupiter's gravity, destroyed by collision with
another object, or even exploded from internal stress. The theory
lasted for decades and appears in any number of stories and novels at
least as far back as *Seola* (1878) by Ann Eliza Smith which suggests that
the destruction of that planet led to the Flood of Noah. In "Invaders
from Outside" (1925) Joseph Schlossel has our solar system invaded
millions of years in the past by an alien world whose inhabitants are
hostile. They take over the fifth planet from the Sun but an error
causes the planet to explode and become the asteroid belt. In the
time-travel romp "Time Wants a Skeleton" (1941) by Ross Rocklynne,
the main characters find themselves on Phaeton just before it is

destroyed by collision with another world. Robert A. Heinlein calls this fifth planet Lucifer and in his young-adult novel *Space Cadet* (1948) his hero is amongst an expedition that discovers the remains of those who had once lived on that world.

In "Collision Orbit" (1942) and its sequels, Jack Williamson (writing as Will Stewart) suggested that the object that destroyed the fifth planet and created the asteroid belt was composed of "contraterrene" material, which he nicknamed "seetee", otherwise called antigravity. The asteroids were full of this dangerous material, but, handled properly with magnets, in "paragravity" generators, it could help adapt the asteroids for human habitation. In describing this, Williamson coined the term "terraform". Out of the series grew the books *Seetee Shock* (1950) and *Seetee Ship* (1951).

A common consideration of asteroids was their use for mining. Asteroids are rich in ores for nickel and iron and there might be much else. One of Clifford Simak's earliest stories explored "The Asteroid of Gold" (1932). There's a platinum asteroid in "Murder on the Asteroid" (1933) by Eando Binder. In "The Talking Stone" (1955), Isaac Asimov suggests an asteroid rich in uranium. He also describes a form of silicon-based life on the asteroids. In his novel for young adults, *The Rolling Stones* (1952), Robert A. Heinlein portrays a growing community when an equivalent of the gold rush hits the asteroids. Likewise, in various stories collected as *Tales of the Flying Mountains* (1970), Poul Anderson considers a community of miners in the asteroid belt. In *Protector* (1973) and others of his Known Space series Larry Niven has the inhabitants of the asteroids—known as Belters, most of whom started out as miners and prospectors—become an independent power in the solar system. Ceres is their seat of government.

The problem of navigating through the asteroid belt is another occasional theme, most recently explored in *The Wreck of the River of Stars* (2003) by Michael Flynn. But the idea dates back at least as far as "Exiles on Asperus" (1933), an early story by John Wyndham (under his real name John Beynon Harris), and for Isaac Asimov's first story "Marooned Off Vesta" (1939). In "Summertime on Icarus" (1960) by Arthur C. Clarke an astronaut is trapped on an Earth-grazer as it approaches perihelion.

The prospect of asteroids becoming homes and playgrounds for the rich was at the heart of Jack Vance's wildly optimistic "I'll Build Your Dream Castle" (1947), whilst Poul Anderson's "Garden in the Void" (1952), reprinted here, shows how an asteroid can be a home from home. Charles Platt realized that the rich and famous would not want their private asteroid homes contaminated by refuse and so has one asteroid as the belt's waste disposal site in *Garbage World* (1966).

However you consider them it is clear that the asteroids have a huge diversity of possibilities and, in the future, may help mankind survive.

Poul Anderson (1926–2001) was one of the genre's leading writers of both hard-sf and fantasy. His work could range from the extreme of *Tau Zero* (1970), where a damaged and ever accelerating space-ship outlives the universe and enters the next, to the Nordic fantasy world of *The Broken Sword* (1954). And he was happy creating worlds anywhere within that range, from those seeking to monitor any attempt to manipulate time in the Time Patrol series, collected as *Guardians of Time* (1960), to the whimsy of *The High Crusade* (1960) where a spaceship turns up in the middle of the Hundred Years' War in fourteenth century England. For his diversity of output Anderson was made both the Grand Master of Fantasy in 1978 and the Science Fiction Writers of America Grand Master in 1997. He explored the lives and liberties of those living and working on the asteroids in *Tales of the Flying Mountains* (1970) but the following story comes from earlier in his career and postulates a most unusual asteroid and its even more unusual resident.

"**A**N ASTEROID. A *GREEN* ASTEROID."
His voice oddly resonant in the metal stillness of the space-ship, he looked through the forward port with an uncertain wonder in him.

There was darkness outside, the great hollow night of space, and a thousand stars flamed cold in the brass frame of the port. The asteroid showed as a tiny pale-green spark that only a trained eye would have seen among those swarming bitter-bright suns. The quality of it was different, a muted reflection of the Belt's weak light instead of naked fire leaping across a universe, and it flickered a little as the irregular stone spun on its axis.

"Green," said Hardesty again, the note of puzzlement grown stronger. "I never saw that before."

His wife shoved off from one wall of the cabin, her tall form weightlessly drifting past the glitter of control board to the instruments mounted on the farther side.

"Shall we have a look?" she asked practically.

Hardesty glanced at the meters and performed a mental calculation; one had to be sparing of fuel on a voyage like this.

"Yes, if the velocity isn't too different from ours," he said.

Marian's dark head bent over the telescope and her long, strong fingers spun a wheel, sighting on the speck that flitted out among the constellations. There was a faint sighing of gears above the murmur of air blown through a ventilator. It was quiet out in space—so quiet. Hardesty's pulse was loud in his own ears.

He unclipped a pencil from a pocket of his coverall and scribbled the figures she announced on a pad clamped to the control board. When her readings were done, he took the slide rule from its rack and manipulated it with the easy speed of long practice. His gaunt frame hung in mid-air, one foot hooked through the arm of a recoil chair to keep him in place.

The *Gold Rush* was moving outward from the Sun with a velocity known closely enough from his last astrogational readings. It was a fair approximation to assume that the asteroid's motion was at forty-five degrees to the ship's path and its speed that to be expected of a body orbiting at this distance. Thus, from the observed transverse angular velocity, the separation could be estimated. It would take so much fuel to kill the ship's outward vector—a deceleration of two-point-five Gs should do it in the allowed distance—and then you added ten per cent for manoeuvring and landing.

"Uh-huh," he nodded. "It's all right, honey."

Marian swam into her chair, adjusted the webbing, and plugged in her throat mike. She'd be taking the reading while Hardesty piloted the ship, but you needed a comcircuit to talk and hear when the rockets were going.

His mind quit gnawing at the problem of a green asteroid and concentrated on the delicate job of working the ship in. Slowly, his whickering gyros swung the hull around. When the rockets started to roar, it was a thunder voice booming and crashing between the vibrant walls, shivering the teeth in his skull, and weight dragged cruelly at a body grown used to free fall. For a moment his eyes hazed, the constellations danced insanely through a suddenly reddened sky, and then his trained reflexes took over and he watched the asteroid swelling in the rearview telescreen.

They shot past it at a distance of ten miles, splashing the great dark with livid flame. Now it rolled in the forward port, and he notched the main switch ahead and felt his tissues groaning. Marian snapped out a string of instrument readings, and gyros whined as Hardesty brought the ship about, changing course, bearing down on the rock. They swung past it in a long curve. When it was centred on the cross-hairs of the rearview screen and could be held there, Hardesty backed down upon it.

A typical piece of space debris, he thought. It was roughly cylindrical, perhaps ten miles long and five thick, but the crags and gashes that scarred its surfaces made it a jumble of blackened stone. Here and there a patch of quartz or mica caught the thin sunlight in a swiftly harsh blink. The greenness was in patches, clustered on such hills and slopes as offered most Sun, but there seemed to be a delicate webbing—of veins?—connecting all those bunches. There were brown and grey and yellow mixed in. Like lichen, he decided, and his mind hearkened back to the cool, mossy rocks of a New England forest and suddenly, almost bitterly, he wished he were there.

The radar screen flickered and danced. Not much level ground, but he had landed on worse places without toppling his ship. Even if he did fail now, it would mean only the nuisance of rigging the derrick to lift her—a bump in that feeble gravity couldn't hurt vessel or crew.

A motor sang above the dull thutter of rockets and the landing tripod slid out around the tubes. Electronic valves glowed, radar-controlled servos adjusting the lengths of the three legs to the sloping, pitted surface. In the sudden ringing stillness, as the rockets went dead, the hull boomed and sagged. Shale gave way beneath one leg, but the servo lengthened it till its foot rested on solidity, and then the whole ship was quiet.

Hardesty shook his head to clear it and looked across at his wife. Her thinly strong features smiled back at him, congratulating him, but no words were needed; they knew each other too well. He unbuckled the webbing and stood erect.

The vision of the sky was like a blow in the face when they stepped out. He could spend a hundred years in the Belt, thought Hardesty, and its eerie unhuman magnificence would be as cold in his heart as the first day he left Earth.

The *Gold Rush* was not a large spaceship—a two-passenger Beltboat with extraction and refining equipment, fuel and supplies enough for a year of cruising—but she loomed over their heads, a squat metal tower against the stars, dully ashine in the pale, chill light. Before them, a harsh raggedness of knife-edged rock swept to a horizon that seemed near enough to touch, the edge of forever lying beyond that wolf-jawed rim of hills. The ground was black, pits and craters and twisted frozen magma, dully lit, shadows like holes of blindness creeping over the rough slope. A tiny Sun, three hundred million miles away, glittered and threw a wash of dim, heatless luminance.

It was quiet, the blank quiet of airlessness and emptiness, the only noise that of the muted scrunch of footsteps carried through the spacesuits, only that and the hot, rapid thud of heart and breath. The sound of his own life was almost deafening in Hardesty's skull, and yet it was the dimmest flicker in a room of night, a tiny frantic fist beating on iron gates of silence.

And overhead wheeled the stars, the million suns of space, fire and ice and the giant sprawl of constellations, the Milky Way a rush of curdled silver, the far, mysterious glow of nebulae, hugeness and loneliness to break a human heart. There went the Great Bear, swinging light-years overhead, and it was not the friendly neighbour of Earth's heaven, but a god striding in flame and darkness, scorning the watchers, enormous and beautiful and cruel. The others followed, and the stars that Earth never sees threw their signals flashing and flashing across the years and the unthinkable distances, and no man knew what they were calling.

Hardesty drew a deep breath and looked over to Marian. The declining Sun flared off her space armour; a sheen on the helmet veiled her face from him. The armour depersonalized her and the voice over the radio was a metallic rattle. It was as if a robot stood at his side.

He threw off the oppression of solitude and forced a calm into his voice: "Come on, let's take a look at one of those green patches before sunset."

"I think there's one over that way." She pointed north with a gauntleted hand.

Hardesty had already located the asteroid's pole star. He noted the position of the other constellations and set off after her. Ten years' experience had taught him how easy it was to get lost in such a jungle of stone, and their tanks only held air for a few hours.

It was ghostly, bounding along in utter silence, almost weightless, between the high, dead crags and under the sharp stars. In all his time out here, Hardesty had not lost the eeriness of it. And yet Earth was blurring in his memory, green fields and tall trees and the feel of an actual wind, a low old house among a thousand shouting autumn colours, beat of wings across heaven—he couldn't always conjure up the images. A blaze of naked stars would rise between.

Well, maybe here, maybe somewhere else, this trip or next, we'll make the big strike. Then we'll go home.

It was the great chimera. For every man who reached it, a hundred broke their hearts or left their withered corpses on some unknown frozen rock.

Hardesty had been one of the luckiest. He'd made enough once to buy his own ship, and since that time enough to pay his costs and even save a little money. And he'd met one of the Belt's few women in an office on Ceres, and married her and made her his partner.

How would Marian look at Earth? She'd never seen it. She'd been born on Mars.

The Sun sloped low as the asteroid spun on its hurried, timeless way. Wan light glimmered off Marian's armour as she topped a high ridge, pinning her against darkness and the scornful stars. Her voice was a sudden excited gasp in his earphones:

"Jim! Jim, come quick!"

He bunched his muscles and reached her side in a soaring bound, floating down and twirling a little like a dead autumn leaf. (*Autumn, a maple scarlet against October smoke, and a leaf scrittling across the sidewalk!*) Together they looked down the crazily tilted sheet of basalt to the seamed ledge jutting out against Orion.

The green was there. In the airlessness, it was as sharp and clear as if it touched his helmet. Leathery domes, coiling vines, thick strong leaves—

He breathed the word as if it were something holy: "Life."

"Life? But it's not possible, Jim. No asteroid has life."

His answer was flat, and a sudden coldness tingled in his hands. "This one does."

★

He strode across the black slabs in the seven-league boots of Belt gravity. The Sun hung between two pinnacles, throwing a horned shadow across the acre of green. Hardesty knelt at the boundary of the patch and grasped one of the cactus-like leaves.

It seemed almost to shrink, and in the vague tricky light he thought that a pulse ran from it, through the webbing of vines, and out of sight along the filaments that reached from this ledge. He drew back his hand and squatted there, staring. Marian came up and stood against his side.

"I—" Her voice was low now, trembling faintly. "I don't know whether to—to be glad or interested or—frightened, Jim."

His long-jawed face slid into the expressionlessness of uncertainty. "I know. We've gotten so used to thinking of the Belt as inorganic that—well, our enemies have been cold and vacuum and distance, impersonal forces. We really don't know how to face something that could be actively hostile. And yet, that life could exist and evolve here is a wonderful feeling." He looked up to the stars as if throwing them a challenge.

"This can't hurt us. Plants. You don't think there could be—monsters here?"

"I wouldn't mind a good hot-breathed dragon. But germs? I suppose I'm being an old woman. But you know what they say about *bold* spacemen never becoming *old* spacemen. They don't live that long."

"How can any life exist here? No water, no air, nothing—"

"I don't know. It's obviously not terrestrial-type life, though I'm pretty sure it's protoplasmic. It's adapted to these conditions, that's all."

Decision brought him erect again. "I suppose we should try to study this out, make analyses and so on, but we have neither the training nor the equipment to do so. We'll take some pictures, and get an accurate orbit for this pebble, and report the whole matter to Ceres. And we'll scout around for minerals as usual, avoiding these green patches. Our work is risky enough without taking even a tiny extra chance."

"You're right." Marian stood looking at the plants. They were small and grotesquely ugly, but—"A garden," she whispered. "A little garden, blooming out here on the edge of nothing."

"Come on," said Hardesty. "Let's get back to the ship."

The Sun sank under the farther rocks and night was abruptly on them. Their flashlights cast dull puddles of yellow haze on the ground, where elsewhere there was a sea of black under the streaming stars. The sky's light picked out the higher crags, etching them frost-grey against the dark, but the humans stumbled in shadow, floating to the ground to continue their careful low-gravity shuffle back toward the ship.

"I can't forget it," said Marian. "Those plants, blooming out here without air or heat or water—do you think that comets hover above them, Jim? Do you think their pollen is stardust?"

"Don't get poetic," he grunted.

In spite of their stellar observations, they had trouble locating the ship, approaching it finally from the other side. Thus they had walked around the massive tripod before they saw the figure waiting in front of the gangway.

Hardesty thought with a flash of disappointment that some other prospector had beaten them to it. He had come far out of the usual lanes, without revealing his course to anyone, to avoid just that; matching velocities and landing was so expensive that, by law, the first man to set down on a new rock held all mining rights. Then, as he looked closer—

The space armour was awkward and bulky, a model which had been obsolete long before Hardesty left Earth, and its metal was patched and battered. There was no air tank. A thick-leafed vine coiled around the square old-fashioned helmet, across the shoulders and down the back, like ivy on an ancient university building. Hardesty saw with a jolting shock that a tendril ran into the helmet, sealed by a clumsy weld, and that tiny rootlets veined the face inside and were tangled in among the man's beard.

The—man?

Marian's stifled scream was loud in his earphones; she clutched at Hardesty's arm and they skipped back together. A dead man, a corpse, a revenant puppet of plants which grew where no life could be—

"Who are you? *What* are you?"

The other took a floating stride toward them. His face was hooded in darkness; they could barely see the glitter of starlight in his sunken eyes. Hardesty stood waiting, braced to meet the thing that neared him. The ship behind seemed infinitely remote.

Metal hands clasped Hardesty's shoulders and the square helmet leaned forward to ring faintly against his own. That close, the miner could see the shaggy head inside, still veiled with shadow—a shattered gravestone of a face with ivy creeping over it and reaching into the cracks. He fought down an impulse to retch.

The voice that came was dim and slow: "You—from Earth?"

"Yes and no. Who are you, man? What is that you're wearing?" Hardesty's mouth was dry.

"My name? It's—I am the gardener." The stranger shook his big head, and the cactus leaves on his helmet rustled where there was never a wind to stir them. "No, wait. Yes, they called me, my name, yes… Hans Gronauer." A throbbing chuckle. "But that was long ago. Now I am the gardener."

"You mean you were shipwrecked?"

"Yes. How long ago? There are not years here. I think it was twenty Earth years ago. That is a guess. It could be more." The newcomer brushed a gauntleted hand over his faceplate, a strangely human gesture, as if he were trying to rub his weary eyes. "You will excuse. It is long since I talked. And my—my talker?—Yes, radio. My radio was broken in the crash. I must talk this way."

"By helmet conduction? Yeah, sure. But—my God, man! That plant growing—growing on you like that—"

The tiny gleam of teeth in the beard, the downcast eyes, it was a shy smile. "The plant gives air. So."

"So—*oh!*" Marian had heard the words over her husband's set. "Jim, of course, the plants release oxygen and he's used them—Twenty years, Jim!"

Turning his face, he saw the cold starlight gleam on her tear-streaked cheeks, and there was a sudden wrench of pity in his own heart.

Twenty years! Twenty years alone in naked space!

"Come into the ship," he said urgently. He didn't think he could stand out here on twisted black stone with a million frozen suns jeering at him. "Come into the ship, man, and get some food. Twenty years! My God!"

"No." Gronauer didn't shake his head, for that human gesture seemed forgotten, but he lowered his eyes. "No. Not yet, please."

"But—"

"The garden would not like it. Not yet."

"The garden?"

"World. We—don't dare. Not till we know. It has been so long."

"I think I see." It was Marian again; Hardesty had never stopped wondering at the cool quickness of her mind. She wasn't pretty, he supposed, but even on Earth he couldn't have had a better wife. "He's adapted in some odd way, or thinks he may have. He's not sure he can stand conditions inside our ship."

"Yes. The plant might die." Gronauer's faded voice held a sudden eagerness. His vocabulary was coming back to him in a rush. "I must think this out. Come with me and let us investigate the problem."

"Come where?"

"My home. It is safe for you. But—yes, bring food."

"You haven't eaten?"

"The garden feeds me. But for you it may not be safe—be safe for you yet. Come quick. Please."

"All right, if it isn't far. We have to watch our air supply, you know."

"The plants give air."

At the thought of tendrils around his head and roots going into him, Hardesty shivered. "No!"

"I mean air is in my house. You can breathe there. It is not far from here."

"Very well." Hardesty disengaged himself from Gronauer and thus from auditory contact. "Marian, fetch some canned stuff. And put my gun into a pocket. It's in the toolbox."

"Gun, Jim?"

"Yeah." His voice was a little ragged. "Never thought I'd need it, but let's not take chances. I'm not leaving you alone with him, either. I'm pretty sure he's harmless, but you can't tell. Twenty years! He's not acting like a normal human being. But who the hell would after living here like that for so long? Yes, I want the gun."

Wordlessly, she stepped up the gangway and disappeared into the airlock. Gronauer stood waiting, making no further attempt at conversation, and Hardesty was satisfied to keep it that way.

The wonder of his discovery was lost in worried calculation. They could certainly not refuse to take Gronauer with them when they left, but his extra mass and the supplies he would need could upset the whole cruise. There wasn't any outpost to take him to within some scores of megamiles. So unless a decent lode of fissionable ores was found soon, he represented a heavy financial loss. Briefly Hardesty wondered if he could leave Gronauer to be picked up by a government rescue ship. After all, scientists would want to investigate this place... But it'd make Hardesty an outcast, being known to have abandoned a shipwrecked spaceman. And he'd have to live with himself. No, he'd have to take Gronauer back, whatever it cost.

All he could do was hope that there was a lode on this asteroid. Gronauer would know about that.

Marian came back, loaded with a sack of cans which Hardesty slung over one shoulder. Gronauer set off at once.

The path was dark, there under the ghostly arch of the Milky Way, but he picked his way with effortless speed. It didn't seem to occur to him that the others were having trouble keeping up. Hardesty cursed and stumbled. He noticed that there was a leathery bladder on the castaway's back, apparently part of the vine system. It glowed with the dimmest of red light. Heat?

After a mile or two of bare stone, they entered a patch of growth that seemed to stretch indefinitely far on every side. The frailer vines and leaves shrank aside from the human feet, and subliminally faint pulses rippled through the garden and over the edge of the little world. Hardesty estimated that they came, in all, some five miles from the *Gold Rush* before reaching the other spaceship.

It was a smashed ruin. Only the central part of the hull seemed intact, and that had been patched and welded. It lay in a small box canyon, against the low bluff at the farther end. The metal ribs and the great broken tubes were scattered around it like raven-picked bones. And everywhere the steel was covered by green growth.

Here the plants had become a thicket, vines swarming over the cliffs and wrapped about the gaunt crags, leaves and tendrils and looming fluted columns hiding the rock in a ghost-grey sea, stirring without wind and rustling without sound under the chill stars. Gronauer's cabin was smothered in the dripping life. Hardesty could not suppress a shudder as the leaves framing the airlock brushed him.

Within the chamber there was a stifling darkness until Gronauer opened the inner door, and then feeble light shone. It was lost again as frost condensed on the space-chilled helmets. Hardesty and Marian helped each other out of their armour, careful not to touch it with bare hands, and followed Gronauer into the room beyond.

The miner's first glance was for the castaway, now that he had removed his ivy-covered, battered old armour. His hair and beard were streaked with grey, and he smelled unwashed, though there was no grime on him. It was the face that held Hardesty's gaze, the cruelly smashed face which had healed into lumps of scar tissue. It was pock-marked on cheeks and forehead, where he had gently pulled out the roots of the plant that still clung to his spacesuit. But the eyes were gentle, mutilated lips curved in a timid smile, and he stood aside for his guests.

The cabin was small, almost unfurnished, yet crowded. It was cold and the air had a musty reek. Plants covered walls and ceiling, made a springy carpeting underfoot, rustled and shivered as the humans walked across them. There were a lot of the red bladders twined into the leafage, and light came from countless tiny—berries?—things which glowed a dull amber in the grey-green tangle.

"It is strange to you, I suppose," said Gronauer apologetically. "But it keeps me alive."

Hardesty touched a bladder. It was warm under his hand. Yes, the plants heated the room and aired it and illuminated it and fed the owner. He had a sudden dark wonder as to just who owned whom.

"It's like a dream," whispered Marian. The unspoken thought ran on: *A nightmare. A surrealist's delirium.* "Have you had this long, Mr. Gronauer?"

"Yes. At first I ate the garden, but then I saw that, that way, one of us must kill the other, and if I killed it there would be no food for me. So I made friends instead, and bit by bit the garden learned my needs and gave them to me."

As if exhausted by speech, Gronauer's rusty voice faded out and he answered no more questions. Hardesty repressed a revulsion. After all, this was a wonderful example of human ingenuity, the greatest Robinson Crusoe story in the universe, and certainly the plants were harmless. But he took out cans and can opener with the eagerness of a man clutching at familiarity in a strange land.

"Shall we eat?" he suggested.

Gronauer shook his head, smiling, when they offered him Bionate and one of their few, cherished cans of beer. "I—have no taste for it," he said. "It might even be dangerous. I will feed."

Carefully, he broke off one of the fleshy cactus like leaves and chewed on it. He held a trailing vine to his face, and Marian looked away as the tendrils stirred hungrily and slid into the pocks. At least, thought Hardesty a little sickly, the plants did everything for him. Everything except furnish human companionship—and it didn't seem as if Gronauer needed that any more.

Not after twenty years.

It was surprising how much difference a full stomach made. Hardesty hadn't really been aware of his own hunger till it was gone and strength was flowing back into his bloodstream. He sat down almost casually on a vine-begrown chair—there was a mossy plant intertwined, making a faintly warm cushion—and began to draw Gronauer out in talk. That wasn't easy; the castaway was too shy to do more than mumble answers while staring at his feet, but piece by piece the story was revealed. It was, in reality, quite simple.

Gronauer had been only twenty or so when he left his native Germany for the Asteroid Belt. That was thirty years ago, when the mineral riches of the flying mountains had just lately come to the attention of an Earth increasingly starved for fissionable ores, and the great companies were outfitting expeditions. A ship which cruised among the scattered worldlets, refining the substances it located, could return in a year or two to one of the asteroid cities with a cargo worth a good many millions of dollars.

Hard, dangerous, and profitable work has always commanded high wages, and no few of the prospectors, Gronauer among them, had soon been able to buy their own ships and go out as independent operators.

He'd had a partner—he couldn't remember the man's name now—and they'd travelled and dug together for about five years. As the most accessible asteroids became worked out, the custom of not revealing one's destination grew up. That way, if you found a rich group of planetoids, you could make several trips without competition—but, of course, if you met with an accident there could be no rescue. Without more powerful radio equipment than a Beltboat could carry, there was no way to get help.

Gronauer had gone north of the ecliptic plane, looking for one of the many groups which travelled in crazily tilted orbits. He'd found this green world and come wonderingly in for a landing. But the asteroid had a satellite, a meteor which had suddenly flashed over the horizon and crashed through the ship's engines and sent it hurtling to its death.

The other man was killed. Gronauer had escaped with broken bones and a smashed face. He'd lain near extinction for a timeless age; only the fact that the weak gravity made no demands on his body had saved him. After that, the only thing to do was to survive somehow and hope that another prospector would happen by. That could be within a year or never. It was safest to assume that he would leave his bones here.

One man could live off the ship's food stores perhaps two years. But there was life, the plants, food. Gronauer had had no means of testing for poison except his own metabolism. A few times he got sick but he learned what he could safely eat. Certain of the fleshy cactus growths were nourishing.

He harvested all of them within five miles or so of his ship. After a few days—or weeks, or months; he lost track—he'd gone out after more, and found that everything was dead in the area which he had exploited. And when he cut some plants elsewhere and ate them, he nearly died again.

Gronauer was no biologist, but a spaceman generally picked up a good knowledge of science and so he had heard of symbiosis. It was clear that the plants were in some way interdependent, that each species was necessary to the survival of the whole. And in some dim way they had sensed the enemy among them and reacted with deadly swiftness. Any type he tried to eat would soon become poisonous to him. Perhaps the garden would try something still more devastating. An unnoticed root, growing between two plates of the wrecked ship that housed him, could split it open and let out the air in a great and fatal rush.

With a quiet, methodical courage that Hardesty had to admire, he had given himself the urgent job of studying the symbiosis. He had no formal education in biology and almost no scientific instruments; most of his conclusions were guesswork from the sketchiest data. But given a year or two of patient slogging, and a good mind driven by a peasant's deep, strong will to live, one could accomplish more than Earth's cold intellectuals would ever admit.

He puzzled it out, observing and thinking in the huge loneliness of his world. The life here was protoplasmic, chemically similar to his own. It even seemed to involve photosynthesis of some kind.

The tough skin of the "cactoids" admitted ultraviolet light—intense in airless space, even this far from the Sun—while preventing the loss of water by evaporation. Instead, the water circulated through vine systems to other species that used it in their own life processes, and carried organic compounds manufactured by various types of plants to the symbiotic whole. The water was obtained from gypsum and other minerals by certain roots which added alcohol to prevent its freezing. Even so, the bitter temperatures would long ago have turned it to ice, except that it circulated through the red bladders and these heated it with energy derived from fermentation or very slow combustion. The oxygen for that could also be cracked from mineral compounds beneath the surface.

Cross-fertilization and the subsequent spread of life over the whole asteroid depended on specialized vines. There even seemed to be hearts for this vascular system, slowly pulsing lumps of tissue scattered through the garden. A vast and unimaginably intricate network, each type fulfilling one of the many functions needed to maintain the whole in existence—

A trained biologist might well have needed as much time as Gronauer to puzzle out the life cycle.

"I still wonder if solar energy is enough to keep such a system going," said Hardesty. "It takes a lot to break up minerals, you know, even if the symbiosis manufactures catalysts."

"We are as far from the Sun as we ever get," answered Gronauer patiently. "The orbit is very—yes, very eccentric. I think the period is about seven years. At least we have three times come, I think, within the orbit of Venus while I was here. It gets hot then, special plants grow up to protect the others, and energy is stored chemically against the long cold which follows."

"I see. And with this highly tilted orbit, the asteroid hasn't been discovered even when it was that close to Earth."

The poor guy! Think of him sitting here, watching the Sun grow and glaze, watching Earth swell to a blue brilliance and her moon visible beside her, and still alone, still forever alone.

"How did life evolve here?" wondered Marian. "You need air and oceans for that, and this asteroid has been dead rock since the beginning of time."

Hardesty shrugged. "We'll probably never know, but I can make a guess. On some other world, maybe the world of another star, air and water disappeared slowly enough for life to adapt. Certain spores of that life were lifted on the last wisps of atmosphere up to where light pressure could drive them from that solar system. The old Arrhenius theory. They survived the trip. There were a lot of spore-clumps landing on many worlds, but this might be the only one in our system that had the conditions they needed for growth. Maybe not—the spores could be the ancestors of all life on our planets, but I doubt it. Too completely alien."

It was an eldritch thought, that the garden had been seeded from across that gulf of space, that it was the child of a world millions of years in its grave, and that—perhaps, in the remote future, when all the planets were airless husks—gardens like this would bloom as the last defiance of the sunless night. He shivered in the chill must of the room.

"Go on," he said. "Tell us what you did."

Gronauer looked at him with gentle, frightened eyes.

"Don't be shy," said Marian softly. "It is a great and wonderful thing you've done. You make me proud to be human."

"Human?" The short laugh was jarring. A vague rustling went among the leaves. "I am—human?" After a moment, looking away: "Please to excuse. I have not been used to talking so much. I will try."

The words stumbled out, awkward, toneless, the words of a man who had begun by speaking German, changed to the English of the spaceways, and then not spoken at all except for the shadowy half-language of the garden. Hardesty had to fill in gaps; the castaway could only hint at a reality too far from human experience for communication—but the outline grew.

It had been plain that the symbiosis was highly adaptable. It probably had to be, to survive the extremes of the asteroid's wildly swooping orbit. Gronauer thought, too, that the impact of cosmic rays, unshielded by atmosphere, induced a high mutation rate; somehow, the garden weeded out unfavourable mutations and took those it could use. The pattern was not a rigid thing. It was constantly evolving.

There even seemed to be a primitive brain some where. Not a human-type brain—there probably wasn't a nervous system as Earth knew it—but *something* had to control that change. Something *had* altered the garden's metabolism and poisoned those leaves that the stranger ate.

Probably it had tried various compounds from the beginning of Gronauer's attacks until it hit on this one. The man had harvested the deadly leaves and disposed of them with a terrible feeling of being watched. But that was ridiculous—or was it? Was not the whole impossibly living world against him, ringing him in and waiting for him to die?

After a few weeks, he ate again, experimentally, and was not sick. He'd fooled the garden. Only it would keep on trying to kill him, and he would never know when it had made a successful attempt until too late. His one long-range chance of survival lay in making peace with the garden; and that could only be done by proving his potential usefulness to it.

Digging around a patch of growth, he discovered that certain thick roots went deep into the hard rock. Those must be for extracting buried minerals. Protoplasm required carbon and oxygen, among other things, and most likely the source of the former element was the various carbonates.

Gronauer went to an area where the plants had not yet penetrated and began to dig. His miner's eye and brain were more effective than the chance gropings of the blind roots, and it was slow work for them, forcing their way into solid rock.

Before long, he had a small heap of assorted carbonates. He macerated them and laid them beside one of the big roots. A few hours later, tendrils had grown around his offering and most of it was being absorbed. Limestone was a favourite, he saw, while iron compounds were hardly touched. He went after more limestone. And there were other elements they must need—sulphates would be especially valuable—and with the tiny atomic heater that remained to him, he could concentrate nitrates.

It took time for the garden to understand. There probably was no conscious mind reasoning out what Gronauer wanted; there was simply a high mutation rate and a completely integrated ecology. By supplying minerals, by loosening rock about new roots, by guiding tendrils in their direction of growth, the man performed a service; and, the energy saved, the whole system could go into proliferation—some of which would be new, "experimental" forms.

Within a few months, there were pale leaves which seemed to be mostly protein. Gronauer harvested and ate them. Presently there were no more such leaves. They had apparently not fulfilled a real function, and the symbiosis had cut them off. Gronauer stopped working for the garden. He waited, and the slow weeks passed, and his supplies from Earth got horribly short. If he had guessed wrong—

No. The flesh-leaves budded out again. Gronauer rewarded the garden with a heap of limestone and copperas. Thereafter the leaves stayed. Whether it was blind natural selection within the framework of symbiosis, or whether there really was some dim brain capable of learned reflexes, the garden adapted to the new fact that flesh-leaves meant free minerals.

"After that," said Gronauer simply, "we were friends. The problem was only to com—communicate our needs to each other."

He needed green food to prevent scurvy. An experimental taste made him ill, and again he withheld his services. Thereafter the garden produced more edible green leaves than it needed for itself, and he gathered the surplus.

It was to his advantage to have the garden change rapidly so that new possibilities would arise. He rewarded each discovered mutation with an extra mineral ration; if it turned out to be useful, he was lavish in his payments. Thus, over the years, he attained a remarkably balanced diet.

Meanwhile, the plants had grown back around his ship, and he transplanted vines inside. They died, and he tried again, and still again, until he struck a variety that would endure the conditions he needed. They gave light and heat to replace his failing generator, and proved to be much more efficient producers of free oxygen than the tanks of Martian swordgrass which was standard on spaceships.

He had been recovering water by the usual condensing methods, replacing losses by baking gypsum, but his new plants "learned" to give him as much alcohol-free water as he wanted. He could have had the alcohol, too, but he didn't like to drink alone. And surely few men had ever been as lonely as he.

"And all the time," said Gronauer, "I was trying other things, learning more about the symbiosis. After a few years I got the—the feel of it. I have not the scientific words to describe, but I can understand in my own way what goes on. I can look at a patch of growth and tell what it needs. I can look at a mutant form and after a while know what it may do. By selecting new strains for several generations, I can create a species which will fit well into the symbiosis. It was thus I made the light-berries, for my own use, and roots which can use ferric carbonate—the symbiosis could not handle that before, and limestone was getting short. And other things."

"The—well, your spacesuit? The air plant on it?" Hardesty felt embarrassed at mentioning that.

"My air compressing pump was going to wear out soon, I knew that, and by then it was more natural for me to work with the plants rather than dead machinery. The plants growing on my helmet, they give heat and light and free the oxygen out of my own breath. They live from my bloodstream. It is not much they need and they give me vitamins in return. Their rootlets entered my skin quite painlessly.

"I have many kinds of food-plants now, with new tastes. You would like them, I think, but they are probably different from what you are used to. Go slow at first, eat only a little of the native food for a year, or however long your supplies last."

Hardesty and Marian did not stop then to consider Gronauer's odd phrasing of the invitation. It wouldn't have meant much to them; in twenty years of solitude, anyone would develop a curious turn of speech.

Gronauer shuffled over to a desk, opened a drawer and took out an old logbook. Routine entries stopped with the shipwreck; what followed was page after page of fine script and painstakingly drawn illustrations.

"Here are my notes," he said with a humble pride. "I have described and pictured everything. It is all that you need to know."

Marian skimmed through it, and her thin intense features lit with a genuine glow.

"It's wonderful, Mr. Gronauer," she said after a moment. "This marks some kind of epoch in biology, you know. Your name will go down in history."

"Um, yes." Hardesty forced himself back to the practical side of things. "Tell me, though, how's this world for radioactives? Any good deposits?"

"A few deposits, but not worth working unless they have changed refining machinery a lot since my time."

"They haven't." The spaceman sighed. "Well, it was just a thought. We might as well blast off, then. Our ship's quarters are rather cramped, Gronauer, but we'll fix up the best we can for you."

"For me?" The soft eyes widened.

"Of course. Did you think we'd leave you behind?"

Gronauer shook his grey-maned head. "But I cannot go. I have to stay here. I am the gardener, you see."

Hardesty took a restless turn about the cabin. His feet fell so lightly in the low gravity that it was soundless; he drifted ghost-fashion between the cluttered instruments and controls of the Beltboat.

"I don't know what to do," he said. "We can't take him along. Imagine having a raving lunatic crowded in here with us for months. But, damn it, we can't abandon him either."

"We won't be abandoning him," said Marian. "No one can say the situation is our fault. We'll let the government know, and he'll be all right till they send a ship for him."

"Even so, it's the principle of the thing." He stared out the port, at the hugeness of night and frosty stars beyond, barren rock and mute loneliness, and the primal terror of it struck deep into him. "Leaving a man alone in *that!*"

"He's done all right for twenty years, dear. He can last one more. After that, it'll be up to the official rescue party. We can suggest that they take a psychiatrist along."

"You had no luck persuading him?"

"None at all. I tried every day. I went over to his place while you were exploring the asteroid and talked to him." Wistfulness tinged her voice. "I told him about mankind and about Earth and summer moons and smoky hills in autumn, the way we've always dreamed it—I've never seen Earth, Jim, except in pictures, but somehow it's more real to me than all this empty universe. He isn't interested. I had to quit when he started getting angry."

Hardesty went over and kissed her. "You're a good kid," he murmured. "Some day, some day *soon*, we're going home to Earth. No more space for us. It'll be roses growing over a house by the seaside." His fists clenched impotently. "If only there'd been a strike right here on this damned lump! But I hunted everywhere. Not a thing worth digging out. Gronauer told the truth."

"Why should he have lied to us?"

"I don't know, except that he isn't normal any more. He doesn't react like a human being, even like a human who's been alone that long. Those plants have done something to him." Decision hardened Hardesty's lean face. "Well, he doesn't get many more chances to come along. We're not hanging around here another twenty-four hours. The sooner off, the sooner we'll find that lode and go home to Earth."

"Yes, I suppose so." Marian turned back toward the microscopic galley. "He's coming over for dinner, you know. I talked him into that much, at least."

"Well, I suppose there's no harm in it. Any special motive other than hospitality?"

"Oh, we'll make it as bright and cheerful as we can. Homelike. It may change his mind."

"I doubt that. But we'll have done our best."

Hardesty glanced out the port again. The Sun was rising, a tiny brilliant disc winged with the zodiacal light. Its thin radiance crept over blackened lava and tumbled granite, seeming only to add to the ruinous desolation.

Marian busied herself, getting the small luxuries they had saved for festive occasions out of the freezer, filling the ship with an aroma that made her husband lick his lips and grin. She hummed as she worked, and somehow the table she set was like a bit of Earth—the gleam of plate and silver, a centrepiece of flame-red swordgrass blooms, even the tiny porcelain dachshund that was their mascot.

"We're putting on the dog," she explained solemnly. "Now you go dress, Jim."

He put on clean dungarees, knotted his one and atrocious tie, and slicked back his sandy hair. Marian had put on a print dress and dainty slippers; she suddenly looked pathetically young. Hardesty wished with irritation that there was no guest coming, that this might be for the two of them alone. Briefly, he knew that they'd never really fit in on Earth, for something of the high, cold solitude had entered them and they were too self-sufficient and aloof.

But that was a well-known psychological phenomenon. It was one reason why few prospectors went back till they'd made their pile and could live independently of society. Another was the difficulty, these days, of getting any kind of decent job on Earth.

It's not mankind we're going back to. We'll have neighbours, but our intimacy has become something that will never really let anyone else know us. It's Earth we want, Earth and clean winds and the tall trees above, Sun and sea and sky. We want an environment that is home instead of deadly foe. We want the heritage of our race's evolution.

The stars wheeled overhead, grand and lonely—he'd miss the sky of space now and then; he'd wonder at the dimness of constellations—but there'd be summer around him, a whisper of leaves, the chirp of crickets and a firefly bobbing through the warm and sleepy dark. No more metal, no more tanked air and canned food and armoured life—they would have come to their kingdom.

Harsh sunlight gleamed off the figure that approached. Gronauer. Hardesty sighed, pumped out the airlock and opened its outer valve. When he closed that again and opened the inner one, a breath of searing cold eddied from the figure which stood there.

Gronauer climbed out of his suit and looked timidly around him. He had dressed in an old coverall given him by Marian. It didn't fit well and he was obviously uncomfortable in it. For a moment, he shrank from his host's welcome.

"It is—warm in here," he mumbled.

"Sorry. Want me to lower the thermostat?"

"No, please not to bother, I will get used to it. You were good to ask me." Gronauer edged nervously into the cabin.

"Sit down. Dinner will be ready in a minute."

"I cannot stay too long." The stooped grey form placed itself on the edge of a recoil chair, as if ready to leap from sudden menace. "In here I am cut off. The garden might need me and I would not know."

"Isn't that the case in your own cabin?"

"No, no. There are roots growing through the plates. My children inside are part of the whole system. I have sealed around the roots so air does not get out, but the garden can still call me." The words were jerky, stammering a little, and the eyes were never still.

"I noticed that every disturbance seemed to set up vibrations in the plants. Is that how they—communicate?"

"Yes. Formerly, before I came, those were just special stimuli causing certain stereotyped reactions. Like if a plant was hurt or killed by a rockfall, the vibrations triggered a reaction elsewhere, seeds were carried to the spot, a new plant was started. But after all these years, I can—read? understand?—more. Often I know just what is wrong even before I go there. By sending my own pulses out, I can usually cause to be done whatever must be done, even without going there to do the work myself."

"A sort of nervous system, then." Hardesty rubbed his chin. "And now you've become its brain." The thought was unpleasant, somehow.

Gronauer leaned forward eagerly. "And the eyes and hands, too. Many of the old functions have died out because I do it quicker and better, so the garden needs me. It would probably die without me. That is why I cannot go with you."

"Soup's on," called Marian gaily.

It was mostly synthetics and dehydrates, but you wouldn't have known it, for she was an inspired cook. Hardesty dug in eagerly. Gronauer, though, only picked unhappily at his share.

"I hope you like it, Mr. Gronauer," said Marian, a little stiffly.

His twisted face tried to smile an apology. "I am not used to such fare for a long time. Garden food tastes different. It *feels* different." He waved a hand inarticulately. "How shall I make clear? It is that *you* eat things you have no kinship with; you kill them and devour them without any emotion. But *I* am nourished by something of which I am a part."

Wryly, Hardesty's mind wandered off on the subject of autophagy. Given perfect surgical tools, shockless and bloodless amputation, how long could a man survive by eating parts of himself?

"At first I wanted to go back." Gronauer's tongue seemed loosened all at once. Perhaps the beer he was not used to had taken hold already. "It is strange to remember how lonely I was—oh, for years I wept because there was no one and nothing else. But now I see that it is you who are lonely, each of you alone in a world of dead metal, shouting at someone else you cannot even be sure exists, cannot be sure what he is thinking of you or even if he is thinking at all."

His grin was rather terrible. "How do you know you are not the only consciousness in a world of robots? Alone, alone, and you go to your grave and that is the end. But I belong. I *feel* the other life. It is part of me and I am part of it. My life has meaning and beauty—my life, married to other sensitive life, all of us together against the void. No, no, I cannot go back to Earth!"

He lapsed into stillness, sat looking out of the port at the cruel brilliance of stars, and did not answer their remarks. Hardesty traded an exasperated look with Marian.

"We're leaving, you know, Gronauer," he said after they had finished and were sitting in the recoil chairs again. "This is your last chance to come with us."

The grey, scarred head shook violently, so that the long hair swirled about the eyes.

"I suppose you'll make out all right," said Hardesty. "We'll plot an orbit that'll get us to the nearest radio station—I think that's Pallas right now—as soon as possible, and from there we can relay word to Ceres. It won't be many months before a government ship comes for you."

Gronauer shrank back and breath hissed between his teeth.

"What then?" he gasped. "What will they do?"

Despite himself, Hardesty was surprised at the violence of the reaction.

"Why, you have a legal right to stay here if you want, of course." *Unless the psychiatrists decide you're insane*, his mind added grimly. "But there'll be scientists to study your garden and your discoveries. There'll be supplies and companionship—"

"I do not want it!" Gronauer stood up, trembling. "I have all I want. I am the gardener. Is that not enough? Do not tell them I am here. They would come and hurt the garden."

"Under the law, I can't abandon you. It's all right to leave you, I guess, seeing that that's what you want, but not reporting a ship-wrecked spaceman? I could get in trouble for that."

"Who would know?" interjected Marian. She threw a wink at her husband over Gronauer's shoulder. *Soothe him, humour him till we're away from here*. "If you wish, of course we'll keep your secret. It's your right to stay here alone if you really want to."

"I want. I want!"

"But think, Mr. Gronauer." She smiled at him warmly. "Think of what that will mean. You're getting old. You can't live forever. You'll die here and perhaps no one will discover this asteroid for centuries, or perhaps never. The garden will die without a human to attend it. If you let the scientists come, they'd preserve it as a natural wonder even when you were gone."

"They would not understand." His voice was harsh and hostile. "The gardener must be part of the garden. He must grow into it, make it his life. Their scientific tending would not be enough."

I think, said Hardesty's mind, *that the old man is right. This is more than a mechanical set of duties to be performed. You can't replace a human brain with an electronic computer, even the best and latest model, even one which actually thinks. You can't replace the gardener with a paid attendant. Even if anyone would consent to live here alone, two or three years at a time, for any wages. Could you be hired to let roots tap your bloodstream?*

"Then that's that," he said aloud, coldly. "The garden will last your lifetime, undisturbed."

Orion wheeled mightily overhead, a glitter of frozen fire against an infinite clear dark. Gronauer sat still. There were trickles of sweat on his face, and he was breathing heavily.

Marian tried to break the embarrassed silence: "It has been a great privilege to know you, Mr. Gronauer. And the garden. Was there anybody you once knew? Any message, perhaps?"

"No," he said abstractedly. "No one. Not anymore."

After another minute, his eyes lifted to theirs with a kind of entreaty.

"I have thought of this before," he blurted. "I am, as you say, old. There should be a race of human gardeners here, to carry on. The garden is still growing, still evolving. It needs men, and it gives them rewards you cannot now imagine. Would—would you think of staying here yourselves, having children here, too?"

The thought was so grotesque that Hardesty had to laugh, a harsh sound jarring against the drumhead of tense silence. It seemed to strike Marian differently.

"Children," she repeated. "Yes, Jim, we have to get back to Earth soon, while we can still be young with our kids."

"You could have them now," said Gronauer. "Here."

"No. It isn't fair to a child to raise it anywhere but on Earth. It isn't right to grow up in metal." There was something haunted in her voice. "I know. It happened to me."

"A child growing up here—" The castaway's words trailed off. He drew a long breath. "Would you come with me?" he asked. "There is something I would like to show you. It will change your outlook on all this. You will at least see why I want to stay here alone."

"What's that?" Despite himself, Hardesty felt a resurgence of interest.

Damn it, the asteroid was unique.

"I cannot explain in words. You will have to see. It is not so far to go."

"Well—"

"It is the last gift I can give you."

"Certainly we'll come," said Marian. "We'll be glad to, won't we, Jim?"

"Sure," he said worriedly. He went to the spacesuit locker and opened it. "We'd better hurry, then. It'll be sunset again pretty quick."

"We will be following the Sun," said Gronauer. He lumbered over to his own suit where it stood in the airlock. Briefly, his gnarled hands stroked the grey-green vines that draped it—an odd, wistful caress.

Hardesty peeled off shirt and pants, revealing the insulated one-piece undergarment which served as padding below his armour. Marian exchanged her dress for a similar outfit. It looked well on her slim figure. Hardesty smiled as he helped her into her suit.

Gronauer donned his own armour. He was still breathing hard. Something very odd here. When he was looking away, Hardesty ambled quietly over to the tool chest, palmed his gun, and clipped it onto his spacesuit. Marian saw the gesture, started to say something, and throttled her words. Maybe he was right. There was at least no harm in it.

Or in Gronauer. He might have been a little crazy by normal Earth standards, but what did those mean out here, three hundred million miles from the Sun? But he was not violent; he partook of the serene, timeless strength of the garden. A couple of hours' jaunt was not too much to please an old man trapped in a loneliness he himself no longer recognized.

They came out under a sky that was flashing ice and bitter dark, with a wan little sun low above ragged black stone. Gronauer led the way, a bounding figure of shadow and dazzling metal, now lost in a gully of night and now outlined grotesquely against the sprawl of stars. Hardesty swore at his speed, lengthened his own flat leaps, and felt rock and scree rattle beneath his boots.

They were moving into the far bleak eye of the Sun, faster than the planetoid's axial spin. As the stars reeled insanely backward and the Sun began to climb again, Hardesty had a sudden weird feeling that he was moving back in time. He choked it down and concentrated on picking his way through the jumbled, looming, crazily tilted stones, down riven gulches and up hillsides that were heaped slabs of igneous rock, a nightmare landscape of ruin and murk.

It was a zigzag path, he noticed dimly, leading into an area he had only skimmed through in his search, but he was too busy keeping up with Gronauer and watching Marian to think more deeply about it. His breath was harsh and loud in a suddenly hot spacesuit.

The Sun was halfway down to the opposite horizon when Gronauer went into another ravine and out of sight. Hardesty followed him, scrambled awkwardly down its steep sides, the undiffused glow of his flash picking boulders out like distorted faces. The crack was long and deep; he had to fumble in shadow for several minutes before he came out at the other end. Then he looked around.

He stood on a gigantic basalt block sloping off to the edge of the world, overhead and around him the stars and the rime-frost arch of the Milky Way, and he was alone.

"Gronauer!" His voice echoed rattling in his helmet. "Where the hell are you?"

Useless, of course. Gronauer didn't have a suit radio. But how the devil could he have gotten lost?

Marian came leaping out of the ravine and over to stand by him. Her breathing was as hard as his.

"What became of the old man?" she asked anxiously.

"That's what I'd like to know. First he takes off like a bat out of Mars, and then he manages to lose us. Just went too fast? No, I was keeping up all right. He must have climbed the canyon wall ahead of me—I wouldn't have seen him—and taken off in some other direction."

"But why, Jim?"

"I don't know. He's mad, completely cracked, of course. Needs psychiatry in the worst way. But let the government worry about him. I'm fed up." Hardesty took a long stride forward. "Come on, let's get back to the ship."

"But he may just have made a mistake—"

"Then he can catch up with us and lead us properly. The hell with him."

"Well, he does seem a pretty hopeless case at that, doesn't he? The poor old man! I hope we see him again before we blast off."

Hardesty shrugged. "Personally, I don't give a hang. Now let's see, which way is the *Gold Rush?*"

"Why, I suppose—that way. Toward the Sun."

"We zigzagged quite a bit, remember." Hardesty's hand rang against his metal leg in a slap of exasperation. "Nuts! We're lost!"

"There's the asteroid's pole star, up there, dear, and the Sun was west of it at setting, so our general direction should be *that* way."

"Yeah. I hope it's not too general. Let's go."

They set off along the sloping hillside toward a razor-backed spine of rock, black against the Milky Way. Neither one said anything.

It was hard to orient yourself, if you didn't know every inch of the path. You had to twist and turn, picking a slow way across a narrow landscape of crags and gullies and craters, sometimes lost in darkness that was like a flowing liquid, sometimes blinded by the thin yet vicious sunlight directly in your eyes. There were no broad outlooks. Vision was bounded on every hand. Only the turning sky had depth.

Men had gotten lost on asteroids and wandered within a few miles of their ships till their oxygen gave out. It was not a comforting reflection. Hardesty shoved it resolutely out of his mind.

After an hour or so, they passed a region of plant growth. Hardesty looked at the stretch of garden with a rising bitterness in him.

Low, silvery shrubs, lichenous growth spotting naked rock with red and brown and yellow, high, gaunt, yuccalike boles and gallows branches, sullen blood-crimson glow of heat bladders, huge, muscular roots plunging deep into the little world's iron heart, delicate fairy tracing of vines looped and coiled between the shrubs, the throb and pulse of the garden's beating hearts—a reach of growth over the hills and out of sight, a frigid world made alive where no life should be, supreme triumph of organism over the chaotic waste of the frozen and hostile Universe—

But it was too alien. The eldritch forms only added to the strangeness and loneliness, and he hated them. He kicked viciously and saw the pulse of alarm ripple out through the garden and over the near horizon, leaves rustling and whispering in the windless vacuum of space, the garden talking to itself.

"Go ahead," he muttered. "Call your brain. That's all he is now, your brain and your hands. You've taken his soul away."

"Don't, Jim," said Marian. "Please don't."

"Oh, all right." He trudged in silence for a while before adding shamefacedly: "I'm being silly, I know. This is nothing but another instance of adaptation. Life on Earth is interdependent, too, a balance of nature. But I still don't like it."

The Sun crossed the sky again and lowered behind them. Hardesty glanced worriedly at his wrist chrono. They'd been out for a good two hours; their tanks didn't hold very much more air.

Don't get excited. That speeds up your metabolism, makes you burn oxygen all the faster, blunts the cool judgment you need. Take it easy. Slow and easy. Lots of time.

Sunset, and darkness like a steel shutter slammed tight. Nothing around them looked familiar yet. Rather, everything looked the same. All these leaning spires and tumbled boulders and gnarled old craters looked alike and there was no way home.

Marian's hand crept into his and he squeezed it, grateful for the touch of human nearness.

"According to the stars, we're in the neighbourhood now," he said as unemotionally as possible. "We'd better follow a spiral path—"

Out of the corner of an eye, he saw the blue-white sheet of flame that spurted up over the horizon, saw it rising and spreading in a terrible brilliance that veiled the stars, and flung an arm across his eyes with a shout. The next moment the ground heaved and

buckled under him, flung him spinning upward in the light gravity
and bounced him against a lurching granite cliff, then tossed him
back to the shaking, sundering rock below.

"Marian!" he cried. "Marian!"

The fire was gone, but half the sky was blotted from sight by a
column of smoke and dust, climbing and climbing like a monster
spirit let out of Solomon's flask, and the ground shivered and rumbled and boulders danced on its surface. Hardesty clung to the rocks,
clawing himself into naked stone, and his own screaming was loud
and mad in his ears.

"Jim! Are you all right, Jim?"

They stumbled toward each other, falling and struggling as earthquake waves raced around and around the tiny world. They locked
arms and lay on the cracking ground together and looked wildly at
the nightmare scenery.

The seasick roll died away. A miniature landslide came down a hill
slope, slowly in the acceleration of feeble gravity, the slowness of
fleeing through clinging mud.

Hardesty and Marian got up and stumbled toward the black jinni
which rose against the stars.

He felt drained of emotion, a machine moving wearily toward
some destined end. He topped a ridge and looked with blank eyes at
the ruin of his ship. It was scattered to the horizon and beyond, and
the molten slag was still aglow beneath its resting place.

"Gronauer," he said, just that one word, but it held loathing for
the castaway and for himself, the time and anxiety he had wasted
trying to help someone who didn't want to be helped, but mostly
for his stupidity.

Marian stared around. "Where?"

"Gronauer? I don't know. He gave us the slip and came back, wrecked the safety controls and blew up the nuclear pile of the ship."

"No," she said. "He wouldn't. It must have been a meteor."

"Not where I landed. A meteor would have had to come straight down to hit the ship. Even then, it wouldn't blow up the pile." He kicked savagely at a boulder, which flew off like a bird winging south. "Gronauer did it. You know that yourself."

"Why?" Marian's whisper, like a dim voice from across that gulf of space that winked and jeered at him with a million hostile eyes, was so faint that even in his earphones he could scarcely hear it. "Why?"

They saw the figure lurching up the slope toward them, hands dangling empty, the helmeted head overgrown with vines like an ancient Greek nature god. Hardesty drew his gun and rested it on his free elbow for steadiness. "Jim! No!"

"Calm down," he said. "After what he did, I'm not taking any chances."

"Are you going to—kill him?"

"It's not a bad idea. He's insane, probably homicidal. We can't watch him all the time…"

Gronauer must have seen the gun, but his slow pace did not slacken. One hand came up, tenderly caressing the vine that trailed off his shoulder.

Hardesty kept the gun level, but he did not fire, merely tensed his finger on the trigger when Gronauer suddenly broke into a staggering run toward them. Marian gripped Hardesty's arm.

The old man fell over a rock and tried to get up.

"First time I've seen him stumble," Hardesty said puzzledly, and lowered the gun. "Come on. The worst he can do is heave something at us. He's unarmed."

Gronauer was still trying to crawl toward them when they reached him. He stopped and rolled over on one side to look up at them. Blood and foam and twisted vines and tangled beard could not hide the smile on his battered lips.

Tears glistened on Marian's face in the keen starlight. Hardesty heard a sob in the radio and wanted to hold her close and tell her it wasn't real, that it had never been real, and that the flame-coloured woods of Earth's October lay just beyond the jagged, airless pinnacles. But he couldn't. Instead, he knelt when Gronauer motioned him closer, and put his helmet against the castaway's.

"Now you will have to stay," said Gronauer with feeble triumph. "I could not get away from the ship in time, but that does not matter. I am old and would have died soon. Then the garden would not have anyone to take care of it. Now it will."

"Killing yourself and marooning us for the sake of some lousy vegetation," Hardesty said bitterly. "I should have known you were crazy and taken off right away and sent help back to you."

Gronauer tried to shake his head. "Not crazy. You will gather the supplies that were not destroyed in the explosion and move into my cabin. You will read my notes and tend my plants… and become part of the symbiosis, as I was."

"I'd shoot Marian and myself first!"

"No, you will hope to be found by someone else. That hope will keep you from committing suicide. When you are ready to give up hoping, you will be—adjusted. You will like it here. This will be the home you were searching for; this will be your Earth. And you will have children—"

"So your damned garden can go on!"

Gronauer nodded and his smile grew wider even while his eyes lost their focus.

"The garden will go on," he said, just before his breath ceased altogether.

Hardesty stood up. Marian was clinging to him and her voice was insistent in his earphones, but he didn't hear her. He was looking at the stars, the bright stars which neither comforted nor mocked, being too remote to care, and the green of the plants in the distance, and he thought with a dull despair that even now it looked like New England in October.

IN JUPITER'S SKY, THE SUN'S DISC APPEARS FIVE TIMES SMALLER
THAN IT APPEARS AS VIEWED FROM EARTH'S SURFACE.

JUPITER

Desertion   Clifford D. Simak

Jupiter is the giant of the solar system, its mass being more than
double the mass of all the other planets combined. It is a gas giant
with no definite surface like the inner planets and probably no solid
core. Its atmosphere is 90% hydrogen and 10% helium and has been
considered a failed star—in Arthur C. Clarke's novel *2010* (1982) it is
transformed into a star, called Lucifer. Its clouds are in constant tur-
moil—there are clear bands of clouds on its outer surface amongst
which is the Great Red Spot, which has been visible since 1831 and is
believed to be a vast anticyclonic storm.

Because of its size and magnitude Jupiter is clearly visible in the
night sky and at times can be the third or fourth brightest object. The
Babylonians named it Marduk after their chief god, and the Greeks
followed suit with Zeus and the Romans with Jupiter.

It is believed that Jupiter was the first planet to form in what was
still an unstable solar system and that early in its life it migrated in
toward the Sun before returning to its current position. This migration has been credited with establishing the solar system as it now is,

with Jupiter's gravity stopping the fifth planet from forming between Mars and Jupiter, and reducing the volume of material available for Mars to become a larger world. Jupiter is also seen as a guardian of the inner planets because its gravity attracts many comets and meteors thereby helping protect the inner planets from a more significant bombardment.

Jupiter has seventy-nine known satellites, most having been discovered recently by the space probes sent to the outer planets, and most being little more than rocks. Of significance are the four Galilean moons, so called because they were discovered by Galileo in 1610 when he first viewed Jupiter through a telescope. These four—Io, Europa, Ganymede and Callisto—comprise over 99% of the mass of moons orbiting Jupiter. Ganymede is the largest satellite of any planet and is larger than Mercury. Ganymede, Callisto and Io are all bigger than our moon. Europa is believed to have a vast ocean of water beneath its deep crust of ice, and is one of the worlds of our solar system considered as a possible target for colonization.

In early science fiction it was long believed that Jupiter had a solid surface and that it was Earth-like. In *A Journey in Other Worlds* (1894) John Jacob Astor, the American millionaire who went down with the *Titanic*, depicted a Jupiter that was a prehistoric earth, with dinosaurs. George Griffith, whose inventor Lord Redgrave tours the planets with his new wife in *A Honeymoon in Space* (1901), avoids Jupiter but visits Ganymede where they discover advanced humanoid beings living in glass-domed cities. W.S. Lach-Szyrma had likewise avoided Jupiter but in his atmospheric "A Trip to Jupiter's Moonlet" (1891) he takes us to an unnamed moon to marvel at the majesty of Jupiter and other moons in the sky, which he calls a "colossal pyrotechnic display." In their short serial "The Star Shell" (1926–7), George and Bruce Wallis depict a Jupiter divided between two warring races, one sophisticated and the other barbaric. The Red Spot is seen as a vast, toxic jungle.

Many pulp stories of the 1930s pitted humans against the hostile environment of Jupiter, especially the Red Spot, as in "The Red Hell of Jupiter" (1931) by Paul Ernst. Scientists even attempt to control the Red Spot in Frank Belknap Long's "Red Storm on Jupiter" (1936). In "Gulliver, 3000 A.D." (1933), Leslie F. Stone has her expedition surprised to discover that Jupiter is populated by Lilliputian-sized natives who capture any explorers who stray there.

Writers recognized that if Jupiter were to be visited by humans then humans themselves needed to adapt. Clifford Simak tackled this in "Desertion" (1944), which is reprinted here. Poul Anderson gave it the full treatment in "Call Me Joe" (1957), where artificial centaur-like beings are created to live and work in the Jovian environment but are controlled from beyond Jupiter by humans—in this case a paraplegic—who experience the world through Joe's mind.

In "Bridge" (1952) by James Blish (later incorporated in *They Shall Have Stars*, 1956), humans attempt to master Jupiter's environment by building a bridge of ice on one of the planet's few stable land masses. The building is achieved by robots controlled remotely from the small moon, Amalthea, the fifth of Jupiter's moons to be discovered. Coincidentally, Arthur C. Clarke has an expedition visit that moonlet in "Jupiter V" (1953), which they discover is a giant spaceship. Blish returned to Jupiter, or its moon Ganymede, to consider further the potential for humans to explore the outer worlds, and in "A Time to Survive" (1956, later included in *The Seedling Stars*, 1957) he elaborates his theory of "pantropy", adapting humans for specific worlds.

Ganymede was for many the preferred world for colonization and appears in *The Snows of Ganymede* (1955) and *Three Worlds to Conquer* (1964), both by Poul Anderson, *Farmer in the Sky* (1950) and other young-adult novels by Robert A. Heinlein, and both *Jupiter Project* (serial, 1972) and *Against Infinity* (1983) by Gregory Benford.

The idea that life might exist in Jupiter's atmosphere continues to inspire writers. Arthur C. Clarke explored it in "A Meeting with Medusa" (1971), where he sees a balloon-like jellyfish. In *Jupiter* (2000) and *Leviathans of Jupiter* (2011) Ben Bova depicts a giant city-sized creature in the oceans of Jupiter.

The sheer scale of Jupiter and its major moons provides endless possibilities for science fiction adventures, scientific endeavour and the creation of truly alien beings.

Clifford Simak (1904–1988) was one of the major contributors to the so-called Golden Age of American magazine science fiction in the 1940s in *Astounding SF* and in the 1950s in *Galaxy SF*. He was one of those writers whose work grew and developed according to the demands of the market and was sometimes ahead of the game. He first appeared in Hugo Gernsback's magazine *Wonder Stories* with "The World of the Red Sun" in 1931, where time travellers find the final remnants of mankind enslaved by a giant brain. Soon his work went beyond the limitations of the magazines of the day. "The Creator", where time-travellers encounter the Being that created the Universe as an experiment, was published in a small-press magazine in 1935. Simak drifted away from the field because he was not happy with the way it was developing, but returned when John W. Campbell, Jr. became editor at *Astounding Stories* and soon became one of its leading writers. Amongst his many stories for Campbell was the start of a series set on each of the planets: "Hermit of Mars" (1939) on the

Red Planet, "Clerical Error" (1940) on Jupiter, "Masquerade" (1941) on Mercury and "Tools" (1942) on Venus, but before continuing the series he began another which grew into the volume *City* (1952) and followed the evolution of human society away from the city to a more bucolic world. Part of this process explored how humans might be adapted to live in other environments and that is the subject of the following story, not planned as part of the series, but subsequently incorporated. Simak went on to even greater fame in the 1950s with a wonderful series of novels and short stories which are uniquely Simakian. In the world of science fiction he was a brilliant and distinctive one-off talent.

FOUR MEN, TWO BY TWO, HAD GONE INTO THE howling maelstrom that was Jupiter and had not returned. They had walked into the keening gale—or rather, they had loped, bellies low against the ground, wet sides gleaming in the rain.

For they did not go in the shape of men.

Now the fifth man stood before the desk of Kent Fowler, head of Dome No. 3. Jovian Survey Commission.

Under Fowler's desk, old Towser scratched a flea, then settled down to sleep again.

Harold Allen, Fowler saw with a sudden pang, was young—too young. He had the easy confidence of youth, the straight back and straight eyes, the face of one who never had known fear. And that was strange. For men in the domes of Jupiter did know fear—fear and humility. It was hard for Man to reconcile his puny self with the mighty forces of the monstrous planet.

"You understand," said Fowler, "that you need not do this. You understand that you need not go."

It was formula, of course. The other four had been told the same thing, but they had gone. This fifth one, Fowler knew, would go too. But suddenly he felt a dull hope stir within him that Allen wouldn't go.

"When do I start?" asked Allen.

There was a time when Fowler might have taken quiet pride in that answer, but not now. He frowned briefly.

"Within the hour," he said.

Allen stood waiting, quietly.

"Four other men have gone out and have not returned," said Fowler. "You know that, of course. We want you to return. We don't want you going off on any heroic rescue expedition. The main thing, the only thing, is that you come back, that you prove man can live in a Jovian form. Go to the first survey stake, no farther, then come back. Don't take any chances. Don't investigate anything. Just come back."

Allen nodded. "I understand all that."

"Miss Stanley will operate the converter," Fowler went on. "You need have no fear on that particular point. The other men were converted without mishap. They left the converter in apparently perfect condition. You will be in thoroughly competent hands. Miss Stanley is the best qualified conversion operator in the Solar System. She has had experience on most of the other planets. That is why she's here."

Allen grinned at the woman and Fowler saw something flicker across Miss Stanley's face—something that might have been pity, or rage—or just plain fear. But it was gone again and she was smiling back at the youth who stood before the desk. Smiling in that prim, school-teacherish way she had of smiling, almost as if she hated herself for doing it.

"I shall be looking forward," said Allen, "to my conversion."

And the way he said it, he made it all a joke, a vast, ironic joke. But it was no joke.

It was serious business, deadly serious. Upon these tests, Fowler knew, depended the fate of men on Jupiter. If the tests succeeded, the resources of the giant planet would be thrown open. Man would take over Jupiter as he already had taken over the other smaller planets. And if they failed—

If they failed, Man would continue to be chained and hampered by the terrific pressure, the greater force of gravity, the weird chemistry of the planet. He would continue to be shut within the domes, unable to set actual foot upon the planet, unable to see it with direct, unaided vision, forced to rely upon the awkward tractors and the televisor, forced to work with clumsy tools and mechanisms or through the medium of robots that themselves were clumsy.

For Man, unprotected and in his natural form, would be blotted out by Jupiter's terrific pressure of fifteen thousand pounds per square inch, pressure that made Terrestrial sea bottoms seem a vacuum by comparison.

Even the strongest metal Earthmen could devise couldn't exist under pressure such as that, under the pressure and the alkaline rains that forever swept the planet. It grew brittle and flaky, crumbling like clay, or it ran away in little streams and puddles of ammonia salts. Only by stepping up the toughness and strength of that metal, by increasing its electronic tension, could it be made to withstand the weight of thousands of miles of swirling, choking gases that made up the atmosphere. And even when that was done, everything had to be coated with tough quartz to keep away the rain—the bitter rain that was liquid ammonia.

Fowler sat listening to the engines in the sub-floor of the dome. Engines that ran on endlessly, the dome never quiet of them. They had to run and keep on running. For if they stopped the power flowing into the metal walls of the dome would stop, the electronic tension would ease up and that would be the end of everything.

Towser roused himself under Fowler's desk and scratched another flea, his leg thumping hard against the floor.

"Is there anything else?" asked Allen.

Fowler shook his head. "Perhaps there's something you want to do," he said. "Perhaps you—"

He had meant to say write a letter and he was glad he caught himself quick enough so he didn't say it.

Allen looked at his watch. "I'll be there on time," he said. He swung around and headed for the door.

Fowler knew Miss Stanley was watching him and he didn't want to turn and meet her eyes. He fumbled with a sheaf of papers on the desk before him.

"How long are you going to keep this up?" asked Miss Stanley and she bit off each word with a vicious snap.

He swung around in his chair and faced her then. Her lips were drawn into a straight, thin line, her hair seemed skinned back from her forehead tighter than ever, giving her face that queer, almost startling death-mask quality.

He tried to make his voice cool and level. "As long as there's any need of it," he said. "As long as there's any hope."

"You're going to keep on sentencing them to death," she said. "You're going to keep marching them out face to face with Jupiter. You're going to sit in here safe and comfortable and send them out to die."

"There is no room for sentimentality, Miss Stanley," Fowler said, trying to keep the note of anger from his voice. "You know as well as I do why we're doing this. You realize that Man in his own form simply cannot cope with Jupiter. The only answer is to turn men into the sort of things that can cope with it. We've done it on the other planets.

"If a few men die, but we finally succeed, the price is small. Through the ages men have thrown away their lives on foolish things, for foolish reasons. Why should we hesitate, then, at a little death in a thing as great as this?"

Miss Stanley sat stiff and straight, hands folded in her lap, the lights shining on her greying hair and Fowler, watching her, tried to imagine what she might feel, what she might be thinking. He wasn't exactly afraid of her, but he didn't feel quite comfortable when she was around. Those sharp blue eyes saw too much, her hands looked far too competent. She should be somebody's Aunt sitting in a rocking chair with her knitting needles. But she wasn't. She was the top-notch conversion unit operator in the Solar System and she didn't like the way he was doing things.

"There is something wrong, Mr. Fowler," she declared.

"Precisely," agreed Fowler. "That's why I'm sending young Allen out alone. He may find out what it is."

"And if he doesn't?"

"I'll send someone else."

She rose slowly from her chair, started toward the door, then stopped before his desk.

"Some day," she said, "you will be a great man. You never let a chance go by. This is your chance. You knew it was when this dome was picked for the tests. If you put it through, you'll go up a notch or two. No matter how many men may die, you'll go up a notch or two."

"Miss Stanley," he said and his voice was curt, "young Allen is going out soon. Please be sure that your machine—"

"My machine," she told him, icily, "is not to blame. It operates along the coordinates the biologists set up."

He sat hunched at his desk, listening to her footsteps go down the corridor.

What she said was true, of course. The biologists had set up the coordinates. But the biologists could be wrong. Just a hair's breadth of difference, one iota of digression and the converter would be sending out something that wasn't the thing they meant to send. A mutant that might crack up, go haywire, come unstuck under some condition or stress of circumstance wholly unsuspected.

For Man didn't know much about what was going on outside. Only what his instruments told him was going on. And the samplings of those happenings furnished by those instruments and mechanisms had been no more than samplings, for Jupiter was unbelievably large and the domes were very few.

Even the work of the biologists in getting the data on the Lopers, apparently the highest form of Jovian life, had involved more than three years of intensive study and after that two years of checking to make sure. Work that could have been done on Earth in a week or two. But work that, in this case, couldn't be done on Earth at all, for one couldn't take a Jovian life form to Earth. The pressure here on Jupiter couldn't be duplicated outside of Jupiter and at Earth pressure and temperature the Lopers would simply have disappeared in a puff of gas.

Yet it was work that had to be done if Man ever hoped to go about Jupiter in the life form of the Lopers. For before the converter could change a man to another life form, every detailed physical characteristic of that life form must be known—surely and positively, with no chance of mistake.

Allen did not come back.

The tractors, combing the nearby terrain, found no trace of him, unless the skulking thing reported by one of the drivers had been the missing Earthman in Loper form.

The biologists sneered their most accomplished academic sneers when Fowler suggested the coordinates might be wrong. Carefully they pointed out, the coordinates worked. When a man was put into the converter and the switch was thrown, the man became a Loper. He left the machine and moved away, out of sight, into the soupy atmosphere.

Some quirk, Fowler had suggested; some tiny deviation from the thing a Loper should be, some minor defect. If there were, the biologists said, it would take years to find it.

And Fowler knew that they were right.

So there were five men now instead of four and Harold Allen had walked out into Jupiter for nothing at all. It was as if he'd never gone so far as knowledge was concerned.

Fowler reached across his desk and picked up the personal file, a thin sheaf of paper neatly clipped together. It was a thing he dreaded but a thing he had to do. Somehow the reason for these strange disappearances must be found. And there was no other way than to send out more men.

He sat for a moment listening to the howling of the wind above the dome, the everlasting thundering gale that swept across the planet in boiling, twisting wrath.

Was there some threat out there, he asked himself? Some danger they did not know about? Something that lay in wait and gobbled up the Lopers, making no distinction between Lopers that were *bona fide* and Lopers that were men? To the gobblers, of course, it would make no difference.

Or had there been a basic fault in selecting the Lopers as the type of life best fitted for existence on the surface of the planet? The evident intelligence of the Lopers, he knew, had been one factor in that determination. For if the thing Man became did not have capacity for intelligence, Man could not for long retain his own intelligence in such a guise.

Had the biologists let that one factor weigh too heavily, using it to offset some other factor that might be unsatisfactory, even disastrous? It didn't seem likely. Stiff-necked as they might be, the biologists knew their business.

Or was the whole thing impossible, doomed from the very start? Conversion to other life forms had worked on other planets, but that did not necessarily mean it would work on Jupiter. Perhaps Man's intelligence could not function correctly through the sensory apparatus provided Jovian life. Perhaps the Lopers were so alien there was no common ground for human knowledge and the Jovian conception of existence to meet and work together.

Or the fault might lie with Man, be inherent with the race. Some mental aberration which, coupled with what they found outside, wouldn't let them come back. Although it might not be an aberration, not in the human sense. Perhaps just one ordinary human mental trait, accepted as commonplace on Earth, would be so violently at odds with Jovian existence that it would blast all human intelligence and sanity.

Claws rattled and clicked down the corridor. Listening to them, Fowler smiled wanly. It was Towser coming back from the kitchen, where he had gone to see his friend, the cook.

Towser came into the room, carrying a bone. He wagged his tail at Fowler and flopped down beside the desk, bone between his paws. For a long moment his rheumy old eyes regarded his master and Fowler reached down a hand to ruffle a ragged ear.

"You still like me, Towser?" Fowler asked and Towser thumped his tail.

"You're the only one," said Fowler. "All through the dome they're cussing me. Calling me a murderer, more than likely."

He straightened and swung back to the desk. His hand reached out and picked up the file.

Bennett? Bennett had a girl waiting for him back on Earth.

Andrews? Andrews was planning on going back to Mars Tech just as soon as he earned enough to see him through a year.

Olson? Olson was nearing pension age. All the time telling the boys how he was going to settle down and grow roses.

Carefully, Fowler laid the file back on the desk.

Sentencing men to death. Miss Stanley had said that, her pale lips scarcely moving in her parchment face. Marching men out to die while he, Fowler, sat here safe and comfortable.

They were saying it all through the dome, no doubt, especially since Allen had failed to return. They wouldn't say it to his face, of course. Even the man or men he called before this desk and told they were the next to go, wouldn't say it to him.

They would only say: "When do we start?" For that was formula.

But he would see it in their eyes.

He picked up the file again. Bennett, Andrews, Olson. There were others, but there was no use in going on.

Kent Fowler knew that he couldn't do it, couldn't face them, couldn't send more men out to die.

He leaned forward and flipped up the toggle on the inter-communicator.

"Yes. Mr. Fowler."

"Miss Stanley, please."

He waited for Miss Stanley, listening to Towser chewing half-heartedly on the bone. Towser's teeth were getting bad.

"Miss Stanley," said Miss Stanley's voice.

"Just wanted to tell you, Miss Stanley, to get ready for two more."

"Aren't you afraid," asked Miss Stanley, "that you'll run out of them? Sending out one at a time, they'd last longer, give you twice the satisfaction."

"One of them," said Fowler, "will be a dog."

"A dog!"

"Yes, Towser."

He heard the quick, cold rage that iced her voice. "Your own dog! He's been with you all these years—"

"That's the point," said Fowler. "Towser would be unhappy if I left him behind."

It was not the Jupiter he had known through the televisor. He had expected it to be different, but not like this. He had expected a hell of ammonia rain and stinking fumes and the deafening, thundering tumult of the storm. He had expected swirling clouds and fog and the snarling flicker of monstrous thunderbolts.

He had not expected the lashing downpour would be reduced to drifting purple mist that moved like fleeing shadows over a red and purple sward. He had not even guessed the snaking bolts of lightning would be flares of pure ecstasy across a painted sky.

Waiting for Towser, Fowler flexed the muscles of his body, amazed at the smooth, sleek strength he found. Not a bad body, he decided, and grimaced at remembering how he had pitied the Lopers when he glimpsed them through the television screen.

For it had been hard to imagine a living organism based upon ammonia and hydrogen rather than upon water and oxygen, hard to believe that such a form of life could know the same quick thrill of life that humankind could know. Hard to conceive of life out in the soupy maelstrom that was Jupiter, not knowing, of course, that through Jovian eyes it was no soupy maelstrom at all.

The wind brushed against him with what seemed gentle fingers and he remembered with a start that by Earth standards the wind was a roaring gale, a two-hundred-mile an hour howler laden with deadly gases.

Pleasant scents seeped into his body. And yet scarcely scents, for it was not the sense of smell as he remembered it. It was as if his whole being was soaking up the sensation of lavender—and yet not lavender. It was something, he knew, for which he had no word, undoubtedly the first of many enigmas in terminology. For the words he knew, the thought symbols that served him as an Earthman would not serve him as a Jovian.

The lock in the side of the dome opened and Towser came tumbling out—at least he thought it must be Towser.

He started to call to the dog, his mind shaping the words he meant to say. But he couldn't say them. There was no way to say them. He had nothing to say them with.

For a moment his mind swirled in muddy terror, a blind fear that eddied in little puffs of panic through his brain.

How did Jovians talk? How—

Suddenly he was aware of Towser, intensely aware of the bumbling, eager friendliness of the shaggy animal that had followed him from Earth to many planets. As if the thing that was Towser had reached out and for a moment sat within his brain.

And out of the bubbling welcome that he sensed, came words.

"Hiya, pal."

Not words really, better than words. Thought symbols in his brain, communicated thought symbols that had shades of meaning words could never have.

"Hiya, Towser," he said.

"I feel good," said Towser. "Like I was a pup. Lately I've been feeling pretty punk. Legs stiffening up on me and teeth wearing down to almost nothing. Hard to mumble a bone with teeth like that. Besides, the fleas give me hell. Use to be I never paid much attention to them. A couple of fleas more or less never meant much in my early days."

"But… but—" Fowler's thoughts tumbled awkwardly. "You're talking to me!"

"Sure thing," said Towser. "I always talked to you, but you couldn't hear me. I tried to say things to you, but I couldn't make the grade."

"I understood you sometimes," Fowler said.

"Not very well," said Towser. "You knew when I wanted food and when I wanted a drink and when I wanted out, but that's about all you ever managed."

"I'm sorry," Fowler said.

"Forget it," Towser told him. "I'll race you to the cliff."

For the first time, Fowler saw the cliff, apparently many miles away, but with a strange crystalline beauty that sparkled in the shadow of the many-coloured clouds.

Fowler hesitated. "It's a long way—"

"Ah, come on," said Towser and even as he said it he started for the cliff.

Fowler followed, testing his legs, testing the strength in that new body of his, a bit doubtful at first, amazed a moment later, then running with a sheer joyousness that was one with the red and purple sward, with the drifting smoke of the rain across the land.

As he ran the consciousness of music came to him, a music that beat into his body, that surged throughout his being, that lifted him on wings of silver speed. Music like bells might make from some steeple on a sunny, springtime hill.

As the cliff drew nearer the music deepened and filled the universe with a spray of magic sound. And he knew the music came from the tumbling waterfall that feathered down the face of the shining cliff.

Only, he knew, it was no waterfall, but an ammonia-fall and the cliff was white because it was oxygen, solidified.

He skidded to a stop beside Towser where the waterfall broke into a glittering rainbow of many hundred colours. Literally many hundred, for here, he saw, was no shading of one primary to another as human beings saw, but a clear-cut selectivity that broke the prism down to its last ultimate classification.

"The music," said Towser.

"Yes, what about it?"

"The music," said Towser, "is vibrations. Vibrations of water falling."

"But Towser, you don't know about vibrations."

"Yes, I do," contended Towser. "It just popped into my head."

Fowler gulped mentally. "Just popped!"

And suddenly, within his own head, he held a formula—the formula for a process that would make metal to withstand the pressure of Jupiter.

He stared, astounded, at the waterfall and swiftly his mind took the many colours and placed them in their exact sequence in the spectrum. Just like that. Just out of blue sky. Out of nothing, for he knew nothing either of metals or of colours.

"Towser," he cried. "Towser, something's happening to us!"

"Yeah, I know," said Towser.

"It's our brains," said Fowler. "We're using them, all of them, down to the last hidden corner. Using them to figure out things we should have known all the time. Maybe the brains of Earth things naturally are slow and foggy. Maybe we are the morons of the universe. Maybe we are fixed so we have to do things the hard way."

And, in the new sharp clarity of thought that seemed to grip him, he knew that it would not only be the matter of colours in a waterfall or metals that would resist the pressure of Jupiter, he sensed other things, things not yet quite clear. A vague whispering that hinted of greater things, of mysteries beyond the pale of human thought, beyond even the pale of human imagination. Mysteries, fact, logic built on reasoning. Things that any brain should know if it used all its reasoning power.

"We're still mostly Earth," he said. "We're just beginning to learn a few of the things we are to know—a few of the things that were kept from us as human beings, perhaps because we were human beings. Because our human bodies were poor bodies. Poorly equipped for thinking, poorly equipped in certain senses that one has to have to know. Perhaps even lacking in certain senses that arc necessary to true knowledge."

He stared back at the dome, a tiny black thing dwarfed by the distance.

Back there were men who couldn't see the beauty that was Jupiter. Men who thought that swirling clouds and lashing rain obscured the face of the planet. Unseeing human eyes. Poor eyes. Eyes that could not see the beauty in the clouds, that could not see through the storms. Bodies that could not feel the thrill of trilling music stemming from the rush of broken water.

Men who walked alone, in terrible loneliness, talking with their tongue like Boy Scouts wigwagging out their messages, unable to reach out and touch one another's mind as he could reach out and touch Towser's mind. Shut off forever from that personal, intimate contact with other living things.

He, Fowler, had expected terror inspired by alien things out here on the surface, had expected to cower before the threat of unknown things, had steeled himself against disgust of a situation that was not of Earth.

But instead he had found something greater than Man had ever known. A swifter, surer body. A sense of exhilaration, a deeper sense of life. A sharper mind. A world of beauty that even the dreamers of the Earth had not yet imagined.

"Let's get going," Towser urged.

"Where do you want to go?"

"Anywhere," said Towser. "Just start going and see where we end up. I have a feeling... well, a feeling—"

"Yes, I know," said Fowler.

For he had the feeling, too. The feeling of high destiny. A certain sense of greatness. A knowledge that somewhere off beyond the horizons lay adventure and things greater than adventure.

Those other five had felt it, too. Had felt the urge to go and see, the compelling sense that here lay a life of fullness and of knowledge.

That, he knew, was why they had not returned.

"I won't go back," said Towser.

"We can't let them down," said Fowler.

Fowler took a step or two, back toward the dome, then stopped.

Back to the dome. Back to that aching, poison-laden body he had left. It hadn't seemed aching before, but now he knew it was.

Back to the fuzzy brain. Back to muddled thinking. Back to the flapping mouths that formed signals others understood. Back to eyes that now would be worse than no sight at all. Back to squalor, back to crawling, back to ignorance.

"Perhaps some day," he said, muttering to himself.

"We got a lot to do and a lot to see," said Towser. "We got a lot to learn. We'll find things—"

Yes, they could find things. Civilizations, perhaps. Civilizations that would make the civilization of Man seem puny by comparison. Beauty and more important—an understanding of that beauty. And a comradeship no one had ever known before—that no man, no dog had ever known before.

And life. The quickness of life after what seemed a drugged existence.

"I can't go back," said Towser.

"Nor I," said Fowler.

"They would turn me back into a dog," said Towser.

"And me," said Fowler, "back into a man."

THE CURIOUS ASPECT OF ONE OF SATURN'S PHASES
VIEWED FROM ONE OF ITS SATELLITES

SATURN

How Beautiful with Banners   James Blish

Saturn, with its stunning ring system, is perhaps the one planet everyone can visualize. It was the last of the five major planets known to the ancients, originally called Phainon by the Greeks, meaning the Shining One. The Romans, however, named it Saturn, after the god of the harvest, and by back reference the Greeks then called it Kronos, the father of Zeus. It is another gas giant and though smaller than Jupiter, between them the two account for 92% of all the planetary mass of the solar system.

Galileo was the first to observe Saturn through a telescope in 1610, and though his was not powerful enough to detect the rings he did observe two anomalies which he assumed must be satellites. When he looked again in 1612, they were not there and he presumed he had made a mistake. In 1656 Christian Huygens, who had discovered the satellite Titan the year before, noticed the phenomenon Galileo had seen but his telescope was still not powerful enough to resolve the image. He wondered whether Saturn had a succession of satellites orbiting the planet in much the same plane, and when he published his findings in 1659, he decided these were not moons but a ring. Huygens also reasoned that Galileo lost track of them because when the rings are edge on to the Earth they are almost invisible. Although the main rings span over 63,000km (nearly 40,000 miles) they are little more than ten metres (about 30 feet) thick.

When Cassini took up the study of Saturn in the 1670s, his telescope was powerful enough to observe the rings and to see a gap, which is called the Cassini division to this day. It has since been discovered that within the ring system are a series of small satellites, called "shepherd moons", and their gravitational hold keeps the rings in order. We now know that Jupiter, Uranus and Neptune also have rings, but none as spectacular as Saturn's. The rings are made up of billions of small rocks of water ice. Isaac Asimov made use of this in "The Martian Way" (1952) in which huge blocks of ice are taken from Saturn to Mars for a supply of water.

Saturn's atmosphere, like Jupiter's, consists mostly of hydrogen (96%) and helium (over 3%). Saturn probably has a rocky core of iron-nickel surrounded by a layer of metallic hydrogen.

The current estimate is that Saturn has eighty-two moons, but only seven are of any significant size. In their order from the planet they are Mimas, Enceladus, Tethys, Dione, Rhea, Titan and Iapetus. Titan is the second largest moon in the solar system and, like Ganymede, is larger than Mercury. It is the only moon to have a dense atmosphere, composed almost entirely of nitrogen. Both Titan and Enceladus are favoured as the likeliest worlds in the solar system to harbour life.

In his satire on egocentricism, *Micromegas* (1752), the French luminary Voltaire has a giant from Sirius accompanied by a lesser giant from Saturn visit Earth, where the humans are almost too insignificant to be seen without aid. The scientist Humphrey Davy, remembered almost solely for his miners' safety lamp, but responsible for so much more, was fascinated by scientific speculation. In *Consolations in Travel* (1830) he describes truly alien inhabitants of Saturn, with wings and long snouts, who create synthetic food in liquid pillars and use the clouds for artistic expression. Saturn is an abode of the spirits of the dead in John Jacob Astor's *A Journey in Other Worlds* (1894), whilst in George Griffith's *A Honeymoon in Space* (1901), Lord Redgrave and his wife discover that Saturn's atmosphere is more like an ocean filled with gigantic vegetation and uncanny monsters. These texts show that from the start Saturn was seen as unusual.

Saturn was not favoured so much by the pulp writers and only a few stories rose above formulaic adventure. The best was "Mad Robot" (1936) by Raymond Z. Gallun. It begins on the satellite Callisto where living, perhaps even intelligent crystals, are being destroyed by miners. One of the miners, who has sympathy for the Crystal Folk, leaves Callisto but his spaceship is taken over by the onboard robot who forces a landing on Saturn. The robot has brought along seeds of the Crystal Folk and it ensures that these are planted on Saturn, which is otherwise barren, and thereby save their lives. In the sardonic "The Men Without Shadows" (1933), Stanton Coblentz has Earth invaded by natives of Saturn, which are humanoid in shape but gaseous, but they leave because Earth is not worth saving. Also of interest is "Hermit of Saturn's Rings" (1940) by Neil R. Jones where the crew of a spaceship is wiped out by a strange gas except for one crew member who tries to survive as his ship is trapped in the ring system. Jones predicted some of the larger moonlets, as he called them, which orbit within the ring system.

Writers were more interested in the moons, especially Titan, although all too often they were seen as the home of hostile natives or the refuge of pirates. Of slightly more originality was "Creatures of Vibration" (1932) by Harl Vincent where strange vibrations from Saturn's rings corrupt the natives of Titan unless they can shield themselves. Stanley G. Weinbaum, who delighted in imagining strange creatures suited to their environment, filled Titan with all manner of dangerous beings in "Flight on Titan" (1935) including ice ants, whiplash trees, a knife-kite and the dreaded threadworm, which lulls its victims to sleep.

As more data emerged about Titan and its sister satellites, so the number of books increased. Alan E. Nourse's *Trouble on Titan* (1954), written for young adults, was well researched for its day. Besides a small silicon life-form, Titan contains a special element, ruthenium, which is important to Earth for its energy supply. But the miners of Titan rebel and demand rights whilst holding back a secret which will help mankind travel beyond the solar system.

Ben Bova, who has a fascination for the entire solar system, first explored the moon in "The Towers of Titan" (1962), later incorporated into the novel *As on a Darkling Plain* (1972). Titan poses a mystery as the moon contains gigantic towers built aeons before by an alien race. Despite its title, Kurt Vonnegut's *The Sirens of Titan* (1959) is only partly set on the moon, though it plays a key role because it is here that an alien has been stranded for millennia and who is going to become important for mankind.

Writers continued to imagine what alien life might exist on Saturn or its moons. One such for Titan will be found in the story reprinted here, James Blish's "How Beautiful with Banners" (1966). In *Titan* (1979) and its sequels John Varley imagines a vast intelligence, called Gaea, that orbits Saturn and provides a home for other creatures, notably the centaur-like Titanides. The book should not be confused with *Titan* (1997) by Stephen Baxter where a few explorers survive massive odds to reach Titan, hoping to find evidence of life, but instead find it a bleak world trapped in its own prehistory. The surviving explorers seed their own bacteria on the moon in the hope of creating life and, several billion years later, we discover the results. Robert L. Forward's *Saturn Rukh* (1997) has an expedition seeking to harvest helium from Saturn and encountering a giant bird-like creature in Saturn's atmosphere which will prove their only hope of survival.

Saturn has always seemed so strange that authors have struggled to produce material that will reflect the planet's uniqueness, and now that its moons are proving so important, writers are paying even more interest to the planet and its children.

Although James Blish (1921–1975) sold his first story in 1940, it was not until the 1950s that he established himself as a writer of significance with a spectrum of stories providing sound scientific thinking to many of science fiction's concepts. Perhaps his most challenging by confronting religious doctrine was *A Case of Conscience* (1958), where an alien race seems to have achieved a state of grace without any concept of God or original sin. His Okie series, which began with "Okie" (1950), saw the invention of an antigravity device, known as a spindizzy, which enabled entire cities to take to the stars. The various episodes were later collected in the omnibus *Cities in Flight* (1970), one of the cornerstone volumes of science fiction. Blish also explored the idea of pantropy, a term he coined to describe the adaptation of humans to a planetary environment. This began with "Surface Tension" (1952), in which microscopic aquatic humans are genetically engineered in order to survive on one particular world.

The stories in this series were collected as *The Seedling Stars* (1957). Towards the end of Blish's all-too-short life he became extensively involved in the novelization of the *Star Trek* television series, so contributed less and less original new fiction, but amongst them was the following story which shows that his creativity had not abandoned him.

FEELING AS NAKED AS A PEPPERMINT SOLDIER IN HER transparent film wrap, Dr. Ulla Hillstrøm watched a flying cloak swirl away toward the black horizon with a certain consequent irony. Although nearly transparent itself in the distant dim arc-light flame that was Titan's sun, the fluttering creature looked warmer than what she was wearing, for all that reason said it was at the same minus 316° F. as the thin methane it flew in. Despite the virus space-bubble's warranted and eerie efficiency, she found its vigilance—itself probably as nearly alive as the flying cloak was—rather difficult to believe in, let alone to trust.

The machine—as Ulla much preferred to think of it—was inarguably an improvement on the old-fashioned pressure suit. Made (or more accurately, cultured) of a single colossal protein molecule, the vanishingly thin sheet of life-stuff processed gases, maintained pressure, monitored radiation through almost the whole of the electromagnetic spectrum, and above all did not get in the way. Also, it could not be cut, punctured or indeed sustain any damage short of total destruction; macroscopically it was a single, primary unit, with all the physical integrity of a crystal of salt or steel.

If it did not actually think, Ulla was grateful; often it almost seemed to, which was sufficient. Its primary drawback for her was that much of the time it did not really seem to be there.

Still, it seemed to be functioning; otherwise Ulla would in fact have been as solid as a stick of candy, toppled forever across the confectionery whiteness that frosted the knife-edged stones of this cruel moon, layer upon layer. Outside—only a perilous few inches from the lightly clothed warmth of her skin—the brief gust the cloak had been soaring on died, leaving behind a silence so cataleptic that she could hear the snow creaking in a mockery of motion. Impossible though it was to comprehend, it was getting still colder out there. Titan was swinging out across Saturn's orbit toward eclipse, and the apparently fixed sun was secretly going down, its descent sensed by the snows no matter what her Earthly sight, accustomed to the nervousness of living skies, tried to tell her. In another two Earth days it would be gone, for an eternal week.

At the thought, Ulla turned to look back the way she had come that morning. The virus bubble flowed smoothly with the motion and the stars became brighter as it compensated for the fact that the sun was now at her back. She still could not see the base camp, of course. She had strayed too far for that, and in any event, except for a few wiry palps, it was wholly underground.

Now there was no sound but the creaking of the methane snow, and nothing to see but a blunt, faint spearhead of hazy light, deceptively like an Earthly aurora or the corona of the sun, pushing its way from below the edge of the cold into the indifferent company of the stars. Saturn's rings were rising, very slightly awaver in the dark blue air, like the banners of a spectral army. The idiot face of the gas giant planet itself, faintly striped with meaningless storms, would be glaring down at her before she could get home if she did not get herself in motion soon. Obscurely disturbed, Dr. Hillstrøm faced front and began to unload her sled.

The touch and clink of the sampling gear cheered her, a little, even in this ultimate loneliness. She was efficient—many years, and a good many suppressed impulses, had seen to that; it was too late for temblors, especially so far out from the sun that had warmed her Stockholm streets and her silly friendships. All those null adventures were gone now like a sickness. The phantom embrace of the virus suit was perhaps less satisfying—only perhaps—but it was much more reliable. Much more reliable; she could depend on that.

Then, as she bent to thrust the spike of a thermocouple into the wedding-cake soil, the second flying cloak (or was it the same one?) hit her in the small of the back and tumbled her into nightmare.

II

With the sudden darkness there came a profound, ambiguous emotional blow—ambiguous, yet with something shockingly familiar about it. Instantly exhausted, she felt herself go flaccid and unstrung, and her mind, adrift in nowhere, blurred and spun downward too into trance.

The long fall slowed just short of unconsciousness, lodged precariously upon a shelf of dream, a mental buttress founded four years in the past—a long distance, when one recalls that in a four-dimensional plenum every second of time is 186,000 miles of space. The memory was curiously inconsequential to have arrested her, let alone supported her: not of her home, of her few triumphs or even of her aborted marriage, but of a sordid little encounter with a reporter that she had talked herself into at the Madrid genetics conference, when she herself was already an associate professor, a Swedish government delegate, a 25-year-old divorcée, and altogether a woman who should have known better.

But better than what? The life of science even in those days had been almost by definition the life of the eternal campus exile. There was so much to learn—or, at least, to show competence in—that people who wanted to be involved in the ordinary, vivid concerns of human beings could not stay with it long, indeed often could not even be recruited. They turned aside from the prospect with a shudder or even a snort of scorn. To prepare for the sciences had become a career in indefinitely protracted adolescence, from which one awakened fitfully to find one's adult self in the body of a stranger. It had given her no pride, no self-love, no defences of any sort; only a queer kind of virgin numbness, highly dependent upon familiar surroundings and unvalued habits, and easily breached by any normally confident siege in print, in person, anywhere—and remaining just as numb as before when the spasm of fashion, politics or romanticism had swept by and left her stranded, too easy a recruit to have been allowed into the centre of things or even considered for it.

Curious, most curious that in her present remote terror she should find even a moment's rest upon so wobbly a pivot. The Madrid incident had not been important; she had been through with it almost at once. Of course, as she had often told herself, she had never been promiscuous, and had often described the affair, defiantly, as that single (or at worst, second) test of the joys of impulse which any woman is entitled to have in her history. Nor had it really been that joyous. She could not now recall the boy's face, and remembered how he had felt primarily because he had been in so casual and contemptuous a hurry.

But now that she came to dream of it, she saw with a bloodless, lightless eye that all her life, in this way and in that, she had been repeatedly seduced by the inconsequential. She had nothing else to remember even in this hour of her presumptive death. Acts have consequences, a thought told her, but not ours; we have done, but never felt. We are no more alone on Titan, you and I, than we have ever been. *Basta, per carita!*—so much for Ulla.

Awakening in the same darkness as before, Ulla felt the virus bubble snuggling closer to her blind skin, and recognized the shock that had so regressed her—a shock of recognition, but recognition of something she had never felt herself. Alone in a Titanic snowfield, she had eavesdropped on an...

No. Not possible. Sniffling, and still blind, she pushed the cosy bubble away from her breasts and tried to stand up. Light flushed briefly around her, as though the bubble had cleared just above her forehead and then clouded again. She was still alive, but everything else was utterly problematical. What had happened to her? She simply did not know.

Therefore, she thought, begin with ignorance. No one begins anywhere else... but I did not know even that, once upon a time.

Hence:

III

Though the virus bubble ordinarily regulated itself, there was a control box on her hip—actually an ultra-short-range microwave transmitter—by which it could be modulated against more special environments than the bubble itself could cope with alone. She had never had to use it before, but she tried it now.

The fogged bubble cleared patchily, but it would not stay cleared. Crazy moirès and herringbone patterns swept over it, changing direction repeatedly, and, outside, the snowy landscape kept changing colour like a delirium. She found, however, that by continuously working the frequency knob on her box—at random, for the responses seemed to bear no relation to the Braille calibrations on the dial—she could maintain outside vision of a sort in pulses of two or three seconds each.

This was enough to show her, finally, what had happened. There was a flying cloak around her. This in itself was unprecedented; the cloaks had never attacked a man before, or indeed paid any of them the least attention during their brief previous forays. On the other hand, this was the first time anyone had ventured more than five or ten minutes outdoors in a virus suit.

It occurred to her suddenly that insofar as anything was known about the nature of the cloaks, they were in some respect much like the bubbles. It was almost as though the one were a wild species of the other.

It was an alarming notion and possibly only a metaphor, containing as little truth as most poetry. Annoyingly, she found herself wondering if, once she got out of this mess, the men at the base camp would take to referring to it as "the cloak and suit business."

The snowfield began to turn brighter; Saturn was rising. For a moment the drifts were a pale straw colour, the normal hue of Saturn light through an atmosphere; then it turned a raving Kelly green. Muttering, Ulla twisted the potentiometer dial, and was rewarded with a brief flash of normal illumination which was promptly overridden by a torrent of crimson lake, as though she were seeing everything through a series of photographic colour separations.

Since she could not help this, she clenched her teeth and ignored it. It was much more important to find out what the flying cloak had done to her bubble, if she were to have any hope of shucking the thing.

There was no clear separation between the bubble and the Titanian creature. They seemed to have blended into a melange which was neither one nor the other, but a sort of coarse burlesque of both. Yet the total surface area of the integument about her did not seem to be any greater—only more ill-fitting, less responsive to her own needs. Not much less; after all, she was still alive, and any really gross insensitivity to the demands and cues of her body would have been instantly fatal. But there was no way to guess how long the bubble would stay even that obedient. At the moment the wild thing that had enslaved it was perhaps dangerous to the wearer only if she panicked, but the change might well be progressive, pointed ultimately toward some saturnine equivalent of the shirt of Nessus.

And that might be happening very rapidly. She might not be allowed the time to think her way out of this fix by herself. Little though she wanted any help from the men at the base camp, and useless though she was sure they would prove, she had damn well better ask for it now, just in case.

But the bubble was not allowing any radio transmission through its roiling unicell wall today. The earphone was dead; not even the hiss of the stars came through it—only an occasional pop of noise that was born of entropy loss in the circuits themselves.

She was cut off. *Nun denn, allein!*

With the thought, the bubble cloak shifted again around her. A sudden pressure at her lower abdomen made her stumble forward over the crisp snow, four or five steps. Then it was motionless once more, except within itself.

That it should be able to do this was not surprising, for the cloaks had to be able to flex voluntarily at least a little to catch the thermals they rode, and the bubble had to be able to vary its dimensions and surface tension over a wide range to withstand pressure changes, outside and in, and do it automatically. No, of course the combination would be able to move by itself. What was disquieting was that it should want to.

Another stir of movement in the middle distance caught her eye: a free cloak, seemingly riding an updraught over a fixed point. For a moment she wondered what on that ground could be warm enough to produce so localized a thermal. Then, abruptly, she realized that she was shaking with hatred, and fought furiously to drive the spasm down, her fingernails slicing into her naked palms.

A raster of jagged black lines, like a television interference pattern, broke across her view and brought her attention fully back to the minutely solipsistic confines of her dilemma. The wave of emotion, nevertheless, would not quite go away, and she had a vague but persistent impression that it was being imposed from outside, at least in part—a cold passion she was interpreting as fury because its real nature, whatever it was, had no necessary relevance to her own imprisoned soul. For all that it was her own life and no other that was in peril, she felt guilty, as though she were eavesdropping, and as angry with herself as with what she was overhearing, yet burning as helplessly as the forbidden lamp in the bedchamber of Psyche and Eros.

Another metaphor—but was it after all so far-fetched? She was a mortal present at the mating of inhuman essences; mountainously far from home; borne here like invisible lovers upon the arms of the wind; empalaced by a whole virgin-white world, over which flew the banners of a high god and a father of gods and, equally appropriately, Venus was very far away from whatever love was being celebrated here.

What ancient and coincidental nonsense! Next she would be thinking herself degraded at the foot of some cross.

Yet the impression, of an eerie tempest going on just slightly outside any possibility of understanding what it was, would not pass away. Still worse, it seemed to mean something, to be important, to mock her with subtle clues to matters of great moment, of which her own present trap was only the first and not necessarily the most significant.

And suppose that all these impressions were in fact not extraneous or irrelevant, but did have some import—not just as an abstract puzzle, but to that morsel of displaced life that was Ulla Hillstrøm? No matter how frozen her present world, she could not escape the fact that from the moment the cloak had captured her she had been simultaneously gripped by a Sabbat of specifically erotic memories, images, notions, analogies, myths, symbols and frank physical sensations, all the more obtrusive because they were both inappropriate and disconnected. It might well have to be faced that a season of love can fall due in the heaviest weather—and never mind what terrors flow in with it or what deep damnations. At the very least, it was possible that somewhere in all this was the clue that would help her to divorce herself at last even from this violent embrace.

But the concept was preposterous enough to defer consideration of it if there were any other avenues open, and at least one seemed to be: the source of the thermal. The virus bubble, like many of the Terrestrial microorganisms to which it was analogous, could survive temperatures well above boiling, but it seemed reasonable to assume that the flying cloaks, evolved on a world where even words congealed, might be sensitive to a relatively slight amount of heat.

Now, could she move of her own volition inside this shroud? She tried a step. The sensation was tacky, as though she were ploughing in thin honey, but it did not impede her except for a slight imposed clumsiness which experience ought to obviate. She was able to mount the sled with no trouble.

The cogs bit into the snow with a dry, almost inaudible squeaking and the sled inched forward. Ulla held it to as slow a crawl as possible, because of her interrupted vision.

The free cloak was still in sight, approximately where it had been before, insofar as she could judge against this featureless snowscape; which was fortunate, since it might well be her only flag for the source of the thermal, whatever it was.

A peculiar fluttering in her surroundings—a whisper of sound, of motion, of flickering in the light—distracted her. It was as though her compound sheath were trembling slightly. The impression grew slowly more pronounced as the sled continued to lurch forward. As usual there seemed to be nothing she could do about it, except, possibly, to retreat; but she could not do that either, now; she was committed. Outside, she began to hear the soft soughing of a steady wind.

The cause of the thermal, when she finally reached it, was almost bathetic—a pool of liquid. Placid and deep blue, it lay inside a fissure in a low, heart-shaped hummock, rimmed with feathery snow. It looked like nothing more or less than a spring, though she did not for a moment suppose that the liquid could be water. She could not see the bottom of it; evidently it was welling up from a fair depth. The spring analogy was probably completely false; the existence of anything in a liquid state on this world had to be thought of as a form of vulcanism. Certainly the column of heat rising from it was considerable; despite the thinness of the air, the wind here nearly howled. The free cloak floated up and down, about a hundred feet above her, like the last leaf of a long, cruel autumn. Nearer home, the bubble cloak shook with something comically like subdued fury.

Now, what to do? Should she push boldly into that cleft, hoping that the alien part of the bubble cloak would be unable to bear the heat? Close up, that course now seemed foolish, as long as she was ignorant of the real nature of the magma down there. And besides, any effective immersion would probably have to surround at least half of the total surface area of the bubble, which was not practicable—the well was not big enough to accommodate it, even supposing that the compromised virus suit did not fight back, as in the pure state it had been obligated to do. On the whole she was reluctantly glad that the experiment was impossible, for the mere notion of risking a new immolation in that problematical well horrified her.

Yet the time left for decision was obviously now very short, even supposing—as she had no right to do—that the environment-maintaining functions of the suit were still in perfect order. The quivering of the bubble was close to being explosive, and even were it to remain intact, it might shut her off from the outside world at any second.

The free cloak dipped lower, as if in curiosity. That only made the trembling worse. She wondered why.

Was it possible—was it possible that the thing embracing her companion was jealous?

I V

There was no time left to examine the notion, no time even to sneer at it. Act—act! Forcing her way off the sled, she stumbled to the well and looked frantically for some way of stopping it up. If she could shut off the thermal, bring the free cloak still closer—but how?

Throw rocks. But were there any? Yes, there, there were two, not very big, but at least she could move them. She bent stiffly and tumbled them into the crater.

The liquid froze around them with soundless speed. In seconds, the snow rimming the pool had drawn completely over it, like lips closing, leaving behind only a faint dimpled streak of shadow on a white ground.

The wind moaned and died, and the free cloak, its hems outspread to the uttermost, sank down as if to wrap her in still another deadly swath. Shadow spread around her; the falling cloak, its colour deepening, blotted Saturn from the sky, and then was sprawling over the beautiful banners of the rings—

The virus bubble convulsed and turned black, throwing her to the frozen ground beside the hummock like a bead doll. A blast of wind squalled over her.

Terrified, she tried to curl into a ball. The suit puffed up around her.

Then at last, with a searing invisible wrench at its contained kernel of space-time which burned out the control box instantly, the single creature that was the bubble cloak tore itself free of Ulla and rose to join its incomplete fellow.

In the single second before she froze forever into the livid backdrop of Titan, she failed even to find time to regret what she had never felt, for she had never known it, and only died as she had lived, an artifact of successful calculation. She never saw the cloaks go flapping away downwind—nor could it ever have occurred to her that she had brought heterosexuality to Titan, thus beginning that long evolution the end of which, sixty millions of years away, no human being would see.

No, her last thought was for the virus bubble, and it was only two words long:

You philanderer—

Almost on the horizon, the two cloaks, the two Titanians, flailed and tore at each other, becoming smaller and smaller with distance. Bits and pieces of them flaked off and fell down the sky like ragged tears. Ungainly though the cloaks normally were, they courted even more clumsily.

Beside Ulla, the well was gone; it might never have existed. Overhead, the banners of the rings flew changelessly, as though they too had seen nothing—or perhaps, as though in the last six billion years they had seen everything, siftings upon siftings in oblivion, until nothing remained but the banners of their own mirrored beauty.

IN THE SKY OF URANUS, THE SUN IS NO MORE THAN A LARGE LUMINOUS
POINT, COMPARED TO THE SUN AS SEEN FROM THE EARTH.

URANUS

Where No Man Walks E.R. James

In March 1781 the astronomer William Herschel believed he had discovered a new comet, but the closer he studied it the more he realized this was no comet, but a planet—the first ever to be discovered. In thinking of a name, and tugging his forelock to his patron King George III, he called it *Georgium Sidus*, "George's Star". Although out of keeping with the classical names of all the other planets the name survived for a surprisingly long time, though a year after Herschel's discovery Johann Bode proposed an alternative, Uranus, after *Ouranos*, who in Greek mythology was the father of Kronos (Saturn). Bode's suggestion eventually won, but it was not until 1850 that a consensus was reached.

While the original name remained, an English satirist, known only by his alias Vivenair, issued a pamphlet called *A Journey lately performed through the Air in an Aerostatic Globe...to the Newly Discovered Planet, Georgium Sidus* (1784). One of the first stories to use a balloon as a mode of transport—the Montgolfier Brothers had made their momentous ascent just the year before—it tells us nothing about the nature of the planet. It was an excuse for poking fun at the chaotic nature of the king's government.

The planet featured little in fiction over the next one hundred and fifty years, no doubt because the accepted name upset Victorian sensitivities. Whichever way it was pronounced it either sounded like "your anus" or "urinous" ("urine-like"). If Bode had kept the original spelling, pronounced Oo-ran-os, we might have had more fiction.

Uranus, the coldest planet in the solar system, is classified as an ice-giant, for although its atmosphere is predominantly hydrogen and helium it includes crystals of ammonia ice. Its surface temperature averages -200°C, but an average is meaningless because Uranus, unique amongst planets, revolves on its side. That means that instead of spinning in its orbit, it rolls along. As it orbits the Sun, which takes 84 years, the south pole faces the Sun for 42 years and the north pole for another 42. Just why Uranus is tilted like this has yet to be fully explained but it is suggested that early in its formation the planet collided with a large object or dwarf planet. The same axial tilt applies to its moons, which suggests that these were formed after Uranus was shifted. It is currently believed that Uranus has twenty-seven moons, but only five have any significant mass: Miranda, Ariel, Umbriel, Titania and Oberon. None is especially big. The largest is Titania, with a diameter of 1,578km (980 miles), or half the width of our Moon.

Uranus is sometimes mentioned in passing in early cosmic tours. Francis Ridley, for example, in *The Green Machine* (1926), which has one of the most preposterous of all space machines—an enhanced bicycle—has Uranus boasting an advanced civilization of giant spiders. Stanley Weinbaum, delighting as ever in his alien flora and fauna, explores Uranus in "The Planet of Doubt" (1935), one of his lesser efforts. He allows Uranus an oxygen-argon atmosphere and a planet shrouded in mist with strange moth-like creatures in the upper atmosphere and their caterpillars on the ground. One fact Weinbaum did get right, to a degree, were the strong winds on Uranus.

The following story, "Where No Man Walks" (1952) by E.R. James, is one of the rare short stories from the 1950s featuring Uranus. Even in the 1960s it was uncommon to land on the planet. Fritz Leiber used Uranus's gravity in "The Snowbank Orbit" (1962) to allow a dangerous braking manoeuvre in the planet's atmosphere to evade pursuers. In the young-adult book *First Contact?* (1971) Hugh Walters has explorers tracking the source of a radio signal from Ariel and discovering an alien vessel.

Of more recent short fiction, "Into the Miranda Rift" (1993) by G. David Nordley, is an adventure on a grand scale where explorers on Miranda find themselves trapped by a quake and have to work their way through the interior of the moon to escape. In "Into the Blue Abyss" (1999), Geoffrey A. Landis takes us on a daring plunge into the atmosphere of Uranus to discover slow-motion life.

Uranus still hides its mysteries and its rarity in fiction makes any story a treasure.

Ernest Rayer James (1920–2012) was a regular and reliable contributor to the British science-fiction magazines but who was never able to secure book publication for any of his works. As a consequence, although he continued to write for over fifty years, he is only remembered by a dwindling body of British sf fans. His first story, "Prefabrication" (1947) in the short-lived magazine *Fantasy*, was about synthetic life. He returned to the idea of artificial intelligence in his only book-length work, "Robots Don't Weep" (1952). Several of his stories are set on the planets of the solar system; "Ride the Twilight Rail" (1953) on Mercury, "Made on Mars" (1957) on the Red Planet, "Blaze of Glory" (1954) on an asteroid heading towards the Sun, and "Training Area" (1958) on Jupiter. The following, though, is one of those rare stories set on Uranus. By day, James was a postman, a job he found ideally suited to creating story plots in his head while he pounded his route around Skipton in Yorkshire.

N THE ADMINISTRATION OFFICE OF THE URANUS
Opencast Mining Corporation, a bell trilled.

Derrick Crocker, resting thoughtfully in the straps of his mechanical limbs, lifted his head. A jerk of his stomach muscles set one of the caterpillar tracks that served him for legs in brief motion. A pull of his shoulder muscles lifted his metal arms to the wall rail to steady himself. He leaned forward.

At the metal desk of the office, Arnold Quillan, lean with the gauntness of those who never put on weight, caught the message container as it came up through the floor from Communications.

He slid out the paper, frowned as he read and reached for the desk pencil. His reply written, he watched the magnetized pencil wriggle back across the desk top to its place.

He sighed and pushed the message back into the container, sending it down.

Derrick let go of the wall rail and his caterpillar tracks carried him into the office. Arnold's deep set eyes watched his approach. "You know," he muttered irrelevantly, "you've got us all beat with those metal and rubber pins of yours." He lifted the bar from across his legs and stood up, catching hold of the wall rail as he did so.

Derrick pointed a metal arm at the hole through to communications. "Message from Munro on the supply ship I suppose?"

"Yes. We've three days left before he gets here." Arnold's face seemed more gaunt than ever. "Do you really think they expect us to increase our shipments of diamonds?"

"What else? Munro's a big noise now, remember. He isn't making a four month's voyage from Mars for the fun of it. We've got to open up that new seam." He urged Arnold towards the control room ramp.

But Arnold resisted the thrust of the metal arm. "But last time…"

"Forget last time." Derrick's square face set like a mask of strength. "I'll not get mangled up again. Don't be a fool."

"Steady, Derrick. Remember I'm Manager—"

"I am remembering, Arnold." Derrick's eyes smouldered sombrely. "And I like it that way. You know well enough that the Three Worlds are building ships just as fast as they can…" He paused, looking over his shoulder out through the observation dome beyond the office. Uranus, from that position beside the desk, filled the entire sky.

Its greenish light coloured the floor and seats of the dome. Its apparent rotation above the mining station was clearly visible as Derrick's gaze passed on where he knew the new mining site to be. There, on a tremendous fold of rock, reaching above the near-solid gases of the lower atmosphere, the scanners had located a new region of blue clay.

Man, with all his marvels, had still not made synthetic jewels of useful size. Here, on this alien world with its enormous pressures and once enormous temperatures there were entire strata of diamonds. Diamonds for tools and engines—and particularly for bearings and spindles on space-going craft that were subjected to the violent, long lasting strains of interplanetary travel.

★

He turned back to Arnold grimly. "The stuff's there, waiting for us. We know it, and the Board knows we know it. Munro will say it nicely, because he worked with us on that first seam, but the fact remains this is a business. If you won't get the stuff, they'll send out someone who will."

"All right," muttered Arnold. "I know. You're the Advisory Engineer." He turned and, with the ease of long practice, shuffled down the ramp below the surface of the inmost moon of Uranus, with only an occasional touch on the wall rail to counteract the almost non-existent gravity.

Derrick, held down to the metal surface by the magnets within his caterpillars, kept easily at the Manager's side.

Neither spoke until they were almost at the in-swinging doors of the lower levels. "We'll try remote, first," said Arnold determinedly.

Derrick shrugged. "You're the Manager."

They thrust open the girdered doors—doors that, in the event of a direct meteor hit on the surface level, would seal automatically—and entered the noise and bustle of the control.

Derrick noted that the shift supervisor had been watching the doors from his central cubicle. Already he was beckoning to the assistant supervisor to take over. News travels fast in a tiny, isolated community such as theirs.

Derrick wondered if the mechanical scouts would be any more use than on the three other tests they'd run since they'd sunk the O.P. the five hundred miles through the atmosphere to the top of the rock fold.

Leaving Arnold to make the final arrangements with the supervisor, he quickened his speed, crossing the floor to the nearer arm of the semi-circle of remote control panels.

None of the operators noticed him. Intent upon the scenes before the machines they operated 80,000 miles below on the storm lashed mountain range, they sweated in tense silence while the work went on.

The excavations group inspector shuffled up to Derrick as he paused to watch over the operators' shoulders. Derrick nodded to him. "Hail worse than usual. What's current speed in this belt?"

"Hundred and two." The inspector's restless eyes flickered briefly at Derrick. "It's washing away all the small stuff for us." He paused as the operator at the No. 4 panel suddenly flung up his arms. "Machines too. Excuse me—"

Derrick sped to the side of the frightened man. One became so immersed in operating the remotes, that nerves, strained by the impression of 'being there,' cracked.

Eyes tightly shut, trembling all over, the man grabbed at Derrick's metal arms. "Help me! Help!" he was moaning.

Derrick snapped him out of it. The inspector slid down into the vacated seat, pressing the button summoning the relief operator.

Derrick watched the shaken man shuffle off. It was no wonder men got top space rates here. Physically there was little danger; mentally the strain was almost beyond human endurance.

He looked up at the master screen picturing the excavation area. Considering the howling gale down there, a lot of rubble was being shifted. But it wasn't good enough. Not to satisfy the boom in ship building. The inspector was running a new "louse" out of the automatic mining garage. "Louse" was a good description. Its segments hugged the uneven ground as, flat and heavy, it churned out of the lee side of the garage.

The relief was shuffling up. Derrick watched the view from the "louse's" TV camera as it went into action beside the others, planting explosives, drawing back, waiting while the blast was swept away in the greenish hail-filled haze, and then jolting forward to bulldoze away debris from the blue-clay covering the diamond seam.

Presently he passed on along the line. Always there was wind, but today it was really bad. And, on Uranus where everything was ten times Earth-size, really bad was incredible. They would be splitting none of the seam, for fear of the diamonds being carried away, until the wind was down to a normal breeze of less than fifty per. It was a good thing there was a back log of jewel fragments to be carried to the automatic rockets shuttling up. All the operators were intent on the scenes before their machines, too absorbed in their tasks to notice him.

At length he looked across at the new, partly assembled semi-circle of remotes that would control operations on the second lode-bearing mountain chain. Mechanics, electricians and electronics men worked over most of its length, but at the right hand arm, Arnold and the supervisor were talking and watching the general scanner of the O.P., as they held on to the rail in front of two fully assembled control panels.

Derrick tracked across to them and ran straight into his position before the panel prepared for him, beside the swivel seat already adjusted for Arnold.

He too looked up at the screen above the panels. Visibility fifty feet: excellent for a depth of three hundred odd miles below the level of the first opencast. Current speed forty m.p.h. H'm. Allowing for the extra pressure of this depth, that was nasty. His eyes glanced at the other instruments recording information transmitted up from the O.P. It was the current speed that was making Arnold hesitate. If the O.P. had been any other shape than a flattened dome, it would have been swept away by the sheer weight of gases compressed to a consistency of light oil.

The scene shuddered and shadows cast by the violent turbulence danced away over the worn surface of the rock, carrying a few loose stones away into the greenish murk.

"See that?" said Arnold tensely.

Derrick nodded. He reached out and cut in power. The eye-level screen of his remote control glowed with a view of the shallow interior of the O.P. Arnold's louse seemed to be at one side...

Derrick looked away. "All right." His own voice seemed far away as his tenseness grew. Half his mind was already down there. "We'll run out a single scout—"

"But Derrick—Derrick, does it stand a chance in that flow of compressed gases?"

"That," muttered Derrick grimly, "is just what we need to know. All the experience we gained at Opencast One may be useless. We have to find out." He settled his torso in the harness and picked up the headphones.

The booming sounds of compressed gases filled his mind as he turned back to the screen.

Now he seemed really there. The concave screen before him was the windscreen of the scout. Ten feet before him, the curved wall of the O.P. was billowing resiliently out, more like canvas than the metal sheets it actually was.

He set his mouth, braced himself and flung the switch to open the panel on the lee side of the O.P.

It slid away, showing the twisting, violent eddies racing away into the bilious green hell of an atmosphere that was mostly methane, hydrogen and helium. He opened the throttle and the cabin floor swayed with the movement of the jointed segments as they clung low upon the weather-worn rock.

Sound boomed deafeningly as he passed outside. The motor growled behind him with changing load as he cut out the left caterpillar track and turned the twenty foot louse in half its own length, with the segments grating all around the cabin.

Forward, edging out around the side of the O.P. into the teeth of the current. Shadows cast by additional compression, caused by his appearance, smeared the rock with flickering shadows. The louse shuddered, but low built as she was, she crept forward surely.

Clear of the O.P., Derrick sighed with relief. The 3,000 mile depths of the atmosphere above the surface glaciers of Uranus were still and silent, with even the light gases of hydrogen and helium solidified by the vast muffling weight above; only near the comparatively rarified upper levels of the atmosphere—in which they had made their first blue-clay strike—were there storms. At his present level, in spite of the rotational motion of the more or less permanent wind belt above and the gale further disturbing it, friction would always slow current speed to something between the two extremes.

He worked the louse steadily around until she was broadside to the current. Eddies streamed from the curved windscreen, but she held steady. He felt sweat start on his forehead and gather coldly upon his back.

Advancing steadily, he watched distance indicator, gyro-compass and the rock outside by turns.

Suddenly the cracked surface of the blue clay was swaying towards his caterpillars. He ran out on to it and stopped. A probe thrust down and picked up a sample from below the skirt of the louse. He examined it in normal light through an inspection panel between his feet. Blue clay all right. He made a pattern of echo soundings, and the hidden diamond seam a few feet below marked his screen in a curve. This was only the beginning of the strata. It was a fault, not worth working. The problem was to locate the main level of the strata where it approached the surface near enough to be a commercial proposition.

He felt the louse lift uneasily beneath his feet. The dry clay was being powdered by the additional current friction at the side of the louse. Like smoke it was rising over the cabin. He urged the machine forward, echo-sounding as he went, picking his way, thankful as the feathering dust died away, trying to distinguish solid surface from debris choked holes.

Sweat trickled down his back. Surely the current speed was still increasing. How close to exactness were their calculations? Were the echo-sounders functioning properly? So little was known of the behaviour of substances at a pressure such as now surrounded the louse.

The floor heaved sideways, hesitated, heaved. The scene before him tilted dizzily. He was being overturned. The boom of the current over the mountain range suddenly increased beyond all proportion. He clung desperately to the control panel, fighting to get the louse down on her caterpillars. Then he noticed that he was being swept sideways and, knowing now that he was clear of the surface and floating in spite of the leadweight of the louse, he knocked at the cut off switch—

And woke to reality with sweat pouring down his face, his heart pounding wildly, chilled by the fantastic thought of plunging slowly down, down until the louse was crushed flat and he was nothing but a freezing smear upon a crumpled tortoise of metal, down, down, very slowly, pushing between crowded, almost motionless molecules and atoms of gases and "free" substances until, at length… But the depths were unknown even yet—

He wiped his face and looked up at Arnold's anxious face. "No good!" he gasped. "Waste of time—and machines." He wriggled in his straps, easing the set of his limbless torso, trying to reorient himself to actuality.

Arnold nodded. He set down the headphones he had evidently snatched from Derrick's head. "What you need is a good stiff drink."

"You've said it."

They passed in silence through the concrete-lined boring to Accommodation. In Arnold's own quarters, they drank the neat spirit without ceremony. Derrick took a deep breath. "I'll want everything ready for a delayed drop... by six tonight. That'll give me a full day tomorrow. I don't want to be caught by darkness and be frost bitten because my power gets low before I locate the O.P. for return... Not like last time..." He drained his glass.

Arnold's voice sounded strangely far away. "All right, Derrick. I'll see to it." Derrick gave an involuntary shudder. That nightmarish cold down there—

Arnold put a hand on his shoulder. "Sure you're all right?"

"Yes!" Derrick lifted his head with a slow grin. "Yes. And don't you suggest anyone else going. You know I stand the best chance... the way I am—the way Uranus has made me."

Arnold stared at him a moment. Then he turned away, speaking back over his shoulder as he left to make the preparations. "All right. You're the engineer..."

"Yes." Derrick picked up the bottle and glass in his metal claws. But he put them down again. A clear head was what he needed.

He tracked across the corridor to his own quarters. First a shower to cleanse him of sweat, then a light meal and finally rest. He called to his man to unfasten him.

Usually he felt unutterably grateful to medical science for his mechanical arms and legs. But at times like these, waiting, with the snap fastenings of artificially lengthened tendons dangling loosely at the shoulders and bottom of his torso, it was difficult not to be impatient.

But Peters, his personal orderly, was a good man. He would know of the imminent descent, but he said nothing of it. By the time Derrick had been carried into the shower, fitted with his light eating arms, been supplied with an after dinner cigar and brought up to date with Earth sports news, he felt able to relax.

When Arnold came back, he was ready.

At his own suggestion, to save fuss, he was run on a wheelchair through the passages to the spacecraft bay.

By five to six, he had been fitted into the harness within the heavy, transparent globe of the manual operated louse, specially designed for him.

Muscles relaxed, he listened to the final preparations for take off. They would be a few minutes late. Uranus turned upon her axis once every 10 hours 40 minutes. The louse could be depended upon to function perfectly for some 25 hours. But the descent and ascent consumed so much time that a single 5 hour 20 minute period of daylight was all that he could manage on her surface. Every minute might count.

As always he experienced a strange feeling of superiority. Sitting before a remote control, he was as other men. It seemed that he had his arms and legs again. But here, in his own louse, he did not have to transmit his orders to the mechanisms through humanly frail arms and legs. He was actually the nerve-centre of the louse, a real part of it. He could do more than was possible to any other Earth man.

"Nearly ready," said Arnold's voice. "Are you comfortable?"

"Yes." Derrick glanced at the intercom, smiled to himself—even ears of metal and dead stuff were his to command. He looked up at the open hatch above him. "Can you hear me all right?"

Arnold, holding a microphone to his lips, nodded. "Loud and clear." He glanced behind him. "We're clearing out now. In two minutes you'll be on your own. Anything else you want?"

"No thanks. Don't finish that bottle until I get back." Derrick permitted himself a final wriggle within the harness. "You can fill the Gravity suit when you like."

"Right." Arnold signalled to a mechanic out of Derrick's sight. "Here it comes."

The rubber cushions encircling Derrick's lower half swelled to prevent the terrible pull of Uranus from drawing too much blood from his head.

"That's fine," he said.

Arnold waved. "Good luck. Don't spend all day down there!" His head drew back and the hatch swung into place and spun into its grooves, tight.

Derrick flexed his muscles gently, taking the strain on the sprung control wires that were now his limbs. He waited.

"All clear, Derrick," said Arnold's voice. "Fire away."

"So long," said Derrick. He cut in the automatic pilot controlling his descent.

And the springs of his harness strained. The light of the space bay flickered and was gone. The greenish light of Uranus settled into the cabin of the louse. He relaxed again. Velocity of escape from this tiny, inmost moon was so low that no great acceleration was necessary.

The automatic pilot was setting course for the O.P. down there, fifteen degrees of latitude north of the Equator, hidden by the darkness of night, in the second of the northern hemisphere belts, to meet it as it swung around in space, guided by the beam it had been set to transmit.

He glanced at the mushroom-like landing tug ahead of him. The rockets around its rim were all firing steadily and already it was beginning to spin, gaining stability ready for the delayed fall into the incredible depths of the giant planet awaiting him.

After reporting back to Arnold, he settled down to wait, his thoughts going ahead of him. This descent would be no different to the other infrequent maintenance descents to the working open-cast—at least not until he was on the ridge of the mountains so many miles deeper than any man had ever been before.

Slowly, as the hours passed, the mighty, greenish globe of Uranus swelled to meet him. The great moving belts of current, parallel to the equator, slowly spread out, ever widening, and the advancing tide of sunlight crept around the giant planet towards his point of contact. The extreme tilt of its axis was not readily apparent to him with only the blackness of space and the stars and the several moons as reference points.

The swinging of the tug and louse, as the gravity pull of Uranus took over control of them, turned his world about. He watched the planet grow through the rear-pointing TV.

With his heart-beats drumming in his ears and his muscles sagging and his entrails heavy against the pit of his stomach, he struggled to keep his consciousness. Uranus's gravity was so very much greater than Earth's. A giant planet. And he was accustomed to the relative non-gravitational field of the inmost moon—a mere pinhead when compared with its mighty captor.

Adaptation was always an agony, a battle against the terrible sensation of weight. This time it seemed worse than the others.

Sweat started from his skin, soaking into the thin, air-conditioned net of his clothing, steaming into the air of his globe, being drawn out, however, before it could condense on the transparency, by the moisture control.

But, as always, sediment collected on his skin, irritating in spite of the cooling lotions with which he was automatically being sprayed.

His skin crawled, and the itching took his mind off the gravity... And his body, left to itself, came to terms with the alien conditions in the same slow manner as the apparent planetary surface flattened out below him.

While the louse sank into the first, thin breath of the atmosphere, the sound of the rockets braking above him screamed faintly. Ever deepening the sound presently growled. The stars faded from his view in the green opalescence. The jets thundered in the thickening atmosphere, beating down and around him.

Earth's hundred or so miles of atmosphere was the thinnest of planetary clothing by comparison with the muffling depths below him. The green gloom seemed to claim him. The tug straining above tending to lose its reality. The drag and turbulence of warring forces chilled his blood-starved nerves.

In delayed fall, eight hundred miles through the atmosphere to the colossal ridge of the diamond-bearing mountain fold took time. The ultra-steel cable on which his life hung twanged and vibrated in the rush of compressed gases.

The ridge swung up towards him and he came out of his faintness, shocked—as on other, shallower descents into this frigid, storm-torn atmosphere—by the angle at which he fell.

His muscles jerked and jumped as he righted the louse. Her flat shape and the current clamped her down on her tracks just as the tug automatically exploded down its anchors and reeled itself down to stand upon its central spike, to wait his return.

He recovered slowly from the jolt. Radar fixed the direction of the O.P. He made tests, current speed and direction, pressure and the rest, to check the O.P. automatics. Arnold sounded as though trying not to be relieved to hear him after he breathed up his report through the throat microphone.

To test the louse's stability, he drove her forward a few yards. She seemed to undulate normally over the current-smoothed rock. He stopped and reported back up to Arnold.

"It's different being here," he breathed, "with luck an hour should be all I'll need."

"Good," said Arnold's firm voice. "Are you sure the magnetic counterpoises are easing the strain on your muscles?"

Arnold always asked that. Electro-magnets, their pull automatically altering directly in relationship with the pull of gravity, eased the weight of the clips and controls fixed to his muscles. It was the nearest they could yet get to antigravity fields.

Here on the surface of a giant planet, anything helped. Although he was further from the centre of gravity because of the lower average density of such planets, the weakness caused by his own weight was only just bearable.

He cast off from the tug. The segments of the louse grated alarmingly because of their own weight as he drove her forward. Every few yards he halted to peer out at the rolling rock and to rest his trembling muscles.

Current-gusts shuddered over the louse, but his confidence grew. TV tended to magnify the shadows of high-pressure turbulence; actually looking out into the racing green hell was, strangely enough, less frightening.

He reached the sloping skirt of the O.P. It looked like a limpet seen below water; but the pressure of the atmospheric gases were greater than that of water. He thought of the remote-controlled louse that would be still sinking into the depths; but refused to let his mind dwell upon that.

Tracking broadside to the current, he reached the blue clay edge and stopped. Actually looking at the sample through the wall of the globe was reassuring.

On he pressed through the green depths. When debris began to shower around him and the skirt of the louse to lift as before, he pushed the nose down with an up-pointing jet and ground over the fragments filling the hole he could not clearly see.

With solid rock beneath him, he pressed on, echo-sounding as he went. At this extra depth, all remote-controlled lice would have to be fitted with such jets to cut down wastage.

A mile along the ridge from the O.P., the echoes showed a strata harder than rock, twenty feet below the surface.

He tried to estimate its extent, forgetting the shuddering and swaying of the louse in his excitement. He reported back to Arnold triumphantly.

"Good," said Arnold. "We've got your position on the chart. Come on up and we'll move the O.P. and blast down for a test sample with remotes."

"No." Derrick rested in his straps. Fatigue was beginning to tell upon him. But he did not want to have to come down again for a second search. Maintenance trips later would be bad enough.

He picked his spot in the lee of a rise, trundled forward to plant explosives, trundled back.

The shock wave lifted the louse from the rock. Blinded, deafened, shaken, he fought her down again, trundled back. Debris and smoke were twirling away in the murk. He waited for them to clear and stared at the shallow, jagged holes he had torn. Three times he planted explosives and retreated to suffer the terrible concussions of pressurized gases. At last he felt he was deep enough—

"Derrick!" Arnold's voice ripped through his concentration. "Derrick, get back now. Meteorological reports that there's a whirlpool eddying towards you."

"Not at this stage," growled Derrick. "I'll risk it. Maybe it'll eddy away as it came."

"But—" Arnold sighed. "All right. It's your life."

His life. Yes, it was his life. Down here he was something superhuman, a being to challenge the might of this alien world. He jolted down into the fuming crater. Rubble and dust was streaming over the lip, showering on the louse, battering on the ultra-steel segments.

Trembling muscles forced him to wait. With the first signs of gaining strength he drove down into the bottom of the crater. Rock. Hard rock. He hammered down again and again with the sampling arm. Suddenly it slid down easily to its full extent. He operated the sampler.

He withdrew it into the inspection chamber and peered at it with straining, bleared eyes. He blinked and stared again, and the blue clay sample filled his mind with triumph.

Now they could be sure. He turned the louse and mounted the crater wall with the motor all out. Over the lip—

The current lifted the louse. Swaying, clear of the crumpled, shifting rock left by his blasting, the louse rose into the heavy atmosphere. He pulled at the nose-jet control. The current struggled against its power. The louse began to be carried sideways.

But now the nose dipped. The concussion of striking down knocked him silly. He hung dazedly in the harness, fighting the blackout that threatened to rob him of his senses.

At length the red mist cleared from his sight. With sweat rolling off him, fatigue adding its weight to the crushing gravity, he came back to coherence.

A gigantic shadow was lying across him. He looked up in awe. A colossal funnel of whirling turbulence was moving in small circles with ponderous slowness.

Gasping, he realized that he was clear of the rock again. His relaxing muscles had allowed the nose-jet to lapse. He pulled it on again. The louse sank slowly, slowly—oh, so slowly.

He thought of the comparative narrowness of the mountain range. How long had he been out of control? Those terrible depths. No time for any check of position. He doubted whether he would be able to see the needles of his instruments.

He struck rock, bounced on the track springs and went skimming up at a fantastic angle with the blood bursting up into his head.

This was it. Success—and failure. He almost laughed. So Uranus would claim him after all. But not without a struggle. He levelled out with the rock below. Down he thrust again. The louse crashed against the smooth hard surface. Sounded as though her skin was punctured.

Yes. Beneath his feet the bilious gases were whistling in. He almost laughed. How one's thoughts ran riot. Uranus had already claimed his feet and legs and arms.

Pressure would be building up around his last stronghold—this globe. The poisonous gases swirled wildly up before his eyes. He noticed that the windscreen of the cabin was starred and cracked.

Would the globe hold? Would it hold? There seemed nothing to do but wait for the result of this trial of strength. The fantastic column of turbulence that had beaten his attempts to touch down and stay down seemed almost upon him. But it would be further away than it seemed. Refraction of light down here made it seem to lean right over him, blotting out the glow from above.

He could hear its tremendous roar—

Helplessly he waited.

And suddenly he knew that the roar was receding. He began to take stock. And at once amazement filled him. Whirlpool from the friction between the vast current belts or no, he seemed to have kept his position flat on the rock.

He had lifted before... What had been the difference? He caught his breath. Of course. Before, the louse had had the buoyancy of the earth pressure gases within it—now, like a submerged submarine, its tanks were full. His weight must have increased enormously. That last crash had saved him.

The trip back to the tug was steadier than the slow advance from it to the lode.

He felt but for this anticlimax he would have failed to make it in his weakened condition. He gathered up the end of the ultra-steel cable in his harnessing magnet, felt it couple and relaxed. Now the automatics were taking over.

The tug let go its hold upon the rock and rose slowly over him, drawing him after. He felt his last strength slip from him and passed into a state between waking and dreaming.

It was over.

He was waiting in the administration office when Arnold came back from meeting the arrivals from the ship. Munro seemed fatter than before, prosperous, sure of himself. The formal earth clothes he and his two companions wore were like the trappings of another race.

Derrick lifted his metal hand in greeting. "Glad to see you again, Munro."

Munro's smooth face creased into a smile. "Good to see you, old man. Like old times."

Yes, thought Derrick, as the preliminary small talk ebbed and flowed, it was like old times. Munro was being diplomatic with his staff, preparing them for the shock of further demands upon them.

"Well," said Munro at last, as he set down his glass upon the sticky plate before him. "I expect you've guessed that I've not come out all this way just for a drink. I've wanted to come many times, of course—but as it happened I had to wait until I was sent."

Derrick smiled to himself. Now for it. He caught Arnold's eye for a moment. It made them both feel good to be prepared. Poor Arnold. It was hard to wait, Derrick supposed. He would never forget how haggard his chief—his friend—had been as he had feverishly unfastened the harness within the globe without waiting for Derrick to speak.

Arnold suddenly gripped the bar across his legs and sat up straight. "All right, Munro. I think this time we've forestalled you. We've got a new diamond strata ready for opening. It's deeper in than the other, but it's ten times the extent. Almost inexhaustible—It'll take us years to work it out. And the wastage of remotes shouldn't be any higher than in the old opencast. Derrick's discovered a means of making them heavier. We'll be atom-blasting to clear the rock away from it within a week—"

"You have?" Munro turned to his two companions. "Do you hear that, gentlemen? Your task has been made that much easier. See what an example has been set for you to maintain!"

"What?" breathed Derrick. His metal arm reached across the desk, gripping Munro's plump wrist in its claw.

Munro winced. "Steady on, old man."

"Sorry." Derrick let go hurriedly. "What was that you said? What d'you mean?"

"Grand news for you, old man." His eyes almost disappeared in the plumpness of his comfortable face as he smiled at Arnold. "For you too. The Corporation has been scanning Saturn and you both are to be transferred there at twice the salary—"

"Opencasting on Saturn!" gasped Arnold. "You don't mean it?"

"Of course. Saturn is very like Uranus in composition. The same forces have been at work there. We believe that the diamond strata is even thicker. It should be because of the superior size of the planet—"

"My God!" said Arnold. He looked at Derrick with his mouth open.

Derrick licked his lips. Well… it was true he was a freak in the presence of other men. He belonged where no man walked.

As his eyes met Arnold's, a slow smile lifted the corners of his mouth. Arnold's eyes began to twinkle, too. They had been working for the benefit of the newcomers. The joke was on them.

FOR NEPTUNE, THE SUN IS REDUCED IN ASPECT TO A SPARKLING STAR, ITS DIAMETER
APPEARING AROUND 30 TIMES SMALLER THAN IT IS SEEN FROM EARTH.

NEPTUNE

A Baby on Neptune   Clare Winger Harris & Miles J. Breuer

Had Galileo persevered with his observations in 1612 he would have been credited with discovering Neptune, but although a record of Neptune's location was in his notes, he believed it was a star. So, Neptune was lost for another 234 years. After the discovery of Uranus, several scientists realized there were perturbations in its orbit that could only be explained by the gravitational attraction of another body. Urbain Le Verrier calculated this effect and identified where Neptune should be. He encouraged astronomer Johann Galle to search and within hours Galle had found it, on 23 September 1846, exactly where Le Verrier had calculated.

Various names were proposed, and for a while it was known as Le Verrier's planet, but the discoverer eventually named it Neptune, because the planet had a greeny-bluish tinge, suggesting the sea, and Neptune was the Roman god of the sea. The name Le Verrier's planet remained for a while, though, and is referred to as such in the misogynistic *The Triumphs of Woman* (1848) by Charles Rowcroft, where Neptune is inhabited solely by men while women are shunned.

Neptune is larger than Uranus and considerably more active—it's the windiest planet in the solar system. Its primary moon, Triton, is unusual, because it's the only large satellite in the system to orbit its planetary host the wrong way round! This suggests it's a captured moon, probably from the Kuiper Belt, and not a true son of Neptune.

Being the outermost planet, Neptune becomes the front line in the war between the Solar System's Anglo-Saxon Empire and the empire of the Sirians in *The Struggle for Empire* (1900) by Robert W. Cole. Neptune is Earth-like, covered in seas, mountains and towns all under a blue sky. In *Last and First Men* (1930), Olaf Stapledon envisaged Neptune as the last refuge of a distantly evolved human race, billions of years in the future, until an exploding Sun destroys everything. In similar mood John W. Campbell, Jr., foresaw a distant future in "Night" (1935) where mankind is extinct and its machine successors await their last days on Neptune.

The pulpsters liked Neptune. "A Baby on Neptune" (1929) by Clare Winger Harris and Miles J. Breuer, which is reprinted here, is an intriguing puzzle as to how radio signals are being received from an apparently barren world. Henrik Dahl Juve portrayed a tropical Neptune in "The Monsters of Neptune" (1930), apparently heated by large deposits of radium. In "The Universe Wreckers" (1930), Edmond Hamilton has his natives of Neptune trying to save their planet by creating a second sun to warm it. Hitherto heat has been conserved first by encasing Neptune in metal and then, after migrating to its moon Triton, encasing that in metal. The novel-length "The Vanguard to Neptune" (1932) by J.M. Walsh has a host of life on an Earth-like Neptune from vicious intelligent giant birds to alien plants from another world.

Neptune fell out of favour for a while but returned with a vengeance in Piers Anthony's *Macroscope* (1969) where—in a long and convoluted plot—Neptune is converted into a world-ship to pursue the source of a signal from across the galaxy. Neptune's primary moon is the locale for Samuel R. Delany's *Triton* (1976) though it's barely a realistic representation of the world. Delany creates a free and libertarian society which has virtually no rules.

Because it's the last major planet of the solar system Neptune and its moons are seen as a likely place for first contact with aliens. Amongst the recent examples are *Neptune Crossing* (1994), the first of the Chaos Chronicles by Jeffrey A. Carver and *Transcendence* (2010) by Christopher McKitterick.

Neptune may be remote, but for anyone visiting us from afar, it's the first major port of call, a true outpost of empire.

———————————

Clare Winger Harris (1891–1968) was one of the first women contributors to the science-fiction magazines. She sold her first story to *Weird Tales* in 1926, "A Runaway World", which suggests that our solar system is like a subatomic world to a greater macrocosm. She entered a story contest run by *Amazing Stories* and achieved third place with "The Fate of the *Poseidonia*" (1927), wherein Martians are trying to draw water from Earth for their parched world. She contributed twelve stories in total to these early magazines including "The Artificial Man" (1929), where a sportsman gradually replaces parts of his body with mechanical parts and so mutates into a cyborg. She later self-published a collection of most of her stories as *Away from the Here and Now* (1947).

Amongst her work was this one collaboration with the physician Miles J. Breuer (1889–1945). Of Czech descent, Breuer had served with the US Medical Corps during the First World War. He operated his own chemical laboratory, which may have inspired his first story, "The Man Without an Appetite" (1916). Breuer was attracted to the first specialist science-fiction magazine, *Amazing Stories*, in 1926, debuting there with "The Man with the Strange Head" (1927). Over the next decade he wrote another thirty stories, a selection of which was published as *The Man with the Strange Head* (2008).

This story dates from 1929 when the pioneer science-fiction magazine *Amazing Stories* sought to educate its readers on scientific discoveries and their potential, which results in the occasional (now dated) lecture. Bear that in mind because beyond the lecture is a remarkably original idea of alien life.

A DYING WISH

IT MUST BE ADMITTED THAT INTERPLANETARY COMMU-nication is still in a rudimentary stage; nevertheless some aston-ishing developments have already taken place. Beginning with the humble experiments of Hertz in 1887, progress has been variable but uninterrupted. Hundreds of brilliant men have devoted their lifetimes to the work. Episodes of intense human interest can be found along the way of this development. This account deals with one of them.

The story of any great achievement is marked by certain epochs, certain milestones, each of which is associated with the name of a genius. After Hertz came Marconi, who, in about the year 1896, expressed the existing theoretical knowledge in his concrete and workable wireless telegraph. He was followed by deForest, who about 1900 developed the three-electrode vacuum tube, making wireless telephony commercially possible. Then for a half a century nothing startling happened; efforts were devoted chiefly to the increase in transmission power and in the range of radio waves.

It was not until 1967 that Takats at Budapest experimentally confirmed the belief of scientists that radio waves, since they were electromagnetic waves of the same nature as light, could be reflected and refracted. Up to Takats' time we lacked the proper media for this reflection and refraction. Using the gigantic crystals of aluminium developed at the Kansas University by H.K.F. Smith, machining them into shape, Takats succeeded in focusing radio rays as accurately as the light rays from a movie projector are focused on the screen.

With his projection system four miles long, he focused radio waves of intensity receivable on the planet Mars. Two years later signals were picked up from Mars, Venus, and from the direction of both Saturn and Jupiter. That is how fast things moved.

It was demonstrated beyond a doubt that these signals were attempts of intelligent beings to communicate with us. Yet, by the time they were comprehended even vaguely, not one person was alive who had lived at the time of Takat's discovery. In 2099 a young kindergarten teacher, Miss Geneva Hollingsworth, at Corpus Christi, Texas, published a paper in *The Scientific Monthly* that gave the fundamental clue to the messages that had kept coming in over the instruments for one hundred and thirty years. The conceptions of number, size, rhythm, geometry, solar-system position, solar-system period are so simple and now so thoroughly understood that it seems ridiculous that it required more than a century to grasp them.

Though the fundamental conception was simple, the development of actual communication was a terrifically complex and tedious matter. Little Miss Hollingsworth was long dead and gone before the interplanetary code was developed. She would have shrunk terrified from the complicated proportions that her simple idea assumed, had she been able to see it put into practice.

But the year 2300 dawned with a fairly fluent communication going on with Mars, Venus, four of Jupiter's moons and one of Saturn's, and an unsolved mystery with regard to Neptune. Astronomers admitted that the bodies from whom intelligible messages were being received were in such physical condition that inhabitation by intelligent beings was a granted possibility. But, living beings on Neptune! That was hardly conceivable. That bleak and distant planet was too cold and dark. Yet signals came from it. Were they intelligent signals from living beings or not? No one knows. Certainly no one had as yet been able to understand them. They were merely noises in the receivers. Yet they were too uniform, too persistent, too regular to be passed over as accidents or as inorganic phenomena. They demanded an explanation of one kind or another.

Then, in 2345, came the first successful interplanetary voyage. Thirty-five years before a daring explorer by the name of Bjerken had gone in a trans-geodesic coaster to the moon, but had never been seen or heard of again. Consequently now the eyes of the world were turned with eager curiosity in the direction of Rex Dalton, the Kentucky physicist, who, on January 7th, was starting out for Venus. The radios, which were buzzing at the last moment with announcements of the preparations for departure, suddenly gave out the news that the famous English astronomer, Myron Colby, would accompany Dalton on his perilous voyage.

The trip of Dalton and Colby was a memorable one, not only in the annals of astronomy and physical-mathematics but likewise in those of biology, since it proved that man's previous conception, that, if evolution progressed on two different worlds it must necessarily do so along parallel lines, was an erroneous one.

The *Pioneer*, which was the name of Dalton's space coaster, descended to the steaming atmosphere of Venus, and its astonished occupants gazed through the transparent walls at a strange sight. Lying beneath the pale fronds of gigantic, stringy and palm-like vegetation were thousands of huge worms!

Their heads were large and contained points which suggested terminal organs of the special senses. If the aggregation of special-sense end organs constitutes a face, the faces of these things were creepy, repulsive. They were intensely active, twitching and writh-ing and darting back and forth, in and out among each other. They seemed to be engaged in a tremendous activity and even handled a good many blocks and sticks and things among them. The earthmen shuddered and were disgusted at the slimy spectacle.

In a few moments the shell of their vessel was so hot that to save themselves they were compelled to start the refrigerating apparatus they had brought with them, in anticipation of just such a situation. They raised their vessel and cruised about, looking for cities, for intelligent beings, and finding nothing but slimy life, settled again. Near them was another intensely active bunch of worms. Suddenly a message sounded on their radio in the interplanetary code:

"Hello! Are you intelligent beings in the crystal sphere that dropped from the sky?"

Dalton coded back:

"We are humans from the planet Earth. Where can we find you?"

Then the two men gasped in astonishment when their radio said:

"You are among us now, looking at us. Come out. We wish to look at you more closely and see if you are as civilized as we are."

The two scientists looked at each other in puzzled bewilderment.

"We'd better test the atmosphere first," Dalton suggested.

They had come all prepared for this. Between double doors was a compartment into which all accumulating waste had been placed during their space journey. The inner door was opened, the waste material was placed in the chamber and the inner door was closed. Then the outer door was opened by electrical means, and the refuse was thrown out electrically, and the outer door was closed again. This always lowered the pressure, which was again made good by drawing compressed oxygen and nitrogen from cylinders.

Now they had registering thermometers, barometers, and hygrometers and buretts for automatically gathering samples of the outside air, which could be analysed in a few minutes with their equipment. The results of their tests showed that the atmosphere resembled that of the earth, with some excess of carbon dioxide and oxygen; the temperature was 60° Centigrade, the pressure 790 millimetres of mercury, and the humidity 50 per cent.

"We cannot come out," Rex Dalton radioed. "Our bodies will not stand your atmosphere." They had to make some plausible excuse for not coming out.

These were the first scientists to return alive from an interplanetary voyage. Their trip may not have been entirely satisfactory from the standpoint of the romantic reader or the sensational news-spreader, but its scientific significance was epoch-making. It certainly gave the first evidence that intelligent beings can be found under other conditions than ours and in a form other than that which we have learned to know as human.

RECORDING ON THE STEEL TAPE

Professor MacLean still retained all the keenness of his mental powers, although he was ninety-two and confined to bed. Recently his death had been expected every day, for he was so weak that he talked with evident effort. Into his room every morning came Patrick Corrigan, his friend, and his successor at the university.

"Corrigan," the old man said, and the younger man leaned forward to catch the faint words, "this is a great day for me. People give me credit for having had much to do with the building up of interplanetary communication. I would be ready to die now, were it not for that mystery about Neptune. That makes me feel like a failure. But, now these young men have returned from Venus, I feel encouraged. Some day the question of Neptune will be answered."

For a moment the aged man's voice trailed off wearily, then he began again:

"Baffling, mystifying this Neptune business. Those low-pitched, tapping sounds that come through our instruments must mean something. There is a rhythm, a sort of mathematical suggestiveness about them. I could die in peace if I knew what they mean."

Corrigan waited respectfully and somewhat puzzled. He had a solution to propose for the Neptunian mystery and hesitated to present it because of a foolish superstition that he might be thus the cause of Professor MacLean's death. Finally he spoke:

"You followed the radio reports of Dalton and Colby's trip. They landed near Phoenix yesterday I've been pondering on their reports since. Do you remember what they said about the quickness of the worm-people? Doesn't that remind you of the uncomfortable speed with which the Venerian messages come in? Only experts can make anything of them. Now, Mars is slower than we are; quite easy to receive in code. Now, suppose—"

The aged man sat up suddenly with an effort, bringing a look of alarm into Corrigan's face. The latter continued warily:

"Now, suppose that the messages from Neptune are so slow that they fail to register with us. Because of their slowness, we cannot synthesize them into sounds!"

Corrigan stopped suddenly. Professor MacLean lay white and still; there was no evidence that he lived. Corrigan stood in stunned silence. Presently the Professor raised a white hand and a wan smile played over his features.

"Correct!" he whispered. "It almost overcame me. Now go and work it out experimentally. I shall wait to hear from Neptune."

For a man like Corrigan the experimental working out of the idea was a simple and straightforward matter. The principle of recording radio impulses electro-magnetically on a steel tape was already well known. Assuming hypothetically that the tappings he had been hearing from Neptune were individual wave impulses, a simple calculation told him how fast they must be recorded in order that they might be reproduced as sound. He rigged up this much of the apparatus and set it to making permanent records of the Neptunian impulses.

In the meanwhile he adapted an ordinary transatlantic dictaphone to reproducing sounds from the steel tape. He had three days of tape when he was ready to try it out for the first time. He wheeled it into Professor MacLean's sick room. The aged scientist looked as though he could not last much longer; Corrigan wanted him to witness whatever the instrument had to tell them. With beating heart he adjusted the tape into the dictaphone and started the tubes.

"—scientists of other planets—"

That is what the instrument spoke, quite clearly. That was the result of seventy-two hours of patient recording of Neptunian messages. About a word a day. Corrigan looked anxiously at the bed.

"I'm still in good shape," Professor MacLean smiled. "I must live long enough to hear the first complete message from Neptune."

No youngster eagerly awaiting Christmas was ever more impatient at the lagging footsteps of time than was Corrigan during the six weeks which he set aside for the accumulation of the first message from Neptune. He tried to get himself absorbed in other work, but it was of no use. He could not stay away from the recorder; he hovered around it continuously, which only made the time drag more heavily. Finally, one momentous day, the apparatus was wheeled into Professor MacLean's room again, and with trembling fingers Corrigan threaded the steel tape. They listened for the voice, which began in the well-known interplanetary code:

"Elzar, physicist on the planet Neptune, sends greetings to the scientists of other planets. The Earth, Mars, and Saturn VIII we can hear. The others are too rapid for us. For ten of our years we have been sending out messages. Answer if you hear this. Elzar, physicist on the planet Neptune, sends greetings to the scientists of other planets. The Earth, Mars, and Saturn VIII, we can—"

Apparently a repetition of the message had begun. Corrigan turned his eyes to Professor MacLean to see how the long-awaited message affected the old man. A smile of peace and contentment rested upon the wasted countenance. Professor MacLean's indomitable spirit had waited long enough to hear from the mysterious Neptune; then it had taken flight to the place where Neptunian affairs matter little or not at all.

Does it mean that the scientist was stronger than the friend in Corrigan's makeup, when Corrigan first dispatched the reply to Elzar of Neptune before making Professor MacLean's funeral arrangements? Not necessarily. While this famous man's funeral was going on, under the lenses and microphones that were broadcasting it over the entire Earth, the slow tapping messages from Neptune were again being magnetized into the steel tape. It was over six months before the following message was heard out of the dictaphone:

"Elzar of Neptune has received the message of Corrigan of the Earth. For many years we have had analysers for receiving the ultra-rapid messages from Mars and Venus; for many years our analysers set to catch Earth messages have been silent. Today we are overjoyed to hear them speak. That tells us that you have understood our signals. Noting that you have already made a successful trip to Venus, and not having ourselves as yet conquered the problems of space-travel, we invite you to visit us on Neptune. You will find no lovelier spot in the universe. Our extensive forests and our wonderful cities will please and amaze you. I live with my child in one of the largest cities, exactly on the equator and turned to the sun at XIX-1118-00Boo. That will help you find me. Our home stands on the edge of a cliff, overlooking a great sea, the greatest on the planet. We live happily, though occasionally sorrow is thrust into our midst, because huge and vicious beasts come up out of the sea and prey upon our people. Just yesterday a fine child was destroyed. Elzar bids you come and welcome."

A TRIP INTO SPACE

The Neptunian scientist's invitation was a startling thing and would give Corrigan no peace. For months his mind dwelt on the idea of going to Neptune. Several other messages came from Neptune, all from Elzar, who had manifestly a powerful and interesting person-ality. Who but an astounding character like Elzar would think of extending an invitation across those reaches of space? And who but a genius like Corrigan would think of accepting it? For accept it he did.

The first thing he did was to call Dalton into the project. However, Dalton's space ship could not be used, for the simple reason that it was too slow for that enormous distance. Theoretically, the velocity of light was the upper limit of speed for spaceships of the geodesic-hurdling type. In practice, there are numerous objections and obsta-cles to such a velocity. Dalton had made his ship so that it traversed the 26,000,000 miles to Venus in ten hours, with a mean velocity of 850 miles per second. At this rate, it would take about forty days to

cover the 2,707,000,000 miles to Neptune at the latter's nearest position. After considerable discussion, a speed of about twenty times
that of the original ship was decided upon. This would give a velocity of between 16,000 and 17,000 miles per second which would get
them to Neptune in two days or less.

Two days is not an unreasonable period, and Corrigan was afraid
of higher speeds, not knowing what to expect from the Lorentz-
FitzGerald contraction. The principle is as follows: a moving body
contracts in the direction of its motion, so that at a velocity u, its
length is $\sqrt{1-(U^2/C^2)}$ of its original length, when c expresses the
velocity of light. Therefore, at the velocity of light, the length of the
moving body would be zero. Most physicists believed that this was
merely a conception of relativism, due to the fact that the velocity
of light is an arbitrarily chosen constant in a world where everything
else is relative. But no one wanted to test the truth of this belief on
himself.

The late afternoon of July 11, 2347, saw the geo-desical flier,
Neptunian, launched into the unknown, taking with it Corrigan and
Dalton. The two occupants had placed themselves face downwards
on the floor of the vessel, and waited with fast beating hearts for
the second of severance from all earthly ties. They watched with
interest the curiosity and anticipation depicted on the faces of those
who crowded about outside. Corrigan manipulated the controlling
levers, and the dark frame beneath them became a blank. For an
instant they were pressed crushingly against the floor, and then they
floated strangely free. There was the earth rapidly dropping away
from them below.

For a few seconds nothing was heard within the vessel but the
sharp intake of breath. Conversation was out of question at such
an exciting moment. The *Neptunian* was one hundred miles above

the surface of the earth before they looked around within the vessel and spoke to each other. Land, water, mountains, valleys beneath them were rapidly coalescing and rounding into a sphere. They had barely begun to feel warm from the friction of the atmosphere when they were out of it. After they left the atmosphere, Corrigan threw the switches into full speed. In a few seconds the earth appeared no bigger than a bass drum.

ELZAR EXPLAINS

There followed a period of space-sickness, during which the explorers were intensely miserable. They were afraid they would die and then afraid they would not die. They wondered what insane idea possessed them to embark on such a trip. Eventually they sank into a stupor of several hours, from which they awoke considerably improved. The disorder did not wear off for about sixty hours, however. Dalton was the first to feel well.

Later researches by competent clinicians on space-trips have demonstrated that space-sickness is due to the removal of the effects of gravity from the fluid in the semi-circular canals of the inner ear. These canals constitute a little organ which controls the equilibrium of the body and which is closely connected with the eyes and with the gastro-intestinal tract. Normally the fluid fills the lower halves of the two vertical canals and the entire horizontal canal. In a geodesic-hurdler this fluid is freely distributed over the entire interior of canals, and severe vertigo, nausea, and vomiting result. Most people become adjusted to the condition in two or three days.

The complete isolation of the passengers of a space-coaster, their curious independence of what we have become accustomed to as natural laws, the blazing glory of the stars and planets in the black sky, the strange emotional experiences through which the travellers pass on seeing their mother earth become a tiny pin-point of light—all these things have been dwelt upon so much in the popular magazines that this is no place for them. One point has not been clearly brought out in any popular writings that I have seen. At their enormous veloc-ity, why are not space-travellers in danger of instant annihilation by collision with loose masses of matter in space?

We know that space is full of flying bodies in size all the way from microscopic specks to small planets. A projectile shot at random stands a strong chance of colliding with one of them before it has gotten very far. But a geodesic spaceflier is in no danger from them, because it is not on a world-line. Stating the same thing in different words, the space flier is moving along a dimension at right angles to the three old dimensions. Theoretically speaking, it is not in the old Euclidean space at all. Practically speaking, space-travellers report seeing numerous bolides and asteroids, which, however, seem mutu-ally repelled by their vessels. On a path at right angles to a geodesic, a repulsion exists similar to that of like magnetic poles, and it is not possible to approach a mass of matter of any size whatever unless power is applied and the course changed.

By means of a telescope with lenses of the marvellously refrac-tive substance, protite, Corrigan and Dalton studied everything they could see from their vessel. They passed within a half a million miles of Uranus, a mere stone's throw.

"I wonder," mused Corrigan, studying the pale-golf-ball sized disc, "whether Uranus is a dead world? Doesn't it seem a logical explanation of his constant taciturnity?"

"It seems to me," said Dalton thoughtfully, "that it is the inevi-table trend of the forces of Nature to build up Life. Life arises out of matter, regardless of what the conditions are. Even on our own planet Life exists in sections that would seem most unfavourable: the burning sands of the desert and the frozen seas of the polar circles. Life, yes. But not necessarily Life as we conceive of it."

"You may be right," Corrigan sighed.

On each of the fifty days observation and calculations of position had been made. Almost at every hour they knew exactly where they were. Therefore, when the disc of Neptune began to fill the entire sky, they gradually altered their angle with the geodesic and slowed down their speed, with a view to landing. For many hours they had been unable to sleep because of their wonderment at the amazing world that filled the observation frame beneath them. Great cloud strata pierced by jagged mountain peaks, which rose to heights of twenty-five miles above the planet's surface, veiled the greater part of the strange world from their eyes.

They had but a dusky twilight by which to see. Shadows were black as ink; a favourable reflecting surface shone dazzlingly. However, with pupils widely dilated and retinas rendered hypersensitive by their long absence from refracted light, they were able to make out all details comfortably and distinctly.

"We seem to have struck an uninhabited portion of Neptune," commented Dalton, unable to keep an undertone of misgiving out of his voice. "Like Martians landing on the Sahara desert or the polar wastes."

"All right, we'll move around and have a look at other places," Corrigan replied and suited action to word. Soon the awful grandeur of the bare, bleak landscape was passing in panoramic review beneath them. One day, two days they circled about, at sixty miles an hour, at a thousand miles an hour, but found no variation from the original scene that had at first staggered them. Nothing but dry, fearful canyons and bare, towering crags tumbled in chaotic masses, their tops forever buried in the cloud strata.

"Hm! This *is* funny," Corrigan mumbled through set lips. They circled the planet about the equator and then from north to south, but saw the same dismal rocks, the same cold, scurrying vapours. Bare rocks, swirls of snow—truly a strange topography for a civilized world!

"There must be some mistake in the messages," Dalton offered.

Dalton didn't understand interplanetary communication as Corrigan did.

"Mistake!" Corrigan exclaimed. "A mistake in the interplanetary code is more difficult to admit than what we see below us."

"Suppose the messages came from some other planet?" Dalton asked.

"Stop and think," Corrigan reminded. "We translated the word 'Neptune' from the code into English. But the code signal for Neptune gives the size, distance from the sun, and position relative to other planets. It is no more possible to conceive that the message came from some other planet, than it would be for me to imagine that some other person is talking to me with your voice. There can be no doubt about the following facts:

"That our message came from Neptune;

"That this is Neptune; and

"That this is an uninhabited world.

"From the bleakest mountain summits to the depths of those black gorges, there is neither plant nor animal life. Now, explain it as you will. I can't do it."

"Perhaps," suggested Dalton, "the Neptunians live in caverns within their planet. Let us land and investigate."

"No," reminded Corrigan. "Remember that Elzar's message said that he dwelt on the equator on a cliff that overlooked the greatest sea on Neptune. Now where's the sea? We've scoured this whole dead globe, and found no sea."

Dalton leaped up in sudden enthusiasm.

"Anyway," he exclaimed, "we can locate the spot he mentioned by means of his bearings, and see what's there."

No sooner said than done. In a couple of hours' travel and a half hour's calculation, they located XIX-1118-00Boo on the equator. There indeed was a looming cliff, and below it a chasm, that was a veritable abyss into nothingness. But the cliff was bare and bleak; naked rocks jutting out of dry ice, with snow sifting about. And the chasm, of which no bottom was visible, was not a sea, for there was no water.

Dalton proceeded to test the atmosphere, as he had done on Venus. When they hauled in their instruments and calculated their data, they were utterly astounded to find the following figures: temperature –260° Centigrade; pressure, 30 mm of mercury; humidity zero; chemical composition, traces of inert gases of the neon type, amounts of hydrogen, oxygen, and carbon-dioxide almost too small to determine chemically.

"That stuff out there must be hydrogen snow," gasped Dalton, sinking into a chair.

"Certainly no form of life can exist there," Corrigan sighed. "I can't explain it."

And so, with heavy hearts they turned the *Neptunian* back toward the Earth.

Once more back in their homes on Terra, the disappointed scientists told the story of their fruitless journey into the depths of interstellar space. But, a surprise was in store for them. During their absence there had been time for the exchange of a few short messages with Elzar. These had been received and answered by a certain promising young man by the name of Sylvester Kuwamoto. (This curious surname is a relic of the epoch, several hundred years ago, when races and nationalities existed separately on earth. His name is suggestive of the Japanese race and nation, which occupied the island of Japan, spoke a curious language, and was quite isolated. However, it was not long before Japan joined the general intermingling of races which has resulted in making the population of the entire globe a homogeneous race.) He had been little more than a sophomore student in Corrigan's laboratory prior to the latter's trip into space. But he had shown such a brilliant aptitude at the message-storing machine, that Corrigan had immediately given him a permanent position in the laboratory, and put him in charge of the Neptunian affairs. He had sent and received the following messages:

Kuwamoto: "Two of our scientists have gone out in a spaceship to visit you on your world. They will arrive in forty-nine of our days. Watch for them."

Elzar: "We are happy because we shall have visitors from the Earth."

Kuwamoto: "Please notify us as soon as you see them."

Elzar: "It is now the sixty-second terrestrial day, and your people have not yet arrived. I fear that the spaceship has met with disaster."

Two days after this message was interpreted, Corrigan and Dalton arrived. Corrigan immediately radioed this message to Elzar:

"There is some great error. We went to Neptune, looked it all over, but saw no sign of life or habitation. We found the spot which you designated as your home, but found nothing. We found conditions there in which no kind of life could exist. Can you explain?"

The reply was anticipated eagerly, but required the usual wait of three months to record, before the few moments of interpretation could be enjoyed. It ran:

"We watched closely for you, but did not see you." Then followed a check of the solar-system data on the Earth and Neptune at critical periods during the voyage.

Direction finders and range computers were put to work. Interplanetary code checks and re-checks were made. Neptune's position was checked back and forth. The messages were from Neptune. Corrigan and Dalton knew they had been there. Could they convince the public that they were telling the truth?

WHAT LIFE ON NEPTUNE?

Fifteen months passed, during which Neptunian affairs remained a puzzle to the entire world. There was some joking at the expense of Corrigan and Dalton, though I doubt if any serious-minded person ever doubted their account of their voyage. On the other hand, there were people who scoffed; scoffed at the accounts of the voyage, and at the Neptunian messages which continued to arrive with systematic precision at comparatively regular intervals of from three to six months—but which shed no light upon the mystery.

Patrick Corrigan and his assistant seemed to live primarily for the moment when, the steel tape threaded, they could sit in their laboratory and listen to the words of Elzar. They had grown very fond of the scientist of another world. His cheerful, philosophizing personality seemed to come out of the void, encouraging them to find him, wherever he might be.

One day in the laboratory, after the interpretation of a particularly encouraging message, Sylvester Kuwamoto, began to speak to Corrigan, thought better of it, cleared his throat to cover his embarrassment, and lapsed into silence.

"What is it?" queried Corrigan kindly. "Never mind me, you know."

"Nothing special," the younger man demurred; "only—I can't quite explain how I feel about Elzar. It is sort of—well, it may sound silly—but like talking with God. We can't see him, we can't find him; yet know that he exists and that he is good. Do you—er—see what I mean?"

"Precisely," Corrigan replied. "To be frank, I've had somewhat the same feeling myself, though I've never tried to put it into words. Elzar's personality is, well a pervading one. We feel its influence through millions of miles of space! Too bad we can't know what he *looks* like. I can't help imagining him as an old man with a flowing beard and a kindly face. We human beings put a lot of stock in our sense of sight, don't we? Unless we can *see* an object, we feel that we know little about it. Yet I'll venture to say that in time we'll develop other senses than our five by which we become acquainted with our environment."

"That may be," replied Kuwamoto musingly; "but I, for one, am not willing to wait until more senses develop. I'm going to use the five I've got, and I want to see Elzar I"

Corrigan merely sighed.

After Corrigan left, Kuwamoto sat buried in deepest thought.

"Man's reason exceeds any of his five senses. Reason is more important at this age than instinct and emotion which have served their terms in the past."

A strange idea, vague and incomplete was hovering about the outskirts of his mind, trying to get in. There was an explanation to this Neptunian puzzle; he almost had it within his grasp, when suddenly, elusively, it evaded him. There was something Dalton had said, that ought to be the key to it. For weeks he was moody and absent-minded. He read minute reports of the Venerian and Neptunian trips, and talked repeatedly with Dalton and Corrigan.

Pretty soon he grew more cheerful, and carried sheets of scribbled paper stuffed into his pockets. Early one morning he raced pantingly into Corrigan's laboratory. By sheer compulsion, he sat down and forced himself to be calm.

"Shut it off!" he said, pointing to the apparatus on which Corrigan was working, also in the effort to solve the puzzle of Neptune. "You'll never find the answer that way."

"You've got it!" exclaimed Corrigan, dropping his instruments. "Tell me!"

Kuwamoto began impressively.

"Exactly 500 years ago, Leverrier discovered Neptune—not with material instruments, not with his five senses, but by abstract reasoning. From the disturbances in the orbit of Uranus he predicted Neptune's position so accurately that Galle in Berlin was able to turn his telescope to that spot and see it. Likewise, *abstract reasoning has discovered the inhabitants of Neptune.* I can tell you how to make an instrument to see them."

Corrigan stared.

"Neptunian processes are slow," Kuwamoto argued.

Corrigan nodded.

"And you couldn't see the people?"

Corrigan shook his head.

"Nor the animals? Nor the plants? No life?"

Corrigan ceased responding.

"Mountains of ice. Hydrogen snow. Low temperature. Low pressure. And yet there is life there. Life that was invisible to you. Can't you see yet?"

Corrigan waited patiently. Kuwamoto went on:

"Out there in that rare atmosphere, so rare that you could just barely detect it with instruments of precision, no life such as we know it, can exist. It must be a different form of life. The living things are gaseous bodies! Don't you see? Composed of cells, with nuclei and chromosomes and everything. But the cells are huge ones, composed of gases instead of colloids."

Corrigan sprang to his feet. His face was pale with sudden excitement.

"By God! You're right!" He slammed his powerful fist down on the table, causing a couple of flasks to topple and crash. He never noticed their contents spreading across the table and dripping down.

"Living creatures," Kuwamoto continued, "intelligent creatures, plants, animals, all composed of gas-cells. Huge cells with slow chemical processes, all going together just like the cells do in our own bodies. Only out there in that cold, metabolism is slow."

They sat a while and stared at each other.

"But it is Life, just the same!" Kuwamoto exclaimed. "Only different from our kind of life. That's all."

Corrigan pondered.

"That hypothesis explains all the data thus far observed. Now to test it further experimentally. That means another trip to Neptune." He slapped his knee.

"A viewing apparatus for seeing Neptunian gas-life will be a simple thing. Some sort of fluoroscope such as is used by medical men in X-ray work. And an apparatus for storage-recording of visual images; we can take motion-pictures at the rate of one a minute, and then project them at the normal speed of sixteen per second."

Corrigan was already figuring with his pencil on a pad, while Kuwamoto talked on:

"A little experimental work right here in the laboratory will enable us to determine in a preliminary way just which type of electromagnetic vibrations are reflected from the surface of masses of gas. Too short a wave will go on through because it gets between the molecules; whereas too long a wave will penetrate molecules and all. When we find approximately the right length, we can get together our photoelectric receiving bulbs, and take them along to make the final adjustments on the spot. An ordinary television screen will do for the viewing end. You see: find the wavelength reflected from the gas-surfaces, devise a photoelectric cell that is sensitive to it; and project the images from the photoelectric cell on an ordinary television screen."

That night Corrigan tossed restlessly in his sleep.

"Gas-cells. Of course!" his wife heard him mutter.

A VISIT TO NEPTUNE

Preliminary experimental work was more tedious than the enthusiasm of the first moment had reckoned on. It was all straightforward stuff, nothing about it difficult to understand; but the mathematics was complicated, the experimental details were numerous and tedious. Thus it was a good two years after its return from the first voyage, that the *Neptunian* was taken out of its hangar and "tuned up." The second successful voyage to Venus in the old *Pioneer*, and the two disastrous expeditions to Mars, which took place in the interval, are too well known to require notice here.

This time the *Neptunian* contained three voyagers, for Dalton would not be left behind, and Kuwamoto had to be there. The vessel could have carried a dozen people, but the very applicants who were most anxious to go on the expedition were the least desirable ones from the scientific standpoint. Corrigan decided that news reporters and curiosity seekers would have to wait until this travel was commercialized. The space that would have served for more passengers was given over to a radio and television apparatus for more perfect communication of the vessel with the earth. They left with as little publicity as possible. Publicity was becoming unwelcome to Corrigan.

The only matters of interest from the fifty-day voyage are Kuwamoto's notes on the passage of time. He states that the time did not seem that long. Time apparently counted according to what they did. There being little or nothing to stimulate them, much of the time they rested passively, and may even have been in a sort of unconscious state produced by the lack of external comatic stimuli. Kuwamoto thinks that the only thing that kept the entire period from seeming like a blank in the retrospect was his period of space-sickness, and the regular calls of the warning-clocks by which they made their observations of position. This suggests that space-voyages ought to prove valuable for invalids of the nervous-exhaustion type.

Corrigan and Dalton felt strange emotions when they saw again the same sterile mountain peaks and bottomless abysses. They cruised about for a few hours before landing, in order to let Kuwamoto see the general features of Neptune. Then they located Elzar's home on the equator, selected a resting spot, and landed the machine. Immediately everyone went to work. Dalton was taking straight photographs, which was possible with large lenses, sensitive plates, and long exposures. Kuwamoto set about erecting the viewing apparatus; he was feverishly busy, with an expression of wonder on his round, wide-eyed face. Corrigan began some radio messages back to the Earth, reporting their arrival.

In comparatively few hours, Kuwamoto's adjustments were finished. The two machines, one for direct viewing and the other for taking the storage-movies, were placed with their huge lenses against the transparent wall of the ship.

From within their warm vessel the travellers gazed out upon the stern and forbidding character of the landscape without. Directly centred in their frame of observation was the gently-sloping, plateau-like area that was midway between a rugged mountain with a cloud-shorn summit and the vast chasm that Elzar called the sea. Bare jagged rocks; ice, dry and solid as rocks; flurries of carbon-dioxide and hydrogen snow—these were printed indelibly upon their brains as they sat before the infrared viewing box, and switched on the current. The two older men calm and silent, the younger man half hopeful, half fearful, waited for the tuning of the machine. Then, abruptly, Kuwamoto switched on the amplifying tubes.

Corrigan remarked afterwards that his first impression was that of looking into a kaleidoscope. Dalton's impression, again, was that of looking at an empty room, and suddenly seeing it richly furnished. The brilliant colouring of the scene took their breath away. The gaunt mountain was covered with great billows of luxurious vegetation, and the plain was a wealth of flowers, trees, and grass, all inexpressibly huge in proportion to the people looking at them. The most beautiful sight of all were the great, opalescent bodies of varying shapes and sizes that were scattered about the landscape at varying heights above the ground. Their colours shimmered and flashed throughout the entire chromatic scale of visibility.

But, it was only the scintillating of the flashing hues that gave any variety to the scene, for everything was motionless. Not a movement, not a stir, anywhere. The immobility of the iridescent, vari-formed object was disappointing. It was like a brilliantly coloured stereopticon picture.

The three men looked at each other with emotions that cannot be described. Has anyone tried to picture what Balboa felt when he first saw the Pacific Ocean from the "peak in Darien"? A few moments of breathless silence, and then some trivial remark to break the constraint; that is the way scientific men take these situations.

"Medusae!" Dalton exclaimed. "Jellyfish, a thousand times magnified!"

"And everything frozen solid," Kuwamoto remarked.

They moved their vessel here and there, to get new views, watching the scenery on the screen of the infrared view-box. With intense interest they viewed the multicoloured festoons that adorned the landscape; huge, umbrella-shaped bodies that clung to the hillsides. Exclamations of delight issued from their lips from time to time, as some amazingly lovely object came within their range of vision.

"These medusoid forms must be the people—the intelligent beings," Corrigan remarked. The others assented.

The vast chasm was now a sea; why it should happen to be a deep greenish blue is not yet explained; but that was its colour. Down in its depths could be seen vast, gloomy bulks; and on the surface, here and there, an enormous, slimy bulk, like a gigantic paramecium—obviously the ravenous beasts that Elzar feared so much. The three observers were hushed for a moment when they noted the contrast between the repulsive bulks of these beasts, and the brilliant and delicate tracery of the intelligent inhabitants. They brought their machine back to their original landing place, after hunting about a few minutes to find the location.

"Here we are," Corrigan finally said; "same old place."

"And yet, not quite the same," Dalton replied. "Look, some of these things have moved. They have different positions. Kuwamoto is right."

It was true; there was a slight change of position throughout the entire group of huge, globular objects.

"That must be Elzar!" Corrigan pointed with suppressed excitement to a brilliant umbrella-shaped body in all hues of purple, floating near a resplendent structure not far from the cliff's edge.

Kuwamoto nodded. He was busy adjusting the motion-picture taking machine. He had it trained on Elzar and his house.

"One picture a minute," he said. "In about six weeks we can see some action on this film. In the meanwhile, why don't you talk to them?"

If waiting for Neptunian messages on the earth was an anxious suspense, imagine the patience that was required of these three men enclosed in the narrow ship, waiting for six weeks, until the message came to them, tick by tick. This six weeks, unlike the fifty days of interplanetary travel, were the longest any of the three men had ever spent. Fortunately, they were all three of them scientific men, and knew how to find intellectual pursuits to pass away a large part of the time.

Immediately on their arrival, Corrigan had coded:

"We are here. Look for us on the plateau near your house."

After those interminable six weeks had passed, after every possible aspect of the scene had been studied, and every animal and plant form studied and photographed (they could not move their vessel because the motion-picture camera was constantly in operation), they finally threaded their steel tape into the dictaphone, and listened to Elzar's voice; through the vacuum tubes and condensers, this deep and kindly voice was coming from that purple, cape-like mass with innumerable streamers that hung up above the others:

"Welcome my friends, I am overjoyed at your arrival. I see your ship now, though you must have waited long and patiently to enable us to see you. Before that, your movements were so rapid that we could not see you. We realize that yours is the difficult end of this communication problem. From your message, I judge that you have recognized my house. Me you will recognize because I am larger than any of the other people in this group. My child resembles me in miniature, and is—wait a moment—oh—oh—help!—" and then silence.

Elzar's wail of distress brought the two men to their feet in instant alarm. All eyes turned frantically to the intra-red view-screen. Could it be possible that consternation reigned over that peaceful scene; that events were at this moment rising to a climax that spelled some terrible calamity?

"We can do nothing!" cried Kuwamoto hopelessly. "Let us run the film through and see what is the matter."

THE BABY ON NEPTUNE

While Kuwamoto prepared the film that had required six weeks to make, Corrigan radioed back to Earth, asking the receiving stations to get their television sets in readiness to receive the first reel of a possible Neptunian drama. Kuwamoto slipped his reel of film into the projector. For the first time the observers saw the frozen scene in motion. Trees swayed, multicoloured Neptunians glided over the ground or floated through the atmosphere; the waves of the sea tossed, and a huge bulk showed itself anon; especially the Neptunians were busy on tasks and purposes of their own.

They all gazed at Elzar in silent admiration, aware of his domi-
nance over the rest of the Neptunians. He was a truly remarkable
organism. If he had been beautiful in mobility, he was a thousand
times more lovely now. He resembled nothing so much as a brilliant, multicoloured chandelier of gigantic proportions, scintillating
throughout the chromatic scale with each pulsation of his delicately
constructed body. Like fairy gossamer were his body tissues; and
yet the vastness of the whole gave an impression of sturdiness and
power. His prevailing hues were purples, though he contained all the
colours of the spectrum, harmoniously interwoven.

"He is the only one whose dominant colour is purple," Corrigan
remarked.

"Appropriate, for both his brain and his body are exceptional.
Look! there is a smaller being with much the same colouring!"
Kuwamoto replied.

"That must be Elzar's child," declared Corrigan.

As they watched, Elzar rose above the other Neptunians about
him, and the observers realized that he was just then talking to
them—making the speech to which they had listened a half hour
before. He remained quite motionless, and the observers, more
interested in the moving objects, allowed their eyes to wander from
him to his diminutive counterpart, who was moving away in the
direction of the cliff edge that overhung the sea.

"Great heavens, look at that!" Kuwamoto's exclamation was
unnecessary, for they all saw it simultaneously.

Out of the depths, a black, slimy form had risen, with the fluid
of the sea splashing off its glistening sides. It seemed to spy the
Neptunian child, for swiftly it turned toward the little purple bell.
The deadly intent of the loathsome entity was obvious to all the
observers. It reached out great pseudopods, slimy, flowing, shapeless

projections, preparing to wrap them all around the bright body of the little one. Swiftly it closed toward its victim, while the men in the spaceship remained rigid, frozen in their positions; the little Neptunian was all unconscious of the impending calamity. Ready to fall upon the child, to close about him completely, when Elzar suddenly woke to the danger, whirled about, and sped toward the scene of the tragedy. Then—the picture was ended, and the men gazed stupidly at the blank screen before them.

"Ye Gods!" shouted Kuwamoto. "Just at the crucial moment, like a cheap novel serial! I suppose all we can do is nothing, and Elzar's child has been devoured by the filthy beast."

"Not at all, not at all!" Corrigan cried excitedly. "Remember it is all going on very slowly. Let's find out for sure!" He rushed toward the window and looked out.

Nothing but bare black rocks and frozen air. In his excitement he had forgotten the viewing machine that rendered visible the tenuous gaseous matter on this cold planet.

Through the infrared visual transformer, the scene which had become so familiar during the past week lay before them. Now it was more comprehensible, since they could read it in the light of what they had seen happen on the moving projection.

"Thank God! It isn't too late… But what can we do? By the time—" Kuwamoto interrupted Corrigan.

"It is true that the distance between the monster's pseudopodia and the little Elzar is decreasing. But, it is slow. Let us think. We can act fast."

"We're enclosed in this machine and can't get out—"

"Those things are so big. Even the little Elzar—far too big for us, we can't handle him. Destroy the monster somehow—if we could do that—"

In helpless despair they stood gazing upon the scene of the tragedy. The monster seemed such a short distance away from the beautiful little creature.

"Blow him away!" Kuwamoto shouted. "The nitrogen tanks!"

The others comprehended his idea instantly. Corrigan moved the space-vessel close to the scene of the tragedy, gradually, with the aid of the infrared screen, working it into a position between the beast and the little medusoid child. On the viewing screen, the two Neptunian creatures towered high above the apparently tiny earth machine; it looked like a toy between them.

Dalton and Kuwamoto placed a cylinder of nitrogen in the air-valve compartment that was used for refuse disposal, retaining control of its stopcock by an electrical connection, and aiming its discharge tube directly at the monster. The outer door was then opened, sending a puff of air into the face of the foe and causing it to sway visibly on the viewing screen, among the frigid, motionless scenery. Almost instantaneously, Kuwamoto turned on the compressed nitrogen.

On the infrared viewing screen, the stream of gas looked like a solid black beam shooting out of their space-vessel. It spread out swiftly into a black cloud that struck the monster and literally blew the beast to nothingness. To the Neptunians, who must have been watching the attack, the sudden vanishing of the beast must have appeared very mysterious indeed. The pressure of the nitrogen in the terrestrial cylinder was to them an almost inconceivable phenomenon; none but their trained mathematical physicists could comprehend it.

For an hour or two, they waited and watched, anxious to see if the vortex of gases had done any harm to the Neptunian child, even though the bulk of the space vessel had protected it from the greatest pressure. In that time, no serious change was visible, and the men, exhausted by the strenuous events of the last hours, slept. Upon awakening, they were gratified to see in the visual transformer that Elzar had reached the little one's side; and that both of them seemed safe.

The men made a quick decision to return to the earth. They had gathered enough data and had enough excitement for one trip; whereas the difference in the perception of the passage of time between them and the Neptunians made it out of question for them to wait for anything else. The most trivial act of a Neptunian required too great a portion of an earthman's lifetime.

They expected at the beginning of their return journey, that they would soon hear from Elzar. On the third day they began to get the purport of his message, which occupied the entire flight homeward.

"My friends from the Earth, I thank you for saving my child. How you destroyed the animal, I cannot understand. It vanished instantaneously. When I looked toward the place you recently occupied, you were no longer there. Often have I warned my little one of the awful dangers from the sea, but I believe it is characteristic of the young of all worlds that they learn by experience rather than by admonition. You averted a tragedy that would have wrecked the life of Elzar. How I can show you the gratitude I feel, I do not know. Perhaps the time will come; but I must act quickly, for any delay on my part might cover the remaining years of your lives. My dream is interplanetary television, and to that I shall devote the remaining years of my life. Never shall I be content until I see the cities and men of your world. Again I thank you and may you live to realize the gratitude of Elzar of Neptune."

Kuwamoto sighed.

"It wouldn't take much," he said, "to go over there some day and clean up that nest of ugly beasts."

COMPARISON OF THE SIZE OF THE SUN'S DISC AS SEEN FROM THE EARTH (TOP)
COMPARED TO HOW IT APPEARS FROM PLUTO AT PERIHELION (P) AND APHELION (A)

PLUTO

Wait It Out   Larry Niven

When the discovery of Pluto was announced in March 1930 it was a gift to the burgeoning science-fiction community. The first all-sf magazine, *Amazing Stories*, had appeared in 1926 and by 1930 there were seven such titles and the genre had been named.

In fact, the newly dubbed science-fiction writers had already considered planets beyond Neptune. In "Out of the Void" (1929), Leslie F. Stone has her adventurers way off course until they stumble across the planet Abrui, beyond Neptune. She correctly predicts that this distant world is smaller than Earth, but in all other respects, including the idea that the planet is warmed by a small second sun, was far from correct. But then so were all the other writers who jumped at the opportunity of exploring a new world. Stanton A. Coblentz recognized that Pluto will be cold, but still gave it a breathable atmosphere in "Into Plutonian Depths" (1931) and has the ancient Plutonian race living underground. In "The Planet of Despair" (1931), R.F. Starzl has it inhabited by giant, black humanoids who are at war with Earth and blast our planet out of its orbit. References to Pluto were hurriedly written into "The Emperor of the Stars" (1931) by Nathan Schachner and Arthur Leo Zagat and the title for "Beyond Pluto" (1932) by John Scott Campbell. Stanley G. Weinbaum, who in his brief life explored most of the planets and moons in the solar system, took his adventurers to Pluto in "The Red Peri" (1935) which has a crystalline form of life.

Pluto is, of course, very distant from the Sun, but it has such an eccentric orbit that at perihelion, when it is 4,436,820,000km (2,756,994,000 miles) distant, it is within the orbit of Neptune. It is now travelling away from the Sun and its greatest distance will be 7,375,930,000km (4,583,200,000 miles). Light, or any message from Pluto, would take 6.8 hours to reach us, whereas it takes just over eight minutes from the Sun. Until recent probes had revealed Pluto to be a fascinating world, little was known about it, although in 1978 it was discovered to have a moon, Charon. It is surprisingly large. Pluto's diameter is 2,376km (1,476 miles) and Charon is half the size at 1,212km (750 miles), compared to our Moon which is a third the diameter of the Earth. Pluto and Charon are therefore more like twin worlds, locked together.

We currently believe that Pluto has five moons, though the others are no more than large rocks. What's more, Pluto, which was downgraded to a dwarf planet in 2006, is regarded as just one of many minor planets which orbit beyond Neptune in the Kuiper Belt. Amongst the largest are Eris, Haumea and Makemake, all larger than Charon and, for that matter, than the largest asteroid, Ceres. None of these outer worlds was identified prior to the discovery of Quaoar in 2002, and they have changed the whole concept of space beyond Neptune.

It is also believed that Pluto might have a subsurface ocean of water, sufficiently well insulated to remain liquid. It is certainly a more exciting world than scientists had long believed.

Science-fiction writers, of course, always saw the planet's possibilities. In *Man of Earth* (1958), Algis Budrys saw it as a terraformed but neglected colony that is ready to rise in revolt against Earth. In his young-adult novel *Have Space Suit—Will Travel* (1958), Robert A. Heinlein has Pluto as a base for aliens from Vega to explore the solar system. In Larry Niven's first novel, *World of Ptavvs* (1966) Pluto, which hides the remnant of a race that had helped establish life on Earth, was once a moon of Neptune until it was thrown out of its orbit by an impact. Clifford Simak's explorers in "Construction Shack" (1973) discover that Pluto is artificial, the equivalent of the workman's hut while the solar system was being built. Gravity experiments on Pluto trigger alien activity which includes the abduction of Earth through a wormhole in *The Ring of Charon* (1990) by Roger McBride Allen.

Possibilities of life on Pluto still exercise the minds of writers. One such is suggested in Larry Niven's "Wait it Out" (1968), included here. There are further discoveries in Robert Silverberg's bleak "Sunrise on Pluto" (1985), and Stephen Baxter's "Gossamer" (1995), where spider-like creatures have created a web between Pluto and Charon.

In *Icehenge* (1984) Kim Stanley Robinson explores across several generations how a series of monuments are erected on the north pole of Pluto. Robinson then used this as the starting point of his solar tour, *The Memory of Whiteness* (1985), which takes his readers all the way from Pluto back to Mercury, our starting point.

Pluto may be on the edge of the solar system, but it isn't necessarily the end of everything. With the Kuiper Belt and the even more distant Oort Cloud, it's really the start of further discoveries.

Larry Niven (b. 1938) is one of the major writers of "hard" science fiction—meaning that his work has, at its core, solid scientific extrapolation. His career stretches back nearly sixty years, though his debut story "The Coldest Place" (1964) treated him unfairly, because it appeared just at the time when it was discovered that Mercury was not tidally locked to the Sun but did indeed revolve on its axis, which rather ruined Niven's surprise ending. Amongst his work, which is firmly rooted in the era of classic sf whilst also showing a transition to modern sf, is his series called Tales of Known Space. This includes his first novel *World of Ptavvs* (1966), the collection *Neutron Star* (1968) and the multi-award winning *Ringworld* (1970). Many of Niven's stories are set in the planets, satellites and asteroids of our solar system. "Becalmed in Hell" (1965) was one of the first stories to be set on a realistic Venus. *Rainbow Mars* (1999) travels into the Martian fictional past to discover a whole series of imaginative worlds. The Known Space series takes us through the Belter colonies in the Asteroid Belt to various major satellites. The following story, though written in 1968, long before the space missions reached Pluto, nevertheless provides us with a realistic glimpse of that distant world.

NIGHT ON PLUTO. SHARP AND DISTINCT, THE HORIZON line cuts across my field of vision. Below that broken line is the dim grey-white of snow seen by starlight. Above, space-blackness and space-bright stars. From behind a jagged row of frozen mountains the stars pour up in singletons and clusters and streamers of cold white dots. Slowly they move, but visibly, just fast enough for a steady eye to capture their motion.

Something wrong there. Pluto's rotation period is long: 6.39 days. Time must have slowed for me.

It should have stopped.

I wonder if I may have made a mistake.

The planet's small size brings the horizon close. It seems even closer without a haze of atmosphere to fog the distances. Two sharp peaks protrude into the star swarm like the filed front teeth of a cannibal warrior. In the cleft between those peaks shines a sudden bright point.

I recognize the Sun, though it shows no more disk than any other, dimmer star. The sun shines as a cold point between the frozen peaks; it pulls free of the rocks and shines in my eyes.

The Sun is gone, the starfield has shifted. I must have passed out.

It figures.

Have I made a mistake? It won't kill me if I have. It could drive me mad, though.

I don't feel mad. I don't feel anything, not pain, not loss, not regret, not fear. Not even pity. Just: *What a situation.*

Grey-white against grey-white: the landing craft, short and wide and conical, stands half-submerged in an icy plain below the level of my eyes. Here I stand, looking east, waiting.

Take a lesson: this is what comes of not wanting to die.

Pluto was not the most distant planet. It had stopped being that in 1979, ten years ago. Now Pluto was at perihelion, as close to the Sun—and to Earth—as it would ever get. To ignore such an opportunity would have been sheer waste.

And so we came, Jerome and Sammy and I, in an inflated plastic bubble poised on an ion jet. We'd spent a year and a half in that bubble. After so long together, with so little privacy, perhaps we should have hated each other. We didn't. The UN psycho team must have chosen well.

But—just to be out of sight of the others, even for a few minutes. Just to have something to *do*, something that was not predictable. A new world could hold infinite surprises. As a matter of fact, so could our laboratory-tested hardware. I don't think any of us really trusted the Nerva-K under our landing craft.

Think it through. For long trips in space, you use an ion jet giving low thrust over long periods of time. The ion motor on our own craft had been decades in use. Where gravity is materially lower than Earth's, you land on dependable chemical rockets. For landings on Earth and Venus, you use heat shields and the braking power of the atmosphere. For landing on the gas giants—but who would want to?

The Nerva-class fission rockets are used only for takeoff from Earth, where thrust and efficiency count. Responsiveness and manoeuvrability count for too much during a powered landing. And a heavy planet will always have an atmosphere for braking.

Pluto didn't.

For Pluto, the chemical jets to take us down and bring us back up were too heavy to carry all that way. We needed a highly manoeuvrable Nerva-type atomic rocket motor using hydrogen for reaction mass.

And we had it. But we didn't trust it.

Jerome Glass and I went down, leaving Sammy Cross in orbit. He griped about that, of course. He'd started that back at the Cape and kept it up for a year and a half. But someone had to stay. Someone had to be aboard the Earth-return vehicle, to fix anything that went wrong, to relay communications to Earth, and to fire the bombs that would solve Pluto's one genuine mystery.

We never did solve that one. Where *does* Pluto get all that mass? The planet's a dozen times as dense as it has any right to be. We could have solved that with the bombs, the same way they solved the mystery of the makeup of the Earth, sometime in the last century. They mapped the patterns of earthquake ripples moving through the Earth's bulk. But those ripples were from natural causes, like the Krakatoa eruption. On Pluto the bombs would have done it better.

A bright star-sun blazes suddenly between two fangs of mountain. I wonder if they'll know the answers, when my vigil ends.

The sky jumps and steadies, and—

I'm looking east, out over the plain where we landed the ship. The plain and the mountains behind seem to be sinking like Atlantis: an illusion created by the flowing stars. We slide endlessly down the black sky, Jerome and I and the mired ship.

The Nerva-K behaved perfectly. We hovered for several minutes to melt our way through various layers of frozen gases and get ourselves something solid to land on. Condensing volatiles steamed around us and boiled below, so that we settled in a soft white glow of fog lit by the hydrogen flame.

Black wet ground appeared below the curve of the landing skirt. I let the ship drop carefully, carefully... and we touched.

It took us an hour to check the ship and get ready to go outside. But who would be first? This was no idle matter. Pluto would be the solar system's last outpost for most of future history, and the statue to the first man on Pluto would probably remain untarnished forever.

Jerome won the toss. All for the sake of a turning coin, Jerome's would be the first name in the history books. I remember the grin I forced! I wish I could force one now. He was laughing and talking of marble statues as he went through the lock.

There's irony in that, if you like that sort of thing.

I was screwing down my helmet when Jerome started shouting obscenities into the helmet mike. I cut the checklist short and followed him out.

One look told it all.

The black wet dirt beneath our landing skirt had been dirty ice, water ice mixed haphazardly with lighter gases and ordinary rock. The heat draining out of the Nerva jet had melted that ice. The rocks within the ice had sunk, and so had the landing vehicle, so that when the water froze again it was halfway up the hull. Our landing craft was sunk solid in the ice.

We could have done some exploring before we tried to move the ship. When we called Sammy he suggested doing just that. But Sammy was up there in the Earth-return vehicle, and we were down here with our landing vehicle mired in the ice of another world.

We were terrified. Until we got clear we would be good for nothing, and we both knew it.

I wonder why I can't remember the fear.

We did have one chance. The landing vehicle was designed to move about on Pluto's surface; and so she had a skirt instead of landing jacks. Half a gravity of thrust would have given us a ground effect, safer and cheaper than using the ship like a ballistic missile. The landing skirt must have trapped gas underneath when the ship sank, leaving the Nerva-K engine in a bubble cavity.

We could melt our way out.

I know we were as careful as two terrified men could be. The heat rose in the Nerva-K, agonizingly slow. In flight there would have been a coolant effect as cold hydrogen fuel ran through the pile. We couldn't use that. But the environment of the motor was terribly cold. The two factors might compensate, or—

Suddenly dials went wild. Something had cracked from the savage temperature differential. Jerome used the damper rods without effect. Maybe they'd melted. Maybe wiring had cracked, or resistors had become superconductors in the cold. Maybe the pile—but it doesn't matter now.

I wonder why I can't remember the fear.

Sunlight—

And a logy, dreamy feeling. I'm conscious again. The same stars rise in formation over the same dark mountains.

Something heavy is nosing up against me. I feel its weight against my back and the backs of my legs. What is it? Why am I not terrified?

It slides around in front of me, questing. It looks like a huge amoeba, shapeless and translucent, with darker bodies showing within it. I'd guess it's about my own weight.

Life on Pluto! But how? Superfluids? Helium II contaminated by complex molecules? In that case the beast had best get moving; it will need shade come sunrise. Sunside temperature on Pluto is all of 50° Absolute.

No, come back! It's leaving, flowing down toward the splash crater. Did my thoughts send it away? Nonsense. It probably didn't like the taste of me. It must be terribly slow, that I can watch it move. The beast is still visible, blurred because I can't look directly at it, moving downhill toward the landing vehicle and the tiny statue to the first man to die on Pluto.

After the fiasco with the Nerva-K, one of us had to go down and see how much damage had been done. That meant tunnelling down with the flame of a jet backpack, then crawling under the landing skirt. We didn't talk about the implications. We were probably dead. The man who went down into the bubble cavity was even more probably dead; but what of it? Dead is dead.

I feel no guilt. I'd have gone myself if I'd lost the toss.

The Nerva-K had spewed fused bits of the fission pile all over the bubble cavity. We were trapped for good. Rather, I was trapped, and Jerome was dead. The bubble cavity was a hell of radiation.

Jerome had been swearing softly as he went in. He came out perfectly silent. He'd used up all the good words on lighter matters, I think.

I remember I was crying, partly from grief and partly from fear. I remember that I kept my voice steady in spite of it. Jerome never knew. What he guessed is his own affair. He told me the situation, he told me goodbye, and then he strode out onto the ice and took off his helmet. A fuzzy white ball engulfed his head, exploded outward, then settled to the ground in microscopic snowflakes.

But all that seems infinitely remote. Jerome stands out there with his helmet clutched in his hands: a statue to himself, the first man on Pluto. A frost of recondensed moisture conceals his expression.

Sunrise. I hope the amoeba—

That was wild. The sun stood poised for an instant, a white point-source between twin peaks. Then it streaked upward—and the spinning sky jolted to a stop. No wonder I didn't catch it before. It happened so fast.

A horrible thought. What has happened to me could have happened to Jerome! I wonder—

There was Sammy in the Earth-return vehicle, but he couldn't get down to me. I couldn't get up. The life system was in good order, but sooner or later I would freeze to death or run out of air.

I stayed with the landing vehicle about thirty hours, taking ice and soil samples, analysing them, delivering the data to Sammy via laser beam; delivering also high-minded last messages, and feeling sorry for myself. On my trips outside I kept passing Jerome's statue. For a corpse, and one which has not been prettified by the post-surgical skills of an embalmer, he looks damn good. His frost-dusted skin is indistinguishable from marble, and his eyes are lifted toward the stars in poignant yearning. Each time I passed him I wondered how I would look when my turn came.

"You've got to find an oxygen layer," Sammy kept saying.

"Why?"

"To keep you alive! Sooner or later they'll send a rescue ship. You can't give up now!"

I'd already given up. There was oxygen, but there was no such layer as Sammy kept hoping for. There were veins of oxygen mixed with other things, like veins of gold ore in rock. Too little, too finely distributed.

"Then use the water ice! That's only poetic justice, isn't it? You can get the oxygen out by electrolysis!"

But a rescue ship would take years. They'd have to build it from scratch, and redesign the landing vehicle too. Electrolysis takes power, and heat takes power. I had only the batteries.

Sooner or later I'd run out of power. Sammy couldn't see this. He was more desperate than I was. I didn't run out of last messages; I stopped sending them because they were driving Sammy crazy.

I passed Jerome's statue one time too many, and an idea came.

This is what comes of not wanting to die.

In Nevada, three billion miles from here, half a million corpses lie frozen in vaults surrounded by liquid nitrogen. Half a million dead men wait for an earthly resurrection, on the day medical science discovers how to unfreeze them safely, how to cure what was killing each one of them, how to cure the additional damage done by ice crystals breaking cell walls all through their brains and bodies.

Half a million fools? But what choice did they have? They were dying.

I was dying.

A man can stay conscious for tens of seconds in vacuum. If I moved fast, I could get out of my suit in that time. Without that insulation to protect me, Pluto's black night would suck warmth from my body in seconds. At 50° Absolute, I'd stay in frozen storage until one version or another of the Day of Resurrection.

Sunlight—

—And stars. No sign of the big blob that found me so singularly tasteless yesterday. But I could be looking in the wrong direction.

I hope it got to cover.

I'm looking east, out over the splash plain. In my peripheral vision the ship looks unchanged and undamaged.

My suit lies beside me on the ice. I stand on a peak of black rock, poised in my silvered underwear, looking eternally out at the horizon. Before the cold touched my brain I found a last moment in which to assume a heroic stance. Go east, young man. Wouldn't you know I'd get my directions mixed? But the fog of my breathing-air hid everything, and I was moving in terrible haste.

Sammy Cross must be on his way home now. He'll tell them where I am.

Stars pour up from behind the mountains. The mountains and the splash plain and Jerome and I sink endlessly beneath the sky.

My corpse must be the coldest in history. Even the hopeful dead of Earth are only stored at liquid nitrogen temperatures. Pluto's night makes that look torrid, after the 50° Absolute heat of day seeps away into space.

A superconductor is what I am. Sunlight raises the temperature too high, switching me off like a damned machine at every dawn. But at night my nervous system becomes a superconductor. Currents flow; thoughts flow; sensations flow. Sluggishly. The one hundred and fifty-three hours of Pluto's rotation flash by in what feels like fifteen minutes. At that rate I can wait it out.

I stand as a statue and a viewpoint. No wonder I can't get emotional about anything. Water is a rock here, and my glands are contoured ice within me. But I feel sensations: the pull of gravity, the pain in my ears, the tug of vacuum over every square inch of my body. The vacuum will not boil my blood. But the tensions are frozen into the ice of me, and my nerves tell me so. I feel the wind whistling from my lips, like an exhalation of cigarette smoke.

This is what comes of not wanting to die. What a joke if I got my wish!

Do you suppose they'll find me? Pluto's small for a planet. For a place to get lost in, a small planet is all too large. But there's the ship.

Though it seems to be covered with frost. Vaporized gases recondensed on the hull. Grey-white on grey-white, a lump on a dish of refrozen ice. I could stand here forever waiting for them to pick my ship from its surroundings.

Stop that.

Sunlight—

Stars rolling up the sky. The same patterns, endlessly rolling up from the same points. Does Jerome's corpse live the same half-life I live now? He should have stripped, as I did. My God! I wish I'd thought to wipe the ice from his eyes!

I wish that superfluid blob would come back.

Damn. It's *cold*.